Rudely Interrupted

Love In The Afterlife

DAVID IVELL

DEDICATION

For all those we've loved and lost in these recent years.

May this book be a small reminder that even when life ends, the story does not. I believe that life doesn't just stop. It carries on, sometimes in memory, sometimes in laughter, sometimes in words, and sometimes in ways we can't quite explain.

There is so much we don't understand, but love doesn't vanish. Hope doesn't end. Maybe, just maybe, we are less alone than we think. And the ones we have lost? Well, who knows what adventures they are having.

RUDELY INTERRUPTED

CONTENTS

ACKNOWLEDGMENTS

Writing a story about ghosts, love, and the sheer chaos of the afterlife would have been impossible without the very real support of the living.

To my family, who patiently endured the crazy ideas, endless conversations about metaphysics, pub hauntings, and whether ghosts can, in fact, get goosebumps, - thank you for your love, encouragement, and occasional reality checks.

Finally, to every reader holding this book: thank you. Stories live only when they are shared, and by stepping into this one, you've given these ghosts a little more life. May it remind you, as it has reminded me, that love and laughter travel farther than we think, sometimes even beyond the veil.

CHAPTER ONE

SHERRY AND THE INCONVENIENCE OF METAPHYSICS

Let's get one thing straight: being dead isn't the worst thing that's ever happened to me.

That particular trophy, gold-plated, slightly dusty, and inscribed with "Most Traumatic Public Humiliation", still belongs to the Year 6 end-of-term talent show at the William Lloyd Garrison Elementary School, nestled in the heart of the South Bronx.

Now, while most kids sensibly opted for a bit of interpretive dance, a magic trick involving playing cards and a reluctant sibling, a pitchy rendition of *Let It Go* or a half-hearted Spice Girls number, I, ever the misunderstood artiste, decided to perform a dramatic monologue from *Mary Poppins*. In a cockney accent so criminal it would have made Dick Van Dyke file a noise complaint. Picture this: a ten-year-old boy swaddled in a shawl that once belonged to his mother, or possibly the living room sofa, delivering lines like "chim chim che-ree" with all the pathos of a drunk BBC weatherman after three sherries and a head injury.

Halfway through my emotional climax, I was struck by a nosebleed of such biblical proportions that someone in the front row crossed themselves. I carried on, true to the spirit of the stage, with toilet roll jammed up both nostrils like a teary, bloodied walrus who'd lost his umbrella and his dignity in one go. So yes, death? Honestly, a bit of a holiday by comparison.

Right now, I'm stamping my ghostly feet outside a 300-year-old English pub called The Rose and Crown, buried in the frosty heart of an English countryside village called Beddlestead, a name that sounds less like a village and more like something you'd find in an Ikea catalogue. If I'm being honest, I am beginning to regret my afterlife choices. My coat, which I no longer need, is buttoned up to the top. My scarf, equally redundant, looped fashionably around my neck. Ghost or not, I have standards. Because you see, there's death… there's style… and I'll be damned, again, if I'm giving that up.

You'd think being dead would excuse you from the elements, but as I can witness, you still feel the cold. In fact, it's so cold I can't feel my fingers, which is remarkable considering I no longer technically have a circulatory system. I don't know how that works, something to do with residual memory or unfulfilled longing or perhaps just cosmic spite. All I know is I am freezing. A dead man with goosebumps. Not a phrase I thought I'd ever say.

The pub, twinkly lights, ivy curling up the brickwork like it's auditioning for a Jane Austen reboot, a roaring fire inside, and some kind of handmade sign advertising a "Cheese and Pickle Quiz Night," which raises far more questions than it answers. Quaint doesn't begin to cover it. If the building had a scent, it would be pipe tobacco, pickled eggs, and mild generational trauma. Inside, the regulars are huddled around the fire, throwing back pints and passionately debating the bins, or in my vernacular the trash cans.

Apparently, and it may be a British thing, but just like discussing the weather at every opportunity, there is *always* something to say about the bins.

So, like I said, I'm dead. Like, not metaphorically, I mean *literally* dead. Capital D. No pulse. Ghost. Boo!

I've been dead for just under a month and, frankly, it's going rather *better* than expected. Seriously. The afterlife, it turns out, involves a lot of hanging around pubs and rediscovering your capacity for sarcasm.

The pub has become, in death, my version of home.

Yes, I know what you're thinking: *"Why a pub?"* Why not a castle with lots of chains to rattle, or a cathedral or a cliffside mansion with dramatic lightning?

Because… because I died inconveniently. Very. That's the thing about murder; it rarely happens on your own schedule.

I was murdered sometime between a Thursday and a Friday, while shopping for Christmas crackers and arguing with a cab driver about whether the song playing on the radio was Bing Crosby or Dean Martin. (It was neither. It was Michael Bublé, and for that alone, I'm not sure I deserved justice.)

Now, I don't remember the murder itself. According to The Reverend, who we'll come onto much more later, says ghosts rarely do. Apparently, it's some psychological defence mechanism built into the cosmic system, like a factory reset for trauma. I suppose it's helpful, but also, I must say, rather rude. If you're going to turn me into a floating wisp of unresolved business, the least you could do is let me remember the part where I got dramatically stabbed, pushed off the tube platform, or if a piano fell on my head! Anything but this vague *"Oops, you're dead!"* energy I've been saddled with.

Snowflakes are now landing on my shoulders and stay there, because, well, there's nothing to stop them. From the perspective of a living passerby, assuming anyone in this village still walks anywhere, they probably just look like they're hovering mid-air, like little frozen UFOs deciding whether or not to abduct something. Then they vanish, presumably melting or drifting off like normal flakes do. But no. Not here. In reality they're starting to pile up on me. Not dramatically, no avalanche situation, but enough that if I had a mirror (and a reflection, which I don't), I suspect I'd look like a festive scarecrow left out too long. Every so often I try brushing them off, which does absolutely nothing except reinforce the illusion that I'm still participating in the physical world. I'm not, obviously. I'm more snowdrift than man at this point.

So here in the snow I wait. Time doesn't pass the same way for us. Not in the "you're immortal" sense, more in the "you're waiting for a dentist who might never call your name" kind of way.

I checked my ghostly wristwatch, which doesn't exist, and sighed for effect. Being dramatic is about commitment.

The road in front of me was empty. No cars. No people. Just the snow falling in sullen clumps and a pub that looked like it would rather not be associated with me, thank you very much.

I don't like waiting. It reminds me of every terrible date I ever had, especially the one where the woman brought her own Tupperware to sneak food off my plate. (I respected the hustle. I did not call her back.)

Anyway, about the advert. The one I placed it in *The Times*, which felt classy and also slightly desperate. Something about serif fonts makes you feel less like a lunatic. The wording was vague on purpose.

No mention of ghosts. No threats. Not even a cheeky pun. Just mystery. I wanted to seem like a reclusive billionaire with a secret will, not a murdered New Yorker with unfinished business and a questionable sense of boundaries.

Still, I was optimistic. Maybe this person would arrive and everything would change. Maybe they'd believe me when I told them I was dead. Maybe they wouldn't scream and run for the hills. Maybe they'd be the kind of person who knew what to do when a ghost asked for help.

So, I'm waiting for the person who responded. Or at least, I *hope* they're coming. For all I know, they took one look at my ad and assumed it was a pyramid scheme involving cryptocurrency and mince pies.

I glance toward the road, which is empty. Again. I've now counted every snowflake that's fallen in the past ten minutes and named the more symmetrical ones.

The pub door flings open with the muffled shout of "George get a round in" as George stumbles out backwards into the snow, pauses, sways heroically, blinking at the cold like it personally offended his mother. Two wobbly feet heading in opposing trajectories. His hands pat down his coat pockets with increasing panic, searching for something, his keys? His phone? His entire purpose? Before arriving at the unmistakable conclusion that he has absolutely no idea why he's out here at all. After a moment of blank confusion and an audible sigh that could've melted icicles, he turns around and totters straight back inside without a word. The door swings shut behind him with a puff of snow, and almost immediately, the muffled chorus of voices rises in delight, as if greeting a hero who'd briefly wandered into the wrong war. Glasses clink. Someone shouts *'He's back!'* The Rose and Crown, it seems, never punishes confusion, only dares you to do it louder next time.

Inside, The Rose and Crown continues to buzz with chaotic cheer, the air thick with laughter, the clink of pint glasses, and the suspicious aroma of something called "bubble and squeak," which, let's be honest, sounds less like a dish and more like what happens to toddlers in waterproof trousers.

Betty waves to me from the window. Betty died in 1943 and has the chic wartime aesthetic of someone who could either knit you a scarf or destroy you in hand-to-hand combat. She has a perfect 1940s British clipped accent and a suspiciously symmetrical face, and she is … delightful, even though she's been dead for over eighty years.

She gives me that quizzical "have you lost your mind" look. I haven't told her why I'm out here, loitering in a blizzard like a door-to-door tax inspector from a particularly gloomy chapter of *A Christmas Carol*. Not because I'm trying to be mysterious, but because saying, *"Hello, I placed a classified ad in the newspaper asking a stranger to help solve my untimely murder because I, being currently between bodies, cannot operate a telephone without filling the ethereal void with blue words of frustration,"* tends to raise eyebrows, even among the already dead. There's only so much dignity one can maintain while admitting you're a ghost with unresolved trauma, limited social skills, and absolutely no thumbs.

Also, the last time I told someone I needed help solving my own death, they tried to exorcise me with a lavender scented candle and a copy of *Reader's Digest*. I'm still emotionally recovering from the lavender fumes.

Then of course, and please, please keep this to yourself, because I do still have *some* pride left. I might have a small, inconvenient crush on her. Just a little one. Harmless, really. The kind of crush that makes you accidentally hover a bit closer than necessary and pretend the snow in your eyes is the reason you're blinking so much.

It's complicated, of course. It always is. Love, death, and spectral boundaries rarely make for tidy equations. But it reaches a particular level of cosmic farce when the girl you suddenly discover you want to spend the rest of your life, sorry afterlife, with has quite inconveniently, already *had* a life… and died in it. Eighty years ago. Which means she still thinks "fancying someone" involves a shy glance across a church hall, a formal invitation to dance, and the shared, intimate unwrapping of a boiled sweet. Possibly in an air-raid shelter.

Here I am, modern, flustered, and utterly unequipped to court someone who thinks "emotional vulnerability" is something you report to your superior officer. I don't even know the etiquette. If indeed there is an etiquette for dating a ghost? Am I supposed to haunt her politely? Float nearby with sincerity? Or just write "Do you like me? Yes/No/Just Fade Away" on a steamed-up pub window and hope for the best? I simply can't recall ever seeing a self-help book that equips you for falling in love with a girl, a British girl, whose been dead twice as long as I was ever alive.

Whatever the rules are, I'm fairly certain I'm already breaking most of them.

So here I am. Tony Ferrari. Yes, like the car. No, I don't have one. Ex-NYPD detective. Reluctant bookshop owner, sorry ex-bookshop owner. Current ghost. Standing in the snow like an idiot in a trench coat he no longer needs, waiting for a complete stranger to show up so I can ask them to do me a teeny tiny favour: Help me solve my own murder and move on. Yes, moving on. More on that later too.

No pressure.

I look up the lane again. Still no sign of anyone. Just the snow, a lonely pub, and my fading dignity.

A gust of wind blew a sheet of snow directly into my face like Mother Nature had had enough of my passive-aggressive haunting and wanted me to do something already. Message received.

Behind me, the door to The Rose and Crown creaked open again, it's starting to get busy. A trio of locals shuffled in, red-cheeked, scarfed, and already mid-conversation about which member of the town council had the least impressive allotment vegetables. It was a hotly debated topic in Beddlestead, second only to whether the new vicar was "too modern" or just "not enough corduroy."

They walked straight past me, of course, because I am now what doctors call "transparently unimportant." I gave a little wave. Nothing. Not even a shiver. Just like that, they were inside, warming themselves by the fire and tucking into something that may have once been a Scotch egg.

Honestly, the Scotch egg deserves a separate haunting of its own.

And then, out waddled the real villain of the piece: the pub dog.

His name is Trevor. He's a spaniel-terrier-collie-whatever mix, the kind of dog you get when two breeds love each other very much and no one has access to contraception. Trevor is ancient, perpetually damp, and smells faintly of burnt gravy. He is also the first living creature that I discovered who could see me. Ok in first instance - smell me. Who knew - ghosts smell?

This might sound like a sweet Pixar subplot. It is not.

Trevor sniffed once, twice, and then gave me the same look my mother used to give me when I said I wanted to join the police, equal parts disappointment and fear that I'd embarrass the family name. He circled me slowly, as if sizing me up for a haunting, and then, because he's Trevor, lifted his leg and peed directly onto my shoe.

Which, again, I don't need, but still. Rude.

"Trevor," I hissed, which is hard to do when you don't have functioning lungs or, you know, vocal cords. It came out more like an emotional sigh on the wind. Which, I admit, is sort of beautiful in a sad poetry kind of way. But not effective. Trevor sauntered off, tail high, mission accomplished.

I dusted off my shoe out of habit. That's the thing about being dead, you forget. You forget you can't feel anything. You forget you can't actually sneeze no matter how cold it gets. You forget, occasionally, that your reflection isn't a thing anymore and try to fix your hair in the glass of the pub door, only to discover that, nope, you're still a wisp of emotional trauma in a trench coat.

The village bell tower struck one. The bells rang out across the snowy square in the key of "you've waited long enough."

I looked down the lane again, hoping for a glimmer of movement, a flicker of life. Still nothing.

Maybe they changed their mind. Got cold feet. Or maybe they Googled "how to respond to a cryptic ad in The Times without ending up chopped into artisanal bits" and wisely chose brunch instead.

Can't really blame them.

I caught another glimpse of Betty through the frosted window. She was now sitting beside Bob, yes, we have a ghost child. Not our child if you know what I mean. He's been dead even longer than Betty. Bob has a Cockney accent, a stutter, and an unnerving fascination with Matchbox cars. Betty was telling him a story, probably about rations or rationing or ration card scandal (there was one, by the way), and they were both laughing.

I love her laugh. It sounds like the first three notes of a Glenn Miller tune.

She glanced out at me again. I gave her a little nod, pretending I was just taking in the scenic snow, not standing in it for over an hour waiting on someone who may or may not be able to hear ghosts and solve murders.

Which, again, is a weird ask. I get that. But it's also very me.

The longer I stood there, the more I started to spiral. Because let's be real: what if no one comes? What if no one else in the entire living, breathing, brunch-eating world can tune into my frequency? What if the only beings I'll ever communicate with again are Betty, Bob, a pub dog with authority issues, and Reverend Myles Abraham, a snobby Edwardian ghost who once told me I smelled like "a discount haberdashery"?

Just as I began plotting my next move, I saw a figure appear at the far end of the lane.

Coat. Scarf. Backpack. Walking like someone trying to remember if they locked their front door. They were looking around like they weren't entirely sure where they were going, which, to me, screamed "responded to a sketchy ad in the classifieds."

I straightened up. Adjusted my coat. Wiped imaginary snow from my ghost lapels.

Here we go.

They were either about to change my (after)life…

…or scream and run away, taking Trevor with them.

The first reaction when someone sees a ghost can be very unpredictable, so I had to give this meeting my best shot.

I only had the one response to the advert, who clearly didn't catch onto the "no need for names" and signed it *Angie*, as if we were pen pals and not cautiously tiptoeing into the supernatural unknown. I can't say I was overly encouraged, but with only one response - beggars can't be choosers.

RESEARCH ASSISTANT SOUGHT – UNUSUAL AUDITORY PERCEPTION REQUIRED

Have you've ever heard something others swore wasn't there? Discreet individual needed to assist with a private historical research project involving voices, memories, and matters of a delicate, immaterial nature. No prior experience necessary, though an open mind, steady nerves, and a fondness for long pauses in empty rooms would serve you well. Must be comfortable working with things that go bump, rustle, or mumble vaguely.

No vicars or priests, no nonsense. Possibly biscuits. Confidentiality guaranteed.

Please respond in next week's Times using the reference: "Still Listening." No need for names. You'll know if it's meant for you

RE: STILL LISTENING

Dear "Still Listening" (which sounds like a Fleetwood Mac B-side, by the way),

I think this is for me.

Anyway, hello. I'm Angie. I hear things. Always have. Sometimes it's music when there's no radio, sometimes it's voices saying things like "Don't go in the cellar," which I obviously ignore, and once, very clearly, "Nigel took the biscuits," which turned out to be true. Nigel absolutely took the biscuits.

I'm very discreet (except for the Nigel incident), good with awkward silences, and have a strong working relationship with the unexplained. I also make an excellent cup of tea and a passable fig roll.

If you're not looking for someone like me, I deeply apologise and hope your auditory problems clear up soon. But if you are looking for someone like me, I'm around. Usually in wellington boots.

Yours strangely,
Angie (of Tunbridge Wells)

P.S. I once had a conversation with a radiator. It wasn't very bright, but it was polite.

As I said I didn't hold out high hopes.

Now before you ask, and I know you're about to, as I can see it in your sceptical expression, I already know the question that's itching in your brain like an itchy thing that's had far too much coffee.

"How," you're wondering, "does a ghost, one without hands, thumbs, or even a reliable postcode, manage to place an advert in *The Times*?"

Aha! That's where you underestimate me. You see, being dead isn't the full stop everyone makes it out to be. Ghosts, as it turns out, are nothing if not *resourceful*. Especially those of us who've died inconveniently and still have admin left to do.

Now, you might be thinking I had help. A living assistant, perhaps? A friendly séance? A typing medium with a vintage typewriter and a fondness for tweed?

No. I had... Trevor.

Now, before you jump to conclusions, no, Trevor didn't write the advert. Trevor has paws and a brain that's mostly a sponge soaked in gravy and squirrel memories. Plus, he has the emotional maturity of a weathered sock and the bladder control of a garden tap. He's also the first living creature to see me, smell me, and, on occasion, walk directly *through* me to reach a half-eaten crisp under the bench by the dart board.

It was during one of his less dignified moments, the sudden and unsanctioned tiddle upon my foot (or the vague ectoplasmic memory of it), that inspiration struck me. Not a thunderbolt of genius, mind you. More like a lukewarm, slightly damp revelation that smelled faintly of Pedigree Chum. But inspiration nonetheless.

You see, *if* Trevor could interact with me, even if only on a scent-based level, then perhaps others could too. Maybe not all. Maybe not often. But some people, in certain states of mind, could catch a flicker. A voice. A spectral hand wafting vaguely in the direction of the peanuts.

That, dear reader, is when I turned to Reverend Myles Abraham.

Now, the Reverend is what happens when you take a man with a PhD in smirking and put him in charge of eternity. He's what you get if an Oxford don died mid-lecture and never got over the fact that nobody applauded. The Reverend has been dead since approximately the invention of pews, and he considers himself something of an authority on spectral mechanics, metaphysical etiquette, and, for some reason, cutlery.

He explained, using the kind of patient tone usually reserved for small children and poorly performing mediums, that all souls vibrate. Not in a *trendy yoga class* kind of way, but in a deeply existential, quantum-frequency-of-being sort of way. Living people vibrate too, just on a slightly different channel.

"It's like tuning a radio," he said, swirling his ghostly sherry with an air of exhausted omniscience. "We're Classic FM. The living are more... Heart FM Radio. Unfortunate, but there it is."

Apparently, most people don't notice ghosts because we're broadcasting on the wrong frequency. We're background static. White noise. The haunted equivalent of an out-of-office email. But if the dials get nudged, say, by trauma, spiritual enlightenment, or just a really decent whisky, then suddenly, the frequencies start to overlap.

Which brings us, in a roundabout and rather obvious way, to *alcohol*.

According to Reverend Abraham (who, despite being dead, is a firm believer in the sanctity of the pub), inebriation is one of the few reliable methods of *lowering the frequency barrier*. The more a person drinks, the more their internal frequency dial spins wildly toward the supernatural. In short: the drunker they get, the more likely they are to hear things that aren't technically audible. Voices, footsteps, ex-girlfriends. The usual.

"Well," I said, putting two and two together and getting roughly the shape of a plan, "I do live in a pub."

"Haunt," corrected the Reverend.

"Live," I repeated.

That's when it hit me. If I could find someone sufficiently marinated in ale and existential openness, someone whose internal radio was halfway between this world and the next, I could *communicate*. Not just knock over pint glasses or write creepy things in bathroom steam, but actually *talk*.

All I had to do was find the right person. The Rose and Crown, bless its beer-soaked beams and structurally questionable chimney, provided no shortage of candidates.

You see, The Rose and Crown is what you'd call a *local*. Not in the geographic sense, though technically, it sits in Beddlestead, a village that proudly boasts one shop, two cows, and three hundred opinions, but in the spiritual sense. It's the sort of pub where people don't just drink; they **contribute** to the atmosphere. Loudly. Repeatedly. Sometimes with involuntary interpretive dance.

It has everything a ghost could hope for in a target demographic: unreliable lighting, a fireplace that occasionally screams (possibly unrelated), and a clientele that treats sobriety like a distant cousin, acknowledged, but never invited to the good parties.

There's Old John, who claims he once saw his own twin brother in the beer garden. (He never had one.) There's Mandy, who talks to the jukebox like it owes her money. Then there's Big Dave, who once tried to arm-wrestle a coat rack and lost. In short, *these* were my people, my tribe.

Now, the trick was figuring out which of these fine, marinated individuals might be able to hear a ghost without immediately soiling themselves or launching into a hymn.

So I began experimenting. Not haunting, exactly. More... *suggesting.* A well-placed chill. A whisper near the dartboard. Rearranging beer mats to spell out "HELLO" in increasingly creative fonts. That sort of thing.

Most ignored it. Some swatted at me. One tried to blame it on gluten.

But eventually, I found her. *Mavis.*

Mavis was somewhere between 60 and 700 years old and wore cardigans like they were armour. She drank only port or sherry and insisted on calling the landlord "young man," with a cheeky highly inappropriate leer, even though he'd been shaving since 1984. Most importantly: she talked to herself. Constantly. The kind of talking where you begin to suspect she *might not* be the only one in the conversation.

One evening, I whispered in her ear, "Can you hear me?"

She replied, without blinking, "Not now, Geraldine, I'm talking to the ghost."

I did take a quick look around in case there was another ghost she was already in conversation with, but there wasn't. Only Trevor sitting beside her eyeing up her pork scratchings.

Bingo.

With Mavis now fully inducted as my one-woman ghost hotline, I devised a plan. I would dictate an advert to her, slowly, clearly, and without the use of poltergeist shorthand, and she, in her tipsy benevolence, would phone it into The Times. The fact she insisted on calling me Geraldine did prompt a few questions, but through a complicated sequence of nods, shuffles, and a brief misunderstanding involving an espresso machine, the message was sent.

RESEARCH ASSISTANT SOUGHT – UNUSUAL AUDITORY PERCEPTION REQUIRED

I dictated every word. Well, most of them. Mavis added "biscuits," which I didn't mind. Biscuits are a universal language, a cornerstone of British society, and I was trying to seem approachable.

… and so my little classified ad was born, nestled between a lost Labrador in Tunbridge Wells and a man selling antique doorknobs "with powerful energies." It was my beacon. My ghostly message in a very expensive bottle.

Would anyone answer? Would they understand?

Well. That's another story.

But I can say this: never underestimate the combined power of spectral ingenuity, canine urination, and a half-cut pensioner with a mobile phone.

It's how most revolutions start.

I guess you're starting to realise, I ramble, not in the hearty walks through the countryside ramble, but I lose train of thought and go off in multiple directions and down rabbit holes.

Angie stood at the low stone wall by the gate that led to the pub, casually kicking the snow off her Wellies. There was a kind of purpose to it, like she'd trained in the art of snow-removal at a Swiss finishing school. One boot. Then the other. Then a little shake, which was less to dislodge snow and more to assert her authority over the surrounding landscape.

The sky above was grey in that specific English way that suggested it might do *something* again soon, but only once it had made you stand around awkwardly for long enough.

Angie glanced about with the sort of scrutiny one usually reserves for locating lost relatives at railway stations or catching squirrels in the act of theft. Her gaze swept the front of the pub, then the pub sign, then the roof tiles, and finally hovered in my direction. Not *at* me, mind. Just *through* me, in that cheerfully oblivious way living people do when ghosts attempt meaningful eye contact.

I stepped forward, arms wide in what I hoped looked like friendly enthusiasm "Angie! It's great to meet you. Thank you so much for coming!"

Nothing. Not a flinch. Not a blink. She might as well have been looking through a particularly unconvincing pane of frosted glass. Or, as it happened, *me.*

I waved. I nodded. I attempted a cheerful little bow that turned into more of a startled stagger (you try balancing with no working muscles). Still, not even a twitch of recognition. Trevor, the pub dog, emerged from the doorway just in time to witness my one-ghost performance art. He glanced at me with the resigned indifference of a creature who has long accepted the supernatural as a mild inconvenience, then looked at Angie, then back at me.

Then he yawned and padded back inside.

That was Trevor's thing. He had the air of a retired wizard who occasionally turns into a dog, mostly for the excuse to nap in public.

I wasn't giving up. I jumped up and down. I tried standing in the way of snowflakes so they would bounce off my ectoplasm and hit her directly in the face. I even attempted to kick a small pebble at her Wellie. That part didn't work for two reasons: one, I don't have working feet, and two, pebbles are surprisingly judgy when it comes to spectral interference.

Nothing worked. I could've performed Hamlet on ice in front of her and the only response I'd have got was a sniff and a vague comment about someone leaving a window open.

Then, without so much as a "pardon me, spectral stranger," Angie looked directly at me and walked *through* me.

Now. Let's pause for a moment and talk about what that feels like. People always imagine it's cold. It's not. It's not warm, either. It's… itchy. Not on your skin, because you don't have any, but in your *sense* of where skin ought to be. Like your soul just wore an itchy jumper and then someone took it off with a blender.

She passed through me and into the pub with the unhurried confidence of a woman who knew exactly where she was going and had absolutely no regard for who she might walk through on the way.

I stood there, stunned and vibrating slightly, like a haunted tuning fork.

Inside, The Rose and Crown was the usual chaos. Warm yellow light, the hum of conversation, the sound of a cork being popped from a bottle, and the occasional "Y'alright, Dave?" shouted at a volume scientifically proven to reset pacemakers. Most of the commotion was coming from the public bar. That's where the regulars sat, men with beards and women with opinions, and all of them with stories about things that happened "before it all went to pot." The Rose and Crown was a kind of retirement home for old jokes and slightly damp coats.

Angie, who had still not acknowledged my presence in any meaningful way beyond a direct phasing-through, plonked herself down at the quieter end of the lounge bar on a tall stool. She gave a contented sigh, the sort usually only made after collapsing onto a sofa or getting into a warm bath and began to gently stroke the radiator beside her.

I blinked. Not literally, obviously, but you get the idea.

She stroked the radiator.

She *smiled* at the radiator.

That's when I knew. This was her. *This* was Angie.

Nobody else could smile at a radiator and make it feel like it had just been complimented on its haircut.

She ordered a large sherry in a voice that suggested she'd done this before. Possibly twice already that day. Then she looked out the window with the wistful air of someone who'd just remembered a dream they'd forgotten to finish.

I pulled myself together, hovered beside her and said, "Right, Angie, it's me. The advert. You replied. Let's talk ghosts."

Still nothing. I could've been a coatrack for all she noticed.

So I stayed. I sat down on the stool next to her, less a "sit" and more a strategic float-and-linger. I tried to chat. I told her about the Reverend. I explained the snowflake experiments. I told her about Trevor and the time he chased a ghost cat into the cellar and then refused to come out until someone bribed him with gravy.

Nothing. She sipped her sherry, nodded vaguely at the fireplace, and continued her psychic romance with the heating system.

It wasn't until her *second* sherry, ordered with the casual elegance of someone doing essential medical rehydration, that she tilted her head and said, quite suddenly, "Oo, there you are. Sorry. Didn't see you arrive. Want a sherry?"

I stared at her.

"You... you see me now?" I asked, trying to keep the disbelief out of my voice and largely failing.

"Of course I do, dear. You've been rattling on about radiators and dogs for the last few minutes. Honestly, I thought you were one of the quieter ones."

I was floored. Figuratively. Literally wasn't an option.

"You could hear all that?"

She nodded, sipping delicately. "You've got a nice voice. Bit echoey. Like a nostalgic kettle."

I wasn't entirely sure what that meant, but I was taking it as a compliment.

She turned to me, eyes sharp now. "So, you're the one who placed the advert?"

I nodded. "Yes. That was me."

"And you're..." she waved a hand vaguely in the air, "...all floaty and not-quite-there?"

"Yup. Ghost," I said, with the kind of sheepishness only the dead can muster.

"Hmm," she said, as if I'd just told her I collected spoons. "That does explain the coat."

I looked down. I was wearing the same trench coat I'd died in, which had seemed like a good idea at the time. It looked, in the right light, vaguely noir. In the wrong light, it looked like a wardrobe decision made during a blackout.

"I get this sort of thing now and then," Angie went on. "Always been a bit sensitive to the other side. Family trait. My gran used to chat with dead husbands during tea. Not hers you understand, she'd never been married, she was just a flirt."

She smiled fondly into her sherry.

I looked at her, properly this time. Hair like it had once been styled and then unionised, scarf knitted from optimism and leftover wool, eyes twinkling with the sort of mischievous clarity that meant she absolutely knew what was going on and intended to make the most of it.

She could see me now. She could *hear* me. More importantly, she had just offered me a drink.

It wasn't a séance. It wasn't a ritual. It wasn't Latin incantations or ritual salt circles.

It was Angie.

… and, to be honest, she might be exactly what I needed.

Even if she did flirt with radiators.

"Let's move to the comfy chairs," she said, with the confident air of a woman who had claimed many a cushioned seat in her time and dared anyone to challenge her right to it.

The Rose and Crown, by now, was entering its late afternoon lull, having just survived the lunchtime rush of bubble and squeak. Now, for the uninitiated or those not raised on British pub menus written in chalk, bubble and squeak is what happens when leftover vegetables band together for one last dramatic performance. It's cabbage and potato fried until they admit defeat, often served with bacon, eggs, or a hangover. It makes a sound like a wet sock being startled when it hits the pan, hence the name.

The pub had done a fine trade in it that day. There was a sort of post-bubble-and-squeak haze in the air. A gentle fog of contented digestion is standard in most English pubs around 2:45 p.m.

The comfy chairs were upholstered in the kind of fabric that defied modern classification, part floral, part tweed, part disappointment. The sort of chairs that had survived generations of elbows, dog hair, and philosophical debates about the correct pronunciation of "scone." (It's "scone," of course, like "gone," unless you're wrong.)

Angie settled into hers like a queen into a throne that smelled faintly of ale and polish. I hovered slightly above mine.

The barman brought over her next sherry without being asked, which either meant she was a regular or that sherry was simply summoned by sitting in a certain chair at a certain time. You never quite know in pubs like this. There are ancient systems at work: unspoken rules, invisible timetables, and possibly one elderly landlord who remembers your order because he hasn't forgotten anything since 1986, when he briefly blacked out during a game of darts and woke up married.

She accepted the drink with a nod and continued her conversation with me, or rather, from the barman's perspective, continued her conversation with herself, the fire, or possibly the ghost of her last sherry. Judging by the complete lack of alarm, this was not an uncommon sight.

This is the thing about pubs: once the alcohol reaches a certain saturation point in the bloodstream, social rules become more like guidelines, and the line between "chatting with a friend" and "having a full-on debate with a bar stool" gets worryingly fuzzy.

It reminded me of when Bluetooth earbuds first appeared, those tiny, nearly invisible things that allowed people to walk around talking animatedly to no one at all, while the rest of us tried to determine whether we were witnessing a live podcast or a minor psychotic episode.

There was a regular customer in the bookshop, Roly. Cornish. Ancient in the way that suggested he might have once personally offended Time and was being punished by being left alive longer than everyone else. Roly had strong opinions about everything, particularly the price of marmalade, the dangers of processed cheese, and people who talked to themselves on the street. He'd stand near the fiction section, peering suspiciously over his glasses and mutter, "Talkin' to the pixies, they are," with a firm shake of the head, as if he'd seen it happen once during the war and wasn't about to let it become fashionable again.

Sorry, I digress. But then, I'm dead. I have *nothing but time* to digress with.

Back in the pub, Angie was settling into her sherry with the efficiency of a woman who knew precisely how long it took for her blood to turn conversational. She had that way of sipping between thoughts, punctuating her sentences with the clink of glass and the occasional satisfied "ahhh," like each sip was a small reward for surviving another half hour of reality.

"You know," she said, "I've always been a bit tuned in. Sensitive, you might say. I mean... aware."

I nodded. Ghost-nodded, really. It's a lot like regular nodding, but with slightly less chin and more wistful sadness.

"Had it since I was a girl. Used to talk to things. My mother said I was just imaginative. My father said I'd grow out of it. The vicar said it was probably a phase, like Beatlemania. But then I kept doing it. When the voices started answering back, I stopped telling people."

She smiled as she said it. I liked her. She was calm in that maddeningly British way, like someone who would calmly finish a crossword while watching a horror movie.

I attempted to respond, to keep the momentum going. I told her about The Reverend Myles Abraham and his belief in ghost-frequencies, about the pub dog Trevor and his spectral bladder, about the snowflakes and the classified ad and the fact that I hadn't been this anxious since I had to give a speech at my ex-wife's second wedding. (Long story. Short toast.)

She listened. Sort of. She made the right noises, at least - hmm, ah, oh dear - and gave me occasional glances that might have indicated interest or might simply have been checking if I'd finished so she could order another sherry.

"So," I said, "you saw the ad. You replied. You said you've got... experience."

"Oh, I've got *experience*, dear," she said. "Ghosts, spirits, echoes, spectres, the whole ghastly catalogue. Most of them are harmless, though I had a bit of a spat with a poltergeist in '98. Nasty piece of work. Lived in my pantry. Moved all my tins alphabetically. Took me *weeks* to unlearn the system."

She leaned forward slightly. "Thing is, you lot are usually looking for something. A message to pass on. A memory to share. Or just someone to notice you before you fade out entirely. You're like dreams people keep having after they've forgotten why."

I wanted to say something profound. Something that would neatly sum up my reason for being, my unyielding quest for justice, my identity as a spirit of purpose and urgency.

Instead I said, "Would you like a crisp?"

She accepted without hesitation. We shared a quiet moment, ghost and woman, over a bag of salt and vinegar, watching the fire and the pub and the endless slow swirl of snow out the window. She ate hers I sucked on mine.

It wasn't a grand spiritual awakening. It wasn't some cosmic sign. It was just... comfortable. A small, strange peace in the middle of a long, complicated afterlife.

In that moment, I knew I'd picked the right person.

"So what are you?" she asks, with a twinkle in her eye that suggests she already knows and is just waiting to see if I get the answer right.

Now, this is an odd question. It's the sort of question that sounds deceptively simple until someone actually asks it out loud and you realise you haven't the faintest idea how to answer.

In life, people mostly ask "Who are you?" That's a manageable question. It has structure. You can throw out a name, maybe a job title, and the world nods and continues. "Who are you?" assumes we all come pre-labelled with some kind of identity badge, and all you have to do is read it. But "What are you?" ... well. That's something else entirely.

It's the kind of question you expect philosophers to wrestle with in a smoke-filled room while stroking a beard or a pipe or a cat, possibly all three. It's not the sort of thing you're prepared to be asked in a pub by a woman who's already halfway down her third sherry and talking to a ghost.

"I suppose… I'm a ghost," I say eventually, holding my hands up in the universal shrug gesture that means "this is a stab in the dark and I reserve the right to be completely wrong."

Am I a ghost? A memory? A dream? A bit of badly stored energy rattling around the psychic plumbing? I honestly don't know. More annoyingly, nobody has given me a proper user manual for this.

"Time is the problem," Angie says, swirling her glass and peering into it like the answer to everything might be hiding beneath a sliver of lemon peel. From the look on my face, she can tell I'm lost.

"Oh yes," she continues, patting my hand, which she obviously can't actually touch, so it's more of a dignified hover. "We ignore time for most of our lives, don't we? We measure it, complain about it, occasionally try to kill it, but we don't really *understand* it. So whatever you assume to be true about time, dear, it probably isn't."

The fire crackles in approval. Fires are always good at that. They sound like they're agreeing with the conversation, even when they're really just digesting logs.

I sit forward, intrigued despite myself. Knowing *what* I am might be a lot more important than *who* I am. Names are easy to forget. Ask any substitute teacher. But understanding why you exist, or don't, is another matter.

"Time is directional," she says, nodding as if this is obvious. "Who knew?"

"Not me," I say honestly.

"Well, the Kuuk Thaayorre Aboriginal community knew. Brilliant people. They don't see time as a line at all, more like a location. They remember the future the same way we remember the past. Einstein knew, of course he did. Bright lad, wild hair. Very clever. Thought time was all relative, which, frankly, it is. Especially at family weddings."

She sips again and continues. "See, during life, we travel. Geographically. Emotionally. Spiritually, if you're into that sort of thing. But it's time that stitches all those places together into a neat little timeline, so your brain doesn't explode trying to figure out why you're six years old and paying a mortgage. Time puts everything in order. It's the glue. When that glue comes unstuck, say, because you die messily or unexpectedly or violently, you don't always stay where you're supposed to."

I raise an eyebrow. At least, I think I do. Ghostly eyebrows are tricky things. They work mostly on intention.

"So, you're saying I'm… unstuck?"

"Yes," she says brightly, as if she's just described me as charming or well-dressed. "You're unstuck. Dislodged from your linear narrative. You've shaken up the snow globe of your life, and now bits of you are stranded in all sorts of places. The part of you that felt deeply about something is stuck *there*" pointing with a wave the Queen would be proud of, somewhere in the vague direction of the beer garden, "the part that wanted something badly is stuck *here*, and the rest of you is trying to pick up the pieces and make some kind of sense of it all."

"Like an emotional jigsaw," I murmur.

"With half the pieces missing," she agrees. "… and some of them belong to a completely different puzzle. Possibly one about horses."

She takes another sip, then adds, "That's what ghosts are, really. Bits of soul with no glue. Fragments of stories that were rudely interrupted… and when the story ends too suddenly, the bits go wandering. Looking for the plot."

It's all making an unsettling amount of sense. "I've lost the plot."

"So, you were murdered?" she asks suddenly, leaping from metaphysical theory to small talk like it's a casual transition. I'm still processing the glue metaphor, and now we're onto homicide. It feels a bit abrupt.

"Yes," I say slowly. "So I'm told. It's why I'm still here, apparently. The Reverend, one of the older ghosts reckons that's what anchors me here."

"Sounds about right," she says with a nod, not missing a beat. "Murder's a messy way to go. Rips a hole in the story. Big, ugly tear right down the middle. No wonder you're leaking bits of soul all over the place."

She sips again, then adds thoughtfully, "When you shake up time, the glue goes. When the glue goes, you don't get to be a neat little memory in someone's photo album. You end up in a pub, talking to a radiator and waiting for someone to notice."

"That's… bleak," I say.

"It's *true*," she counters, "and those two are often related."

I lean back, well, hover back, and glance around The Rose and Crown. The cracked wood, the faded wallpaper, the slow whirl of dust motes performing a lazy ballet in the firelight.

"…and you're saying I'm stuck here because part of me is… what? Is still here?"

"Exactly," she says, pleased. "This place holds a bit of you. A memory. A moment. Something important happened to you here, whether you remember it or not."

I furrow my brow. "I don't recall ever being in The Rose and Crown before I woke up here, just under the dart board."

"Oh, you were, dear. You just have to find out *when*."

It's a disconcerting thought. Being somewhere and not remembering it. Like finding your name carved into a tree you've never seen or getting a birthday card from someone you don't remember dating.

We lapse into a companionable silence. The fire pops gently, as if eavesdropping. The barman glances over, presumably to check if Angie has fallen asleep mid-sip. She hasn't. She's just thinking. Very deeply. With her eyes closed. With a tiny snore.

A man approaches the seat I'm in, clearly intent on claiming the comfy chair for himself. Angie, without opening her eyes, lets out a tremendous and theatrical snore that would have made an opera singer proud. The man startles, mutters something about "not disturbing the elderly," and backs off.

She winks at me without looking.

That's when it hits me. This might be the first person who really *gets* this. Not just the ghost thing. The *me* thing. Angie sees the whole messy tangle of soul-bits and timelines and still decides to sit beside it, offer it a sherry, and protect its seat with weaponised snoring.

"I think you might be the most unusual person I've met," I say.

"Probably," she replies. ".. and thank you, but I'm also the *only* one talking to you. So, let's just go with *most qualified* for now."

She clinks her glass against mine, which makes no sound because mine doesn't exist. But the gesture's there.

Outside, the snow starts again.

Inside, the glue begins to stick. Just a little.

CHAPTER TWO

SPIRITS, SIGNALS, AND MARY BLOOM'IN POPPINS

I watched Angie tottering off down the snowy lane like a woman entirely confident in her ability to negotiate frozen cobblestones with nothing but a pair of bargain wellington boots and raw determination. I watched her go with the air of a man who had just met his only hope of solving his own murder and was now watching said hope, wobble, meander from one side of the lane to the other, while humming a tune that may or may not have involved ukuleles.

"You're staring," said a voice beside me.

Which wouldn't have been surprising had I not been entirely alone, dead, and facing in exactly the opposite direction of anyone who should have been talking to me.

I turned, swivelled really, ghosts tend to swivel more than turn, and there she was. Betty.

Betty had a talent for appearing beside you without making a sound, which would have been unnerving enough without the added bonus of her habit of leaning slightly too close, as if haunting was a contact sport. She looked like she'd just stepped out of a wartime poster for tea rationing: hair perfectly set, coat buttoned, lipstick unreasonably immaculate for someone who'd been dead since 1943.

"Honestly," she continued, folding her arms in a way that suggested she was judging both my posture and possibly my entire afterlife, "you look like a ghost who's just seen a ghost."

"I'm not used to people who think they see ghosts walking away from me," I muttered.

She raised an eyebrow. "Tony, you're dead. People walk through you."

Fair point.

Betty peered down the lane. "Friend of yours?"

"Potentially. She answered an ad."

"The ad you got the dog to send?"

"You knew about that?"

"We didn't stop reading newspapers in 1943 you know"

"Technically, I dictated it to Mavis, who was drunk enough to think I was her cousin Geraldine. Trevor just barked at the bar stool she sat on."

"That explains the biscuits," she said.

There was a pause while we both considered Angie's retreating figure. Betty, in that disconcerting way she had, hummed tunelessly.

Then she said, "The Reverend's turned off the Wi-Fi again."

I blinked. Or rather, performed the ghost equivalent of blinking, which mostly involves looking surprised and slightly translucent.

"The pub has Wi-Fi?"

"Had. Past tense. The Reverend said it was interfering with his signal."

"His what?"

"His signal," she repeated. "You know, the frequency. The cosmic vibration. The Wi-Fi was apparently 'muddling the spirit waves. When it happens he starts slurring, like he's drunk'"

"It explains why WIFI signals drop so often I suppose"

"He started quoting Mary Poppins."

That stopped me.

"Which part?"

"'Winds in the east, mist coming in…' and then he stared into the fireplace like he wanted to pull a lamp stand out of it. He's very theatrical when his reception's off."

The Reverend, of course, was the pub's oldest ghost in both the chronological and spiritual sense. He believed in order, hierarchy, metaphysical etiquette, and correcting other people's grammar.

We watched Angie disappear around the corner, her bright red scarf flapping behind her like a flag of chaotic good.

"She saw me," I said quietly.

Betty looked at me sideways. "And?"

"She spoke to me."

"And?"

"She offered me a sherry."

Betty nodded slowly, as if this was indeed a development of ghost-shaking proportions.

"You're smitten," she said mischievously.

"I am *not* smitten."

"You are absolutely smitten. It's all over your face."

"My face doesn't even work properly anymore!"

"It's *hovering* with smitten."

I tried to look nonchalant. This mostly involved crossing my arms and accidentally phasing through the gate of the pub.

"Look, she's just… interesting, alright? She didn't scream, she didn't run, she didn't throw salt at me. She listened. Properly… and she knew what I was."

"So, you like her." Same mischievous smile. She knew what she was doing. Women do.

"She stroked a radiator and made it feel appreciated."

Betty smiled. "Tony, you do realise that you're flirting with a woman who talks to central heating?"

"Not flirting! …and yet somehow, she's the most together person I've met since dying."

Betty was quiet for a moment. Then she said, softly, "Be careful."

"Why?"

She didn't answer. Just turned to look at the pub.

We stood in silence. Well, I stood. Betty sort of hovered in that way women do when they're wearing sensible shoes and emotional armour.

"Well," said Betty, brushing snowflakes off her coat in a way that was entirely unnecessary but extremely stylish, "don't just float there. Let's get inside before The Reverend decides to start quoting *Sound of Music* and banishes all electric kettles."

With that, she disappeared.

Not walked. Not faded.

Just *pop*. Gone.

I stood there a moment longer, feeling the snow pile on my shoulders like increasingly passive-aggressive frosting. Then I sighed, squared my trench coat, and followed.

This wasn't going to be easy.

But then again, nothing worth doing ever was.

Especially not in Beddlestead.

Especially not when you're already dead… and in love with ghost.

The interior of The Rose and Crown had adopted its usual late-afternoon hush, the kind where sound dared not echo too loudly for fear of waking someone's digestion. The usual crowd had stumbled out into the cold, most of them in the approximate direction of home or something that passed for it. Only the landlord remained now, methodically wiping the same pint glass he'd been drying for what could easily be the past six years.

Well, he had been wiping it. Currently, he was squinting at the back of the bar's Wi-Fi router with a "don't mess with me" expression, that indeed you wouldn't want to mess with. A dog-eared instruction manual sat open beside him, held together by Sellotape, hope, and dried beer. Clearly this was not the first time this had happened.

I drifted through the door and made my way to the hearth, where Betty had materialised with the same grace as a disappointed schoolmistress. The Reverend Myles Abraham was already there, sitting, or rather floating just enough above the cushion to ensure no mortal ever found it comfortable again.

The Reverend looked up from a leather-bound copy of *The Book of Rituals, Rites, and Slightly Unreliable Psalms,* which he only ever seemed to consult when pretending to be tolerant of other opinions.

"Ah, Ferrari," he said, like he was reading my name off a particularly confusing tax return. "Back from your vigil in the snow. Discover the meaning of death yet?"

"No," I said, sinking into the empty chair by the fire. "But I did meet someone who talks to radiators."

"Excellent," said the Reverend, as if this confirmed a long-standing suspicion. "I've always said the plumbing is more spiritually receptive than the clergy."

I watched the fire for a moment. Ghosts don't feel warmth, not exactly. But we remember it, the same way you remember a melody or the smell of someone you loved. The fire *suggested* warmth, and that was almost enough.

The landlord let out a heavy sigh behind the bar.

"Still at it?" Betty asked The Reverend, nodding towards the bar...

"He's been trying to reset the Wi-Fi for half an hour," he said. "I think he's entered the spiritual stage of frustration."

"That's usually when he starts talking to the coasters," Betty added.

As if on cue, the landlord muttered something and gently tapped the side of the router with a spoon.

The Reverend looked over his glasses. "That will do nothing, of course. The interference is metaphysical."

"You mean *you* broke it," I said.

"I disengaged its influence," he said primly. "It was clouding the frequency."

"It was letting people post pictures of their dinner. That's not clouding, that's community." Said Betty with an almost edge of envy.

"Mmm," said the Reverend, turning a page with such force it almost fluttered.

There was a pause. The fire crackled. Somewhere, Trevor let out a long, contented snore that suggested he had, at some point, annexed an unattended slipper.

"She saw me," I said aloud, not meaning to.

The Reverend raised an eyebrow. "The radiator woman?"

"Angie," I said. "She replied to the ad."

"Ah the ad" smirked the reverend "we had a chortle over that one"

Betty went a little pink. Clearly she didn't want me to know she had a giggle over it too. I didn't care, I had just discovered that ghosts can change colour, a bit like an octopus. In Betty's case a very pretty one.

"She saw me. She *heard* me. Properly."

"And she offered him a sherry" said the pink lady. I threw a scowl her way.

"That's rare," said the Reverend. "Even among the gifted, perception fades."

"Then why hasn't hers?"

He closed his book. Slowly. Like it offended him less to consider the question than to leave it unanswered.

"There are a few people in every generation," he said, "who carry a kind of... permeability. An open door in the mind, if you like. Most learn to shut it. Too many strange things knocking. But some… they hang a little bell on the handle and invite them in for tea."

Betty tapped her foot on the hearth rug, which didn't move but looked offended nonetheless. "So what now, Tony? You going to tell her everything? That you were murdered? That you don't know how or why or by whom?"

I hesitated. "Eventually."

"Eventually?"

"Look, I don't want to scare her off."

"You're a ghost, darling. That's *literally* your only job."

"Not the point."

The Reverend leaned forward, elbows ghosting slightly into the armrests. "The girl is a tether. An anchor in the current. But be warned, tethers fray."

"Oh good," I muttered. "Another metaphor. I was running low."

"If she sees you," the Reverend went on, "then she's part of this. Whether she likes it or not."

"She said she was used to it. Voices, whispers, radiators."

"Then she's either gifted or mad. Possibly both."

"Aren't we all?"

Betty stood abruptly. "I'm making tea."

"We don't drink tea," I said.

"Exactly. It'll give me something not to do."

She vanished through the kitchen wall.

The Reverend resumed his reading with the dignity of a man who had clearly chosen this page specifically to ignore me.

I watched the fire again. The flames danced like they were trying out for something.

The landlord, having apparently reached the 'bargaining' stage of tech support, tried to coax the router into life with a biscuit. It refused, with blinking lights of disapproval.

Outside, the snow continued to fall.

Inside, something had started to shift.

Something small.

Something important.

Possibly involving sherry.

Possibly involving fate.

After Betty ghosted off to not-make-tea and the Reverend buried himself back in scripture or sulking, I slipped out of the hearth's circle of flickering light and wandered over to the far side of the pub. The good thing about being dead, if we're assigning any points at all, is that you can loiter dramatically without the pressure of ordering anything. Or being asked to leave. Or, you know, existing properly.

I found my usual perch near the window. Not too drafty, decent view of the lane, and just far enough away from the fireplace to avoid being pulled into theological debates with a dead Edwardian. This was as good a time as any to introduce myself to you, dear reader.

Like I said, Tony Ferrari. Yes, like the car but unfortunately no family relation.

As you've probably guessed by now, accent, trench coat, general aura of having seen too many crime dramas…   I'm not from around here. Born and raised in the Bronx. Used to be a cop. A detective, in fact. With the NYPD. Which, I'll admit, sounds cooler than it usually was.

Now, if your only reference point for 'detective work' comes from TV, I'd like to take this moment to gently and respectfully shatter your illusions. There were no tropical islands. No unorthodox Belgian moustaches. No quirky amateur sleuths solving murders in a cake shop.

What it was, mostly, was paperwork. Endless, soul-wilting paperwork. The kind that gave you repetitive strain injury and made you doubt the Theory of Evolution.

I had a great partner, though. Thomas Clifford. Smart, solid, the kind of guy who never missed a detail and always bought the good coffee. We made a good team. He was the kind of man you trusted to watch your back, fill out the right forms, and remember to bring donuts to stakeouts.

Then one day, he wasn't.

Heart attack. Just like that. No warning. No drama. One moment he was standing by the vending machine, telling me off for forgetting lunch again, and the next… gone. I thought I might bump into him somewhere around here in some ghost like state, but he's "moved on". Apparently moving on is important, so I'll come to that in a few moments.

I lost the buzz for police work after he died. Every day became the same endless loop. Same faces. Same crimes. Same suspects doing the same stupid things. I stayed for another year, but I wasn't really there. Not really.

Then, to my complete and utter surprise, I got a letter. From a lawyer. A proper old-school one, with a waistcoat and everything, who handed me an envelope like it contained the will of a distant baron.

It turned out Tom, Thomas, had left me something in his will. Or rather, his father had. The old man passed away five days before Tom, and in some final twist of timing, everything had been wrapped together.

His dad was British, a fact I only vaguely remembered from some old stake out conversations about cricket, marmalade, and how Americans ruin tea.

The inheritance? A bookshop.

A real one. Wooden sign, narrow door, tiny bell that jingled every time someone opened it and tried not to sneeze at the dust.

Finsbury Books. Tucked away just off Finsbury Square in London, wedged between a falafel place and a dry cleaner that never once looked open.

So, I moved. Packed up what little I had, cashed in a few favours, and boarded a plane to a country where traffic comes from the wrong direction and people apologise when *you* bump into *them*.

Running a bookshop wasn't exactly on my bingo card for life, but it grew on me. Fast.

Finsbury Books started as a modest little shop with some modern fiction and a lot of creaky floorboards, but over the years, it built up a reputation. Not for new titles. No, no. Our strength was in the hunt. The rare stuff. Out-of-print editions, obscure tomes, things with the kind of margins that make collectors whisper like cult members.

We became the place people called when their eccentric uncle died and left behind a library of volumes no one in the family could pronounce, let alone appreciate. We'd sort, assess, and.. yes, occasionally offer them far less money than the books were worth.

Don't judge me. Those people weren't in it for the love of literature. They wanted space. Money. A place to park the peloton.

But I loved it. I really did. There was something about tracking down a long-lost edition of *The Principles of Steam and Parapsychology* for a collector in Wales that gave me a sense of purpose again. It was detective work, in a way. Just with fewer bullets and more mustiness.

… and now here I am.

Dead.

Haunting an English pub.

Trying to solve my own murder.

Which, let's be honest, is the most genre-appropriate twist my life has ever taken.

I sighed, leaned back against the window (without technically touching it), and glanced toward the fire, where spectral domesticity was now in full swing. Betty had returned, not with anything as crass as a real teapot or the vulgar clink of crockery, but with a phantom tea tray so dignified, so absurdly ceremonial, it might have warranted its own coronation. She was now pouring nothing into nothing with the poise of a duchess hosting the afterlife's most exclusive luncheon. The liquid did not steam. The cups did not clink. The sugar did not sweeten. But somehow, it was still, undeniably, *tea*.

Now, I could write an entire volume on the subject of British tea. Not just a chapter. A *volume*. Possibly with footnotes, appendices, and a bonus fold-out timeline charting the psychological significance of 'tea o'clock' as a national coping strategy. Because tea in Britain is not a beverage. It is not even a concept. It is a *response*.

You see, when an English person offers you tea, they are not merely suggesting hydration. No, no. What they are really saying is, "The world is on fire, my emotions are all trying to sit in the same chair, and someone's just reversed into my dustbin, but if I can put the kettle on, *something* can still be done."

Tea is the national emotional duct tape. It is Britain's go-to tool for addressing grief, stress, awkward silences, diplomatic incidents, mild inconvenience, and the recurring national crisis that is British weather. If you stub your toe, make tea. If someone dies, make tea. If a foreign dignitary says something vaguely insulting about crumpets, *definitely* make tea. If there's an alien invasion, rest assured someone, somewhere, will be filling the kettle and muttering, "Well, better get the good mugs out, then."

Betty, of course, had been British since before the invention of the humble teabag. She held the act of making tea in the same reverence a surgeon gives to scalpels, or a Victorian butler to secrets. Even in death, she performed the ritual with all due decorum: warming the phantom pot first, swirling the invisible leaves, and pouring the ghostly brew into non-existent bone-china that nonetheless *judged you* if you didn't raise your pinky.

The point, I realised, was not the tea. It never had been. It was the performance of calm. The illusion of control. The quiet statement that no matter how strange, how unsettling, or how catastrophically absurd life, or in this case, afterlife became, one could still boil water, pour it over something dried and crumbling, and declare with great national pride: *this will help.*

Betty sipped her nothing-tea with a satisfied air, pinky ever so slightly raised, gaze locked firmly on the fire. The Reverend, meanwhile, was deep into his third philosophical argument with a barstool he had named Gerald. (Gerald was a good listener, terrible at Latin declension, but there was no one else to listen)

I watched them both for a moment. The spectral domestic bliss. The ancient arguments. The illusion of a functioning routine, built on the fragile scaffolding of habit and hot beverages.

Somewhere out there, Angie was walking back to wherever she came from. With her ghosts and her radiators and her very excellent boots. She struck me as the kind of woman who would make her own tea, thank you very much, and never trust a bag unless she knew where it had been. The kind who didn't take sugar, not because she disliked it, but because she once decided not to and had never revisited the decision. You could build a society around people like that, an empire even. Or at the very least, a functioning neighbourhood watch.

I left Betty to her tea and the Reverend to his theological barstool battle and drifted off for a little constitutional about the place. You'd be surprised how much wandering a ghost can do without ever going anywhere. But every haunting needs a route, and mine often took me down the corridor that led to the loos, what the

British charmingly call 'toilets' with the sort of cheerful understatement that suggests they expect you to bring a hat and perhaps write a postcard.

The corridor was narrow, creaky-floored, and would have been too cold even before I was dead. It had that peculiar quality of most British pub hallways, as if it had been added as an afterthought by a builder with very long arms and absolutely no spatial awareness. But what made it worth the stroll was the wall on the left, which had become a kind of unofficial Rogues' Gallery. A shrine to drinkers past, landlords gone, minor local celebrities, major local scandals, and once, memorably, a horse.

Old black-and-white photos jostled for space with more recent colour prints, all in mismatched frames that looked like they'd been rescued from a boot sale and then tactically rearranged by some halfwit halfway through their third pint.

I'd walked past them a hundred times. Floated, mostly. They were the kind of thing you barely notice until you do, and then you can't help but look a little too long.

I admit, I hadn't paid much attention to the faces before. A lot of tweed. A lot of moustaches. A few mullets. But for some reason, one photo caught me.

This one.

Betty.

She's standing in front of the old wooden bar, younger than I'd ever seen her in my memories or her current ghostly form. Hair pinned perfectly. That no-nonsense glint already there in the eyes. A smile, yes, but one held in reserve, like it had places to be and a timetable to keep.

Her father once owned The Rose and Crown. Ran it like a ship, apparently. A quiet man with loud eyebrows, according to the Reverend. Betty grew up here, lived above the pub, played under the tables, learned to pull a pint before she'd figured out long division. She used to chase a predecessor of Trevor out of the cellar and tell the drunks when they'd had enough, and they listened, because no one says no to a girl with that kind of certainty in her voice.

I'm glad her photo's here. It belongs.

The Reverend told me once that he saw Betty grow up here, from a little girl with scuffed knees and questions about ghosts, to the teenager who packed her bags with military precision and left to join the RAF. Said she walked down this very corridor in her new uniform, straight-backed and unsmiling, like she was off to have stern words with the Luftwaffe.

But even the Reverend doesn't know what happened after that.

No one does. Not exactly.

She came back. That much is certain. Her photo wouldn't be here if she hadn't. Someone took this picture. Someone framed it. Someone remembered.

Then she died.

Murdered, she said. Not 'passed away', not 'a bit of bad luck'. Murdered. Which makes two of us.

But she doesn't remember by who either and that, more than anything, is what keeps her here.

It's a cruel twist, really. That the dead remember everything except the thing they need most. The thing that tethered them to the land of the living in the first place.

I hovered there, staring at her photo. She looked so alive. Not just in the obvious way, the heartbeat and the breathing, but in the sense that she was going somewhere. That the world hadn't caught up to her yet. That she had one hand on her suitcase and the other in her coat pocket; fingers curled around something important.

Now she poured invisible tea into imaginary cups and watched over this pub like a guardian who refused to rest.

We're not so different, I suppose. She has her mystery. I have mine. Maybe we'll solve them together.

Or maybe we'll just keep drinking tea and arguing with barstools until the end of time.

Still, there are worse afterlives.

Now, you might be wondering: what's the point of all this? Why am I still here, besides a deeply ingrained inability to leave a pub without finishing a conversation? Why don't I just float off into the eternal light or hop on the celestial escalator or whatever it is ghosts are meant to do?

Well, apparently, it's more complicated than that. Of course it would be...

You see, there's a thing we ghosts call *moving on*. No one knows exactly what it means. Some say it's peace. Some say it's closure. Some say it's just a particularly smug form of existential smugness followed by an echoing harp solo and the removal of one's unfinished business. I personally suspect it involves admin. Possibly a cosmic form with tick boxes for "haunted satisfactorily" and "returned library books".

The story, at least in the sermons delivered by The Reverend, goes that ghosts move on when they get justice. Justice is linked with Time apparently. Or, at least, a solid answer. Some kind of emotional full stop. But here's the kicker: the longer it's been since you were murdered, the harder it gets. Justice, it turns out, has an expiry date. It's like milk, or goodwill at a family reunion.

… if the person who murdered you dies, or indeed is murdered themselves, before you get justice? Well, then you're out of luck, sunshine. No forwarding address. No appeals process. Just a spiritual shrug and the ongoing joy of existing as a foggy remnant with commitment issues.

Which is why I'm not taking any chances.

I'm going to find out who murdered me… and why. Not in a vague, poetic, floating-through-the-hedgerows way. I mean actual detective work. I've got the coat. I've got the brooding. All I need now is a witness who won't scream when I introduce myself.

Hence, the advert.

I needed someone who could hear ghosts. Properly. Not just a "Oh, did someone say something? Must've been the pipes" sort of way. I needed a proper living, breathing, wellington-boot-wearing human who could not only hear me, but help me. Understand me. Get the evidence. Talk to the police. Fill in the forms that I physically cannot fill in because I don't have a corporeal thumb.

I need justice. So that I can move on.

Or at least *try*.

But here's the thing they don't tell you in Ghost School (which doesn't exist, but if it did, it would be held in the upstairs room of a condemned schoolhouse, and the headmaster would no doubt be an Edwardian foghorn with opinions). When you *do* get justice, when the case is solved, the mystery untangled, the villain named and presumably very awkward in court, it's not necessarily *you* who decides what happens next.

You don't get a note saying, "Congratulations, Tony Ferrari, your murder has been solved. Please proceed to the light. Or not. Up to you."

No, apparently, the moment your soul ticks the last item off its cosmic to-do list, you just… pop.

Gone.

Vanished. Disappeared. Out. Like a particularly smug lightbulb.

That, frankly, is what's keeping me up at night. Not the being dead. I've adjusted to that. Not even the murder. That'll come out in the wash. No, what I'm really struggling with is…

What happens if I don't *want* to go? If I don't *want to move on?*

What happens if, after all this haunting and monologuing and uncovering the truth, I finally have what I want, and it means I *have* to leave?

Because here's the truly inconvenient truth.

There's Betty.

She's infuriating. She's bossy. She's British with attitude. She once corrected my grammar *in Latin*. She pours imaginary tea like she's performing a ballet in honour of Queen Victoria. But she's also… well, she's *here*. She's the closest thing I've got to a friend in the afterlife. Possibly more than that. Possibly quite a lot more actually, but the whole death thing makes that difficult to clarify.

If I get justice, do I *have* to go?

Would I even get the chance to say goodbye?

Would I *want* to?

Because leaving Betty behind, leaving this weird, creaky, beer-soaked limbo where ghosts argue about the bins and dogs can smell your disappointment, it suddenly doesn't feel like freedom. It feels like loss.

But what's the alternative?

Stay? Float around indefinitely like a haunted novelty item, hoping someone writes a very niche travel guide about me? Spend eternity drifting around The Rose and Crown while Trevor ages out of spite and the Reverend starts quoting *The Railway Children* when the WIFI is on the blink?

Ghosts aren't meant to linger. That's the deal. We're meant to unravel, not knit ourselves more tightly into the upholstery.

But no one ever asked me what I *wanted*.

I stared into the photo of Betty again, and felt the knot tighten.

Maybe I'll get a choice.

Maybe I won't.

Maybe I'll solve my murder, and in that very moment, pop, I'll be gone. Off to whatever's next, without so much as a thank-you or a farewell cup of spiritual tea.

Or maybe I'll find out who did it, choose not to get justice and still get to stay. Maybe I'll just… fade a bit more slowly. Or become a guide. A ghost with tenure. A full-time spook-in-residence.

But I doubt it.

No one gets to retire from the afterlife.

Which means I've got to make this count. Solve the case. Say what needs to be said. Tie up the threads, even the ones I'm afraid to pull on.

Because justice is justice.

… and Betty…

Well. Let's cross that spectral bridge when we come to it.

52

CHAPTER THREE

GHOSTS DON'T HAVE THUMBS

It is a truth universally acknowledged, though rarely discussed over tea, that ghosts are remarkably bad with modern technology. Mostly because we don't have fingers. Or bodies. The finer points of touchscreen navigation are tricky when you're composed entirely of unresolved emotion and passive-aggressive static.

Which made phoning Angie… difficult.

I had taken her phone number without thinking. I mean that quite literally. She'd scribbled it onto a beer mat, placed it on the mantlepiece above the fire, wedged under a Toby Jug wearing a pirate hat.

Of course, I couldn't use the phone myself. Even in life, I was the kind of person who got unnerved by QR codes. In death, my ability to interface with anything battery-powered had been downgraded from "barely functional" to "radioactive poltergeist hazard."

Which is why I needed Mavis.

Mavis was, depending on your definition, a pensioner, a psychic, and possibly a witch, though only if the word "witch" also meant "devout bingo champion with a fondness for port, sherry and crosswords"

She could see me. Sometimes. Usually after 2 p.m. and two sherries. The psychic veil, you see, is a bit like a net curtain, it lets in just enough light to see something's out there, but not quite enough to be sure it isn't just your neighbour hanging out laundry in the shape of a vengeful spirit.

I found her in her usual spot, table by the darts board, humming something that could either have been a hymn or a suspiciously aggressive jingle from the 1950s. Trevor the pub dog was asleep at her feet, dreaming of a world where squirrels moved slower and ghosts weren't so drafty.

"Mavis," I said.

She didn't respond.

"Mavis," I said again, a little louder.

Still nothing.

I leaned forward, placed a hand gently near her glass (you couldn't touch, but you could *suggest* presence) and said, "Mavis, dear, it's Geraldine."

She jolted upright. "Oh! Geraldine, love, you gave me a turn."

"Sorry," I said, though we both knew I wasn't.

"What is it, then? Need me to light a candle? Tell Fred to stop moving the teaspoons again?"

"No, nothing like that," I said. "I need to make a phone call."

She blinked. "You?"

"Yes."

"With a *phone*?"

"Yes."

"But you're—"

"Yes. I know. That's why I need *you*."

Mavis looked at me the way someone might look at a pigeon requesting the Wi-Fi password.

Eventually, she reached into her handbag and produced a mobile phone roughly the size of a paperback and twice as heavy.

"Alright, Geraldine," she said, squinting at the keypad, "who are we calling then?"

I had just re read the beer mat and memorised the number. "Her name's Angie. She gave me her number. I need you to dial it."

Mavis punched in the digits with the slow intensity of someone defusing a bomb by following instructions written in Klingon.

"Calling..." she said. "Now what?"

"Hold it to your ear. If she picks up, hand it to the radiator."

"The what?"

"Trust me."

The phone rang.

Once. Twice. A third time.

And then: click.

"Hello?" came a voice.

It was slightly muffled, slightly curious, and ever-so-slightly slurred in the way only sherry can do.

Mavis stared. I gestured dramatically at the radiator.

"Oh for heaven's—" she said and leaned the phone against the nearest pipe.

I put my mouth as close to the radiator, without burning. I couldn't feel any heat of course but some bits of common sense you can't unlearn in a hurry. "Angie! It's me! Tony! From the pub! You walked through me! I'm the ghost, remember?"

There was a pause.

"Oh," said Angie's voice. "Hi."

She sounded entirely unsurprised, which was either comforting or deeply concerning.

"I need your help; I think to get justice for my murderer we need to start looking for clues" I said. "I have been thinking and I think we should go to London, to the book shop. It's the first place to look"

Another pause. Then: "Are you using a radiator to call me?"

"Yes."

"Okay," she said. "Just checking."

"Angie," I said trying to get her to focus, "I think we need to go to Finsbury Books."

There was a rustle on the other end, possibly a biscuit being consulted.

"Is that a metaphor for something or an actual bookshop?"

"Actual bookshop. It's in London. Mine. Well, was mine. Before I died. Now I suppose it's under the management of dust and mild confusion."

"Right… and you think the clue to your murder is there?"

"It's a hunch. But a good one. The murder didn't happen here, I'm almost certain. I mean, what's to murder me *for* in Beddlestead? The pickled eggs? Even my ex-wife and I are on good terms these days, and that's saying something. She even sent me a Christmas card last year with only *mildly* passive-aggressive penguins on it."

"That's progress," Angie agreed.

"Exactly. Which means the motive's not here. If there's any clue at all, it'll be at the bookshop. I need to go there. I need to see it again."

"Right. So we meet there, then?"

I hesitated.

"Slight problem with that plan," I said. "I can't leave the pub."

"What do you mean you *can't*?"

"I mean I physically, spiritually, metaphysically *can't*. Believe me, I tried. Once got as far as the post-box down the road and had a full existential nosebleed. I'm sort of anchored. Like a particularly dramatic lamp."

"So how do we get you to London? Parcel post? Poltergeist catapult?"

"I might be able to haunt a car. Temporarily. Ghost-hitch. If you had one."

There was a pause.

"I failed my driving test eight times," she said. "Once on the theory."

"That's okay," I said, trying not to sound like a disappointed sat nav. "We could take a taxi. If the driver doesn't mind picking up an extra passenger who isn't technically there."

"So… I call a taxi to Beddlestead, tell the driver I'm collecting a ghost, and we're going to London?"

"You could leave out the ghost bit. Maybe say you're doing some kind of unconventional research project. People believe anything if you say it with confidence and a clipboard."

"Fine," she said. "But I'm not paying for a hotel if you get stuck haunting the car radio."

"Deal."

Just like that, we had a plan.

Angie would come to the pub. She'd find a taxi willing to drive to London with a woman who talks to ghosts, or herself, and a trench coat full of unresolved trauma, and together, we'd go to Finsbury Books.

To find out why I'd been murdered.

Or, failing that, to finally dust the philosophy section.

Possibly both.

The snow was still coming down in that particularly British way, tentative, and determined to cause maximum inconvenience while pretending it wasn't really trying. The road outside the pub looked like a postcard scene from a Christmas card designed by someone who'd never driven in winter.

Then, as if summoned by a particularly whimsical bit of fate, the taxi appeared.

It wasn't one of those soulless minicabs. No, this was a proper black cab, the kind that could survive nuclear war, a zombie apocalypse, and the full brunt of a hen party from Romford. It pulled up with a sigh of slush and brake pads, headlights flickering through the swirling snow like they were trying to blink the flakes away.

Out stepped Angie.

She looked exactly how you'd expect someone to look after convincing a cab driver to drive to a haunted pub in the countryside: mildly frazzled, a bit defiant, and wearing boots that had clearly seen things.

She stomped up to the door, opened it, and popped her head inside.

"Be right out!" she called back cheerfully over her shoulder. "Just got to pick up a package!"

She winked at Betty who was standing to one side of the fireplace, who stood up with a jolt, not expecting to be seen so easily. Angie gave me a knowing look that suggested the "package" in question had unresolved trauma and a strong opinion on literary categorisation.

I turned to Betty.

"Come with me."

She raised a very British eyebrow. "To London?"

"Yes. An adventure. We'll haunt the cab together. Like Thelma and Louise, but with more tea and fewer cliffs."

"Thelma?"

"Another time" I said, "were ready to leave."

She looked toward the fire as if trying to make her mind up. "I've never left before", then back to me, "will it work? then sighed. "Alright. But I need to tell Bob. He's still working on his Matchbox car pyramid, and if I vanish mid-stack he'll be inconsolable."

Bob, for the record, is the ghost child with a Cockney accent I told you about earlier, a speech impediment, and a deep suspicion of vegetables. He also collects tiny cars with the kind of obsessive energy usually reserved for Cold War spies.

"Five minutes," she said. "… and if this cab smells like pickled onions and regrets, I'm not sitting in the middle."

Outside, the cab driver leaned against his vehicle with the bored dignity of a man who had seen everything and judged most of it wanting. He wore a flat cap at a defiant angle and sipped from a travel mug with "World's Okayest Grandad" written on it.

"London, is it?" he said when Angie re-emerged.

"Yes," she said, hopping into the back seat. "But we just need to collect one more thing."

He grunted, which could have meant anything from "Fine" to "I'm on the meter".

Betty and I drifted toward the cab, managing to hover just enough to avoid the worst of the snow.

"He's got the look of a man who knows at least three types of chutney," Betty muttered.

"Perfect," I said. "I always wanted to haunt someone who appreciates preserves."

We slipped into the cab, phasing neatly into the back seat just as Angie settled in and shut the door.

The driver glanced in the rear-view mirror.

"Name's Gary," he said. "Been drivin' this route since before GPS was a thing and Google didn't know where Croydon was."

"Lovely to meet you, Gary," said Angie.

"You're not one of them influencers, are ya?"

"Absolutely not."

"Good. Last time I had one in the back, she livestreamed my dashboard and said it gave her 'nostalgia anxiety'."

"That sounds medically implausible," I whispered to Betty.

"Shh," she replied. "I like him already."

Gary pulled away from The Rose and Crown with the slow, determined authority of someone who'd once reversed out of a riot. The snow crunched under the tyres, the engine grumbled in protest against rural winter, and the cab inched forward into the drifting mist of Beddlestead.

Inside the taxi, Angie was perched on the edge of the seat, boots already shedding snow onto the rubber mats, and Betty sat beside her with the measured calm of someone who had faced far greater dangers than upholstery.

I, however, was still hovering exactly where I'd been. Just outside the pub.

You see, I hadn't quite mastered the complexities of haunting a moving vehicle. There's something profoundly unnatural about wheels to a ghost. We're used to bricks, mortar, creaky floorboards and haunted mirrors. Motor vehicles are a whole other kettle of metaphysical fish. They move too fast, turn too sharply, and operate on a principle that seems fundamentally opposed to the gentle, ethereal drift most ghosts are accustomed to.

So, as the taxi crept away, I didn't go with it. I stayed right where I was.

I watched.

Watched as Angie turned and looked around to look out the back window.

Watched as Betty frowned and leaned toward the foggy window.

And then—

The brake lights flared.

The cab screeched to a halt with the noise of an angry teapot.

The door flung open.

"Forgot something!" Angie shouted, her voice cutting through the snow like a particularly determined dessert fork. She sprinted back down the road, slipping once, catching herself with a yelp that sounded like an insult to Newtonian physics, and skidded to a stop in front of me.

"You didn't come!" she panted.

"I *couldn't*! I haven't figured out vehicular haunting yet."

Betty appeared behind her, utterly unfazed by the cold or the drama. She grabbed my arm, which is a strange thing to say given that neither of us technically had arms in the traditional living sense. But she grabbed what there was to grab, and I felt it.

Oh, I *felt* it.

A connection. A tether. Something ancient and warm and entirely inappropriate for someone whose heart had stopped beating over a month ago.

"Come *on*, Tony," she said. "You're embarrassing the entire spectral community."

"I'm telling you, I can't—"

"Yes you can. You just need to *commit*."

"Commit?"

"Like when you jump into a freezing lake. Do it all at once, or you'll lose a foot."

She tugged.

I resisted.

She rolled her eyes, leaned in, and whispered, "Imagine the cab is just an extension of the pub. A very loud, metal pub."

"A pub on wheels?"

"Yes. Now get in it."

I took a deep non-breath, focused on the taxi, which was now idling anxiously with Gary looking at his watch like he was considering charging double, and let Betty pull me.

I don't know how to describe it exactly. Haunting a moving vehicle feels like trying to step onto a treadmill that's already going, while also holding a Martini and questioning your life choices. But somehow, with Betty's hand on what might have been my elbow, I made it.

I was in.

She didn't let go.

Honestly? I didn't want her to.

It felt good.

Safe, in a way that very few things in the afterlife can claim to be.

She gave me a look, one part fond exasperation, one part relief, and settled back into the seat like nothing had happened.

I hovered awkwardly beside her.

Angie jogged back to the cab, got in, slammed the door, and gave Gary a winning smile.

"Sorry," she said brightly. "Had to grab a... mumble."

Gary squinted at her in the rear-view mirror. "You lot always forget something. Last week someone left their wedding cake on the roof. Whole thing slid off by Milton Keynes."

With an indignant sigh from the suspension, the taxi rolled back into motion. This time, I was in it.

We trundled away down the lane outside The Rose and Crown, tyres grumbling against the packed snow, the lights of the pub glowing dimly behind us like a slightly judgmental memory.

The pub disappeared behind us.

But Betty didn't let go.

For the first time in weeks, I felt like I might be going somewhere important.

So just like that, we were off to London.

Two ghosts.

One psychic.

A taxi driver who clearly believed that thermos etiquette was able to drive and swig chicken soup at the same time.

The drive was slow going at first, Beddlestead's roads being what they were, more suggestion than infrastructure. Gary handled it like a man personally insulted by winter. He drove with the confidence of someone who'd once delivered a baby during a snowstorm in the backseat of a cab and had only charged double.

The countryside slid past in a haze of white, tree branches bent under the weight of snow, hedgerows frosted like forgotten pastries. The roads gradually widened, the landscape shifted from rural to suburban to stubbornly metropolitan, and the slushy curves gave way to the gridlocked certainty of London proper.

By the time we hit the outskirts, I could feel the city hum beneath us.

Not literally, obviously, ghosts aren't great with asphalt, but emotionally. London is a mood. A nervous breakdown wrapped in bricks and ambition, and you could feel it pulsing through the fog.

We passed red-bricked terraces and corner shops, tower blocks that stared at the horizon like concrete philosophers. Then the cab swerved round a roundabout with the kind of centrifugal force that makes ghosts reevaluate their commitments, and suddenly we were crossing Westminster Bridge.

Big Ben loomed in the distance, snow flurries swirling around it like confetti at a very solemn wedding.

Gary grunted. "Always a jam here."

Betty was mesmerised looking out every window turning around and around "It's changed" she whispered in my ear. Not sure why she was whispering unless the taxi driver really had sherry in his thermos. "Last time I was here there were big tethered balloons everywhere" She was looking up at the sky half expecting to see a Spitfire in a dog fight.

Angie peered out the window, nose nearly pressed to the glass. Clearly she hadn't been to London for a while either.

Me? I looked at the faces.

Because now, in the thick of it, I started to see them.

Other ghosts.

One perched atop a lamppost, legs swinging lazily like a kid on a swing. Another hovered through a crowd at the crosswalk, unseen and unbothered, arms folded like they were late for an appointment that no longer mattered.

They were everywhere.

Most looked content. Some were smiling. One was doing the Times crossword on the side of a red bus and muttering, "Six across, eternal torment, five letters..." as he scratched his chin with the tip of an incorporeal umbrella.

I hadn't realised how many of us there were.

None of them looked in a rush to leave.

Then, just as we rumbled into the edges of Piccadilly Circus, past those great neon signs flickering with relentless optimism about soft drinks and designer shoes, I saw him.

An American Indian chief.

He was bare-chested, towering, and magnificent. His headdress was impossibly elaborate, each feather pristine and defying both gravity and time. He sat astride a ghost horse, yes, a ghost horse, that clopped silently through the traffic, unfazed by the horns and taxis and the man on the corner shouting about vegan cheese conspiracies.

He looked directly at me.

Tipped his spear and nodded.

I nodded back, because what else do you do when a centuries-old warrior-ghost on horseback gives you a moment of solemn spectral solidarity in the middle of London?

"Did you see him?" I whispered.

"The chief?" Betty said, smiling. "How did he get here?"

"His horse had better posture than I do," I muttered.

"That's ghost horses for you," said Betty. "Proud creatures. Very particular about curbs."

Angie, meanwhile, was trying to convince Gary not to take the longer route via Euston, and Gary was arguing that no one, not even the Queen, had ever enjoyed Euston Road.

We turned right at Leicester Square, where a ghostly busker in a bowler hat was singing something that only the dead could hear, and for a moment, it felt like the city was alive in a whole new way.

Not just the London of queues and complaints and overpriced crisps, but the London underneath it all, the city of layers, of stories half-told, of people who hadn't quite left.

Angie leaned close.

"You see what I meant, Tony? About time not being a line? It's more of a tangle here. You pull one thread and you get a Victorian chimney sweep, a lost tourist from 2003, and someone who still thinks the Millennium Dome is the future."

"I see it," I said.

Because I did.

The ghosts here might be stuck, but they weren't lonely, didn't look unhappy, and if I'm honest they looked slightly happier than the living who were rushing past them.

That meant something.

As the taxi rolled on toward Finsbury Square, I sat back, well, floated politely in the general vicinity of sitting, and for the first time since my murder, I allowed a sliver of possibility to creep in.

Maybe there was more to being dead than justice.

Maybe there was something after that.

…. and maybe, just maybe, Betty would be in it, too.

As we neared Finsbury Square, I nudged Angie. Or rather, I nudged the air just near her, which she was fortunately attuned enough to interpret.

"Tell Gary to take the next left," I said. "There's a one-way system right outside the bookshop."

She leaned forward. "Gary, next left, please."

"This one?"

"Yes."

"That's a tight turn," Gary muttered.

We turned into the little street off Finsbury Square and there it was, Finsbury Books. My shop. My life-before-death. The front windows were steamed slightly, the display a mix of poetry anthologies and wonky old maps. The sign above the door was the same: brass lettering that read "Finsbury Books – Rare & Used Treasures," slightly tarnished, probably still hosting at least two generations of pigeon.

"Here it is," she said.

Gary pulled the taxi over with a bump on the curb that nearly threw me out through the windscreen. Angie opened the door and paid him with cash. Too many pound coins for Gary's liking, but he took them anyway.

I drifted out of the cab, heart metaphorically in my mouth, Betty floating beside me like she was evaluating property.

Inside, it smelled the same. A little musty, a little warm, a lot of old paper and ink and dust. The kind of smell that makes book lovers weep and librarians sigh with approval.

Books towered everywhere. Not neatly stacked on shelves, oh no. This was a *system*, not a display. Piles of uncatalogued hardbacks leaned into one another like gossiping pensioners. First editions poked from beneath piles of gardening encyclopedias. There was a small carved bear holding up a stack of German philosophy, and a box labelled "Might Be Magic, Ask First."

Then there was the clock, one of the few belongings from my childhood in the Bronx.

The slow, deliberate tick of it echoed through the silence.

Tick.

Tock.

Tick.

Somewhere in the corner, an electric heater hummed like it was nursing a grudge. "That will be costing me a fortune" I said "who left that on?"

Angie took one step forward. "Probably you"

Then stopped.

"There's someone here," she said quietly.

Betty and I looked around.

"What do you mean?" I asked.

She turned her head slowly, eyes scanning the air like a cat sizing up a ghost mouse.

"I can hear him," she whispered. "A voice. It's soft. But it's here. He's hiding."

"Hiding?"

She nodded. "Behind something. Books maybe. Or in the walls. But he's definitely here. You've got a ghost."

"I've *what?*"

"A ghost. In your bookshop. Didn't you know?"

I blinked. Which is harder than it sounds without eyelids.

"No. I mean… the Wi-Fi used to go out sometimes, but I thought that was just BT being BT."

Betty gave a low, knowing hum.

"Or maybe it was Brian," she said.

"Brian?"

"It's always a Brian," she muttered.

Angie moved carefully between the book piles, ears tilted like antennae.

"He's shy. But he's here… and scared."

"Scared of *me*?" I asked.

"No," she said, and gave me a serious look. "Scared of *why you're here*."

I turned to Betty. She gave me a tiny nod.

"Well," I said, bracing myself. "Let's go find our ghostly flatmate."

Apparently, being dead still didn't exempt you from surprise houseguests.

"Brian?" I called out, feeling absolutely ridiculous. "Brian, mate, if you're in here... I'm not here to evict anyone. Just trying to figure out who killed me. You don't have to hide."

There was a long silence.

Then, from somewhere behind a stack of atlases and a cardboard box of Regency romance novels: "Evict me? *Evict me*? I've been here since 1923, thank you very much. I practically *am* this shop."

Betty turned toward the voice with the kind of subtle satisfaction only ghosts can properly express. Angie gave a little yelp and pointed at the books.

"There!"

The pile rustled. A few dusty volumes slid aside with the grace of a sleepy cat, and then he emerged.

Brian.

He was tall, pale (obviously), and wore the slightly crumpled suit of a man who'd once cared very deeply about waistcoats. His moustache was grand and bristly, the kind that might once have been used to command respect or sweep stairs.

"Good heavens," he muttered, eyeing me. "You're the new one, I wondered where you went."

"I'm not new. I own the place," I said.

"Owned it? You mean. You're as dead as I am. You took over from Wiggins?"

"Wiggins?"

"Bald man. Smelled of onions. Had a hat for every day of the week."

"Oh! Yes. Briefly. I took over when the shop passed to me after a friend passed away."

Brian gave a sniff. "He never dusted."

"No, I don't think he did."

"Not like me. I dusted."

"With what? You're a ghost."

"Willpower."

He crossed his arms with an expression that said: *You may own the deeds, but possession is nine tenths of the law or something to that affect.*

"Brian," I said slowly, "I didn't know you were here. Honestly. I'm just trying to figure out who killed me, and I thought the answer might be here."

"In doing so, you've brought living people stomping around my metaphysical conservatory and ghost companions with suspiciously sharp eyebrows."

"Thank you," said Betty, smiling.

Brian adjusted a non-existent cufflink.

"Look," I said, "I don't want to turf anyone out. This is clearly as much your place as it ever was mine. But if you know anything, anything at all, about what might have happened to me, or why someone would've wanted me dead..."

"I don't," Brian said, and for a moment, he looked genuinely sorry. "I keep to myself these days. Do a bit of cataloguing. Whisper to the dust jackets. Listen to the shipping forecasts. You died long after I stopped paying attention. People come and go, you never know what happens to them"

"You listen to the shipping forecast?" Betty asked.

"Every night. I like the rhythm. 'Viking, North Utsire, South Utsire, impending betrayal, moderate or good...' very soothing."

"Brian," I said carefully, "would you be willing to let us look around? Maybe talk a bit more later?"

He sighed the sigh of a man whose afternoon nap had been indefinitely postponed.

"Fine," he said. "But if you move the Dickens collection, you put it back *exactly* how you found it."

"Deal."

Brian floated back into the stacks, muttering something about alphabetisation and people with no respect for bookshop ghosts.

Angie turned to me. "You really didn't know he was here?"

"Not a clue. I thought the Wi-Fi just hated me."

"Well," she said, glancing into the shadows, "you've got your hands full now."

"None of them ever paid any rent," I muttered.

With that, the three of us ventured deeper into the shop. To find a clue. Or a ghost. Or maybe just a slightly overdue revelation.

We searched for over an hour. Or what felt like an hour. Ghosts don't track time in the traditional sense, we don't age, we don't wrinkle, and we definitely don't own wristwatches. But Angie started looking peckish around the forty-minute mark, and I took that as a reliable sign of time having passed.

We combed through the shop with great care, stepping over towers of hardbacks, peering into alcoves, rifling gently through boxes marked "Unsorted and Slightly Judgemental." Betty glided with the air of a seasoned librarian on patrol.

But there was nothing. Not a single overturned volume. No scrawled messages in the dust. No ghostly crime scenes. Not even an ectoplasmic smudge.

"It all looks… normal," Angie said, finally standing in the centre of the shop and twirling in a slow circle. "No signs of violence. No energy bursts. Not even a cursed bookmark."

"I never did like violence in the shop," I said. "Bad for business."

"That would make sense," said Betty. "You were killed elsewhere. Whatever trail might've led here, it's long gone cold."

Just then, Brian floated back in.

"You've had visitors," he announced casually, as if he were discussing the weather or the merits of marmalade.

"Visitors? Since I died?" I said.

"Indeed. A man in a rather itchy-looking suit. A policeman. Walked in, poked at a few things with a pencil, stared at your desk like it had called him a rude name."

"Did he say anything?"

"Mostly muttered to himself. Something about 'wrong postcode' and 'bloody paperwork'. He did sneeze twice. That was the most spirited thing he did."

Angie scribbled something into her notepad.

"Anyone else?"

"Yes, a rather sharp-tongued estate agent. Turtleneck jumper. Too much hair gel. Was on his phone the entire time, walked in jabbering and walked out jabbering, but with significantly more disdain. Tried to open a secret door behind the travel section. There isn't one, obviously, but he was very disappointed when all he found was the Moldova guidebooks."

"So... he wasn't exactly spiritually tuned-in," I said.

"Not unless the afterlife communicates via Bluetooth," Brian replied.

He floated in a slow circle above the reading chair. "There was one more. Interesting fellow. Ghost. Not local."

Betty's eyebrows rose. "Oh?"

Brian nodded solemnly. "Native American. Chief. Enormous headdress. Very dignified. Rode a ghost horse right through the front window. Didn't break anything, mind you. I rather liked him. Said he was passing through. Wanted to see where the 'unravelling soul' had been tied."

I blinked. "Unravelling soul? He said that?"

"Verbatim. Then he bowed to the history section and galloped back out."

"We saw him in Piccadilly," Betty murmured. "On the horse."

"Lovely form, that horse," Brian said. "High knees. Excellent gliding."

"Why would he come here?" I asked. "I don't know him."

"Ghosts travel in circles of intuition," said Betty. "Sometimes we just know when something's out of joint. Like bees before a thunderstorm."

Angie tapped her pencil against her chin. "So we've got a possibly clueless copper, a very disappointed estate agent, and a spectral chieftain who thinks your soul's been tied up like a balloon."

"… and still no idea who actually killed me," I sighed.

Brian floated toward a stack of boxes and nudged one gently with his foot.

"Might want to check these," he said. "Wiggins used to hide all kinds of things in his unsorted pile. Receipts. Whiskey. One time, a duck egg."

Betty looked at me. "What do you think?"

"I think," I said, "that we're going to need a very large pot of tea, a corkboard, some string, and a lot more time."

The thing about the Indian ghost, it was poking at something in my memory. A tickle in the attic of my brain, dust-covered and a little ashamed of itself. I drifted back toward the unsorted pile, the one Brian had indicated with a weary flick of his foot.

Somewhere in here… something about the Percy family sale. December. I remembered now, vaguely. The three books. Yes. Three volumes I never got around to cataloguing. Because, well, murder tends to disrupt your admin schedule.

"The Percy family sale," I murmured aloud. "I never finished sorting it."

Betty looked up eagerly "What are we looking for?" Before peering into a box marked 'UNHOLY MISC.'

"Three books," I said. "They were Native American history, I think. Not valuable, not that I remember, but unusual. Illustrated. Big volumes."

Angie, flipping through papers with a practiced eye, paused. "I think I saw something about that sale. Here, Percy family probate. December. You made notes."

I hovered closer. In my old, scribbled handwriting, complete with circles, arrows and one doodle of a confused bear, were the entries:

McKenney & Hall's History of the Indian Tribes of North America Vol. I – 1837 Vol. II – 1842 Vol. III – 1844

"That's them!" I said. "I remember now. Beautiful illustrations. Paintings of tribal leaders. Biographies. The sort of thing that belonged in a museum, or a very eccentric uncle's drawing room."

"You didn't catalogue them?"

"I meant to. I wanted to check some provenance details. Then I guess I got murdered."

"That'll do it," Betty said kindly.

"There must be a record somewhere," Angie said, rifling now with the intensity of a truffle pig hunting narrative significance.

"Something about where they went. Or who might have seen them."

"Try the upcoming auction pile," I suggested. "Braithwaite's catalogue. They handle most of the high-end estate sales."

Betty floated over and within a minute let out a triumphant little gasp.

"Here! Look!"

She held up a glossy booklet, the kind that makes dusty old paper smell suspiciously like profit.

"Braithwaite's Winter Auction Catalogue. Lot 17 through 19. McKenney and Hall. Three volumes. Reserve price..."

She paused.

"What?" I said.

"Three hundred thousand pounds."

"Pardon?"

"Three. Hundred. Thousand. Pounds."

We all went silent. Even Brian paused mid-mutter from somewhere behind the architecture section.

"That can't be right," I said. "They weren't in perfect condition. One had a cracked spine."

"Apparently they're rare as hen's teeth and twice as collectible," Angie said, squinting at the description. "Original lithographs. Hand-coloured. Early American frontier documentation. High academic and collector interest."

"That's got to be it," I muttered. "That's the motive."

"You think someone murdered you... for books?"

"It wouldn't be the strangest motive in history. I once saw a man attempt to smother someone over a first edition Beatrix Potter."

"This explains the Indian ghost," Betty said. "He came because those books carry weight. Memory. Spirit. Ties to real lives, maybe family ties, not just paper and ink."

"Thinking back," I added slowly, "there was something odd about the day I picked them up. The Percy place was full of artifacts. Masks. Spears. Carvings. There was this old chap at the auction. Beautiful suit. But he looked like he'd just stepped out of a teepee in an old cowboy film."

"Ghost?" Angie asked.

"I don't know. No, not a ghost. He bid on a few things. Didn't say a word. Just nodded and vanished before the auction ended."

"Then we've got our first lead, a real clue," Betty said.

"We need to stop that auction," I said.

"We need to find out who's selling those books," Angie added.

"… and possibly," Betty said, turning toward the front door, "we need to go dancing."

"What?"

"To celebrate," she said with a more regular mischievous smile, as though it were obvious. "First lead. Case momentum. Also, I haven't danced since 1942 and I'm itching for a swing."

I looked at Angie. Angie looked at me.

"Is she serious?" I asked.

"She's a ghost," Angie said. "Serious stopped being relevant sometime before rationing."

"I'll take that as a yes," I said.

Which brings us to a new question: where exactly *does* one go ghost dancing in London?

After a brief conference, and by brief, I mean Betty announced her intention and we all nodded like people who knew better than to argue with a woman who'd lived through rationing, we decided on Betty's suggestion of the Royal Opera House.

"During the war," Betty explained, adjusting her ghostly gloves like she was heading to afternoon tea with Churchill, "they turned it into a dance hall. It was all swing and stomp and sore feet. Perfect place for a celebration."

"Do you think it's still got... atmosphere?" I asked.

"Oh, darling," she said with a grin, "I'm sure it *never* left."

So off we went. Angie hailed a taxi and pretended to have a dodgy leg, giving Betty and me time to squeeze past and onto the back seat.

The Opera House, in the early evening snow, looked less like a cultural institution and more like a building trying not to brag about being extremely haunted.

We slipped inside. No tickets. No ushers. No queue. Ghost perks. Then let Angie in around the back. Being an ex-policeman, I should have felt more guilty about breaking and entering but this was fun.

The foyer was dark and empty, echoing with that peculiar sense of importance theatres have when no one's around. But as we drifted toward the grand hall, something began to shift.

A light flickered.

A trumpet trilled somewhere above us.

And then—

The room bloomed with ghosts.

They appeared like memories too fond to fade. Men in RAF uniforms and army khakis, American GIs with big grins and Brylcreem-slicked hair. Women in dresses that defied wartime rationing rules, curls pinned and heels polished, each of them radiant with the soft glow of having once felt invincible.

The lights came on, not with electricity, but with a sense of purpose. Then the music started.

Glenn Miller.

"In the Mood."

"He made it here," Betty whispered. "I always wondered."

"Made it where?"

"He went missing, remember? Plane vanished in '44. Officially unsolved. But here he is. Or his music, anyway. Someone kept it playing."

"You're saying he was murdered too?"

"Let's not ruin the party," she said, and pulled me onto the floor.

I didn't resist.

Betty danced like someone who'd waited decades to spin… and I, well, I mostly tried to keep up.

We jived. We swung. At one point, I may have accidentally waltzed into a passing airman. He saluted me anyway.

Angie clapped from the side, a cup of something ghostly and fizzy in her hand, laughing like a woman who had decided that ghost-hunting should always come with live music and ghostly GI's.

The music soared. The ghosts twirled. Time folded in on itself like a well-used handkerchief.

For one night, in the heart of London, among the dead who hadn't quite let go and the living who refused to be surprised anymore, we danced, danced and danced.

We danced like we weren't just chasing a murderer.

We danced like we'd already won.

Unfortunately, you can't dance forever.

Eventually, Glenn Miller played his last invisible encore, the ghostly couples faded back into the ether like polite mist, and Angie's phone buzzed to remind her that reality, such as it was, still existed.

We couldn't find a black cab. Turns out, ghosts aren't great at hailing them, and Angie's charm only goes so far with cabbies named Gary who have a very strict after-7pm chutney schedule.

So she got us an Uber.

The driver's name was Tariq. Mid-fifties, proudly moustached, and possessed the supreme confidence of someone who had *absolutely no idea* where he was going but had no intention of admitting it.

"Beddlestead?" he said, typing it into his phone. "Oh yes, yes. Very familiar. Go there all the time. Lovely place."

"Really?" Angie asked, mildly incredulous.

"Yes, yes. With the ducks, right? Lots of... trees?"

"It's mostly a pub and an aggressive duck who lives in the pond."

"Exactly! Very scenic."

He promptly took a wrong turn and spent the next five minutes pretending it was part of a scenic shortcut.

In the back seat, Betty curled her arm around mine and dozed off. Ghosts don't snore, but they *radiate* sleepiness. It was like being hugged by a lullaby.

I didn't sleep.

I couldn't.

Because I had a plan to make.

The books were real. The price was shocking. The murder? Still unsolved. I was starting to realise I had a very short window in which to do something about it.

Option one: find the ghost chief. The one with the horse and the wise nod and the line about my soul being unravelled. Not exactly listed in the phone book under 'C' for Cryptic Apparitions, but maybe Betty could help.

Option two: crash the auction. Subtle sabotage. Something involving ghostly breezes and dramatic flickering lights. Maybe I could knock over a chair at a significant moment. Ghosts are excellent at disrupting ambiance.

Option three: the Percy Mansion. Where the books came from. Where I'd first seen that peculiar man with the beautiful suit and the aura of a travelling legend. There might be something there. A clue. Or maybe another ghost with a better memory than Brian.

I stared out the window, watching London disappear behind us, the city lights blinking their sleepy goodnights. Tariq was humming to himself and occasionally turning the satnav sideways as if that would help.

We turned off the motorway sometime around midnight. The roads narrowed. Trees grew denser. Snow began falling again, light at first, like nervous confetti.

Then we reached Beddlestead.

Or, more precisely, the outskirts of it.

As the car crested the final lane toward the Rose and Crown, I saw them.

"Stop the car," I said.

Tariq, being a warm blooded living human, ignored me entirely.

"Angie," I said urgently. "Get him to stop."

"Tariq, pull over a sec."

"Here? But we're nearly—"

"Now. Please."

The car rolled to a reluctant halt.

Across the village green, by the duck pond, was a line of ghostly teepees.

They shimmered gently, as if woven from memory and moonlight. A fire crackled invisibly in the centre. Shadows moved between the tents. Not scary shadows. Just... present ones. Solid in their silence.

One of them looked up.

It was the chief. Same headdress. Same stare.

He didn't wave.

But he nodded again. A slow, deliberate motion that felt more like a message than a greeting.

"He's waiting," I said softly.

"For what?" Angie asked, peering through the fogged-up glass.

"Me," I said.

Betty stirred beside me. "Or for justice."

Tariq turned around in his seat. "Everything okay?"

I gave him a nod he couldn't see.

"Yes," Angie said, voice steady. "Let's go home."

The teepees didn't fade as we drove past. They stayed. Watching.

Waiting.

CHAPTER FOUR

GOOGLING GHOSTS ON THE GREEN

Angie had stayed the night, curled like a human question mark in one of the battered leather armchairs by the pub's fire. She hadn't meant to, of course. At least, she hadn't announced it. But sometime around two in the morning, after a long, half-muttered conversation with Betty about the virtues of toast, she'd dozed off, clutching a tartan blanket like it held secrets and snored softly into the middle cushion.

By morning, the fire was down to the barest embers, glowing faintly like the pub's own heartbeat, and Angie was still snoring. Betty and I hovered nearby, trying to look respectfully quiet and failing because the only thing ghosts can't do stealthily is be interested.

Outside, the sun hadn't quite made up its mind. The sky was a dull pewter, as if someone had misplaced the blue and decided grey would have to do. A dusting of fresh snow softened the outlines of everything, and in the middle of the village green, opposite the

Rose and Crown, the ghostly teepees still stood.

They shimmered faintly in the morning gloom, like memories that hadn't quite agreed to leave. There were maybe half a dozen of them, arranged in a loose semicircle around the old duck pond. Smoke, or the suggestion of smoke, drifted upward from the central fire pit, though there was no heat, no crackling, just a sense of quiet reverence that made you want to speak in whispers.

Not that anyone *was* speaking. The village was asleep, the pub was asleep, Angie was definitely asleep.

Well, not everyone.

The duck was awake.

To be specific: *the* duck. The one with the territorial issues and a stare that could curdle milk. He surveyed his kingdom from the little pond house on an island surrounded by reeds. It was a small structure with the kind of tilted roof that suggested it had once hosted fairytale mischief and now mostly hosted grudges.

… and he could *see* them. Intruders on his property.

In a full state of furious waddling, wings flared, tail twitching, the duck honked with the righteous fury of someone whose local bylaws had been violated.

He darted in and out between the ghostly legs of seated warriors, snapping at ankles that no longer existed. One particularly noble spirit lifted his foot slightly, more out of respect than pain, and the duck glared up at him with all the loathing of a civil servant at closing time.

"That duck's got attitude" I muttered.

"That duck," said Betty, appearing beside me like a sigh with intent, "once chased a Labrador into the post office. He is *not* to be trifled with."

We stood there, the two of us, side by side at the frosted window, watching the ghostly camp shimmer in the rising light.

"They didn't go," I said.

"No," said Betty softly. "They're waiting for you."

"For what and why?"

She didn't answer. Or maybe she didn't know.

Behind us, Angie snored again. Not a dainty, ladylike snore, but a proper boots-on, battlefield honk. The kind of snore that suggested her body was still fighting a war with gravity and had decided the chair was winning.

"She's going to have a crick in her neck the size of Warwickshire," Betty noted.

"Worth it," I said. "She stayed."

We turned our attention back to the green.

One of the teepee flaps stirred. A young woman stepped out, maybe twenty, draped in soft furs that whispered of snowy trails and long nights under stars. She didn't look at the village. She looked up. At the sky. At the pub. At *me*.

Just for a moment.

She didn't speak. Just gave a single, solemn nod, then ducked back inside.

"Well," I said, after a long pause. "That's new."

"They know who you are," Betty said. "… and they're watching."

"Here to help?"

She tilted her head. "Maybe. Or maybe to *see* what you do."

I sighed. Or at least made the effort, which for a ghost is 90% of the effect.

"I wish I knew what came next."

"You will," she said.

Behind us, Angie snorted herself awake, blinking reproachfully at the fire.

"Mmph. What time is it?"

"Half past duck," I said.

"What?"

"Don't worry," Betty added, already gliding away, "he'll explain it. Just give him tea first."

Angie stretched, yawned, and finally sat up from the chair with the look of someone who'd briefly become one with the upholstery.

"I think I fused to the armrest," she mumbled, blinking toward the window. "Are they still out there?"

"They are," I said. "And so is the duck. Still angry."

Angie stood slowly, groaning as she realigned various mortal joints. "I think I'd better leave this part to you two. Feels a bit... ghost-centric. I don't want to intrude."

"You're not intruding," Betty said kindly.

"No, but I'm also not dead. Yet. Hopefully. I'll head back, but let Mavis know to call me via the radiator tomorrow, yeah?"

"Of course," I said.

She pulled on her boots and coat, gave Betty a gentle pat on the arm (which went through her, though it was a nice gesture), and disappeared into the morning fog with a last sleepy wave.

Betty and I turned toward the green.

"Shall we?" she asked.

"We shall."

The snow crunched softly beneath our intangible footsteps as we drifted across the road. The teepees shimmered gently in the dawn light. The duck spotted us the moment we passed the pond gate.

He charged.

Not waddled. Charged. Like a tiny, feathery linebacker with a vendetta.

I braced for impact, but Betty stepped forward.

She crouched.

Looked that duck straight in the eyes.

Whatever passed between them in that moment, ancient warrior to ancient waterfowl, it was enough.

The duck's eyes widened. He stumbled, let out a strangled honk of disbelief, and fled. He scuttled back to the duck house like he'd remembered an urgent appointment with some breadcrumbs and his therapist.

I stared.

Betty stood slowly and dusted off hands she didn't physically have.

"What just happened?" I asked.

"I reminded him," she said.

"Reminded him of what?"

"Of who's really in charge of this green."

We didn't have long to ponder, because just then, the flap of the central teepee stirred and out stepped the chief.

Tall. Proud. Draped in ghostly furs and feathers that swayed in a wind that wasn't blowing.

He looked at me. Then at Betty and smiled.

"Greetings," he said in a voice that felt like it had travelled through time, mountains, and very wise silences. "You have brought the duck-whisperer"

Betty blinked. "I'm sorry?"

"In our tongue," he said solemnly, "we name you Ageyui'ga Tsutsastanv'I - 'She Who Terrifies Ducks.'"

I choked on a laugh. Betty gave the ghost of a curtsy.

"It is an honour," she said. "Though I prefer tea to terror, on most days."

He nodded respectfully.

"You have courage," he said. "… and you," he added, turning to me, "have questions."

"That's putting it mildly," I said.

He gestured for us to follow him into the teepee.

As we stepped inside, the snow, the duck, and even the pub seemed to fade into the background.

Just like that, the conversation began.

Between ghosts. Between timelines. Between lives long past, and one not quite finished yet.

The inside of the teepee was warm, not physically, but emotionally. The kind of warmth you feel when someone looks at you and sees not just what you are, but what you've endured. There was no fire, and yet a glow lit the canvas walls from within. Betty sat cross-legged on a low ghost-log. I hovered politely.

The chief, still standing tall, began without preamble.

"In 1887, the United States government passed the Dawes Act," he said, his voice steady, though there was something ancient and weary beneath it. "It promised to give land to native families. What it *did* was divide tribal lands into small, scattered allotments, and sell the rest to white settlers."

"That sounds... targeted," I said.

"It was. Ninety million acres lost. Traded for promises. Stolen through paperwork. Often for pennies. Not even good pennies. The bad kind, with suspicious faces."

Betty frowned. "I've read about it. It was supposed to 'assimilate' the tribes."

The chief gave a short, bitter smile. "Yes. Because nothing says 'we respect your culture' like giving away your home and calling it progress."

He reached behind him and pulled out something that shimmered like paper but felt older than the country that printed it. A folded clipping from The Times, ghost-inked and oddly elegant.

"This," he said, holding it up, "is from your London Times. Published this week."

I peered at it. The headline read:

'Cherokee Nation Present Exciting New Evidence to British Courts in Landmark Land Reclamation Bid'

My eyebrows, ghostly though they were, rose.

"Wait. British courts? Why not American ones?"

"Because," he said, eyes glinting, "sometimes the fox shouldn't be in charge of investigating the henhouse. Britain was there when the treaties were made. Britain's law is tied to ours by the chain of empire. If they acknowledge the case, others will follow."

Betty nodded slowly. "If the Cherokee win their claim..."

"Then other nations may, too. Australia. Canada. New Zealand. Even parts of South America."

My head spun. "That would change *everything*."

"Yes," he said. "Which is why some people would very much like it *not* to happen."

I felt a coldness that wasn't ghostly. "You think there's something in the books. The ones from the Percy estate."

"I know there is."

"Proof?"

"Witness. Details. Evidence of early British involvement. Private letters. Perhaps drawings. Maybe even a map. But more than that, context."

Betty looked grave. "You think that's why Tony was…"

"Removed," the chief said, voice like thunder muffled in snow. "A man in the way. An accidental custodian."

"But... why *me*?" I asked. "Why not just steal the books? I wasn't doing anything with them. I hadn't even catalogued the blasted things yet."

The chief met my eyes. "Because you were going to. Someone knew that and that someone knew the value these books would hold to the American Government, The British Government, Australia, and so on..."

"So if they have the books now, why don't they just destroy them and their problem, poof, goes away. Why auction them?"

"The governments didn't realise they existed. Someone only recently stumbled on what they contained and why it was so important. That person is going to make the governments bid against each other, driving up the price. The three hundred thousand pounds is only the starting bid. To stop this the governments will pay millions."

The silence that followed was thick with the weight of unfinished justice.

I cleared my throat. Pointlessly.

"So, what do I do now?"

He stepped closer.

"You find the truth. You stop the sale. You give justice to my ancestors. You follow the trail. You finish what you started."

I swallowed hard. Or at least mimed it.

"... and then?"

He placed a firm, respectful hand on my shoulder. I felt it. I *felt it!*

"Then, Tony Ferrari of Finsbury Books... you get your justice too."

I blinked and looked at Betty who looked away. She knew what that meant. That I would move on.

"Right," she said with a stiff upper lip. "Then let's stop an auction, save a tribe, and possibly annoy a few very rich people."

The chief nodded.

"… and if there's dancing after," Betty added, "all the better."

Just like that, we had a mission… and I, a recently murdered bookshop owner, had the backing of an ancient warrior, a ghost librarian, and possibly the entire duck-watching community of Beddlestead.

Which, let's be honest, is probably more than most people ever get.

We walked back to the pub in companionable silence, Betty and I. The ghostly teepees slowly faded into the morning light, but the duck remained. Perched on his little house near the pond, he was watching Betty with the kind of expression normally reserved for war generals or disgruntled traffic wardens. He gave a low, rumbling honk that suggested he'd filed an official complaint.

"He's scared of you," I said.

"He should be," said Betty, with a satisfied little smile. "One good stare and he nearly moulted."

Inside the pub, the fire had been coaxed back to life. Someone, possibly Mavis, possibly divine intervention, had left out a fresh pot of tea. We settled into our usual chairs like ghosts with purpose.

"I get it," I said, staring into the flames. "I get the books, the case, the history. I get that it matters. But... I still don't understand why *I* had to die."

Betty stirred her tea, even though there was nothing in her cup. Ghosts do that sort of thing. Force of habit and an underlying suspicion that someone might be watching.

"Sometimes," she said gently, "being in the way is all it takes."

"But I wasn't *doing* anything," I protested. "If I'd known they were important, maybe. But I hadn't even catalogued them. I barely remembered they existed."

"Someone else remembered," she said.

I slumped back in my chair. Or rather, I attempted to slump. Ghosts don't slump well. We drift mournfully and lean wistfully, but we never quite master the proper art of the huffy recline.

"I still don't know *how* I was murdered," I muttered. "Without that, I can't know *who* did it, and if I don't know that, how am I supposed to know who has the books now?"

Betty was quiet for a long moment.

"You said Brian didn't notice anyone robbing the shop."

"Exactly! If the books were stolen, he would've noticed. He's nosier than a hedgehog in a garden party."

"So maybe they weren't stolen. Maybe someone used the keys. Maybe someone had access. Maybe... " I was thinking "maybe I had the books with me when I was murdered."

I blinked. "But then... that would mean someone I *knew*. Someone I let in or had arranged to meet."

The fire popped, almost as if it agreed.

I stared into it. Into the dancing light. Into the mystery that had become my entire afterlife.

Then it hit me.

Not the revelation, not yet. Just a sense of something unsaid, hanging there between us like the awkward silence at a séance when nobody's quite sure who should go next. It was Betty's voice that did it. The way she'd said it, "Sometimes, being in the way is all it takes." Gentle. Measured. But with a note of something else.

Something wistful.

Like she was speaking from experience.

I turned to her.

"Betty," I said, quietly. "How did *you* die?"

"It was the war," she said finally. "The second one."

"You were in the RAF, right?"

She nodded. "WAAF. Women's Auxiliary Air Force. But the plan was that after the war I was going to America."

That surprised me. "You were?"

She smiled, softly. "I fell in love. With a GI. We were stationed at RAF Biggin Hill. Name was Raymond. Ray, for short. Big smile, bad haircut, and a drawl like maple syrup. We met at a dance in the village hall, he asked if I wanted to jitterbug and I told him only if he promised not to drop me. He didn't. Not once."

"You were going to marry him?"

"That was the plan. I said no the first time, but eventually I said yes. He was from Missouri. Said he'd take me home and build us a house near the Ozarks. I'd never seen a mountain before. He promised me pie."

"What happened?"

"War happened. Orders changed. He was due to ship out. We said goodbye, and he kissed me like we were already married. A week later, a telegram came from him, saying he'd put in for a transfer to extend his station so we could marry. Said I just needed to meet him at the airfield the next morning."

She paused, and for a moment I saw the echo of a girl barely twenty, full of hope and lipstick.

"I never made it," she said. "There'd been a last-minute reshuffle. Some confusion. A group of higher-ups had diverted resources and redirected the jeep that was supposed to pick me up. I decided to walk. Snowy morning. Quiet roads. Took a shortcut across the runway."

I winced. I didn't have lungs, but I still felt like I'd lost my breath.

"That's all I remember!" she whispered.

"Do you know what happened to Ray?"

She shook her head. "No. But then, how would I? We didn't know of people like Angie in those days."

"But…" I paused, piecing it together. "If you're *still here*, then that means it wasn't an accident. That something… prevented you from moving on. That you were murdered. Purposefully. But by who? Why?"

Betty didn't answer immediately. She sipped her imaginary tea like it might suddenly provide historical insight. I couldn't tell if she was trying to remember… or trying *not* to.

We sat in silence for a while, just the fire crackling and the occasional distant honk of the duck outside, sounding suspiciously like someone swearing in mallard.

"Could someone have… known?" I asked slowly. "About the transfer? About the marriage? Maybe someone didn't want it to happen."

"Tony, stop! It's all too late for me. You think I haven't thought about it the last eighty years? Wanting to know what happened, wanting revenge, yes, revenge, but that passes. That kind of rage, it burns bright and then it just… smoulders. Eventually, you either find peace or you learn how to make good tea."

She stood up, her ghostly form casting no shadow but every ounce of her carrying weight. "Whoever murdered me will have long since moved on themselves. Which means there will be no justice for me. No tribunal, no gavel, no satisfying ending where the music swells and someone shouts 'Guilty!' This is where I will remain."

She paused, looking out the window at the village green, now silvered with frost and early morning light. "It's not such a bad place to be, is it? I grew up here, you know. Have good memories of the pub, the village… I kissed my first boyfriend behind that shed next to the allotments. Laughed so hard I almost inhaled a ladybird. I watched the summer fetes from this very pub window. Danced on the bar once when Tatsfield beat Woldingham at Cricket. Got told off by my mum and then danced again when she wasn't looking."

Her voice softened. "… and I have responsibilities. You think even if I could move on, I would leave Bob behind? I couldn't do that. He's just a boy. Dead, yes, but still a boy. He needs someone. He needs a family. For better or worse, I'm what he's got."

We sat in silence for a while, just the two of us and the low hum of history wrapped in pub wallpaper.

Then she looked up, caught my eye and said, "… and then you turned up. Looking like a confused detective and making tea with the enthusiasm of a man who's never been allowed near a kettle before."

"In my defence, the kettle was haunted."

"You needed help. Not just with the tea. With your murder. With your afterlife. Suddenly, I matter again. Not because someone needed saving or because I had unfinished business, though apparently I do, but because someone needed *me*. That's a powerful thing."

I sat there for a long moment, like the universe had given me homework.

Then I said, softly, "You matter, Betty. You matter more than most of the living people I knew."

She gave me that look again, the one that could reset bones and make a vicar blush.

"Thank you," she said. "But you need justice Tony. The duck-fearing Indians need justice., and I'm going to help you."

"Betty," I said, as she rummaged, head buried in her handbag, which despite being both ghostly and ancient, still managed to jingle like it had a haunted tambourine in there somewhere, "can I ask you something else?"

Her hands stopped rummaging and went still. Continuing to stare into the depths of her handbag for a pause that clearly meant she was avoiding looking at me. "I think not" she eventually replied, voice slightly broken, without looking up, as if she knew what I might ask.

"I have a question for *you*, though," she added.

"You do?"

"Yes, it's about Brian's dusting."

That came out of nowhere. "What about his dusting?"

"He said he could do it by willpower." She looked up from her handbag with a pointed expression. "I can press keys on a typewriter with willpower."

"You want to write a letter?"

"No. I want you to show me how to use the computer in the office. I want to learn how to search the internet."

I blinked. "You... what?"

She stood up, suddenly all business. "Look, if I'm going to be part of this little ghost-detective agency you've accidentally founded, I want to be useful. I'm tired of waiting around for whisperings and tea leaves. I want Google. I want databases. I want to type in 'Flight Officer Emory' and find out if that insufferable cake-faced liar made it to retirement or died choking on his own medals."

"You want *internet justice*? ... and who is Flight Officer Emory?"

She grinned. "Emory was my CO, insufferable. I want *facts*. Maybe a few blurry photos. Possibly a scandal. But mostly facts, and so do you. We need to research if your death was in the news"

"You know the computer is in the office, right?" Betty was all business now "Tony, chop chop" she gave me that look, you know the look. "Show me how to Google." She said it like she was asking me to teach her a new dance step "come on Tony!"

So, moments later, I stood in the office of the Rose and Crown, feeling like a spectral IT consultant about to train a wartime poltergeist in basic keyboard navigation. The keys were ok. The mouse was the bloomin problem. A ghost moving a mouse is like blowing a droplet of water across a tabletop with a straw.

It didn't take long before Betty was zooming through headlines like a ghostly librarian on a caffeine high. We searched everything: obituaries, accident reports, news snippets from the day I died. Finally, there it was.

"Found it!" Betty said, tapping the monitor with an ethereal finger. "Local news site. The News Shopper. Obscure. But here it is: 'Tragic Christmas Accident Claims Life of Bookshop Owner.'"

I leaned in. There was a grainy photo of the crime scene, or as they'd called it, the accident scene. The twisted remains of a red phone box with a taxi half-embedded in the side. Some poor bystander holding a cappuccino like it had all gone terribly wrong.

According to the article, a black cab had mounted the pavement, skidded on icy cobbles, and crushed me, yes - me, against the phone box. Broken neck. Instant death. It even quoted a police officer saying, "It was a tragic accident. Wrong place, wrong time."

Don't get me wrong, I'm glad I don't remember. Because being slammed into a phone box by a runaway taxi and snapping like a breadstick is not the kind of memory I'd cherish. But at least now I *know* how I died. It's a strange feeling learning of your own death, looking at the place where I drew my last breath.

Betty looked at the screen with a frown. "The driver swerved to avoid a motorbike. Witnesses said he didn't have time to react."

"That," I said, "is probably why no one was ever brought to justice. Because they all thought it was just some freak event. A terrible, tragic accident."

Betty's brow furrowed. "Except you're a ghost… and ghosts don't happen unless something goes... unfinished."

"Exactly. And you know what the article says? The motorcyclist gave a statement. Said he lost control slightly going around the corner. Swerved, the taxi reacted, bam."

"The motorcyclist?" I leaned back reading the page "I know him," I said grimly. "Harry Barker. Introduced himself to me once at the Percy estate. Called himself Mr. Percy's butler."

Betty's eyebrows climbed so high I thought they might go independent and start a jazz trio. "The *butler*?"

"Yep. The butler. At the same estate we got the Native American history books from. The books now on auction."

"Tony," she said slowly. "Are you telling me the butler did it?"

"It's beginning to feel a bit like a particularly on-the-nose Agatha Christie plot, yes. But I don't believe in coincidences. You know how far The Percy Estate in Hexham is from the bookshop?"

She shook her head.

"Three hundred miles at least. That's not a coincidence. That's a *plan*."

"If he was driving that motorbike in London, the same day you died, right by your shop…"

"Then either he has very bad luck, or very good aim."

We sat in stunned silence. Betty leaned back, arms folded.

I looked back at the screen. At the photo of my body outlined under a sheet. The wreckage. The phone box. A red one. Of course it was red. Knowing there will never be another photo of me, ever, this was the last. I was dead under that sheet but it was my body.

"You're sure you've met this Barker?" she asked.

"More than once," I said. "We picked up the books from the Percy mansion. He was the one who showed me around. Said Mr. Percy wasn't available. That I'd be dealing with him directly. Very formal. Very smooth. Very unsettling."

"Do you think he knew what he was doing?"

"I think," I said, "he absolutely did… and I think he's more than a butler."

Betty nodded. "Shall we pay the Percys a visit?"

"Definitely," I said. "But we'll need a plan. Maybe a map and a car."

Betty smiled. "You know what this means, don't you?"

I looked at her. "What?"

She leaned in. "Road trip with Angie."

"I wonder if Angie has an email address."

She clapped her ghostly hands together. "We'll need snacks!"

"You can't eat snacks!"

"We'll *buy* snacks," she said. "Then stare at them longingly. It's what ghosts do."

Just like that, the next chapter in the case of my own murder had begun.

…and this time… I was coming for the butler.

RUDELY INTERRUPTED

CHAPTER FIVE

FLAMINGOS AND HALF A PINT OF STOUT

Angie turned up in the taxi just after eleven, a swirling figure in a long coat and a woollen hat so aggressively orange it could stop traffic without even trying. Which, to be fair, may have come in handy given the weather. The taxi slid slightly on the thin frost coating the road, then came to a dignified stop in front of the Rose and Crown with all the ceremony of a royal visit.

Same driver. Same taxi. Gary.

Gary had the face of a man who had witnessed things, births, weddings, funerals, at least three goat-based emergencies, and one alien abduction (allegedly), and was now resigned to the fact that life rarely made sense, especially once you crossed the M25 motorway.

"What a lovely morning," Angie said, climbing out of the taxi and thudding the door shut with a kind of efficiency that suggested she had once packed bags in a thunderstorm.

"Picking up something again are we?" said Gary, smiling in a way that could be interpreted either as fondness or slow-burning flirtation.

I watched from the pub window as Betty floated to my side.

"Someone's got a fan," she said, eyes twinkling.

"What, Gary?" I replied.

She gave me a sly look. "Oh yes. You might have competition, Mr. Ferrari… and I don't mean from the duck."

I raised a ghostly eyebrow. "Gary's old enough to be her uncle."

"So?" said Betty. "He's charming. Wears a hat. Offers boiled sweets to strangers. Some women go for that sort of thing."

I glanced at her. "… and you're going to have to stop acting like you don't enjoy stirring the pot."

"Never," she replied, practically glowing with self-satisfaction.

The front door creaked as Bob floated down the stairs, all knees and enthusiasm.

"Ooh! Is that a taxi?" he asked, peering out the window.

"It is," Betty replied. "Do you want to have a look?"

"Can I *sit* in it?"

"I don't see why not. But ask nicely."

Bob didn't need telling twice. He zipped through the pub wall and landed on the pavement outside just as Angie turned to retrieve a bag from the backseat. Bob, in his charmingly awkward way, floated up to Gary.

"Excuse me, Mister Taxi Man, can I sit in your car? I've never been in one before."

Gary blinked and looked around for whatever caused that tingly odd feeling he just felt. Angie, quick on the uptake as always, smiled sweetly and stepped in.

"Oh, I say, Gary, would you mind terribly popping into the pub for a moment? I'm parched. A half-pint of bitter? Just a quick one. You've earned it, what with all the driving and not skidding into a hedge."

Gary looked between her and the taxi, visibly torn between professionalism and mild romantic intrigue.

"Just a half," he said. "I'm still on shift."

"Of course," said Angie, ushering him toward the door.

Bob whooped and immediately phased into the back seat of the cab. He popped up through the upholstery like an excited meerkat in a wartime jumper.

"Look at this!" he cried. "Buttons! Knobs! Oh, I could drive this thing. I *would* drive this thing. I shall name it: The Phantom Vroom!"

Betty chuckled and drifted toward the taxi.

I stayed where I was, watching them in the taxi from afar. Betty was happy.

I'd seen Betty go into the office yesterday. She'd spent a good couple of hours in there, bathed in the ghostly glow of the computer screen, clicking away with the kind of fervour usually reserved for eBay auctions and intense crossword competitions.

But we hadn't spoken about it. She hadn't raised it, and I assumed, for now, it was private. I didn't push. But I would ask her. Later. When we weren't distracted by taxis and six-year-old spectres attempting to hotwire reality.

Inside, Gary perched on a barstool, pint in hand (half, true to his word), and began regaling Angie with tales of his more unusual fares.

"Once drove a woman to Glastonbury dressed as a flamingo," he said. "Didn't blink. Feathers everywhere. Smelled of rum and cinnamon. Told me she was spiritually aligned with Elton John's chi."

Angie laughed. That same snorting, helpless laugh that managed to say, "I find you ridiculous, but in a way that makes me want to hear more."

Betty leaned over to me as I joined her by the taxi. "She's warming to him."

I crossed my arms. "He's not that funny."

"He told her about the flamingo, didn't he?"

"Everyone's got a flamingo story."

"No, Tony. No, they don't."

Bob stuck his head out the passenger side window. "This thing has *cup holders!*"

"Progress marches on," Betty replied.

We all stood there in the wintry air, the strange little tableau of half-alive, mostly dead individuals gathered around a black cab and the pub we call home. There was something oddly comforting about it. Something almost normal. If normal involved spectral children joyriding stationary vehicles and middle-aged taxi drivers flirting with ghost-whisperers over discounted bitter.

Then, just like that, I realised something.

We weren't just solving mysteries anymore.

We were building something.

A team.

A family, even. That stopped me in my tracks. I tried to push the thought out, but it hung on in there expanding to fill every space until it would be impossible for it to be pulled out.

"Bob, sweetheart," Betty said gently, "you are not haunting the horn again."

"But it goes *BEEP*," Bob said with a pout.

"Yes, and the last time you did that, Trevor dug up Mrs. Wilberforce's entire rose bed."

"Worth it," Bob mumbled, but floated away.

"Ready?" Betty asked me.

I looked toward the pub, where Angie and Gary were still chatting, and back at Betty and Bob and the rattling, ghost-infested taxi.

"Let's go find a butler."

Hexham greeted us with drizzle and cobbled stubbornness. The town looked like it had been built by a mason with trust issues and a surplus of grey stones, and possibly by-laws preventing too much excitement after 7pm.

By the time Gary pulled the taxi into the car park behind The Grapes, the sky was a heavy blanket and the pub windows glowed with the promise of mediocre chips and below-average jazz. We were, as far as timing went, firmly in the territory of Too Late to Visit the Percy Estate Without Getting Shot At By Groundskeepers or Startled Deer.

Angie climbed out first, stretching the kinks from her back like someone uncorking a bottle of sarcasm. Gary followed, making a show of looking at the sky and saying, "Long way back to London this time of night."

"Oh? Planning to stay?" she asked, tone light.

"Booked a room too. Only one left, apparently," he said. "Wasn't going to risk a night drive. Roads'll be a nightmare."

The roads, I should mention, were not a nightmare. They were damp and sparsely populated by the occasional hedgehog with a death wish. But Gary's voice had that casual, *no really I'm just here for my own convenience* lilt that translated, roughly, to: *I'm flirting and trying not to make it weird.*

"Convenient, isn't it?" Betty murmured beside me, arms folded. "Don't be jealous."

"Stop it! I'm not jealous. I just find his hat too jaunty for my taste."

We followed them into the pub, which was loud and full of people who looked like they came with their own anecdotes. Gary went to check in. Angie stayed at the bar, idly spinning a beer mat. Betty and I lingered near the coat rack.

Then came the moment.

"You got the last room," said the barman, whose beard looked like it had aspirations to be a sentient being. Our living companions had each grabbed their keys. "Except the bridal suite, I assume….."

"No said Angie" grabbed her bag and heaved it up the stairs.

Betty and I glanced at each other.

"Awkward," she said.

"Very."

"I'll sleep in the fireplace," she offered.

"No. No. I'll hover in the bathroom. It's the ghostly equivalent of sleeping on the sofa."

"Generous," she smirked.

"Don't mention it."

We could have collected the key (with a key fob shaped like a badger) but as it was of no use to us, we climbed the stairs in a floaty jaunt, past portraits of fox hunts and one deeply suspicious-looking stuffed ferret. We took possession of the bridal suite.

The room was fine. A four poster, so high there was a footstall to help get on top, for those without the ability to float. Betty looked at the bed and then at me.

"Looks really comfy" she teased.

I nodded and retreated into the bathroom, hovering just off the cold tiles.

"Comfortable?" she called.

"Like a cloud with trust issues," I replied.

Downstairs, Gary was telling Angie about his time transporting a celebrity llama.

Upstairs, I was rethinking the entire nature of spectral etiquette.

How **do** you tell a girl who died 80 years ago that you're interested, but equally you might just go 'pop' at any moment and disappear the moment justice is done. Life, I mean death, is so unfair.

Tomorrow, we'd visit the estate. Tonight, we'd navigate the trickier terrain of floating together with things unsaid.

The next morning, the scent of frying bacon wafted up the stairs with all the subtlety of a brass band in a cathedral. I knocked on the bathroom door then phased through to find Betty already upright and perfectly composed, as if she'd spent the entire night floating in a dignified seated position.

"Morning," she said cheerfully. "You look translucent."

"It's a look," I muttered, rubbing at my temples out of sheer ghostly habit.

We drifted down to the dining room where Angie was already seated, Gary was trying to use a coffee machine that had little plastic pouches that needed inserting somewhere unmentionable. Angie halfway through a full English breakfast that smelled so good I almost achieved reincarnation on the spot.

"Morning, sleepyheads," she said with an inappropriate wink, gesturing to the seat opposite her. "We saved you a plate. Well, not physically, obviously."

I stared at the sizzling plate with a longing that bordered on spiritual crisis.

"Boy, I could *murder* a full English," I said.

Betty looked at me. "Bit soon for murder jokes, don't you think?"

We took our usual position at the edge of the table, hovering, invisible to everyone except Angie, and occasionally, I thought maybe Gary was starting to tune in, although that might have been my imagination. Either that or he was developing a sort of sixth sense usually reserved for minor prophets and overly sensitive cats.

"Gary's heading back to London this morning," Angie said between bites. "He says he has other clients to ignore."

Breakfast concluded with the ceremonial wiping of mouths and settling of bills. Gary tipped his hat, literally, to Angie, then gave us a strange little wave that suggested he knew we were there but didn't want to make a fuss about it.

"Stay safe," he said. "Don't go poking any butlers without backup."

"Wouldn't dream of it," Angie replied.

"You told him?" said Betty "about us"

"Oh yes, a man who has experience with flamingos and llamas can handle a ghost story"

With that, Gary climbed into his cab and drove off with a modest toot of the horn and the weary resignation of a man who knew he'd left something behind but didn't know what.

The three of us stood outside The Grapes, looking down the lane toward the edge of the village.

"Percy Hall is that way," Angie said, pointing toward a road flanked by high hedges and draped in morning mist. "Ten-minute walk, give or take."

"Ready?" I asked.

Betty nodded. "Always. Got my handbag and everything."

"I still don't know what's in that thing."

"Secrets," she smiled "did you learn nothing in the living world?"

We set off, a woman and her two spectral companions, passing cottages with names like *Pudding Hollow* and *Thistle End*, and the occasional suspicious ginger cat.

As we crunched along the lane that led toward Percy Hall, I drifted a bit closer to Betty. Her handbag was slung over her shoulder, swinging with quiet purpose, walking like someone who had spent decades preparing to confront a stately home.

I cleared my throat. Again, ghost habits die hard.

"Betty... can I ask something?"

She glanced sideways. "You're asking anyway. Go on."

"Yesterday. Before we left. You were on the computer for quite a while. Did you... find anything else? About Ray, I mean."

There was a pause, just long enough to notice the chirp of a far-off bird wondering if it had migrated too early.

Betty nodded, slowly. "Yes. I did."

She didn't say anything for a moment, and I let her take her time. We passed under the curling iron arch of a gate, the vines having long ago given up trying to strangle it.

"I found his wedding certificate first," she said. Her voice was steady, but soft. "He got married in 1947, after the war. Nebraska. A girl named Clara. She looked... sweet. Big smile. I could tell from the photos."

"So he did go home," I said, gently.

"Yes, and he lived. He had a good life, I think. I found photos from a newspaper piece about his retirement. He worked for the postal service. Had three boys."

She stopped and turned to me, a small smile forming. "He had a life, Tony. A full one."

I watched her face, trying to read it, not the words, but the subtext. The flickers behind her eyes. But all I saw was peace.

"You're glad," I said. Not a question.

"I am. I thought it might hurt," she admitted. "But it doesn't. Not in the way I thought. It's like... like some part of me was frozen, wondering if he'd waited. Wondering if I'd failed him. But he didn't wait, or at least not forever. That's good. That means he lived."

"You're not angry?"

"It's strange. It's like being released from a story you didn't realise you were still trapped in."

We walked on, the hall looming closer now.

"He died in 1999," she continued. "Just missed the millennium. His obituary said he was surrounded by his family."

"Just missed the fireworks," I said quietly.

Betty chuckled. "He hated loud noises."

I gave her a look. "You knew that?"

"We talked, Tony. I knew his favourite pie, blueberry and cheese, and that he once got into a fight with a rooster. Of course, I knew he hated fireworks."

I smiled. She smiled back. It wasn't a big, triumphant smile. It wasn't even sad. It was the kind of smile you give someone when you've finally let go of something you didn't know you were holding onto.

"Thank you for asking," she said. "I wasn't going to bring it up yet. Thought I might need time. But now... I feel lighter."

"Betty, you're floating six inches off the ground. You can't *get* lighter."

She rolled her eyes. "Ghost jokes. Always classy."

The road curved gently uphill until we crested a small rise, and there, nestled beyond a wrought-iron gate and a line of yew trees, stood Percy Hall.

It was every bit the stately home you'd expect from a place with a name like Percy Hall, stone chimneys, gables, the sort of windows that made you feel like you were being judged. Even from here, I could tell it had that special kind of chill only old money and older secrets could generate.

Angie whistled. "Nice place. Terribly murderable."

"I like it already," Betty said.

We stopped just outside the grand front doors of Percy Hall.

Betty took a breath she didn't need, squaring her ghostly shoulders.

"You ready for this?" I asked.

"Are you?" she replied.

"Not even slightly."

"Perfect," she said. "Let's meet the butler."

CHAPTER SIX

SPOONS AND OTHER THINGS THAT SKITTER IN THE DARK

The heavy brass knocker was shaped like a lion eating a pineapple. Of course it was! Percy Hall didn't seem like the kind of place to leave a door unguarded by tropical symbolism.

Angie raised it and gave three firm raps.

We waited. Somewhere inside, something shifted. A curtain twitched. A grandfather clock coughed meaningfully. Then the door creaked open just wide enough to reveal a man in a waistcoat so crisply ironed it could slice ham.

He had the butler look: tall, impeccably dressed, eyebrows like sculpted hedgerows, and the haunted stare of a man who had been quietly judging people since the Victorian era.

"Good morning," he said. "May I help you?"

Angie smiled sweetly. "Good morning! I'm Angela Robbins. We spoke by email. I'm here to follow up about the antique silver spoon collection you're selling."

There was a beat. A pause so deliberate it may have had choreography.

"Of course," he said. "Please, come in."

He stepped aside, and we entered the cavernous entrance hall.

Percy Hall had that unmistakable air of money, mothballs, and secrets stuffed into the wainscoting. The floors were waxed within an inch of their lives. The portraits on the wall stared down like they knew your internet history.

"This way," the butler said, gliding rather than walking.

As we followed, I leaned into Betty.

"That's him," I whispered. "Harry Barker. The motorcyclist. But look at those portraits on the wall Betty, the old Lord Percys. Every one of them with that same startled set of the eyes, and a nose like a proud Roman statue that's just heard a mildly offensive joke. It's him. I'm telling you. That's not just a butler; he's Lord Percy himself."

We passed under a chandelier so enormous it had its own gravitational pull and entered what could only be described as the Grand Sitting Room, which contained precisely no one sitting.

"I'll fetch the spoons," he said, bowing ever so slightly before disappearing into a corridor that definitely led to either an office or a secret passage to a cheese pantry.

"I'll just have a little look about," Betty murmured, already absently tottering toward a display cabinet with a disturbing number of antique horse brasses.

Angie waited until the door closed.

"You're sure it's him?"

"As sure as a ghost can be," I said. "That's Harry Barker. But he's not a butler."

"Let me guess," she said. "He's Lord Percy?"

"Bingo."

We had only a few minutes before he returned, but that was enough. Angie found a framed photo on a sideboard, Lord Horace Percy accepting an award for "Local Preservation Efforts." It was clearly him, sans waistcoat but with the same unblinking eyes and air of tax evasion.

"I'll keep him talking," Angie said. "You two snoop. But quietly."

Betty nodded. "I can snoop like a whisper in a library."

I drifted toward the massive fireplace, feeling for anything… off. Behind me, the sound of Barker/Lord Percy's shoes returned. Angie straightened, smile in place.

"Oh good, you're back," she said brightly. "Did you say the spoons belonged to Lord Wellington himself? I'd love to know more about the collection. The lineage of pieces like this must be fascinating."

He paused, just slightly.

"Ah. Yes. A prized set. Very rare."

Behind the bookshelf, Betty found a drawer. She gave me a meaningful nod.

Lord Percy smiled with wonky teeth. "Indeed, indeed. This particular piece, for example, was allegedly used by Queen Victoria's second cousin, on a picnic, no less. A gooseberry tart was involved."

"Good heavens," Angie said, leaning forward with all the earnest interest of someone who had once owned a novelty teaspoon shaped like Sherlock Holmes. "… and the one next to it?"

"That one," he said, with a touch of reverence, "belonged to a Russian countess who later defected to Belgium. It's said she used it to stir rebellion… and porridge."

Betty rolled her eyes behind a silver teapot. "Porridge. The revolution of champions."

As Lord Percy launched into a tale about the origins of a spoon possibly connected to a brief diplomatic incident involving Portugal, I nudged Betty.

"Let's see what else this place is hiding."

She nodded, and we slipped deeper into the shadows of the sitting room.

That's when we felt it.

Eyes.

Not living ones. These were colder. Still. Watching from between the curtain folds, from the dusty crevices of grandfather clocks, from portraits whose subjects knew too much and said too little.

Percy Hall wasn't just haunted.

It was *crowded*.

They began to emerge slowly at first, glimpses in doorframes, a shimmer of movement near the stairwell, a reflection in the polished mahogany that didn't belong to any living person in the room. One by one, the ghosts of Percy Hall revealed themselves.

An elderly woman in a sweeping blue gown drifted halfway through the wall near the piano and peered at us through gold-rimmed spectacles as if checking for dust. A footman in stiff livery appeared just behind a curtain and gave Betty a respectful nod.

Then there was the gardener, who trudged silently through a Persian rug with a wheelbarrow full of Cheese.

They were watching us.

Not menacingly, but not passively either. It was the look people give at bus stops when someone suspiciously good-looking joins the queue. Curious, a bit wary, and already writing imaginary dialogue.

More ghosts began appearing as we crept through the far end of the hall, an elderly gentleman with a beard like two duelling squirrels stared down from the landing; a pair of children, pale and identical, skipped silently through a closed door; and near the ceiling, a man in Edwardian garb was levitating upside-down while reading a newspaper.

"Why is he upside-down?" I asked.

"He died that way," said a maid with half-tied ribbons as she drifted past us, dusting the air itself with an invisible cloth. "The chandelier incident of 1903. He insists the view's better." The maid smiled a little too provocatively for my liking "I'm Elsie by the way" blew me a kiss and swirled off.

Betty gave me a grin, or it might have been a scowl. Not always easy to tell.

A portly man in a powdered wig shuffled past muttering to himself. Something about Napoleon and misplaced canapés.

We passed a mirror, cracked, but still reflective. Except it didn't reflect us. Only Angie and an animated Lord Percy trying to bend a silver spoon with his teeth.

"Classic," I muttered.

Then, a new ghost appeared at the top of the grand staircase. A man in a tweed suit, eyes shadowed beneath a bowler hat.

He pointed directly at me.

"You," he said. "You saw it. You saw what he did.""

My ghostly blood ran cold.

"You remember me?"

He nodded slowly. "I was watching. I always watch. He meant to switch them, the books, well in fact he did. But he got confused and forgot he had already switched them. You got the real ones by mistake."

Betty gasped. "Tony… he's your witness."

"I don't know your name," I said in my best NYPD police accent.

"They called me Mr. Fletch. I used to handle inventory. Died of shame in 1972. Badly mislabelled a Fabergé egg. Never got over it."

"Where are the real books now?" I asked.

He looked around nervously. "Not safe to say here. He listens. Even when he's pretending not to."

"Who?" I asked, though I already had a sinking feeling.

"Lord Percy," he whispered. "The walls talk to him. Or maybe he talks to the walls. Either way, they're on good terms."

I looked at Betty. She raised an eyebrow.

"But I'll find you," Fletch continued, stepping back into the shadow of the stair rail. "Later. In the rose garden. After lunch when the estate has its afternoon snooze. It's safer there."

Then he vanished.

Betty looked at me. "Well. That was dramatic."

I nodded. "We've got our first real lead."

Behind us, Lord Percy launched into a story about a spoon once confiscated by Neville Chamberlain.

Angie, bless her, smiled and nodded.

I drifted back toward Angie, trying not to draw the attention of the other spirits still silently observing from the wings of the hall. Checking I was far enough from the walls in case they did have ears and were listening, I leaned in close.

"We need more time," I whispered. "We have a lead who wants to meet us in the rose garden."

Angie, never missing a beat, turned back to Lord Percy "I say, all these spoons are marvellous, but I must admit I'm not quite used to so much walking before tea. Do you think we might sit down for a moment?"

Lord Percy blinked, a man momentarily derailed by a civilian breaking from script. "Ah. Of course. The Blue Salon is just through here. I'll have tea brought in."

As they stepped into the adjoining room, Betty lingered near the door, turning to Elsie the maid, who was still wiping down invisible grime with stubborn pride.

"Elsie, love," Betty said softly. "Could you show us to the rose garden later? There's someone we're hoping to meet."

Elsie gave an excited nod. "Will he be there" she said looking over at me under her eyelids.

"Most definitely" said betty with the air of collusion.

"Course. Still smells nice out there, even with no noses."

We regrouped in the Blue Salon, where Angie was now seated on a faded floral sofa that had the posture of a disappointed aunt. Lord Percy, unfazed, was ringing for tea. Moments later, a young woman entered with a tray so polished it could double as a lighthouse.

"Cream?" Lord Percy offered.

"Two lumps and a great deal of caution," Angie replied cheerfully, and laughed loudly at her own joke.

Betty and I took up our station near the window, pretending to examine the view while the human conversation carried on behind us. The garden was visible beyond the glass: symmetrical hedgerows, gravel paths, and rows of dead rose bushes that still blushed in ghostly colour.

We watched as Angie continued her feigned interest in the spoons while steering the conversation away from anything auction related. Lord Percy, for his part, was indulging her with increasing enthusiasm. Perhaps he sensed in her a fellow admirer of shiny things and scandalous histories, or perhaps he was simply grateful to avoid questions about provenance.

After a well-timed compliment about a French olive spoon, Angie excused herself to 'freshen up' and joined us near the window.

"I've bought us until after sunset," she said. "He's invited me to stay for dinner. I'll keep him distracted. You two meet your lead. See what else he knows."

"You sure you're alright with that?" I asked.

She gave me a look. "I've been on tinder for three years love. I can endure one more evening with a man who thinks spoons have a personality."

"… and Betty…"

She nodded. "We'll be careful."

The rest of the afternoon was spent in slow reconnaissance. Betty and I wandered through the less-populated wings of the house, drawing rooms untouched for decades, libraries full of dust and secrets, corridors where the air grew inexplicably colder.

We climbed the narrow back staircase up to the servants' quarters, each step giving off a mournful creak, like it remembered being trod upon by generations of weary boots and gossiping housemaids. The ceiling bowed slightly, the wallpaper curled like old letters, and the windows were so dusty they might as well have been murals of fog.

When we finally reached the attic corridor, it was obvious: Percy Hall was in trouble. The roof was clearly rotten.

Rain had left ghostly stains along the beams, patches of plaster sagged like tired eyebrows, and we could see faint daylight through several ominous cracks. A few buckets sat strategically placed, as if in a feeble attempt to catch time itself leaking through the rafters.

Elsie, who had appeared the moment we arrived, as all good servant ghosts do, nodded grimly.

"Yep," she said. "Whole thing's been falling apart since the '80s. Lord Percy kept patching it, but you can't slap spit on woodworm forever."

I floated through one of the beams experimentally. It shuddered.

Betty winced. "That's not comforting."

"I've seen softer bones in a cemetery," Elsie muttered.

Elsie raised her ghostly duster like a sceptre. "He's been flogging bits and bobs from the estate for decades. Selling off heirlooms, pawning silver, forging artefacts, he even sold the piano stool once. Claimed it was Napoleon's loo."

Betty gasped. "Was it?"

"Absolutely not. But the cheque cleared."

"If you know he's a bit of a crook, why not do something?" I asked.

Elsie gave me a look that could have peeled wallpaper. "Because this place is ours too. We worked here, lived here, died here. This roof leaks on our memories. You think we want the whole place condemned and turned into a bloomin spa hotel with wellness pods and avocado toast?"

Betty nodded solemnly. "She's right. If Percy Hall goes under, it all goes under. Even the ghosts. They'd be scattered. Lost."

Elsie folded her arms. "So, if Lord Percy has to sell the odd priceless spoon to keep the ceiling out of our teacups, well… most of us look the other way."

"But Tony was murdered," Betty said quietly.

Elsie looked at me with something almost like guilt. "We didn't know. If we'd known…"

"Would you have stopped him?" I asked.

Elsie didn't answer.

But the silence spoke volumes.

I looked up at the buckling ceiling. Somewhere above it, storm clouds were probably gathering.

Below it, ghosts were clinging to a past that was rapidly decaying.

Beneath it all, Lord Percy was counting his silver spoons and praying nobody noticed some were silver plated.

"Fletch better show up," I muttered.

"He will," Betty said. "This house is whispering. It's ready to tell its story.""

Elsie led us back down the stairs, floating obviously, but still skipping an odd stair the way she did whilst in the living. I followed, and we stepped through a side door into the twilight of the estate gardens, where roses bloomed as though lit from within.

Now, it was just a matter of waiting.

Waiting for a ghost with a memory full of auction house errors and buried truths.

Right on cue, as if summoned by dramatic tension and possibly a minor key piano chord, Fletch appeared. He stepped out from behind a crumbling pillar near the rose arbour with the reluctant poise of a man who had once tried haunting subtly and then changed tack halfway through in favour of dramatic entrances.

"I wasn't followed," he muttered, glancing over his shoulder in the manner of someone checking for unwanted paparazzi, or possibly Lord Percy's eyebrow.

Betty raised one perfectly arched eyebrow in response, the kind that suggests its owner had once terrified an entire parish council with a look. "By who?"

Fletch rubbed at his translucent chin. "There's a lot of unrest in the walls. Old ghosts, newer ones. The gardener who drowned in the goose pond thinks I should keep my mouth shut. Elsie says I've got a flair for drama and it's all gone to my head. Even the twins from the nursery chimed in, and they only speak in rhyming couplets."

"But you remembered me," I said.

"I did," he nodded. "From the auction. You stood there, hands, feet, hair, breathing, everything, alive, and now here you are, deader than a scone at a slimming club buffet. The moment I saw you arrive today I knew things were bad. You being dead, it means something, means things are... moving"

"I need to ask... why did you bid on that lot? Those books. Why those?"

I blinked. "Honestly? I didn't. I was trying for a set of first edition Jules Verne novels. Nautilus and tentacles, that sort of thing. The Native American collection came bundled in. Could've been novelty teapots and I'd still have walked out with them."

Fletch's ghostly complexion changed in a way that would have made a chameleon jealous. "So... you really weren't supposed to win them."

"No. But once I had them, I opened them. They were beautiful. Important. Full of... weight. I planned to catalogue them properly. Do them justice. But...I didn't get the chance."

Fletch's face shifted through three different expressions: confusion, recognition, and a deep ghostly version of 'oh no.'

"Because someone parked a taxi between him and a phone box and broke his neck," Betty added, emphasising the gravity of it all.

"Exactly," I said. "So no, I didn't know."

Fletch nodded slowly. "Umm, then you really, really didn't know, did you?"

He glanced around again, as though expecting Percy Hall itself to interrupt. "Those books… they aren't just old paper. They're proof. Hidden in plain sight. Not just in the art, but in the marginalia. Notes. Names. Dates. Proof of treaties broken. Promises made in writing and ignored. Proof that could collapse entire property holdings, international treaties, maybe even governments if they ever saw light."

"They were historically explosive," I said.

"Percy would've buried you under the garden himself if he weren't so afraid of worms."

Betty crossed her arms. "So he had someone else do it. The motorbike. The taxi."

"Likely someone on the payroll. Percy doesn't like getting his own hands dirty. Makes his spoons tarnish."

"The other ghosts?" I asked. "They knew?"

"They suspected. But they're afraid. This place… it's their home and the Native Indian books are the golden ticket to save Percy Hall. Ghosts don't relocate well. The housing market for the afterlife is brutal. But they didn't know that he had your murdered, so sorry about that old chap."

Betty looked at me. "So now you've got your own death to deal with, a centuries-old conspiracy, the weight of hundreds of the Cherokee ancestors, and now the existential security of dozens of ghostly squatters in Percy Hall. Feeling overwhelmed yet?"

"Only slightly."

Fletch stepped back into the shadows. "I shouldn't be seen with you. Not until I know who else is listening. But I'll leave something for you. Something Percy missed."

"What is it?" I asked.

"You'll know it when you see it," he said, already dissolving like a Victorian mystery. "It's in the library. Look behind The Collected Sermons of Bishop Tiddles. It's not what it seems."

Then he was gone, leaving the scent of old ink and quiet guilt hanging in the air.

Betty turned to me. "Well, this is escalating."

"I didn't expect to be at the centre of a posthumous land rights thriller," I admitted. "I thought being dead would be simpler. You know. Ectoplasm and a nice eternal lie-down."

Betty grinned. "Oh, Tony. You poor sweet fool. You're almost British now. We don't *do* simple. It's probably time for tea."

Somewhere in the rose garden, a petal fell with dramatic timing. Inside Percy Hall, a sermon book was hiding something it really shouldn't.

The library, when we arrived, did not disappoint. It was the sort of room that had never been dusted properly because everyone was too intimidated by the books. Floor-to-ceiling shelves groaned with leather-bound volumes, each one looking like it had been read once by a Viscount and then left to contemplate its own legacy.

We scanned the titles until we reached the S section, where sermons and other moral pronouncements appeared to breed like rabbits.

"Here we are," Betty said. "Bishop Tiddles."

"Who names a bishop - Tiddles?" I asked.

"Someone who clearly didn't like him," Betty replied.

We found the spine: *The Collected Sermons of Bishop Eustace Tiddles, 1853–1868: Morality, Muffins, and Misery.* It was wedged tightly between *The Art of Proper Bell Pull Etiquette* and something ominously titled *An Inquiry into Staring Too Long at Servants.*

Betty reached for it, her hand half-phasing through the spine. "This is your moment, Tony. Ghost up and give it a tug."

I reached out, and with a little willpower and a lot of passive-aggressive grunting, managed to ease the book from its spot. It gave way with a soft *thunk*, and the shelf behind it swung inward on old hinges.

"Secret passage?" I breathed.

We both peered in.

It was cobwebby, dark, and the sort of ominously quiet that made your ears feel like they'd just been scolded by a particularly disappointed librarian. The air was stale in the way that suggested it had been breathed once in 1883, found wanting, and left behind in protest.

Now, here's the thing about ghosts.

You might think we're immune to fear. That we float through walls and social awkwardness without a care in the ectoplasmic world. That fear is something for the living, like haircuts and income tax. But fear is deeper than flesh. It's older. It's stitched into the very fabric of who you are, or who you were, or who you almost managed to become before the taxi got involved.

So, when we looked into that tunnel, Betty and I did not feel brave. We felt, if you'll pardon the phrase, deeply hauntable.

"There's something moving in there," I whispered.

"There's always something moving in tunnels," Betty replied calmly, as if she were listing ingredients for a shepherd's pie. "That's why tunnels exist. To move things that shouldn't be seen."

She crouched slightly, peering further in, and I noticed even her ghostly eyebrows had gone into caution mode. This is the supernatural equivalent of DEFCON 2.

"You think it's another ghost?" I asked, hoping the answer was "Yes" because that's a manageable level of weird, as opposed to say, cursed moles, undead badgers, or something that glows green and hums show tunes.

Betty shrugged. "Might be. Might be rats."

We stepped in together, both hovering an inch above the floor, because old habits die hard and neither of us fancied brushing our incorporeal toes on a centuries-old bat poo. The cobwebs were thick enough to knit into an unsettling sort of jumper. I swore one spider was wearing a tiny bonnet and had a suspicious number of eyes.

"Spiders," I muttered, brushing at my face instinctively even though, strictly speaking, I didn't have a face that could itch anymore.

"I never minded spiders," said Betty, brushing a particularly lacy one aside. "It's the way they move. Like they know something. Like they're plotting. Spiders always look like they've just been to a very informative meeting."

The tunnel narrowed in that classic ancient estate way, where practicality had long since taken second place to draughts, superstition, and the notion that rich people wouldn't be caught dead down here, though, as it happened, we were.

"Who do you think built this?" I asked, mostly to distract myself from the cold spot developing somewhere around my ghost-stomach.

"Victorians," Betty said. "Or monks. Or secret society members with too much time and far too many bricks."

At one point we passed a stack of crates marked *Tea 1872*.

… and that's when we heard the whisper.

Not the kind that says "hello," or "beware," or even "I put the kettle on." No. This was the kind of whisper that says, "I've been here for a very long time and I've had thoughts."

We both froze.

Now, freezing as a ghost is more of a psychological state than a physical one. But we managed it, standing perfectly still in the way only people who are deeply aware of their own doomed curiosity can.

Betty turned her head slowly.

"Tony," she said, very calmly, "that was not wind."

Another whisper. This time behind us.

"I think we're being followed," I said.

"You think?" she replied. "You didn't hear the bit where something said your name?"

"I was trying to be optimistic," I said.

There was a pause. A long, creepy, cinematic pause.

Then something skittered.

I don't know what. I didn't look. I may be dead, but I still know the universal truth: if something skitters in a tunnel, *you do not look.* That's how horror movies happen. That's how low-budget documentaries with titles like *Britain's Most Haunted Gutters* happen… and thank you very much, I had no intention of becoming a ghost who gets talked about in other ghost stories with the phrase "and that's why we never go near the west wing."

It made a sort of noise that can only be described as a whispering scuttle. The kind of noise that suggests legs, many of them, and opinions. The kind of thing that's been living here longer than time and doesn't appreciate being disturbed by a couple of ectoplasmic nosey parkers.

"Don't look," I whispered.

"I'm not," Betty whispered back.

"You're looking with your third ghost eye, aren't you?"

"I am aggressively *not* looking in any spectral capacity. You?"

"Staring firmly ahead and pretending I didn't hear anything that could scuttle up a trouser leg."

We picked up the pace. Float-walking, if that's a thing. Not quite running. More… brisk haunting. A hasty reconsideration of our entire tunnel-based decision-making process.

The skittering stopped.

Now, in horror logic, a noise stopping is infinitely worse than it starting. Because it means the skitterer is either: a) repositioning itself for a dramatic jump scare, or b) thinking.

I don't like things that skitter *and* think.

The tunnel opened up sullenly into a small circular chamber. I say "opened up," but it really more *gave up*. It stopped trying to be narrow and menacing and decided to be slightly wider and deeply unsettling instead.

The room was all stone walls and bad intentions. Shelves sagged under the weight of ledgers that hadn't been touched since Queen Victoria stopped returning ghostly RSVP cards. The books looked like they were bound in optimism and then punished for it. Some of them had titles in Latin. One of them may have been growling faintly.

A single candle flickered on a cracked porcelain saucer. It should not have been lit. It had no business being lit. We hadn't passed any matches, any torches, or even a friendly spectral Boy Scout.

There was a chair.

Of course there was a chair.

It sat in the middle of the chamber facing the wall. Not the candle. Not the doorway. Just a blank section of stone.

"Why is it always chairs?" I muttered. "Why is it never something wholesome, like a ghost picnic?"

I looked at Betty. Betty looked at me.

We shared the classic ghost look that says: *We are fully aware this is a terrible idea, but we're here now and might as well finish the scene.*

Betty stepped forward cautiously, like she was approaching a possessed vicar with a clipboard.

"Excuse me," she said, "do you happen to be—"

The chair spun around slowly.

Dramatically.

Because of course it did.

Empty.

Of course it was.

Nothing sat in it. Just a wisp of dust. Possibly a small puff of resentment. But we could feel it. There was something else here. I had sort of assumed that alive people had one frequency and ghosts another, but perhaps there are other frequencies that neither the living nor the dead can see.

But the air shifted. The temperature, which had already been somewhere between crypt and frozen peas aisle, dropped by a few unnerving degrees.

We both felt it.

The really spooky part?

Is that ghosts aren't supposed to feel things like that. We're not designed for temperature variation or dread-induced sweating. But we felt it. Like something had noticed us. Not a ghost. Not a person. Something... else.

"Well, that's not menacing at all," I said.

Then something grabbed me.

Properly grabbed me.

I don't mean brushed against or nudged politely. I mean *grabbed*, in the full-fingered, I-know-your-insurance-details kind of way. My arm locked.

And here's the kicker, *I felt it*.

As in: I, Tony Ferrari, ghost and former semi-respectable bookshop owner, *felt* someone grab me. It shouldn't be possible.

That's not in the ghost user manual. That's not how afterlife physics works.

"Betty," I whispered, "I'm being held."

Betty stepped forward and stopped.

She looked down at her own wrist. "So am I."

It didn't feel hostile, just... ancient. Cold. Curious. Like something flipping through its ghost mail and going, "Oh, what's this, haven't seen one of these in decades."

Then it let go.

Just like that. Gone. No flash. No noise. Just a sense of something withdrawing, satisfied.

We hovered in the silence for a beat, staring at our arms like they might have grown polite labels.

"That," Betty said eventually, "was not one of the usual suspects."

"No. That was something… else."

The candle went out.

Naturally.

Back up the tunnel we went. No discussion. Just action. Tactical float-retreat. Our pace increased. Speed records were shattered. The cobwebs parted before us like even *they* didn't want to get involved.

As we reached the tunnel mouth and emerged into a back corridor somewhere behind the library, we stopped and wheezed.

I say wheezed. Ghosts can't wheeze. But if we could, we'd have sounded like a harmonica being stepped on.

I turned to her.

"So," I said, "are we brave? Or just stupid?"

"I've never seen those as mutually exclusive," Betty replied, brushing spectral lint off her lapel with the air of someone who has just survived something they intend to file a formal complaint about.

There was silence for a moment.

Then the whisper came.

Just one word. From the tunnel.

"Again." In the same way a golden retriever would bring a ball back and want you to throw it again.

We stared into the darkness.

"Nope," I said. "Absolutely not, not on your life."

"Seconded," said Betty. "Come on. Let's go find Bishop Tiddles and demand answers."

We turned our backs on whatever had just audited our spiritual frequency and headed back to the library. Behind us, the tunnel sighed. Or maybe it was laughing. Either way, we weren't sticking around to find out.

Not without tea.

Somewhere, a dinner bell rang. Somewhere else, Lord Percy was almost certainly telling Angie about a spoon once owned by a minor viscount and used in a duel over soup.

We didn't speak. We didn't need to.

We had books to check. A sermon to investigate. And a Bishop to question.

Well… his books, at least.

With quite possibly some holy water on standby.

Because the truth, much like the tunnel, was getting darker the deeper we went.

Before we could dig deeper, we heard the clinking of cutlery and the echo of polite chuckles coming from the dining room down the hall.

"Shall we check in on our distraction?" Betty said.

We floated off, sticking to the shadows like two overcaffeinated breezes.

Inside the grand dining room, Lord Percy was mid-anecdote about the time he met a spoon collector who believed silverware had psychic energy. Not emotional resonance, mind you, *psychic energy*. According to the collector, a well-tuned dessert spoon could pick up messages from the astral plane if stored properly near a jar of marmalade. Apparently, the teaspoon of Marie Antoinette once made a medium sneeze for fifteen consecutive minutes.

Angie, composed as ever, was nodding with just the right amount of interest that said, "I'm listening," while simultaneously projecting the spiritual essence of "I could be home with a nice cup of Earl Grey" Her performance was a masterclass in social civility, somewhere between polite curiosity and desperate internal monologue. She'd clearly reached the stage of conversation where you mentally start redecorating a shed just to stay awake.

We left them to it.

The library was as we had left it: tall shelves, deep gloom, and the faint lingering odour of academic despair. Dust coated everything like it had been carefully applied with a pastry brush. There was a solemnity to the room, the sort that made you feel like whispering even if your mouth hadn't technically moved in decades.

"Right," Betty said, heading for the theology section. "Let's see if our dear Bishop Tiddles has left us anything else worth disturbing the undead about."

Now, Bishop Eustace Tiddles had not been known for brevity, humour, or a functional understanding of the common man. He had been known, however, for three things: sermons that exceeded the length of many novels, an unhealthy obsession with muffins, and a facial expression that suggested he permanently smelt something off about your character.

We hovered before the hallowed shelf.

There was our: *The Collected Sermons of Bishop Eustace Tiddles, 1853–1868: Morality, Muffins, and Misery.* That had been the lever to the secret passage. We wouldn't be pulling that one again.

On the shelf below, we found the follow-up volume: *The Sermons of Bishop Eustace Tiddles, 1869–1887: Purgatory, Punctuality, and Preserves.*

"Oh good," said Betty. "I was worried we wouldn't find the one with theological jam."

The spine resisted slightly, like it didn't want to be involved, but eventually gave in with a grumble and slid free. Behind it, nestled in a shallow recess in the wooden shelf, was a key.

Not just any key. A gothic key.

You know the sort, long, heavy, and unnecessarily curvy, like it had been designed by someone whose only concept of doors came from nightmares and organ music. This was not a key for anything as mundane as a cupboard. This was a *plot key*.

Wrapped around it was a small scrap of aged paper, folded with obsessive neatness.

Betty delicately opened it. "'Look under the fuse box under the stairs.'"

"Very modern," I said. "Nice to see Bishop Tiddles embraced 19th-century electrical innovation."

"Either that," Betty said, "or this was added by someone a little more contemporary. A ghost with access to practical knowledge and poor handwriting, like Fletch."

We floated down the hallway to the grand staircase. The fuse box was tucked underneath, predictably behind a small, creaky door held shut by the mutual agreement of dust and spite.

The box itself looked like it had been installed during the Crimean War and updated by a man with shaky hands and deep distrust of instructions. Wires sprouted from it like ivy. There were labels, all faded, and one suspicious toggle marked simply *DO NOT TOUCH* in Gothic script.

Beneath the main panel, I noticed a slight discolouration in the wood.

"Here," I said. "Looks like a hidden panel."

"Very Agatha Christie," Betty murmured.

I inserted the key, which clicked with all the theatrical satisfaction of a prop sword being drawn at the exact right moment.

The panel creaked open, revealing a staircase.

Stone.

Narrow.

Leading down.

Because of course it did.

We both peered in. The stairs were lined with an equally dour set of cobwebs as the last *adventure*, and a smell that floated up suggesting mildew, secrets, and faint disappointment.

"You must be kidding me!" we looked at each other. "Do we?"

Betty sighed with the sort of long-suffering grace only British ghosts and primary school teachers possess. "This is clearly the next chapter, come on."

We descended. The light dimmed behind us, swallowed by stone. We glided past old wall sconces and carved brickwork, our forms trailing the ancient air like forgotten promises. It was quiet. Not peaceful.

"I don't like the vibe down here," I said.

"Good," said Betty. "Means we're in the right place."

At the bottom of the staircase, the air changed. Not dramatically, there was no sudden burst of wind or chorus of whispering Latin, but subtly. Like the walls had all looked at one another and collectively decided to be quiet. That sort of silence where your own thoughts feel too loud and the shadows seem to be rehearsing for something sinister.

A final twist in the corridor revealed a door that looked newer than it had any right to be. Metal. Institutional. The kind of door you'd expect to find at the back of a slightly illegal laboratory or a government facility marked "Definitely Not Aliens."

The door wasn't locked. It opened with a hydraulic sigh, as though disappointed we'd actually come this far.

Inside was a storage room. But not the sort you'd expect under a grand English manor. There were no crates marked "Curse This End Up," or sarcophagi labelled "Do Not Open Except on Tuesdays." No, this was disappointingly… modern.

Strip neon lighting buzzed on the ceiling, casting everything in the unforgiving glare of an overstressed office cubicle. The walls were painted a kind of institutional beige that screamed of mid-90s budget constraints. There were filing cabinets. An old desktop computer sat on a steel desk, humming with the eternal hope that someone might turn Minesweeper on. There was a mug next to it. It said "#1 Lord." The handle had been cracked and superglued. Twice.

But in the centre of the room, on a large oak table polished to the point of insecurity, lay the real prize.

Three volumes.

Ancient. Leather-bound. Weighty in the way only books that could ruin careers tend to be.

McKenney & Hall's History of the Indian Tribes of North America.

Volume I – 1837.
Volume II – 1842.
Volume III – 1844.

They lay open slightly, as though someone had been reading them recently and gotten up to make tea...

Each cover was worn but proud. The leather cracked, the gold lettering dulled, but the presence, oh, the presence, was undeniable. These weren't books. These were statements. Testimonies. Maybe even warnings.

We drifted closer. Betty leaned in, reverently. She had the expression of someone entering a cathedral where the saints were watching. She didn't touch the pages, not out of fear, but respect.

The lithographs inside were stunning. Full-page portraits of Indigenous leaders, rendered in such fine detail it felt like they might step off the page and tell you off for breathing too loud.

Notes in the margins. Scribbled names, dates, references to treaties, meetings, betrayals. Someone had annotated these with obsessive purpose. These were not casual collectors' items. These were working documents, documents meant to prove something. Or expose it.

"Tony," Betty said softly, "these are the real ones."

I didn't reply. I was already opening Volume II.

There it was again. That strange hum. Not a sound exactly, more of a vibration through the ghost-marrow. A sense that these books were awake. Watching. Waiting.

"I knew it," I said. "These are what they didn't want anyone to find."

A faded stamp inside the cover confirmed it:

Property of Percy Hall Archive. Not for Public Loan.

And under that, in a different hand:

To be retained. Not for auction.

"So if these are the originals, and I'm sure they are. What do Braithwaites have that they are auctioning?" I muttered.

"Forgeries" was the answer in a clipped female British accent,

Betty pointed.

We turned to look at the computer.

It blinked at us with the sort of smug patience only an early Windows system can manage.

"You going to try it?" Betty asked.

"I can't even guarantee I'll be able to touch the keyboard."

I floated over, hovered my hands over the keys, and concentrated.

Tap. Tap. Tap.

Password required.

"Try 'Percy'," Betty said.

Access denied.

"McKenny"

Access Denied

"Indian"

Access Denied

"Try spoons?" whispered Betty "with a capital S and a !"

Access granted.

I stared.

Betty smirked. "Men are so transparent." Then looking over at me "yes especially you these days"

The desktop opened.

There were folders. So many folders. But one caught my eye.

Auction_Proofing_Confidential.

Click.

Spreadsheets. Provenance lists. Notes. And one file:
Redacted_Lots.

There. Lot 42.

McKenney & Hall volumes. Withdrawn. Proxy sale arranged.

Next to it:

Bid winner: T. Ferrari. Error. Correction pending.

I stared at my name. *"T.Ferrari – Error"* Typed in a box on a spreadsheet that might as well have read "Target."

I wasn't supposed to win them.

It had been a mistake… and I had paid for it with my life.

Betty floated beside me, silent, her face unreadable. I felt the gentle presence of her hand on my shoulder.

There was more.

Origionals: Sub-Basement Archive. Verification process incomplete. Access restricted.

One final note.

Facsimile volumes prepared by Cartwright & Doyle, Edinburgh.

It began to make sense. They had already swapped them out. The fakes would be auctioned, the government bidders would get their books and bury the truth of stolen land and broken promises, the generations of Cherokee Indians wouldn't get their justice, I lost my life and my future. The only winners were the ghosts of Percy Hall who would get a new roof.

In the end Percy wanted the money but like all book collectors he couldn't let the originals go and that's what I had on the desk in front of me.

Only I'd messed up the plan… and now… I was dead. But not done. Not yet.

Together our senses twitched and we looked at each other. A sound.

There's something about footsteps in an underground tunnel that completely ignores logic and jumps straight to horror. You don't think, "Oh, good, someone's coming to deliver biscuits." You think, "Well, this is how the film ends," and start mentally drafting your last words.

The sound echoed long before the source appeared, deliberate, uneven steps. One solid footstep, one scrape. A limp. A slow one. Rhythmic. Like someone was being careful not to trip over their own sense of menace.

We froze. I know, I know, we're ghosts. We couldn't technically be seen, heard, or tripped over unless we *wanted* to. But instincts are hard things to override, especially when your death was recent, your nerves still remembered panic, and your brain hadn't quite got the memo that you were now technically immortal.

"Hide!" I whispered, dragging Betty behind the large oak table, as if that would help. She gave me a look.

"Tony," she said, her voice calm but dry as Yorkshire gin, "we're incorporeal."

"Yes, but he doesn't *know* that," I hissed.

Betty looked at me in the most British way possible, disappointed politeness laced with just enough passive aggression to make wallpaper peel.

"We're *invisible*, darling!"

"…oh. Yes. Right."

Still, we crouched there behind the table, as if muscle memory had its own ghost. We peeked around the edge, our vapourised forms somehow holding their breath. Footsteps drew closer, the sound louder now, echoing off the cold stone walls.

Then he appeared.

I recognised him immediately.

The man from the auction. The one with the nice suit.

He hadn't been bidding, not exactly. He had hovered nearby, quiet, watching the proceedings with the kind of sharp-eyed focus you normally only see from cats. I remembered his perfectly tailored coat, and now, here he was.

In the flesh. Well, most of it.

His left arm was in a plaster cast, slung in a navy-blue strap. His coat was the same one, only slightly more crumpled, and he had a look about him, tense, exhausted, still trying to appear in control but failing at the edges like a pie that had cracked in the oven.

The newspaper article had said the taxi driver involved in my death had been injured. Broken wrist, nothing serious. But they never named him. Said he was cooperating with police.

This man had a broken something.

Betty glanced at me.

"That him?"

I'd most definitely seen him before. The man I suspected had been *meant* to win the lot but hadn't bid for some reason. The man who'd glared like someone who had just watched their lunch order go to the wrong table. Now, here he was again. " I think so".

With a satchel.

He approached the table where the three volumes of *McKenney & Hall's History of the Indian Tribes of North America* lay, looking like he expected them to hiss at him. He opened the satchel slowly, methodically, like someone trying not to wake up a sleeping bear, and reached for Volume I.

That's when Betty pounced, ok, stepped forward.

Well, not just forward. She closed her eyes, pinched her nose in a way that seemed more mystical than nasal, and began to hold her breath even though she didn't have one.

I was about to ask what she was doing when she began to flicker.

Not gently. Not that elegant, ghostly shimmer we sometimes do when feeling especially Victorian.

This was full-on strobe lighting.

Her edges fuzzed and blurred, her colour changed with the tint of old sepia photographs, and the strip lights above us began to react.

One blinked.

Then two.

Then all of them joined in like they'd just discovered rhythm and jazz hands.

"I didn't know you could do that," I whispered, staring at her with the slack-jawed admiration usually reserved for sword swallowers and very large cakes.

"It's how the Reverend breaks the WIFI," Betty replied through clenched teeth, her voice warping like a radio signal from space. "I've been practising."

The lights overhead began to blink in time with her frequency shifts. On. Off. On. Off. A light show with a vendetta. The man froze.

He looked up, then around.

"Hello?" he said to the room, which, to be fair, had no intention of replying.

The lights went out.

Not dimmed. Not flickered.

Out.

We were plunged into the kind of darkness usually reserved for horror films and family Christmas or Thanksgivings.

There was a pause. Then the click of a lighter.

An old Zippo flared into life. He held it aloft with trembling fingers, casting a soft glow over the table and his nose.

I took a step closer… and blew.

Dust. It's the one tool every ghost has at their disposal. It follows us. Accumulates, and, in sufficient quantities, becomes weaponised atmosphere.

A puff of old library funk and ancestral pollen sailed across the room and straight into his face.

He recoiled instantly. Coughing. Spluttering. Eyes wide with the realisation that something he couldn't see had just *interacted* with him.

He dropped the book, thankfully onto the table, and backpedalled so hard he nearly fell over his own fear.

Then he turned… and ran.

Not a dignified retreat. Not a brisk jog.

He *ran dragging a leg, more of a very fast hop*. The heavy metal door slammed shut behind him. We heard the lock engage. Not a quiet click. A *clunk*. A noise with purpose. With finality. Stumbling up the stone stairs with the energy of a man who had just decided that every horror story he'd ever laughed at might have been a documentary.

Then silence.

A long, echoing silence filled only by the sound of both of us slowly standing up (or at least, levitating with purpose) and examining the room once again.

"Well," Betty said, dusting off her ghostly skirt as the lights flickered back into life "That went better than I expected."

"You flickered the lights," I said.

"I did."

"You shorted the entire room."

"Correct."

"You scared a living bejeezers out of a human into fleeing."

"I'm rather proud of that one."

There was a long pause.

"Did you learn that from the Reverend?" I asked.

"Of course."

We approached the table again. The books were unharmed. The satchel had been abandoned. The lighter sat on the floor where he'd dropped it, flickering feebly as if trying to pretend the whole thing had never happened.

Betty ran her hand just above the surface of Volume I.

"Still intact," she murmured. "Still real."

"I think we just scared my murderer," I said.

"That's poetic," Betty replied.

I sat down on the air next to the table. Ghosts don't need chairs, but sometimes your dignity insists on pretending.

I looked at her.

"You were incredible."

She adjusted an imaginary brooch. "I was *adequate*."

"You were terrifying."

She beamed.

She placed her hands to rest gently on my shoulders. Not in the vague, fluttery way ghosts usually make contact, more of a suggestion than a sensation, but with actual intent. It wasn't physical, not exactly. Not like warm skin on skin. But there was a presence to it. A weight. A kind of emotional gravity that made my ectoplasmic knees go a bit peculiar.

"That's the nicest thing anyone's ever said to me," she said, and then added, "...this century."

She looked into my eyes.

Now, I should clarify: ghosts don't technically have eyes. We have the memory of eyes, the idea of eyes, the general *vibe* of vision. But still, when Betty looked at me, it *felt* like she could see everything, like I'd just turned inside-out, and she was reading the label on my soul.

If I had been alive, I think I know what I would have done next. There would have been a lean. You know the one. The slow, tentative, heart-thudding lean that precedes either a kiss or a very awkward apology. The one that movies do in soft focus and candlelight, just before the soundtrack swells.

But I wasn't alive and Betty is dead.

I had absolutely no idea what the rules were.

Suddenly, I was fourteen again. Not in the magical, time-travelling way. Just mentally. Emotionally. Spiritually fourteen. Back at William Lloyd Garrison Elementary School in the Bronx. Acne. Confusion. Hormones. All of it. I remembered Beatrice St. Clair, the girl who once let me borrow a scented gel pen during Geography and ruined my concentration for a solid academic year. She'd smiled at me once, and I'd spent three weeks composing the perfect sentence to say back. Never used it. Forgot how to speak every time she walked by.

Now, here I was. A grown man. A former NYPD detective. Dead. Still baffled by women.

Because nobody, absolutely nobody, explains how love works when you're a ghost.

There's no handbook for it. No Ghostly Guide to Romantic Entanglements. No "Haunting & Dating for the Recently Departed." You just sort of… guess, and when you guess wrong, I assume you float around kicking yourself through walls for the next fifty years. Zippidy do da.

I mean, what do you *do*?

Do ghosts go on dates? Do they?

Do you buy each other spectral flowers?

Can you even hold hands properly if you don't have nerves or bones or a cardiovascular system?

Do we… fade into each other romantically? That sounds nice. Or horrific. One of the two.

Her gaze didn't waver. She was calm. Confident. Almost amused. There I was, doing my best impression of an emotionally constipated mist.

I thought about asking her what this meant. But how does one say, "Are we… haunting each other now?" without sounding like the world's worst pick-up line?

So instead, I said something stunningly intelligent.

"Erm."

Smooth, Tony. Real smooth.

She tilted her head. Not unkindly. Just… amused. Like a woman watching a ghost try to tie his shoelaces without feet.

"Are you alright?" she asked.

"I think so," I replied. "It's just… I don't know how this works."

She smiled. Not a full-blown grin, just the gentle kind that says, "Neither do I, but I'm game if you are."

"Well," she said, "I don't suppose many people do. We're all just… feeling our way."

"Even in the afterlife?"

"Especially in the afterlife," she said. "The rules get a bit… floaty."

She let go of my shoulders then, with a little pat. Just enough to make my soul shiver slightly.

I had to ask and blurted out. "Is this a… thing? Us?"

She blinked at me. "Tony. We're investigating your murder, helping Cherokee ghosts reclaim their ancestral land, and avoiding an aristocrat who may or may not have orchestrated a deadly antique book heist. *Everything* is a thing. Us? That's just a *nice* thing, but we, we shall solve your murder and deal with everything that comes with that."

Suddenly, everything made slightly more sense.

I wasn't sure if I was in love. Is that possible in death?

I wasn't sure if *she* was.

But I was sure of one thing.

I wanted to be wherever she was, even if it meant lurking in basements and arguing with candlelit chairs for eternity.

CHAPTER SEVEN

THE CUNNING GHOSTLY PLAN

"...and now you've got a witness, you know the motive, and you know where the books are!" Betty said with the kind of triumphant finality usually reserved for detective reveals or winning bingo cards.

We were sat at one of the more settled tables in the back corner of The Grapes after our day of adventure. The Grapes is the sort of pub where time didn't just pass, it slouched comfortably into an armchair, ordered a pint, and occasionally dozed off mid-century. The beams were low, the hearth was warm, and the wallpaper was peeling in an artistic sort of way, like it had ambitions of becoming a rustic fresco. The seats had more personality than comfort, and the tables wobbled as if unsure of their place in the world. In other words, as British pubs go, it was perfect.

Angie, sipping something that smelled faintly of apples and rebellion, was beaming across at Gary, who had just joined us with the kind of enthusiasm that suggested his day had drastically improved.

Betty, full of energy after a day of scheming and poking around ancestral conspiracies, was practically glowing with delight. Actually, not practically, she was really glowing, a gentle ochre. Me? I was lost in thought. Not the murder part, the *other* part. The part about us.

"Sorry, what?" I blinked. I'd missed a bit. Probably the important bit.

Betty rolled her eyes, lovingly. "You're meant to be the detective, darling. Try and keep up."

I cleared my throat. "I was just... going over the previous thing in my head."

"The previous thing?"

"You know. The us thing."

She smiled. "Ah. That."

Before she could say more, Angie chimed in. "Gary's here, by the way."

"Noticed," I muttered.

"I told him you two were with me. He can't see you, of course, but he's very open-minded about it."

Gary, returning from the bar with two pints of something that looked locally suspicious, sat down and nodded cheerfully. "They doing alright?"

"They say yes," Angie replied, ever the translator of the dead. "Tony says he likes your coat. (I hadn't). Betty says you should have gone with the Old Peculiar."

Gary blinked. "She's sharp."

"She's dead," Angie whispered. "But yes. Also sharp."

Betty leaned closer. "Tell him I like his shoes, but he clearly doesn't polish them."

"She likes your shoes," Angie said. "But you've been judged."

Gary looked down at his footwear and shrugged like a man who'd accepted defeat long ago in the battle of fashion versus comfort.

The fire behind us crackled in a conspiratorial sort of way, and someone's terrier barked at a shadow, then promptly apologised with a whimper. Gary took a long sip of his pint.

"Anyway," I said, gathering my thoughts, "we know that Lord Percy, aka Harry Barker, was at the scene of my murder. On a motorbike. Because apparently subtlety was not on the menu that day."

Betty nodded. "Yes, and Clarence."

"Sorry who?"

"Clarence"

"Who's Clarence?"

"Your murderer, the taxi driver, the sharp suited guy with a limp, scared of flickering lights, chap who radiates confusion. Was supposed to bid on the books but probably pointed at the wrong lot. Ended up with a Georgian bookcase and no clue.'"

"Yes, I know who he is, but how do we know his name?"

"We don't silly, I just made it up. We can't call him *the taxi driver* as that would confuse Gary, and we can't keep calling him *sharp suited guy with a limp* all the time. So Clarence, him."

Angie explained to Gary "Clarence was driving the taxi that rudely pinned Tony to the phone box." Then with a slightly airy wave. "It's very symbolic, really. Like your life was about to take a call from the afterlife but he got there a bit early."

"Yes, thank you for that visual reminder." I said.

Gary leaned back in his chair, wiping a bit of foam from his upper lip with the back of his hand. "Look," he said, tapping the side of his pint for emphasis, "not just anyone can drive a proper London black cab. It's like joining a secret society but with more traffic and fewer robes. You've got to pass *The Knowledge*, every street, every back alley, every one-way system between Wapping and Wembley. Takes years. You can't fake that. If this Clarence chap was driving one and it was reported as an accident, the police would've had to check his licence, his badge, the whole lot. If he was legit, it'll be on record. If not… the police would have nicked 'im" He trailed off with a shrug that said everything. "Then he's got a hell of a lot more to answer for than bad navigation."

"Then there's Fletch," I continued, "who saw the whole book-switching plan flop like a wet cravat. Percy flubbed it. I got the real books. That made me dangerous."

"Dangerous to Percy's wallet," Betty added. "Which, let's be honest, is where he keeps his soul."

"Sounds like a solid case to me," Betty said annoyingly cheerfully.

I waved a frustrated dangly arm at the ceiling like I was trying to conduct an orchestra made entirely of anxiety. "I may have witnesses," I grumbled, "but one of them is reluctant and ghostly. Being dead tends to complicate courtroom appearances. It's hard to swear an oath when your fingers phase through the Bible."

"… and sure," I continued, "we've got a motive. Or at least, something *that looks like* a motive, or something vaguely *motive-*

shaped. Greed. Family honour. Antique auction skullduggery. All very dramatic, yes, but not provable. Not in a mortal court without producing a séance, three psychics, a Ouija board, and a barrister with a strong stomach for the supernatural."

Betty raised an eyebrow in the kind of withering way only the British can pull off.

Then one of her patient smiles. "Then maybe it's time we got creative."

"Creative?" I repeated. "I was a detective, Betty. I dealt in facts. Procedure. Chain of evidence. The thrill of catching someone mid-lie with a warrant in one hand and a file of damning evidence in the other."

"…and now you're a ghost," she pointed out. "So, adapt… or haunt sulkily. Your choice."

Yes, I know I was sulking. "Yes, we know where the books are, and that they're the real ones. But we can't touch them. We can't move them. We might be able to float through the door, but the books can't. That means he'll be back. Percy. Or one of his hired hands. Probably Clarence with a sandwich and a set of bolt cutters. Those books are valuable. Historically explosive. Unfinished business is irresistible to villains and ghosts alike."

"Why would he need bolt cutters?" Gary asked after Angie translated, his brow furrowing the way it always did when trying to apply mortal logic to ghost-related problems.

"Because" Angie said, gesturing toward Betty like a proud coach introducing their star player, "Betty here… jammed the lock. From the inside."

Gary blinked. "She what?"

"Phased into the door," trying to keep the grin off her face. "…
and then messed around with the lock mechanism until it forgot or
gave up the knowledge how to be a lock."

Betty gave a prim nod, as if she'd merely adjusted a curtain rather
than tampered with physical reality. "Well, I couldn't just let them
come back and walk off with them, could I?"

Now, for clarity, ghost lock-tampering isn't standard ghost fare. It's
not something they hand out instructions for when you pass over.
There's no YouTube spiritual induction video with a floating
clipboard and a dead instructor going, "Right, now class, today
we're covering post-mortal lock-picking, don't forget to like and
subscribe." It's more of a… discovered-it-yourself-while-bored-on-
a-rainy-afterlife-Sunday kind of thing.

Betty, however, had learned it. Because of course she had. 80 years
dead you tend to pick up stuff.

"It's not lock-picking in the human sense," she explained, warming
to the topic like a ghost giving a TED Talk. "It's about resonance.
Everything physical has a frequency. Even locks. If you can match
it… you can confuse it, get the cogs all confused. Not unlock it
exactly. But persuade it not to lock either."

"Ghost hypnosis," I added.

"Ghost lock therapy," she corrected. "It's all very intuitive."

According to Betty, it involved phasing inside the lock and aligning
her own residual energy with the tumblers and pins and whatever
other fiddly bits locks were made of. Not to move them more than
a millimetre, but to vibrate around them in just the right way until
the lock became… uncertain.

"It's like whispering your doubts into a mechanism until it forgets
it has a job," she said cheerfully.

The end result? The door was now in a kind of metaphysical sulk. It wouldn't open, but it wouldn't close properly either. The key didn't work. The electronic lockpad had stopped blinking. The handle had, according to Betty, developed a mild case of existential doubt and was contemplating a career change.

"So, the doors now locked in a full-blown identity crisis."

Gary was staring, equal parts fascinated and alarmed. "So the only way to open it again is...?"

"Physical force," I said. "Tools. Metal. Bolt cutters. Maybe a sledgehammer."

"Or" Betty added with a slight twinkle, "a very persuasive exorcism."

Gary whistled. "Remind me never to cross you."

"Too late," Betty said sweetly.

Now, as amusing as it was to watch Betty effectively gaslight a lock into non-functionality, the situation wasn't all jokes. Because while we'd bought ourselves some time, it wasn't going to last forever. Percy, or someone like Clarence, would come back. Sooner or later. When they did, they'd bring tools. Tools that didn't care how haunted a door was.

Still, we had a little breathing room. Well. We didn't breathe, obviously. But you know what I mean.

Gary looked impressed. "So, what you're saying is, she ghost-hacked a security door. She's like the James Bond of the afterlife," he muttered.

Betty preened. "I prefer Miss Marple with unfinished business."

Angie, translating all this to Gary while sipping her tea, finally burst out laughing. "You realise," she said between giggles, "that if anyone overheard us, they'd assume we were all mad?"

Gary raised his glass. "Let 'em."

Betty, never one to miss a cue, raised her translucent teacup with ghostly pride. "To confused locks, unfinished business, and making a proper nuisance of ourselves."

"To ghosts with grit," I added.

The toast echoed softly into the rafters of The Grapes, and somewhere in Percy Hall a door handle wobbled... just a little. Almost like it was trying to decide what to be when it grew up.

At that moment, a new voice joined us from the ether.

"Cheers, I'll drink to that," said a man in tweed, who materialised beside the table with the kind of casual grace that suggested he'd done this often. "Name's Alf. I haunt the snug, mostly, but the conversation sounded lively."

Betty smiled. "Welcome, Alf. Pull up a chair."

"Can't," Alf said. "My legs don't remember how. But I'll hover pleasantly."

Gary rubbed his arms. "Anyone else feel that chill?"

"That's Alf," Angie translated. "He says hello."

Alf gave a little salute. "Been here since '53. Coronation night. Too many pints then made a pass at Mrs Wipply from the undertakers... Mr Wipply spotted. You know how it goes."

The fire crackled again. This time, in a more approving manner.

"So" Betty said, raising her voice slightly, "we have witnesses. A motive. The means. The prize. Even a local pub ghost for flavour."

"I was saying the same thing to myself," I muttered.

"Then what's the problem?" she asked, bright as ever.

I looked around the pub, thought about the books we couldn't move, the murder we couldn't prove, the witness who wasn't legally viable, and the very real fear that Percy, or Clarence, might come back before we had a plan.

"What's the problem?" I echoed. "Everything."

"Tony," she said, reaching ghostily for my hand, "Look around you, we have a whole team on this now. What did you have a week ago?"

I looked at her, at the fireplace, at Angie, Gary, even Alf the pub ghost now humming along to the jukebox, and I sighed.

"Alright," I said. "Let's save the books. Solve my murder. Bring down a corrupt aristocrat… and try not to get murdered again."

Betty grinned. "I knew you'd come round."

"Tell Gary we'll need him again tomorrow."

"Will do." Said Angie

Gary sipped his pint. "Anyone want crisps?"

"Only if they're salt and vinegar," said Alf.

I nudged Betty and learned into her ear. "You're not just doing this for me, are you?"

She hesitated, and in that moment, something passed over her face. Not doubt. Not fear. Something... softer.

"No," she whispered for my ears only. Then after a pause. Her voice was quieter, more deliberate. "I'm doing it for me Tony… and for Bob. For Fletch. For Elsie. For all the ghosts who are stuck in that place, clinging to a past they didn't ask for. For the Cherokee, who lost everything and still have the courage to keep asking for it back. For justice… and …. yes, for you too."

"So what's the plan Mr Detective?"

I stared into the middle distance as I thought, and finished my non-existent pint of Old Peculiar, because dramatic planning always begins with a good middle-distance stare, and then leaned forward over the table, folding my ghostly hands like a spectral general convening his war council.

"Right," I said. "I have a plan."

"About time" Angie quietly muttered

Everyone, living and otherwise, turned toward me.

"Gary, he has a plan!" said Angie

"Well," I corrected. "I have the beginning of a plan. A skeletal outline. A… wishful list of semi-organised thoughts."

Betty gave me a look that suggested she was both proud of me and deeply concerned about what came next.

"We need time," which is unusual as that is the currency us ghosts have most of. I began, fingers tapping on the table in a rhythm I found particularly strategic. "First and foremost. Time to act before they realise the books are trapped. Time to investigate. Time to recruit… and time, crucially, to make a proper nuisance of ourselves."

"Sounds like your area of expertise," Gary muttered into his pint.

"Correct," I said without missing a beat. "Which is why the ghosts of Percy Hall need to up their game. They've been lingering like half-forgotten wallpaper, but now? Now they need to haunt. I'm talking chains, moans, cold spots, spooky paintings with eyes that follow you down corridors. Real classic material. We need to make Percy Hall unmanageable."

Betty perked up. "Oh, I *like* this bit."

"We can't let the books be moved or hidden," I said, my voice steady. "They're not just artefacts, they're evidence. We lose those books, we lose everything. If they disappear the Cherokee are back to square one."

Angie nodded. "So we distract Percy?"

"…and I think you're the ideal person for the job" I said pointing my ethereal finger at her.

"The silver spoon collection was a winner last time and still probably your best in. Talk spoons, breathe spoons and the most lavish tales of spoons. Flatter him. Nod at all the right times. Laugh as though the story about Queen Victoria's dessert habits is the highlight of your year. But most importantly, woo the ghosts."

She paused mid-sip, which was a mercy because following a snort, the tea might otherwise have come out of her nose. "I beg your pardon?"

"Not like that," I clarified hastily. "Not woo like... woo."

"You want me to waft into Percy Hall, bat my eyelashes at disembodied dukes and moaning maids, and coyly whisper, 'Tell me your secrets, darling. I adore what you've done with the cobwebs"

"I wouldn't go that far," I said, although frankly it wasn't a bad idea. "But yes. If we're going to get them to revolt, really rise up, metaphorically and occasionally literally from the dead, they need someone they trust. Someone living. Someone who doesn't float through furniture or cause power surges when they get emotional."

"They've seen you now," Betty added. "You weren't screaming or waving incense. That's a good start."

Angie gave a long, theatrical sigh, followed by a smile that said she'd already accepted her fate. "Back into the cutlery mines I go."

She gave me a look. "You're enjoying this."

"Only slightly," I replied. "It's just rare I get to send someone else into danger while I hover nearby dispensing witty commentary."

Betty leaned in. "You do realise you're asking her to walk into a house full of suspicious ghosts and one megalomaniacal aristocrat who keeps pretending to be a butler, and who has had people murdered, you for instance, and strike up casual tea-party banter with the damned?"

"Yes" I said. "And I have every confidence in her."

Angie abruptly stood up, placing her hands on the table, head tilted just slightly to the side, an angle carefully honed to deliver maximum disdain with minimal effort.

"Confidence!" She blurted out. Clearly I had hit a nerve. "You know," she said, voice calm and clear like a headmistress delivering her last warning before an expulsion, "it never fails to amaze me how often I'm underestimated. I could be on fire, juggling chainsaws and reciting Shakespeare backwards, and someone would still offer to explain how matches work."

Betty opened her mouth, possibly to offer encouragement or a biscuit, but Angie steamrolled on.

"I'm not some timid little tea lady stumbling into a haunted mansion with a nervous giggle and a cardigan full of holy water. I've stared down year sevens high on sugar and unaccountable rage. I've outlasted Ofsted inspections, parent WhatsApp groups, and a school secretary named Marjorie who once physically wrestled a goose out of a tuck shop. You think Lord Percy and his whispery little phantoms are going to rattle *me*?"

Gary let out a low whistle. "Remind me never to cross you either."

Betty chuckled. "Well, someone's had her Weetabix."

Angie turned toward me, eyes sharp as a librarian catching a teenager dog-earing pages. "You think I'm scared of a haunted stately home? I once lived above a butcher's that was haunted by a Victorian vegan. Do you know what it's like having your windows rattled by a man in a waistcoat whispering 'quinoa' at 3am?"

"I do now," I offered eyes wide open.

She pointed a finger at me. "… and, and you asked me to woo ghosts. Woo! As if this is some ghastly episode of *Spectral Bachelor*. I don't need to flirt with the dead, Tony. I *network*. Ghosts love me. I'm relatable. I bake. I listen. I don't judge their incorporeal state. Have you even tried my fig rolls?"

Betty leaned back, grinning. "This is better than theatre."

Angie threw her hands up with a dramatic sweep that could've taken out a chandelier. "I will walk into Percy Hall, armed with nothing but sarcasm and shortbread, and I *will* charm those ghosts. I will infiltrate the upper crust of the spectral elite and get them to spill their secrets, air their grievances, and possibly share their jam recipes. I shall lead the haunting like a union organiser in a séance."

She began pacing now, stumbling briefly over her wellington boots that were propped against Gary's chair. "We'll hold meetings in the drawing room. Sit-ins in the conservatory. When Lord Percy walks in with his smug, spoon-polishing smile, we'll be waiting, with placards! Or at least dramatic sighs and the smell of wet tweed."

I blinked. "You've thought about this more than I expected.

"I *prepare*," she snapped. "Unlike some of us who float into situations with nothing but a trench coat and unresolved trauma. I, Anthony Ferrari, have read every pamphlet the Society for the Friendly Spiritually-Inclined has published. I've done cold readings in community halls, communed with a Welsh ghost trapped in a coat rack, and once taught a poltergeist how to knit to calm his nerves. So, no, I will not *woo* them. I will *recruit* them. I will rally them to the cause like a spectral Joan of Arc with better biscuits."

Gary, who had quietly returned from the bar with a pint and a look of polite bafflement, sat down just in time to hear, "… and if I have to lead a ghostly conga line to the front steps of Percy Hall while shouting 'Down with forgeries!' I *will*, so help me." "I missed something, didn't I?" he said, glancing in the direction he expected Betty to be.

"She's becoming the ghost whisperer general," Betty said with a shrug. "Apparently using jam and biscuits as diplomatic tools."

Gary turned to say something. Mistake. Angie turned on him. "Don't interrupt Gary," she snapped playfully. "I'm on a roll."

"You're talking to a woman who once talked down a poltergeist possessing a Year 9 vending machine."

"It owed him a packet of Quavers," I suggested.

"I got it for him!" she said, triumphant. "Peace was restored. Year 9 got their crisps. The ghost found closure… and I didn't have to flirt with a single ectoplasmic entity to do it."

Betty was laughing now. "Honestly, Angie, I don't think you even *need* us. You're going to topple Percy Hall on sheer indignation and fruitcake alone."

Angie took a calming sip of her tea, then straightened her scarf like a general preparing for battle.

"But let's face it" she said with a grin "… this is *exactly* the sort of ridiculous mess I was born to untangle."

We all looked at her, this perfectly ordinary woman, red scarf, muddy boots, tote bag filled with supermarket receipts and emergency bourbon creams, who was about to walk into the heart of a supernatural conspiracy like it was parents' evening.

Somehow, we all felt better.

Gary held up his pint. "To Angie. May ghosts everywhere tremble politely in her wake."

We all raised our respective glasses, cups, or translucent hands.

Alf re-appeared "Cheers!"

With that, Angie plonked herself down, took a biscuit from her bag, and began making strategic notes in a little leather notebook labelled *Polite But Firm Conversations with the Dead*.

Flipping the notebook shut. "Alright. I'm ready. I'll go in, chat spoons, flirt with spectres, and make sure the dead aristocracy see me as their confidante instead of an exorcist-in-disguise."

"That's the spirit," I said.

Betty gave me a side-eye that could boil milk. "If you say that again, I will poltergeist your favourite trench coat."

"Angie, I need you to translate" I said turning to Gary. "Gary, we need you to dig. Find out who Clarence really is, his real name. He might not just be a bumbling fool with a limp. If he's driving a black cab without a licence, possibly under an alias, and has a direct line to Lord Percy. As you say, the police would've checked his licence after the 'accident.' If he's clean, that's one thing. If he's not..."

"Then we've got leverage," Gary finished. "Alright," Gary said, already reaching into his coat pocket for his phone. "I'll do some asking around. I've got mates who still drive for the Met, proper old-school cabbies. Some of them still know a bloke or two in Transport Command. Might be able to dig up some old files. Cabbies are the biggest gossips and accidents are top of the bill. Someone will know something."

"Everyone leaves a trail. Especially the dodgy ones. Cabbies talk. If someone's driving without the proper badges, the other drivers know. If he's operating under a fake ID, then someone along the line helped him get it. Even crooks need paperwork."

Angie raised her eyebrows. "This is starting to sound very cloak and dagger."

Gary grinned. "Nah. This is just London. Everything's cloak and dagger if you scratch deep enough."

Betty nodded approvingly. "Well, it's good to have a man on the inside. Or at least someone with mates who know the inside."

"I'm not promising miracles," Gary said. "But if there's dirt on Clarence, or whatever his name is, I'll find it. Might take a few favours. Possibly a bottle of whisky and a Chelsea bun or two. But I'll get something."

"and Clarence," Gary added, "might just be the weakest link in this whole messed-up antique-laden, ghost-haunted chain."

"Let's hope so," I said. "Because if we can't get justice for me, we sure as hell won't get it for the Cherokee, or for the rest of the ghosts still stuck behind Percy's curtains."

Gary stood up, pint in hand, and gave a little salute. "I'll start as soon as we get back to London. I know where the old black cab boys drink. If there's gossip to be had, I'll hear it. Especially if it's about a posh bloke with a limp and a tendency to drive phone boxes into people."

Ok I was starting to like Gary.

Angie gave him a thumbs-up. "You're a star, Gary. Just make sure you don't end up with a ghost of your own."

He smirked. "Please. I'm a London cabbie. I already talk to people who aren't all there most of the time."

I nodded. "Beautiful. That leaves me and Betty."

Betty raised a perfectly arched eyebrow, the sort that had once caused an entire Women's Institute to lower their scones in shame. "Do tell."

"We're going to Braithwaite's."

"The auction?" she said, perking up like a cat spotting a careless pigeon.

"We have to stop the sale," I said. "Percy's going to try to sell the forgeries. We have to be there. Cause havoc. Stir ghosts. Rattle some artefacts. Whatever it takes to disrupt the sale."

Angie tilted her head, part curiosity, part concern, all deeply British. "How exactly do you plan to stop an auction as ghosts?"

I hesitated. "I was hoping to make that up on the way there."

Betty chuckled, with that dry humour reserved for women who'd faced worse and made tea afterwards. "Classic you."

"We've got spirit." I smirked at Betty "That counts."

She folded her arms, giving me the kind of look that could curdle milk, stop a clock, and reconfigure your childhood trauma so effectively you'd be ringing your therapist before you even finished your tea. It was the kind of look that could make hardened criminals confess and vicars forget their sermons mid-sentence. The sort of look that had once, following the discovery of a bite taken out of a pork pie, I swear, made Trevor the pub dog slink behind the dartboard for the better part of a day.

"Tony," she said, her voice calm and precise, like someone explaining fire safety to a toddler holding a flamethrower, "you are suggesting we infiltrate an auction house. Not just any auction house, but Braithwaite's… The Braithwaite's … The one with the catalogues printed on paper so thick it could stop bullets. The one where the staff wear gloves just to handle the *doilies*. The kind of place that has cameras, security guards with laminated ID badges, and possibly, just possibly, a man with a large moustache whose entire job is to shout 'SOLD!' every fifteen minutes while gesturing at baffled European millionaires in salmon-coloured trousers."

"If we must."

She paused. "Brilliant, I'm in."

Angie blinked. "Wait, what?"

"I've always wanted to knock over a Ming vase with intent," Betty said, entirely too cheerfully.

Angie stared at us. "You do know this is potentially a crime?"

"Only if you can hold a ghost accountable," I replied. "Currently, British law is woefully silent on the supernatural."

Gary sighed. "You're going to make me the getaway driver, aren't you?"

"Think of it as spiritual support," Betty said brightly. "Literally."

"We'll need a distraction big enough to stall the sale," Betty said. "Something dramatic. Grand. Possibly with organ music."

"I'll see if I can find an organist ghost," I offered.

"This is ridiculous," Angie muttered, though she was already making notes.

As Angie drank the last of her tea and wiped her mouth with a napkin, she sighed again. "Well. I suppose if I'm going to charm a building full of stubborn souls and decorative serving ware... I'd better get some sleep." Packing up her handbag.

Halfway to the stairs, she stopped abruptly, rummaged through her handbag like it was a bottomless magical cauldron, and triumphantly produced a half-squashed packet of Chocolate Hob-Nobs. "Found them" she announced with passion, and then without ceremony, she shoved them back into the bag with a flourish.

"Ghosts are people too," she said over her shoulder. "Just with worse lighting."

Then, as if she hadn't just dropped one of the more profound supernatural truths of the day, she started humming a show tune, something vaguely Rodgers and Hammerstein with the defiant lilt of someone who fully intended to face down centuries-old spirits armed with nothing more than sarcasm, biscuits, and musical theatre.

Gary, a few steps behind her, gave us a friendly wave over his shoulder. It was the kind of wave that said, "I'm not entirely sure what I've signed up for, but I like this woman and I'm following her into the abyss anyway." He adjusted his jacket, straightened his cabbie hat, and disappeared after her.

I turned to Betty, who hadn't taken her eyes off the couple as the meandered to the stairs. "Do you think she'll be okay?"

Betty didn't answer immediately. Her expression was thoughtful, amused, and just the tiniest bit fond.

"She is a force of nature," Betty said at last, smiling. "The kind that rearranges furniture in someone else's house and refuses to apologise afterwards."

I watched the last shadow of Angie's scarf vanish around the corner, her humming now accompanied by what might have been a brief and passionate soliloquy on the importance of shortbread diplomacy. Somewhere in the distance, Gary was already trying to talk her out of waving a spoon around like a wand.

"God help Percy Hall," I murmured.

With that, we turned toward our own mission, the faint scent of Hob-Nobs and impending rebellion still lingering in the air like the calm before a very sarcastic storm. The bathroom I should add, was as comfortable as it had been the night before.

CHAPTER EIGHT

THE GREAT BISCUIT
REBELLION

Angie gave us a jaunty wave as Gary pulled away in his taxi with
Betty and me in the back, leaving her standing at the ornate, slightly
rusted gates of Percy Hall. She adjusted her scarf with the air of a
woman about to storm the Bastille armed only with a tote bag, a tin
of biscuits, and an unshakable belief that everything could be
improved with a nice cup of tea.

As she began walking up the long gravel drive, a figure shimmered
into view beside her. A ghost, translucent and faintly greenish
around the edges, pushing a wheelbarrow filled with what appeared
to be spectral compost. He wore a flat cap at a jaunty angle and had
the long-suffering expression of someone who had once gardened
for aristocrats and never quite recovered.

"Morning," he said, with the cautious friendliness of a man who'd
seen a lot of strange things in his afterlife and was braced for more.

"Lovely day for a haunting," Angie replied, not missing a beat.

The ghost blinked. "You can see me?"

"Oh yes," she said, patting her tote bag. "I brought biscuits."

"I'll let the others know," the ghost gardener said, as if Angie was an expected guest and not the opening act of a supernatural revolution. He wheeled along beside her, falling easily into step as if this sort of thing happened every Tuesday. Angie explained the problem.

Her mission was simple in its madness: cause an uprising among the ghosts of Percy Hall. Not a violent one, no rattling of chains or head-spinning antics, but a thoroughly British haunting. Polite disruption. Passive-aggressive rebellion. Spectral civil disobedience. Her targets were clear: the guided tours, the day-to-day running of the house, and, most importantly, the final day of the Pheasant Shooting Event, a ghastly display of tweed and gout organised for the executives of the local Sanitary Manufacturers' Union for Rotational Ceramics (SMURC). *We Stand Behind Every Throne.* *(Usually because we installed it.)*

It was the kind of event where you'd find men named Clive or Nigel loudly discussing tap pressure while downing whisky from personalised hip flasks and arguing about the correct way to load a shotgun. Angie had read about it in the brochure she'd nicked from the front desk the day before. It had been nestled between an advert for artisan chutneys and a full-page spread about the estate's heritage curtains.

She was halfway up the drive when more ghosts began to appear. First, a pair of footmen arguing about starch. Then an Edwardian lady floating regally above the path as if she disapproved of touching gravel. A faintly glowing scullery maid trailed behind, muttering about someone stealing her gooseberries in 1897.

"Hello!" Angie beamed, waving like a local politician who also brought cake.

They stared.

"Right," she said, clapping her hands together. "Let's have a chat, shall we? I've got fig rolls, biscuits and a plan."

By the time she reached the front entrance, she had an entourage. It looked a bit like a very disorganised period drama, one where the costume budget had been stretched over two centuries and several tragic backstories.

Lord Percy, still masquerading as Mr. Barker the butler, was standing by the grand front doors, polishing a doorknob.

"Miss…" he said, clearly struggling to remember what name Angie had given the day before. "Glad to see you back."

"Lovely to be here," she replied, stepping inside. "The spoons were simply too intriguing to ignore. I've had dreams about your apostle spoons, you know."

"You have" Lord Percy said, slightly thrown off.

"Oh, forgive me, where shall we begin today? I'd love to hear more about the ceremonial ladle from 1762. The one rumoured to have cursed Lord Biddlesworth's knees."

Lord Percy blinked.

"I read up," Angie said cheerily.

In the shadowy corners of the hall, ghosts leaned in.

As Percy led her through to the east wing, where the spoon collection was held in reverent display inside a glass case that probably would have cost more than Angie's car insurance, if she had past her test. She continued to chat, planting seeds.

"…and the staff?" she asked innocently. "Do they ever report any… odd happenings?"

Percy hesitated. "We pride ourselves on maintaining a calm and historical atmosphere."

"Of course," Angie said. "But you know how it is with old buildings. Echoes. Cold spots. Flickering lights…. Disembodied sighs."

Behind her, a portrait tilted itself slightly to the left.

Percy's eye twitched.

Meanwhile, in the west wing, the disruption had already begun during the 11am guided tour of the estate by some impeccably polite Japanese, American and Canadian tourists armed with cameras, guidebooks, and an enthusiastic appreciation for fine architecture and even finer tea sets. They were being shepherded by a junior guide named Rupert, who had only been working at Percy Hall for six days and still harboured the faint hope that one day he might be promoted to the position of senior guide, or at least be allowed to wear the blazer with the crest.

Unfortunately for Rupert, today was not going to help that dream.

The ghost gardener, known in life as Cedric Nettles, former head of horticulture and amateur poet, had rallied his groundskeeping comrades at the crack of dawn (or what passed for dawn when one is incorporeal and immune to sunlight). There were four of them now, all translucent, all wearing spectral wellington boots, and all inexplicably armed with ghostly hedge clippers.

They were now gliding through the topiary in a sort of military formation, giggling like schoolboys as they re-trimmed the hedges into increasingly suspicious and, frankly, anatomically questionable shapes. Rude.

"Oh my goodness," one of the tourists said in a heavily accented English accent, hand covering her mouth in shock, pointing to what had once been a perfectly clipped badger and now absolutely wasn't.

Rupert turned and paled. "It wasn't like that this morning!" Turning bright pink.

The gardeners snickered and vanished into the next hedge, like horticultural poltergeists with a flair for the inappropriate.

Inside the house, the footmen had begun manifesting with the sort of precision usually reserved for Swiss watches and dramatic irony. They timed their appearances with uncanny flair, popping into existence the very moment poor Rupert was mid-sentence about something wholesome like Georgian cornicing or the historical significance of tea cosies.

They never stuck around long. Just long enough to mutter something deeply unsettling, such as, "He always said the curtains would be the death of him," or "Not since the soup incident of '94..." Then they'd disappear again in a puff of existential regret, leaving behind the faint scent of starch and moral ambiguity.

One tourist let out a gasp so delicate, so refined, that it sounded less like fear and more like a teacup discovering it had been placed on a coaster without consent. It wasn't just a sound; it was a social commentary in breath form. The sort of gasp that would have followed the announcement of a cancelled cucumber sandwich course at a royal garden party. It hovered in the air like a disappointed aunt and was followed almost immediately by a flutter of activity.

Three other tourists, all women of a certain composure and handbag fortitude, clutched their pearls in synchronised horror. Not just any clutching, mind you, this was a coordinated reaction, as if rehearsed in the mirrors of a very posh boarding school. It was the kind of pearl-clutching that deserved its own orchestral accompaniment. If it had been put to music, it would have involved violins, a thunderclap, and a chorus of butlers fainting in sequence.

Meanwhile, a fifth tourist, an older gentleman who had maintained the quiet stoicism of someone secretly hoping for ghosts but pretending to be above it, finally spoke. He adjusted his cap with the solemnity of a man preparing to file a tax return and, in perfectly polite English, asked the most British question imaginable in the face of supernatural events:

"Excuse me, but does the estate have a formal refund policy in place for spectral interference during architectural appreciation?"

There was a beat of silence. Even the ghosts paused.

Rupert, the tour guide, blinked several times. He was holding the laminated "Welcome to Percy Hall" sheet with both hands, gripping it with the same tightness one might use to hold onto the last lifeboat of sanity.

"I… I'll have to check with the admissions desk," he said eventually, with the voice of a man who was beginning to realise that employment might not be for him after all. "I'm not sure if… if there's a dropdown option for 'haunted staircases' on the feedback form."

The gentleman gave a single, solemn nod. "Quite right. I suppose if there isn't, I shall simply note it down under 'miscellaneous grievances.' Thank you."

This, more than anything, rattled Rupert. Ghosts he could now just about handle. Rude topiary with attitude, fine. Pianos with minds of their own, manageable. But a customer with a well-organised complaint system? That was too real.

At that moment, a footman ghost materialised next to a grand four-poster bed in the East Wing and whispered, "Don't look in the chamber pot if I were you… It's been there since 1842" before vanishing again with the subtle rustle of an unpaid invoice.

Another tourist, possibly American, judging by the slow, dawning realisation that she was very far from Disneyland fumbled in her handbag for something. Possibly a crucifix. Possibly pepper spray. She pulled out a small guidebook instead and began waving it like a wand at the architecture. When this failed to banish the bad vibes, she turned to Rupert with a slightly manic smile.

"Is this part of the experience?"

"Technically?" Rupert said. "No. Spiritually? Very much yes."

Just then, a cold spot passed through the group like an emotionally distant grandparent. Everyone shivered. One of the synchronised pearl-clutchers sneezed daintily into a lace handkerchief. It was the kind of sneeze that said, "I do not believe in vulgar eruptions but nature has betrayed me."

Lady Wilhelmina's ghost drifted through the back wall at that precise moment at 45% transparency, her expression a perfect blend of aloof disapproval and mild indigestion. Her presence dropped the temperature by about five degrees and raised everyone's anxiety by fifty.

She did not speak. She did not need to. Her mere presence suggested that no one here was living up to their full potential.

The man with the refund question bowed slightly in her direction. "Ma'am," he said, with old-world politeness.

Wilhelmina inclined her head in acknowledgement. Then she passed through a young tourist's phone, which promptly died, displayed a calendar from 1872, and then rebooted in Latin.

"Right," Rupert said, perspiration sticking to his temples, tucking the laminated sheet under his arm like a shield. "Onwards, everyone. Let's move along now to the Orangery."

He said it with the bravado of a man who knew he was out of his depth but had chosen denial as his flotation device. His tone was too bright, too brittle, like fine china used as a cricket bat.

A Canadian, still clutching her traumatised smartphone like a lifeline, muttered, "British ghosts are really something else."

"Haunt with dignity. Die with scandal," came the response, spoken so softly and sagely it may well have been passed down through generations. The speaker, a tweed-clad woman with a handbag large enough to smuggle contraband jam, continued past and out through the wall the far side of the room above an antique chair with a red rope holding a sign saying, "Do Not Sit".

There was a collective pause, as if everyone mentally agreed this would make an excellent motto for the gift shop.

A suit of armour groaned ominously as they passed, sounding either haunted or deeply unimpressed by the quality of modern tourists. Rupert flinched and muttered something unprintable under his breath that rhymed with "ducking bell [A] ." (which resides in the lower meadow)

Still, he pressed on, earning must be said some brownie points from the ghosts that laid traps in hos path.

"The Orangery," he announced with the forced cheer of a man trying to distract a toddler from a wasp, "was once home to Lord Percival's prized citrus collection. Oranges, lemons, and, allegedly, a grapefruit that correctly predicted the 1929 stock market crash."

He gave a weak chuckle.

No one else did.

Above them, a draught whispered down the hall like a cold rumour. Somewhere in the rafters, a pigeon, or something that resented being mistaken for one, made an ominous sound not found in any reputable bird book.

The group hesitated. One of the women with the pearls made the sign of the cross with a complimentary map.

The American whispered, "Do haunted fruit bite?"

Rupert opened the Orangery doors with all the pomp of a man leading troops into battle and said, "Let's find out."

The hallway lights flickered.

Somewhere in the distance there was a squark as a biscuit hit a pheasant.

Rupert whispered to himself, "Just three more hours. Then I can go home." The tour notes were beginning to dissolve in his sweaty hands. Looking at his party he tried to reassure them with a smile that said, "Everything is fine" and eyes that said, "I have seen too much."

The house, for its part, creaked ominously in agreement.

Then at all once came the scullery maid skipping through the Orangery. A diminutive woman named Maud who had died under mysterious circumstances involving a pie, a rolling pin, and a deeply misplaced recipe for rabbit stew. She had taken it upon herself to hide ladles in increasingly baffling places: behind portraits, inside grandfather clocks, and one tucked neatly into the waistband of a mannequin wearing 18th-century cavalry dress. Her logic, if it could be called that, was that no one should ever have more ladles than they had hands.

The Edwardian lady, Lady Wilhelmina Tuppence-Finch to give her full title, drifted gracefully behind the group, leaving an unmistakable trail of chill behind her, like a silent disapproval fog. She had perfected the art of, what Betty might have called, the "Disappointed Dowager Stare", and deployed it with the kind of precision that made even the hardiest tourist feel as if they'd just tracked mud into a cathedral.

One gentleman from Kyoto, previously full of questions about the Georgian panelling, found himself apologising profusely to no one in particular and bowing several times before tripping backwards into a set of reproduction banisters.

Then, there was Horace.

Horace had been a valet in his living days, and he brought that same meticulous attention to detail into the afterlife. Somewhere between death and ghostly eternity, he had developed a burning passion for alphabetisation. On this particular morning, he had taken it upon himself to rearrange the display cabinets in the west wing.

What had previously been a thematic display titled "Tea Through the Ages" was now divided into sections labelled A to Z. The Agate Teapot sat next to a book about Azaleas. A Biedermeier sugar bowl was awkwardly sharing shelf space with a copy of *Beekeeping for Beginners*.

Rupert walked into the room and froze. "No… no no no, this was Victorian ceramics ten minutes ago!"

One of the tourists tilted their head. "Your exhibit is… postmodern?"

"It's haunted!" Rupert blurted, before remembering that this was not in the official tour script.

The group moved on quickly after that, several of them whispering to their guidebooks and one taking very deliberate video footage of the teapot display.

By the time the tour reached the conservatory, the piano had begun playing itself. Badly.

A ghost child, probably one of the nursery twins, though it was hard to tell when they never spoke above a whisper or below a rhyme, was plinking out a very halting version of "Greensleeves" while invisible feet tapped softly in time to a beat only the dead could appreciate.

Rupert had stopped trying to explain by this point. He simply opened a door with a strained smile, peered inside and around the corner of the door before gesturing people through like a man who had seen the very fabric of his employment contract unravel before his eyes.

Meanwhile outside in the Rose Garden Elsie the maid turned to Cedric who hovering beside her "Well?"

He nodded approvingly. "This lot haven't had this much fun in decades."

"Progress," she said.

From inside the drawing room came the sound of faint hysteric laughter and the unmistakable jingle of a bell that should not, under any circumstances, have been ringing.

The ghost rebellion had begun… and it had done so in the most British way possible: with passive aggression, culinary retribution, and some very stern glances.

Percy Hall, for the first time in centuries, was properly alive.

If Percy Hall had a proud tradition of anything besides dry rot and passive-aggressive portraits, it was the annual Pheasant Shoot. Attended by various rotund executives from a local sanitary ware society, it was considered the jewel in the porcelain calendar, a symphony of tweed, overindulgence, and the reckless discharge of firearms in the general direction of birds.

But today the ghosts had other plans.

It began with the ammunition.

Horace, the spectral valet with a flair for alphabetical systems and light anarchy, had worked alongside Cedric the gardener to pull off a feat of posthumous sabotage so perfect it should've come with its own BAFTA. The ghosts replaced all the shotgun cartridges with bourbon biscuits.

Don't ask how. Ghost physics is mostly about willpower, regret, and the ability to appear exactly where you shouldn't be at the most inconvenient moment.

When Nigel Pomfrey, CEO of FlushCo, raised his double-barrelled shotgun to the sky and shouted "Pull!" he did so with the confidence of a man who believed gravity applied to other people. He squeezed the trigger expecting a satisfying blast of controlled destruction.

Instead, there was a gentle "fwup" and a chocolate-covered biscuit sailed lazily through the crisp January air and smacked a pheasant squarely on the beak.

The pheasant blinked once, then calmly picked up the biscuit and strutted off like it had just closed a property deal.

"What in the name of Royal Doulton…" Nigel muttered, opening his shotgun. Two more bourbons sat innocently in the chambers.

Across the field, chaos was erupting.

Instead of buckshot, digestives and custard creams were firing out in rapid succession. One hobnob ricocheted off a sign reading "No Trespassing" and lodged itself in the pocket of the local poacher, Alan Ponking, where it would be found three weeks later, slightly nibbled and still smug.

The pheasants, meanwhile, were positively thriving. With their natural predators inexplicably flinging snacks instead of death, they began staging what could only be described as a feathery parade. One performed a small but enthusiastic tap routine on a picnic basket.

Cedric and his topiary brigade took things further by continuing to rearrange hedge animals into obscene silhouettes. The box squirrel now seemed deeply illegal. Guests stopped to photograph them, convinced they were part of a controversial new art installation called "Nature Gets Saucy."

Lady Wilhelmina, dead since 1910 and still unimpressed with most of existence, glided through the event trailing a cold draft and the unmistakable aura of withering judgement. Every time someone aimed their shotgun, she murmured something deeply ominous like "Your sins will outlive you," causing misfires, emotional breakdowns, and one attempted phone call to a therapist.

Inside the lounge, the self-playing piano now kicked into "The Ride of the Valkyries" just as the team from LavéLux Industries attempted a synchronized skeet shot. The ensuing chaos saw a whole tray of sausage rolls airborne and one executive diving into a hedge to avoid a flying scone.

By late morning, the ghost of a long-dead butler named Forbes had taken to reciting haiku on the wind, while the twins from the nursery sang eerie nursery rhymes at pitch-perfect volume from inside the loos.

"Three little lads with barrels of bread, fired at a pheasant and hit cake instead…"

It was unsettling, lyrical, and somehow got stuck in everyone's heads.

By noon, only three pheasants had been fired at, none had been hit, but seventeen bourbons had landed in the hat of the Deputy Chair of PlumbWise Ltd, who mistook them for compliments and kept thanking everyone.

Angie, watching the entire debacle unfold from a conservatory window with a cup of tea and a glint in her eye, turned to the ghost of the cook beside her.

"They're revolting," she said.

"In several senses," the cook agreed.

Leaning slightly toward the nearest tapestry Angie whispered, "Now. While he's gone. Spread the word. Revolution with tea at four."

The tapestry rustled in response.

As Percy returned from popping out to see what the *"bloomin heck that bell ringing is"*, Angie standing before a velvet-lined spoon cabinet, nodded solemnly as Percy lectured her on the unique spiritual resonance of gravy ladles.

"So many layers to cutlery," she murmured, as if absorbing deep cosmic truth.

Upstairs, in the forgotten linen closet that doubled as a ghost break room, Fletch raised an eyebrow.

"Did she just declare war with a biscuit?" he asked.

The nursery twins nodded in unison. "The shortbread rebellion has begun."

So, with crumbs in her pocket and conviction in her heart, Angie the Unexpected Ghost-Wrangler had laid the first stone in the campaign to save Percy Hall, stop a fraudulent auction, avenge the dead, and, if time permitted, finally get to try that cursed ceremonial ladle.

Revolutions come in many forms. Some arrive with pitchforks. Some with pamphlets… and some arrive in a sensible cardigan, holding a Tupperware of fig rolls and a clipboard of spiritual grievances.

The moral of the story, heaven help the aristocrat who underestimates a woman with a mission and a firm opinion about custard creams.

The day past with absolutely no effort to gain access to the cellar with the original McKenney & Hall volumes. Operation Bourbon Biscuit had been executed marvellously, everyone agreed.

Footnote A

The Ducking Bell: A Brief and Alarmingly Specific History

In the late 14th century, particularly in the more eccentric abbeys of East Anglia, the Ducking Bell was devised as a *moral deterrent* and *public spectacle*, which, as far as medieval purposes go, was second only to "something involving turnips."

Originally commissioned by Abbot Thurstan of Wibberley-on-the-Wold, who famously mistrusted anything that quacked, the Ducking Bell was designed to *chastise and/or mildly inconvenience* those accused of one of the following civic sins:

- Gossiping in church

- Overly enthusiastic mummering

- Witchcraft-adjacent cheese-making

- Duck impersonation without license

The device itself was deceptively simple: a large iron bell suspended over a shallow pond (often the village duck pond), rigged with pulleys, counterweights, and an unnecessarily complicated system involving at least one reluctant goat.

How It Worked

1. The accused would be seated in a chair attached to the clapper mechanism of the oversized bell.

2. With great ceremony—and the blowing of a recorder by someone called Ethelred—villagers would gather.

3. The goat (named something like "Sir Quavers") would be led up a ramp, triggering the mechanism.

4. The bell would ring *once* (for suspense), and the accused would be unceremoniously dunked into the pond.

5. The bell would ring again as they resurfaced, drenched, repentant, and usually covered in irate duckweed.

It wasn't meant to be fatal—just humbling. Though records show one unfortunate incident involving a particularly large woman, a stubborn goat, and a bell that got stuck mid-duck.

The Ducking Bell eventually fell out of favour when people realised:

- It didn't stop gossip.

- Ducks got in the way.

- Goats were unionising.

However, one original Ducking Bell survives in the private collection of Lord Percival-Percy of Percy Hall.

CHAPTER NINE

GOING, GOING… GHOST

Gary's cab rumbled to a halt outside Braithwaite's Auction Rooms with the kind of weary sigh only a London taxi can make when it knows it's about to be parked somewhere posh and judgmental.

"Alright, then," Gary muttered, peering out the windscreen at the looming sandstone facade. "This is it?"

He glanced into the back seat and found it, as usual, completely empty.

Except it wasn't.

I was there. Betty was there. But as far as Gary was concerned, he'd been chatting to himself for the last hour and a half, and frankly, it was beginning to suit him. Cabbies are used to talking, knowing full well no one is really listening.

I leaned forward and blew a long breath of concentrated ectoplasmic effort against the window. A gentle mist bloomed on the glass. With a ghostly finger, I scratched out the words:

THANKS GARY

He stared at it. "Blimey," he said, his voice dropping to a conspiratorial mutter.

Betty leaned close to me and whispered, "Do you think we're traumatising him?"

"He's a London cabbie," I whispered back. "They've seen everything."

Gary squinted at the words, then nodded slowly. "You're welcome, I guess."

He gave the fogged-up message a final look, did the thumbs up gesture, tipped his cap to the empty back seat, mouthed the words, *Good Luck*, silently for no explicable reason and pulled away.

We turned toward Braithwaite's.

The building itself was the architectural equivalent of a harrumph. Huge, pale stone columns. Brass fixtures polished like mirrors. A front door that looked like it refused entry to people based solely on shoe polish standards. Gary would not have gained admittance.

Betty floated up beside me. "This place reeks of ancestral entitlement."

I nodded. "… and the tang of furniture polish."

We glided through the doors, straight past a doorman with a waxed moustache and an expression of chronic suspicion. Inside, Braithwaite's was dimly lit in the way expensive places always are, because only rich people can afford to squint.

We floated down the main hall. Cameras tracked every angle. Security guards stood around trying to look like they weren't bored stiff. One of them leaned into another and muttered, "If I see one more cabinet full of teaspoons, I'm going to defect to Sotheby's."

Betty giggled and waved at a camera. I told her to stop. She didn't.

Upstairs, in a humming little room filled with CCTV monitors, two guards named Kev and Dave were deep into their second mugs of tea and their fourth shared existential crisis.

Kev leaned closer to the monitor showing Gallery Two.

"Dave."

"What?"

"Did you see that?"

"See what?"

Kev pointed. "There. That shimmer.

Dave sighed. "That's probably glare from the case lighting."

"Case lighting doesn't hover, Dave."

They both stared at the screen as another shimmer passed, vaguely coat-shaped. Possibly trench.

Kev squinted at the monitor again, which had just flickered for the fifth time that morning. "You ever think the cameras are trying to tell us something, Dave?"

Dave leaned back in his chair with the careful precision of a man who has once broken a swivel chair and swore never to repeat the shame. "Yeah. They're tellin' us we need better lightbulbs."

Kev tilted his head. "No, I mean, like, *messages* What if they're blinking Morse code? Like, *help me, Help me, I'm stuck in this vase* kind of thing."

Dave blinked slowly. "Kev. You alright mate? Are you sleeping ok and everything?"

No not really, have things on my mind"

Dave gave him a sideways glance. "You mean you have Melony on your mind. You spend every afternoon break loitering near the canteen tryin' to impress. It aint working"

Kev turned a suspicious shade of pink. "I don't loiter."

"You loiter, Kev. You loiter with intent. You made that lasagne comment last week."

Kev looked defensive. "I was bein' supportive. She tries hard."

Dave snorted. "You said, 'that's a brave use of spinach. Seriously?'"

They both stared back at the monitor, where another flicker passed across the screen.

Kev muttered, "Did you see that"

"Camera on the blink, I'll radio it in"

We drifted through Braithwaite's like a pair of particularly well-dressed draughts. The corridors were lined with glass-fronted cabinets and framed catalogues from auctions long past, all of them filled with treasures that had once sparked bidding wars and whispers over champagne. Now they sat gathering dust and mild disapproval.

"Betty," I whispered, floating beside her, "I think this is the most expensive lost property office I've ever seen."

She grinned. "If someone left a Fabergé egg on the Number 12 from Clapham, this is where it would end up."

The main hallway split into three branches, each leading to its own showroom. A neat little plaque near the junction read:
GALLERY ONE – Fine Art
GALLERY TWO – Rare Books & Manuscripts
GALLERY THREE – Curiosities & Decorative Antiquities

Betty glanced at me. "Books?"

"Books," I nodded. "But let's have a nose around first. You never know where a clue might be hiding."

We turned into **Gallery One**, and the temperature dropped like a disappointed aunt. The walls were covered in oil paintings, all of them involving pale people in elaborate wigs looking down their noses at either a pheasant, a harp, a small boy with hair like a girl, or each other. Beneath each portrait was a little placard with their names and estimates written in tiny, terrified handwriting.

A grand marble statue of something Roman and heroic dominated the centre of the room. It was missing a toe. Betty leaned close.

"He's definitely judging us," she said.

"The statue?"

"No, the ghost behind the statue."

There he was: a translucent gentleman in a powdered wig and a perpetual frown, muttering about "the declining quality of portraiture since 1814."

We made our apologies and backed out swiftly.

Gallery Three was even stranger. This was the domain of the truly odd. Gilded snuffboxes shaped like ducks. A porcelain toothpick dispenser in the shape of Napoleon. An entire case devoted to Forks of royal provenance, each one displayed like a jewel, complete with little backstories that all suspiciously ended with:

"Thought to have once belonged to the Dowager Countess of Shropshire."

"I can feel Angie's spirit vibrating with envy," I muttered.

Betty pointed to a glowering set of matching brass candlesticks labelled: *Allegedly casted from the brass monkeys of the flagship HMS Victory. No refunds.*

She nodded, approving. "Nice touch."

Finally, we reached Gallery Two. The Rare Books Room. It smelled like ancient paper, beeswax, and secrets no one had dusted in years. The lighting was dimmer here, the kind that flickered gently, not in a faulty way, but as if the room itself were trying to blink away tears of literary nostalgia.

Glass display cases lined the room, each one angled perfectly for potential buyers to lean in, squint, and feel mildly inadequate about their own reading habits.

We floated past illuminated manuscripts from monasteries, first editions of Austen and Dickens, even a playbill advertising the first-ever production of *Macbeth* performed with a live goose. The goose now long dead stood stuffed to one side.

"Honestly," Betty said, "this room's full of paper, and still the most haunted thing here is that goose."

There were a few ghostly figures loitering among the shelves. A scholarly chap in round spectacles who seemed to be eternally lecturing no one. A woman in Victorian mourning dress muttering about overdue library fines… and a small boy in short trousers attempting to pull a fountain pen through the glass case by sheer willpower.

"Do you think he was trying to write something important?" I asked.

"I think he was going to draw moustaches in the margins of a first edition," Betty replied.

We finally spotted the display in the back corner. The lights were set just a little brighter here. A plinth, low and solemn, enclosed in thick glass.

And there they were.

McKenney & Hall's "History of the Indian Tribes of North America"

Three volumes.
Vol. I – 1837.
Vol. II – 1842.
Vol. III – 1844.

They were resplendent. The kind of books that looked like they knew more than they were letting on. Gilt-edged. Too clean. Almost… too perfect.

Betty floated a slow circle around the case. "These are the best forgeries I've ever seen,"

The three volumes sat in reverent stillness beneath the glow of a specially positioned spotlight. Volume I bore a finely detailed portrait of a Cherokee chief whose expression suggested he wasn't terribly impressed with the 21st century. Volume II showcased an intricately hand-inked map, its routes and rivers delicately dancing across the parchment. But it was Volume III that gave me pause, as volume III displayed pages of marginalia, notes scrawled in a loopy handwriting.

I pointed. The hair I didn't have on the back of my ghostly neck tingled. "Betty," I said slowly. "That handwriting…"

"Is it familiar?"

"It's mine!"

"Yours?" Her ghostly voice pinged an octave higher. "How can it be yours?"

"I don't remember writing these. I don't remember much of that day since about breakfast. But that's my handwriting. I must've been cataloguing these when, well. When everything stopped."

Betty squinted at the page. "They must've copied your notes when they forged the books."

"Right. They must have thought it was part of the original. Because apparently my handwriting is so archaic, it's indistinguishable from the 1800s."

Betty smirked. "It is a bit curly. Like your letters all want to be ballerinas."

"It's called penmanship."

"It's called excessive flourish, Tony."

I looked again at the inked notes. My notes. References to treaty discrepancies, tribal population shifts, annotations that I'd only just started to understand when I was, well, you know. Turned into a full-time wisp.

"They copied my handwriting," I said, stunned. "They didn't realise they were replicating modern ink."

Betty whistled through ghostly teeth. "So if anyone compared this to your handwriting in other documents…"

"We can prove they're fakes… and we can prove the original that they were forged from was in my hands the day I was murdered"

"… Right before someone decided to park you in a phone box!"

"Exactly. Enough for any detective from Scotland Yard with an ounce of curiosity to start digging deeper"

She floated backward a bit, giving the display a new angle. "This could be the key."

We hovered in silence, both of us absorbing the weight of what we'd found. It wasn't just ink. It was evidence. Proof. Motive. A paper trail literally written in my own hand.

"You okay?" Betty asked gently.

We stood there, or rather, hovered there, until the overhead lights gave a sympathetic flicker. Somewhere behind us, one of the gallery doors creaked open.

Betty turned. "Are we being watched?"

I sniffed. "This is Braithwaite's. We're always being watched. They've got more cameras than Buckingham Palace on Jubilee weekend."

"Ghosts?"

"Betty, since we met, I've yet to visit a building built before 1950 that isn't stuffed to the rafters with ghosts."

She narrowed her eyes toward the shadows. "You think they're on our side?"

"Probably undecided. Depends on how they feel about auctions."

But I felt it too. That sensation of being watched, not with malice, but with interest. As if the books themselves had summoned someone to stand guard.

Betty leaned in close to the case and whispered, "Don't worry. We're here to help."

I nodded beside her. "We'll figure out what's real and what's forged. We'll make sure the truth doesn't go quietly."

From the far end of the gallery, one of the lights flickered out completely.

We both turned.

"I think we just got approval," Betty said.

"Or a warning."

"Maybe both."

"Well," said Betty, floating around the case again, "we've got motive. We've got evidence… and now we just need to, oh, I don't know, convince a world that doesn't believe in ghosts to take us seriously."

"Easy," I said, deadpan. "Should be done by Tuesday."

She grinned. "You're feeling hopeful."

"No," I said. "I'm just embracing the futility with a slightly more theatrical shrug."

"But still," she said, gesturing at the glass, "this is something. Real. Tangible."

"For everyone else. Not us."

She frowned. "What do we do, then?"

I tried to exhale, but realised, that I didn't need to. That was the strange part of being dead, your instincts kept turning up for work even though your lungs had long since been made redundant. I hovered there for a moment, like an indecisive mist, before saying what we both knew was true.

"We need to somehow get the evidence in front of the police," I said. "Or at the very least, get them to come and see the evidence. If we can't get to them, we need them to come to us.'"

Betty crossed her arms with a fluttery puff of silk and sarcasm. "Do we just rattle some windows until a copper gets curious? Or whisper '*Ooooh, injustice'* into someone's tea until they think to call Scotland Yard?"

I floated a slow circle around the display case, trying to gather what passed for thoughts when you didn't technically have a brain anymore. "The sale is today. It's happening. Soon. Once those books are gone—"

"They vanish, nothing for the police to see." Betty finished for me, her voice suddenly softer, the theatrical bite giving way to something more serious. "Private collections. Safe rooms. Climate-controlled vaults. Out of reach."

I nodded. "… and with them, the notes. My handwriting. The proof that they're fakes. The marginalia linking them back to me. To the day I died. To the moment everything changed. If we lose the books, we lose the only physical tie we have to the murder. Percy wins."

"Everyone else loses," Betty said grimly.

I glanced out the gallery window at the slow-moving clouds. Somewhere out there, real people were walking about their day with no idea that a centuries-old conspiracy, several ghosts, and a very determined dead ex-detective were trying to stop the sale of three books. Just three books. But sometimes that's all it takes to tip the balance.

"We need help," I said finally. "Living help."

Betty's eyebrow arched. "Angie?"

"If she can get the ghosts at Percy Hall to talk… maybe we can get someone living to listen."

Betty rolled her sleeves with dramatic flair. "So, until we get Angie to work her magic, we cause a scene? A display of disruptive supernatural theatrics?"

"Exactly."

She rubbed her hands together like a Victorian stage magician about to produce a rabbit. "I haven't rattled a chandelier in years."

The door at the back of the display room swung open with a self-important creak that suggested it had been practicing for this moment for years. Two orderlies in brown overalls, identical in the way that only uniforms and low enthusiasm can make people, ambled into the room with the solemnity of undertakers who also did weekend removals. They didn't look like curators or book experts or even particularly curious individuals. They looked like men who'd been told to move a thing, and by heavens, they were going to move it or be damned!

They made their way to the display case, the sacred home, albeit temporarily, of the three volumes of *McKenney & Hall's History of the Indian Tribes of North America*, with the slow, inevitable gait of people trying to look busy while mentally calculating how many minutes they could add to their tea break if they stretched out the job.

One of them, the taller one, knelt down at the front of the case with a grunt, revealing a lever cleverly disguised as part of the baseboard. He pulled it. A soft click followed. Then another. Then, with a noise somewhere between a whir and a reluctant groan, three small wheels extended from beneath the base of the display unit.

The shorter of the two gave the case a tap with his shoe and the 4th wheel appeared. The taller one gave a nod that said, "You've done it, Derek. You've mastered levers," and both began pushing the case slowly across the polished floor, the fourth wheel squeaking faintly in protest, as if it too felt this was a deeply unwise decision.

Betty and I watched, helpless and hover-bound.

Betty drifted beside me, arms folded, her gaze fixed on the slowly retreating case. "They're wheeling away the evidence of your murder with all the ceremony of a tea trolley."

I floated in their wake, trying to think of something, anything to do. "Can we tip it over? Can you haunt the brakes? I don't know, Betty, short-circuit the wheels? Make it spontaneously combust?"

"I'm a ghost, not a demolition expert," she said. "Besides, if I go all poltergeist now, we'll alert the wrong people. We need chaos. Controlled chaos. A haunting, not a tantrum."

I pressed my face up to the glass of the hallway, creating a foggy circle, and scrawled the word "STOP" in ghostly finger-writing that immediately began to fade.

"They're not going to stop," I said as they rolled past, voice tight. "Unless we give them a reason."

Betty gave me a sideways glance. "You're thinking of something foolish, aren't you?"

"Very probably."

"Does it involve levitating something heavy?"

"No, but now that you mention it…"

She waved a hand. "No. I've seen this look before. Back when you decided to throw snowballs at Trevor to see if he could catch ghost-snow. It didn't end well for anyone involved. Least of all the postman."

I ignored the reminder. "Betty, if they get those books out there, onto that platform, it's over. The buyers don't care if they're real or not. Percy gets his money. The books disappear. The evidence vanishes. My whole murder becomes a historical footnote."

Betty sighed, watching as the display was rolled through a side corridor and out of sight.

"Then we'd better do something," she said.

Kev and Dave were still manning the CCTV control room, which looked less like a hub of high-tech security and more like a second-hand electronics shop from 1994. Twelve monitors blinked and buzzed in black-and-white fuzz.

Kev, was poking the remnants of his packed lunch, a rather squashed baked cheesecake, while Dave, who had a moustache that looked like it had aspirations to be a broom, sipped instant coffee and nodded with grave seriousness.

"I'm just saying," Kev said, spoon halfway to his mouth, "baked cheesecake has structure. Like, it's got integrity. It's the bricklayer of puddings. Non-baked cheesecake, that's just... creamy disappointment in a pastry crust."

Dave nodded solemnly, staring at Monitor 6. "I get you. Like, the cold ones slide around too much. That's not dessert, that's dairy-based chaos."

"Exactly!" Kev jabbed his spoon at an invisible enemy. "A pudding should hold its shape. You cut a slice; it should remain a slice. Not collapse into a dairy landslide."

"Speaking of speed," Kev said suddenly, without transition, "you reckon a dolphin's faster than a shark?"

Dave blinked. "What?"

"Well," Kev said, gesturing vaguely at Monitor 2, where a motionless corridor flickered peacefully, "dolphins are streamlined, right? Proper torpedo shaped. But sharks have that murder energy."

"Sharks look fast, but dolphins've got intelligence… and they've been in the Olympics. Sort of.

"They've never been in the—"

"Figure of speech, Dave."

"Oh." Dave sipped his coffee. "Still think the shark would win if it knew it was racing."

Then Dave pointed at Monitor 4. "Look. The Dereks are on the move."

Monitor 4 showed two brown-overalled orderlies, both named Derek by some cruel twist of admin fate, wheeling a very expensive-looking glass display case down one of the gallery corridors. Inside was a gleaming set of books that practically screamed "touch me and lose your inheritance."

Kev leaned forward, spoon hovering like a satellite dish. "That's the book lot going to the auction, innit?"

"Looks like. Why's it wobbling like that?"

On screen, the case had begun to veer gently but insistently to the left, like a shopping trolley with a vendetta against straight lines. One Derek tried to correct course, while the other leaned into the drift with the body language of a man trying to prevent disaster through sheer optimism.

"They're drifting," Kev muttered, munching on his cheesecake. "That's not secure. That's wobbly book chaos."

The case continued to swerve. Derek One pulled, Derek Two pushed, and somewhere between the two of them, the wheels had clearly decided they were freelance now and were doing their own thing.

"It's going to hit the Ming!" Dave barked, standing so quickly his coffee sloshed over the edge.

On Monitor 4, the case narrowly avoided a 17th-century Ming vase, which teetered on its plinth in a way that suggested it was seriously reconsidering its career in pottery.

Kev gasped. "That vase is worth more than my mum's bungalow."

"It's worth more than your mum," Dave replied, watching the display case continue its aimless roll toward a Grecian urn.

Kev tapped a few buttons on the control panel. Nothing happened. Then he smacked the side of the monitor, which briefly cut to static before resuming its fuzzy feed.

"Can we get someone down there?" Dave asked.

"To say what? 'Excuse me, could you not crash the priceless display into ancient history?'"

On screen, Derek Two produced a walkie-talkie and appeared to shout something unintelligible. Derek One gestured at the wheel, pointing like he'd just discovered it for the first time.

"Do you reckon both of them are called Derek by coincidence?" Kev asked.

"Doubt it. Admin cock-up. Bet they gave up correcting people and just started responding together."

"Derek," Kev said, mimicking. "Yes? Yes?"

They chuckled.

"LEFT, DEREK!"

"I AM LEFTING!"

"THE OTHER LEFT!"

The cabinet jerked right suddenly, nearly decapitating a marble bust of Queen Victoria.

Kev whistled. The camera feed wobbled slightly as the cabinet passed under a low beam, sending one of the Derek's hats flying off like a startled bat.

"Should we tell Marcus?" Dave asked.

"What's he gonna do, shout at the wheels?"

"True."

They watched in silence for a moment longer as the Dereks finally regained a semblance of control and steered the case out of frame.

"So," Kev said, turning back to his cheesecake with a poke, "but is it better than Spotted Dick and Custard"

Dave just gave a don't be stupid, Spotted Dick trumps everything look.

Betty was exhausted. Not in the traditional ghostly sense, since, technically, ghosts don't have cardiovascular systems and therefore don't tire in the way living people do. She was tangled in a battle of will and wobble with wheel number four of the display cabinet, which, unlike the other three, had clearly made a pact with chaos.

The two Dereks, our hapless orderlies of identical name but not of stature, seemed to have the other wheels under complete control. Wheel one responded to Tall Derek's gentle coaxing like a well-trained Labrador. Wheel two obeyed with the kind of docility you'd expect from a monk who'd taken a vow of stillness. Wheel three was a little wild, but willing to follow orders if it wasn't being watched too closely. But wheel four? Wheel four was a gremlin with a vendetta. It shimmied, it jutted, it made spontaneous ninety-degree angles. Betty, in her effort to assist the team (or more accurately, subtly sabotage them), had taken it upon herself to haunt wheel four directly.

It had been a good idea in principle but now she hovered by the corridor wall, arms crossed, looking utterly deflated. Ghost-deflated, which is difficult to spot unless you know the signs: a slight flicker at the edges, a sigh that seems to echo from another century, and a general air of 'why me' that hung around her like ectoplasmic perfume.

"I swear," she muttered, watching the case roll onward, "that wheel just wasn't trying. All bark and no bite"

I was keeping pace just a few feet behind. The corridor was narrow, sleek, and painted the sort of neutral beige you only find in government buildings and places that don't want you to emotionally connect with the décor. A single security camera blinked overhead.

At the far end of the corridor stood the double fire and security doors, large, metallic, stern. They were the kind of doors that made you feel guilty for not having a security badge, even if you weren't doing anything wrong.

I'd watched this procedure before. The Dereks had followed it to the letter earlier: roll the case to the doors, press the green wall-mounted security button to open them, wheel the priceless object through like a ceremonial sacrifice to the gods of auctioneering, then press the button on the other side to close the doors with bureaucratic finality. Simple.

Now, they were doing it again.

The case rolled to a halt.

Derek One (Tall Derek) was muttering something to himself.

Derek Two (Short Derek) moved towards the green button, fingers poised with the same level of seriousness typically reserved for launching torpedoes.

The doors began to swing open towards them, humming like something from Star Trek but with the threatening growl of British engineering.

I waited.

Then, just as they almost reached halfway, I phased through the widening gap and threw myself at the interior button on the opposite wall. Not literally, of course. Ghosts can't throw themselves at things. It's more of a concentrated willpower-and-floating approach, a sort of determined gliding that feels like someone trying to swim through thick soup.

But I did it.

With all my not-quite-corporeal might, I pressed the inside security button. The lights above the doors flickered red in that ominous way that suggested a system not quite designed for paranormal interference. The doors, as if sensing their own betrayal, shuddered and began to close.

The Dereks, still under halfway through, reacted with the sort of swearing normally only heard from people who've stepped barefoot on a LEGO brick.

"What the?"

"Back, back! Don't wedge the Ming again!"

The display cabinet, in fear of being trapped between doors like a cow in a revolving gate, had to be reversed with all the grace of a three-point turn on a cliff edge. Betty watched from the wall, hands to her ghostly mouth, stifling laughter.

"Nicely done," she whispered.

"Wait for it," I said.

The Dereks, thoroughly flustered, tried again. They straightened the case. Derek One gave Wheel Four a good kick for good measure. Betty hissed.

"That's not how you treat a possessed wheel," she muttered.

Once again, Derek Two pressed the outer green button. Once again, the doors began to open with a sort of reluctant mechanical sigh. They braced themselves, gripped the handles on either side of the cabinet, and started to push forward.

Once again, just as the doors reached the halfway point, I hit the interior button.

Red lights.

Closing doors.

Swearing, louder this time.

"WHAT THE HELL IS GOING ON?!"

"THE SODDING BUTTON'S GOT A MIND OF ITS OWN!"

They dragged the cabinet back once more, its glass sides rattling slightly in protest, and now both Dereks looked as though they were about to demand hazard pay.

In the CCTV room, Kev and Dave were watching all of this unfold with the same wide-eyed wonder usually reserved for natural disasters and competitive cheese-rolling.

"Did he just press the inside button again?" Kev asked.

Dave shook his head. "No one's in there."

On another monitor, the auction room had become a theatre of tension. Rows of polished wooden chairs were now filled with bodies that radiated mild panic and colonial guilt. The room buzzed with the low murmur of money preparing to change hands, mixed with just a hint of existential dread. The auction had already begun, and the previous lot, a hand-carved ivory paperweight shaped like a narwhal task embedded in a grapefruit, was commanding far too much attention.

Kev and Dave, still stationed in the CCTV room and surrounded by flickering banks of screens, were observing the drama unfold with the rapt attention of two men who had no idea what was happening but were delighted that it was happening anyway.

"Look at that bloke with the moustache," Kev said, nodding at the main screen where a severely over-groomed man was shifting uncomfortably in his seat. "He's from the British Museum, isn't he?"

"Yeah," Dave confirmed, sipping something from a mug so discoloured it could no longer legally call itself 'tea'. "Looks like his face was designed by a committee that ran out of budget halfway through."

"That guy next to him, what do you think American, right? All modern tweed and tension."

"Yep, you can always spot the Americans. Do you think they know they all wear a uniform?"

"Definitely CIA," Dave said, then added, "or possibly accounting. Hard to tell. They've got the same haunted eyes."

Monitor 9 flickered, showing a wide-angle view of the room. In the centre row sat a representative from the Australian National Archives, nervously tapping a pen against his leg. The British delegate kept adjusting his cravat like it was trying to strangle him. The American envoy's knee was bouncing so fast it threatened to launch him into orbit.

Clarence, sans limp, resplendent in velvet and hubris, was tucked towards the back, trying to look nonchalant. It was the facial expression of someone who'd just hidden a stolen Fabergé egg in a trifle and didn't know whether to confess or sell the recipe.

"They're all here for the books, aren't they?" Kev said, unwrapping a second custard cream with the precision of a bomb disposal expert, eyes darting to the Dereks scratching their heads on monitor 4.

Dave nodded. "Oh yeah, Governments don't show up for narwhal paperweights."

Kev stared thoughtfully. "You know dolphins jump higher than sharks?"

Dave blinked. "What?"

"Dolphins. Jump higher. Than sharks."

Dave, who had clearly been down this conversational cul-de-sac before, closed his eyes. "Do go on."

"Well," Kev continued, "sharks move side to side, right? That's their tail action. Dolphins go up and down. It's why dolphins jump and sharks just sort of... menace. It's biomechanics. Shark tails are horizontal. Dolphin tails are vertical. Up-and-down equals springiness. Side-to-side equals evil."

"You're saying shark posture is inherently villainous?"

"Absolutely. It's like comparing someone in a Volvo to a BMW with a stick-on spoiler. Kind, affable, verses evil."

Dave stared at him with the expression "how much longer will I have to work here". but before he could rebut with something scathing about echolocation or apex predators, the screen flicked to the next lot.

Lot 17. The books were called. "Here we go," Dave muttered, straightening in his chair.

The room below stilled. The paddles froze mid-hover. The British envoy had stopped fiddling with his cravat. The American had finally remembered how to blink. The Australian started nervously whispering into a very official-looking earpiece. A hush fell over the room.

"This is it," Kev whispered, reverently. "The dolphin moment."

Dave squinted. "I don't follow."

"You've got your sharks in the room, right? The government people, CIA, British Secret Service, that American with the titanium cufflinks. They're circling. But the dolphins...the private collectors... they're gonna leap in. Soar over the lot. Splash some cash around. Metaphorically."

Dave opened his mouth, thought about it, then closed it again. "You know what? I'm just going to let that one sit."

They both stared at the screen.

But the books were still stuck in the corridor, on monitor 4. Tall Derek was leaning his forehead against the cool wall trying to calm his nerves. Short Derek was gingerly pressing the button on and off.

Dave tapped the monitor. "You wanna call Marcus and explain that the case is going to be late?"

Kev thought about this for a moment and then picked up his cheesecake again.

"Let's give it a few more minutes, I'm quite enjoying this."

Back in the corridor, Betty floated up beside me, positively glowing with ghostly pride.

"You're enjoying this, aren't you?"

"Immensely."

We hovered a safe distance back as Derek One decided to switch sides with Derek Two, convinced that perhaps the right hand had better button-pressing energy. They rolled forward again. The door opened halfway.

I made my move.

This time, as I pressed the button, I made sure to let out the faintest ghostly chuckle. Not a full-blown moan. Just enough to make the hair on the back of your neck try to file a complaint.

Derek One froze.

"Did... did you hear that?"

Derek Two nodded very, very slowly.

"Mate... let's just take the freight lift."

Derek One looked at the doors, now closing again.

"Right."

With that, the Dereks wheeled the cabinet away, very slowly, with multiple glances over their shoulders, back the way they came.

Betty turned to me, her laughter now fully uncontained.

"Tony," she said, wiping imaginary tears from her eyes, looping her arm through mine. "That was jolly fun!"

"Very Jolly!"

"Listen Mister, don't mock my accent"

Back in the auction room, the atmosphere had shifted. Not drastically. Not yet. But in that peculiar, uneasy way that happens when people dressed in expensive clothes start checking their watches more frequently and pretending they're not worried.

The auctioneer, an upright man named Lionel who wore his authority like a car dealer's cravat, picked up his walkie-talkie with the reluctant posture of someone who had hoped never to use it in anger. A quiet crackle emerged from the device, followed by several strained syllables that sounded like "stuck... wheel three...?" and what might have been "custard cream crumbs in the security keypad."

Lionel scowled. Not a theatrical scowl, but a true British scowl, the kind honed over years of disapproving of things silently. Then he returned the walkie-talkie to his pocket, straightened the cuffs of his jacket like they had personally let him down, and raised his voice with a tone that carried the weight of several centuries of passive-aggressive disappointment.

"Ladies and gentlemen," he announced, his vowels landing crisply in the heavy air of anticipation, "I regret to inform you that there will be a brief delay in the presentation of Lot 17."

There was a pause.

The room, full of diplomats, curators, deep-pocketed eccentrics, and men who owned too many cufflinks, shifted uneasily. Like a herd of antelope sniffing something distinctly lion-flavoured in the wind. You could feel the tension rising, not in a melodramatic, music-swell sort of way, but in that very British way that involved increasingly aggressive tea-drinking and very firm whispering.

From his place towards the rear of the room, Clarence's brow furrowed.

Clarence, whose real name may or may not have been Clarence, depending on which passport he was using, was Lord Percy's go-to fixer, chauffeur, messenger, and, as it happened, murderous taxi driver. He wasn't particularly bright. In fact, if minds were lightbulbs, Clarence was one of those antique bulbs that took a while to warm up, flickered inconsistently, and mostly buzzed when you needed it to shine. But what he lacked in intellect, he made up for in loyalty, muscle, and a very convincing impersonation of someone who always knew what was going on.

His expression tightened now. Not because he understood the full implication of the delay, but because he had been told very clearly by Lord Percy, "If anything delays the sale of Lot 17, you are to act swiftly, discreetly, and with all the subtlety your considerable lack of subtlety can muster."

Clarence, bless him, took that to heart.

He stood abruptly, knocking over his program, which flopped to the floor like a disappointed soufflé, and shuffled out the side entrance with all the grace of a wounded badger trying not to be noticed.

This did not go unnoticed.

The American delegation glanced at each other. The British representative raised one eyebrow and pretended not to text his superior under the table. The Australian fidgeted and took another look at his notes. A woman from UNESCO began fanning herself with her paddle like a southern belle at a séance.

The murmuring intensified.

Lionel, who'd returned to the podium, offered his most apologetic smile, the kind of smile usually reserved for funerals or explaining the concept of boarding zones at airports, and said, "Do please bear with us, ladies and gentlemen. Lot 17 will be joining us shortly. In the meantime, please enjoy a complimentary water infused with something vaguely cucumber-adjacent, available at the rear."

Backstage, Clarence was on a mission. A mission he didn't entirely understand but was committed to anyway. He stormed down the corridor with what he imagined was military precision, but in reality looked more like a confused penguin with a mild limp. As he strode in the vague direction of the display cabinet he could hear the words "Clarence, your salary is about to be redirected into the roof fund," ring through his head in the tone of Lord Percy.

Reaching the secure corridor, he was just in time to see two thoroughly unimpressed orderlies, one tall and angular, the other built like a potato, manually jabbing at the override buttons on either side of a thick security door. The red LED above blinked in what could only be described as bureaucratic contempt.

The taller orderly, Derek One by badge and birthright, was halfway through a spirited explanation into the intercom.

"We told you, twice, the flippin door opens on its own. Then it slammed shut. It's like it's developed a vendetta."

On the other end, a voice crackled from Maintenance Support, First Line. It had all the energy of someone halfway through his fourth shift.

"Doors don't do that," the voice intoned, like a haunted fax machine. "It's probably user error."

"User error?" Derek Two leaned in with the kind of expression usually reserved for bad curry and worse opinions. "How can there be user error in a door? There are only so many options available to pushing a button?"

"Were you pressing it in and out multiple times, or too quickly, were you jabbing at it. They can be quite sensitive"

"Sensitive, sensitive?" Derek 2 held the mouthpiece away for a moment while he expelled a directed expletive."

The Maintenance Voice sighed. "Have you tried turning it off and on again?"

Clarence groaned internally. "It's not a kettle."

"All electronic systems have a restart protocol. Page seven, subsection B. "ask if the device is connected to the power supply"

Derek One blinked. "Is that… is that an actual policy?"

"Yep"

Clarence pinched the bridge of his nose. Somewhere nearby, a CCTV camera blinked. Not ominously. Just with the smugness of something that's seen it all and knows you're not getting your deposit back.

"Look," Derek Two said, taking a calming breath that did nothing to calm him. "We're just trying to move a display case. But the door has a mind of its own. "

"Subsection C: Is it making noises?" the voice asked seriously.

"No, but it groaned."

"Might just be the hinges. We've had budget cuts. They're using reclaimed iron now. From China apparently."

Clarence leaned in to speak on the intercom. "Do you have an override code?"

"Technically yes, but legally no."

"Can I speak to your manager?"

"I am the manager. I'm multitasking. I'm also Sandra from HR between 3 and 5 on Thursdays."

"You're joking."

"I wish I was."

Back in the security booth, Kev and Dave watched the scene play out on a bank of monitors, mugs of tea cradled like sacred relics.

"Sunspots," Kev said with the air of a man who'd read half a Wikipedia article and considered himself an expert.

"Don't start," Dave said. "And you mean solar flares"

"They fry the electrics they do. Was the same when the fire alarm went off yesterday"

"That was Gary. He poked the *break glass thing* with his mop."

Kev sipped his tea. "Gary's never touched a mop in his life."

On the monitor, the two Dereks were now trying to back the case up and push it forward again, like it was a shopping trolley with one sentient, malevolent wheel.

"This place is cursed," Derek Two muttered as the cabinet veered sharply left and nearly clipped a Viola once played by Anne Bolyn.

Whilst everyone was standing around I decided to close and open the doors again in quick succession. Everyone looked at each other.

"We can escalate it to Level Two Support. They have an actual manual."

"How long will that take?" Clarence asked, though he already feared the answer.

"Oh… well… Level Two is currently covering the canteen break rotation. Best I can do is get Darren to pop down with the forklift. You can then get through the doors quicker, before they close.!"

"Or you could always lodge a Facilities Request Form, of course. Then we'll fax it to Extension 804."

"Fax?!" Clarence looked like he might throw himself through the door. "Who even uses fax anymore?"

Clarence pressed the intercom again. "Right. We are *not* letting a door win," he muttered. "This is your last chance. If this door doesn't open in the next sixty seconds and stay open, I will personally walk upstairs, find your department, and … and … God help me"

"Why don't you try holding it open," came a new voice through the intercom, slightly tinny but with the unmistakable smugness of someone from Help Desk Level 2 who had just returned from a long, sandwich-heavy lunch and was now feeling terribly efficient about things.

Dave and Kev leaned forward on their creaky chairs, eyes twinkling with amusement. From the CCTV monitors, they watched the three men in the corridor, the two Dereks and Clarence (who they didn't know was called Clarence), whom Dave had now dubbed "the limping penguin man", freeze like bad actors caught between scenes. The pause was pregnant with the silent realisation that none of them had thought of the most obvious solution in the universe.

The words weren't said aloud, but the look that passed between them was unanimous: "Why didn't you think of that?"

Kev chuckled, nearly spilling his tea. "You can see the thought process happening in real time. Beautiful."

"Okay," Clarence muttered, trying to claw back a sense of authority. "Here's what we'll do. I'll press the button. This button. Derek One, you hold the left door. Derek Two, you hold the right. I'll wheel it through."

"Right," said Derek One, who didn't sound convinced.

"Right," echoed Derek Two, already bracing like a man about to confront a particularly hostile barn owl.

Back in the control room, Dave was wiping his glasses. "You think it'll work?"

Kev shrugged. "I think it's going to be a ballet of incompetence. But I wouldn't miss it for the world."

With that, the security camera zoomed in slightly, as if the system itself was intrigued by what would happen next.

Clarence narrowed his eyes at the door and braced himself like a sprinter in the blocks. The LED light above the door blinked green once and then fell back into ominous silence.

Back in the auction room, the mood was rapidly approaching what one might call "civilised chaos." Conversations were getting louder. Questions were being whispered behind manicured hands. Someone was definitely drafting an email to their lawyer on an iPad.

"Do you think the books are missing?" someone whispered.

Meanwhile, Lionel took another call on his walkie-talkie, nodded grimly, and made a note on his clipboard. It was the kind of note that made you feel like something had definitely gone pear-shaped, possibly sideways, and quite possibly off the edge of reason entirely.

In a very secure room not far from the chaos, two men named Kev and Dave watched all of this unfold on monitors with the slow dawning realisation that they might not be dealing with a normal situation.

"You seeing this?" Kev asked, chewing thoughtfully on a jelly baby.

"Yep," Dave replied. "You don't think someone's stealing Lot 17?"

Dave gave him a long, level look. "A heist, like Mission Impossible?"

Kev leaned in. "The penguin chap, he shouldn't be back there, now he has his hands on the display cabinet."

"I'm calling Marcus, it's all looking very suspicious"

The doors were now open and Clarence was now taking aim at the gap in the middle.

As soon as he started pushing, the case lurched 45 degrees to the left as wheel number 4 aided by Betty, froze solid. The books inside jostled slightly, and Clarence swore under his breath but between all three of them the men pushed the display case through, lurching, squeaking, as if mocking them with every wobble.

Clarence checked the time. The delay had cost them fifteen minutes. Lord Percy would not be pleased.

Lot 17 and the display case rolled into view like the Holy Grail had been mounted on a wheelie bin. The lighting caught the glass, throwing dramatic shadows. You could feel the mood shift. Even the narwhal paperweight looked tense.

The room settled with the hushed reverence of a cathedral moments before a miracle. Rows of bidders, academics, collectors, and jittery representatives from governments who usually didn't attend such affairs, all leaned forward with an almost sacred anticipation. Lionel, a tall man with a voice like vintage port and eyebrows that had opinions of their own, stepped back up to the lectern. He adjusted his bow tie with solemn gravitas.

"Ladies and gentlemen," he began, his voice smooth enough to butter crumpets at twenty paces, "thank you for your patience. We apologise for the brief delay in presenting Lot 17, but as you will soon see, it has most certainly been worth the wait."

A ripple of quiet murmuring rustled through the room like silk against velvet.

Behind him, the display case, finally coaxed down the corridor, was now centre stage, lovingly spotlighted. The glass gleamed. Inside, the three volumes lay as if posed for a national portrait.

"Lot 17," the auctioneer intoned, lifting a single gloved hand as if invoking an ancient spirit, "is a rare, extraordinary, and some might even say miraculous offering: a complete three-volume set of McKenney and Hall's History of the Indian Tribes of North America."

A quiet gasp, the collective intake of intellectual breath, swept through the audience.

"Published between 1837 and 1844, these volumes represent not only an iconic achievement in American ethnographic illustration, but also a vital, deeply human archive of Indigenous history and culture. Each volume is hand-coloured, each page a portal to a past that was almost erased. These books do not just sit on shelves. They speak."

He paused for dramatic effect. One gentleman from the Smithsonian looked visibly moved. A private collector dabbed at his spectacles.

"In Volume I," the auctioneer continued, gesturing to the first open book, "we find a portrait of a Cherokee leader, rendered in exquisite detail. A man whose very expression whispers dignity, resilience, and centuries of unacknowledged pain. Volume II includes a rare map, detailing ancestral trails and lands. In Volume III, we encounter marginalia, notes made, we believe, by an early collector or researcher. Personal. Intimate. A dialogue across time."

Unseen by the living, Tony and Betty hovered near the back wall, watching intently. Tony narrowed his eyes at the marginalia. His own handwriting. It stung like a forgotten birthday.

"These books," the auctioneer went on, lowering his voice to a reverent murmur, "are a testament to preservation. To survival. To cultural endurance in the face of extinction. There are fewer than three complete sets of this calibre known to exist. Most are incomplete, faded, or locked away in institutional vaults. But this set…"

He paused again, letting the weight of his words fill the room like incense.

"This set is pristine. Unblemished. Bound in calfskin leather, restored with care and authenticity. Estimated value begins at £300,000, but I assure you, its cultural worth is beyond measure."

One of the American government representatives was now whispering urgently to a colleague. The Australian envoy scribbled something in a notebook, eight individuals were on earpieces relaying the situation to benefactors abroad. Online there were probably dozens more.

"Let us not forget," the auctioneer said, lifting his gavel and raising his voice a touch, "that we are not simply purchasing paper and ink. We are bidding on legacy. On heritage. On the rare chance to rescue something irreplaceable from the slow oblivion of time."

A smattering of nods spread through the room like a slow wave of cultural guilt and acquisitive hunger.

"So," he said at last, his voice warm with purpose, "let us begin the bidding."

But even as he brought the gavel to the ready, Betty leaned toward me and whispered, "Not if we can help it." She pinched her nose delicately, eyes closing with theatrical concentration, and turned a rather alarming shade of purple, like a spectral aubergine with purpose.

You can guess what happened next.

The lights, which only moments before had bathed the volumes in reverent gold, began to flicker like a haunted rave. A strobe of indecision. A hesitant disco. Then they started popping, one by one, with audible fizzles followed by delicate plumes of smoke curling upward in ghostly spirals. The auction room, previously a temple of high-stakes antiquity, was now a stage for absolute chaos.

There were screams. Honest-to-goodness screams. The kind normally reserved for haunted houses or unexpectedly personal tax audits. The auctioneer, mid-step as he turned to cue the bidding, lost his balance and tumbled from the podium like an elegant sack of confusion, flailing for the lectern, which escaped his grasp with the sort of grace only mahogany can muster. He missed the display case by inches and landed with a wheeze somewhere near Lot 19, a medieval chamber pot that had now been christened by panic.

A groan from the ceiling announced the activation of the emergency lighting system, a greenish hue better suited to alien invasions than historical transactions. It cast a sickly pall over everything, illuminating the emergency exits with all the urgency of a librarian whispering "fire."

The auction house staff, trained for elegance, not existential terror, scrambled. One man tried to herd a group of panicked collectors towards the fire exits.

Then came the siren. Somewhere deep in the bowels of the building, a security alarm began its mournful wail, long and low and somehow accusatory, like a Victorian widow who just discovered the will wasn't in her favour. This part hadn't been intentional. Clearly, in the process of flickering through frequencies like a spectral radio tuner, Betty had accidentally tripped something. Possibly everything.

"Oops," she said, eyes still glowing faintly. "That might've been a bit too much."

I glanced at her. "You think?"

In the control room, Kev and Dave were having what could generously be called *a moment*. Dave was gripping his chair so tightly it creaked in protest. Kev had dropped his Kit Kat.

"Is it a power cut?" Dave asked.

"No," Kev said. "That's the emergency lighting. Look at that monitor, the main fuseboard's lit up like a Christmas tree."

"So not the fuse, then?"

Kev squinted at the flickering monitors, some of which were now cycling through static, while others showed priceless artefacts being abandoned in favour of raw panic. "Mate... I think we are being robbed."

"Call 999" Said Dave "That the policy.

"If the alarms gone off they are probably already on their way"

Back in the auction room, Clarence remained sat in his seat, head in hands. He had seen the lights flicker and go poof before. This couldn't be a coincidence.

I surveyed the scene: the auctioneer attempting to stand upright, collectors evacuating like nervous ducklings, a security guard trapped behind a falling curtain, and the books, still miraculously safe in their case, now bathed in emergency gloom.

Somewhere behind us, a particularly posh woman shrieked, "This is an outrage!" and immediately tripped over her husband.

"So," Betty said, adjusting her ethereal scarf, "What next, general?"

"Now," I said, "We get Angie back down from Hexham and in front of the police. It will take at least a week to re-arrange the auction, if not longer."

"Kev," Dave said quietly, his eyes narrowing as he leaned toward the glowing screens. His voice had that strained, tea-too-hot tone, the sort you used when something was very wrong.

"Yeah?" Kev replied without looking up, still half-focused on poking a custard cream into his mouth with the concentration of a man performing surgery.

"Can you see those figures in the static on Monitor 7?"

Kev squinted, crumbs tumbling down his uniform like ancient masonry. He leaned in. Monitor 7, usually as thrilling as watching beige paint dry on a beige wall, was now alive with a fizz of ghostly static. In the midst of the white noise, two faint silhouettes shimmered and twitched.

Kev blinked. Once. Twice.

"Is one of them… dancing?"

"Yep," Dave said, the word dragging itself reluctantly out of his mouth like a child late for school. "Looks like it's doing the Charleston."

"Blimey," Kev muttered. "Is the shorter one waving at the camera?"

"Yep," Dave confirmed, "I think it just mouthed 'Hello Dave.'"

There was a long silence.

Kev reached for his walkie-talkie, thought better of it, then reached instead for his Kit Kat. "Right," he said, breaking off a finger. "I vote we pretend we didn't see that. Agreed?"

Dave nodded. "Agreed."

With that, they turned the volume down slightly on Monitor 7… just in case.

CHAPTER TEN

I'D LIKE TO REPORT A MURDER: MINE

Gary's taxi smelled faintly of bacon sandwiches, existential resignation, and a brand-new pine-scented air freshener bravely losing the battle against both. I slid into the passenger seat, or at least hovered convincingly, and Gary grunted a greeting without taking his eyes off the road.

"Morning, Tone," he said. "Ready for our little outing?"

"As ready as a dead man can be for a police interview," I said, but of course he couldn't hear me, being dead and all...

He snorted at the lack of response, which in Gary-speak meant he was either amused or unsure if he was actually just talking to himself.

The taxi rolled out of the sleepy lanes near the Rose and Crown and pointed its way towards the local police station in Biggin Hill. It was only a short drive, but the scenery as ever in this part of Kent was worth the attention, low hedges, slightly apologetic cows,

233

and road signs that seemed almost embarrassed to suggest directions. Everyone around here knew everyone else, where they lived, probably what they had for supper. So they didn't need road signs.

Gary drove like only a London cabbie forcibly exiled to the countryside could; confident, a little insulted by roundabouts, and determined to believe that every road map was wrong unless personally confirmed by three generations of cabbies and a pub landlord.

"So," he said after a while, as we rattled past an abandoned shoe shop that had reinvented itself as the "Vintage Sneaker Emporium," "you ready for this?"

I shrugged. "As much as you can be when you're relying on someone else to do the talking."

Gary gave me a sideways glance as if waiting for the response he knew wouldn't come. "You trust Angie?"

"Completely." I said.

"She's mad, she is," he said, nodding approvingly. "Good mad, though."

We fell into a companionable silence, broken only by the occasional squawk from Gary's ancient radio and the soft whirr of ghostly unease I hadn't managed to shake since breakfast.

Finally, the police station came into view.

It was wedged uncomfortably between a tax office that hadn't seen joy since decimalisation and a bakery now boldly rebranded as *Artisan Gluten Haven*, which, judging by the number of forlorn faces inside, was still waiting for its first happy customer.

The station itself looked like it had once aspired to be important but had given up somewhere in the early '80s. Its faded white bricks sagged like a cardigan left too long in the rain, and every window wore a misted glaze that suggested there was a cannabis farm inside. There wasn't.

Above the door, the flickering "POLICE" sign buzzed and fizzed like it was trying to communicate in Morse code: **S.O.S. SEND PAINT.**

Gary pulled the taxi up to the curb opposite with the attitude that *a London Cab can park anywhere at all.* Even on a double yellow line outside a police station.

I floated out through the door, because I can, and because I can't use a door handle. Even though I don't have to open the door, you cannot imagine the frustration of knowing, such a simple task, is beyond reach. It's like being a toddler who can't reach the fridge door. Gary followed, but at a slower, more stompy human pace.

The automatic doors gave a sad little shudder and opened half a second too late, catching Gary neatly on the shin.

"You rotter"" he barked at the inanimate object. Ok he didn't use the word "Rotter", that was an editorial replacement.

Inside, the place was exactly what you'd expect: grey chairs, greyer floors, and walls painted in a shade of beige so noncommittal it could run for mayor.

A few people sat in the waiting area, nursing bruises both physical and emotional. The air smelled faintly of instant coffee and despair.

The desk sergeant was a man built like a wardrobe full of sandbags, slumped behind a desk littered with paperwork, a stale croissant, and a crossword puzzle that appeared to have defeated him somewhere around 6-Across.

His badge said **Sgt. P. Wicks**, but I couldn't help but feel he looked more like a "Barry" or possibly a "Neville."

Gary approached first, because technically I didn't have a working voice for official purposes.

The sergeant grunted without looking up. "Yeah?"

Gary cleared his throat. "Not me, mate. Her." He thumbed toward the door.

At that moment, the automatic doors shuddered again, and Angie swept in.

There's no other way to put it. She *swept*. Full coat, full hair, full purpose. Like Mary Poppins but with a to-do list that included "solve murder" instead of "take tea."

The sergeant raised an eyebrow, visibly recalibrating his estimate of how much trouble this was going to be.

"Yes, miss?"

Angie smiled sweetly, the kind of smile that ought to have had its own permit. "Good morning. I'd like to report a murder, please."

A small, stunned silence fell over the room.

Someone in the waiting area dropped their coffee. A child looked up from a sticky lollipop with sudden, horrified interest.

Sgt. Wicks put down his pen very slowly, like it might explode if moved too fast.

"I'm sorry…. what?" The last murder in Biggin Hill, or surrounding parishes had been in 1976, the last and possibly only heatwave in the UK. Even global warming, it seems, gives British weather a wide berth, as if uncertain whether to intervene or just let it play out like a weird cousin's wedding. Jeremy Philpot who had been stabbed, quite ineffectively, with a cake slice during a particularly intense argument about whether trifle should contain jelly.

His assailant, a local librarian named "mad" Mavis Dipple, had claimed she acted in self-defence, citing Philpot's use of the phrase *"I don't believe in trifle layers"* as psychologically violent.

Her case based on the grounds of extreme provocation, hadn't carried favour and she was relaxing at the pleasure of her majesty, until 1980 when she joined the cast of the hit British soap opera, Housewives of Croydon. Philpot's death or folk legend *"The Dessert Tragedy"*, is often whispered about in church fêtes and printed annually in the Women's Institute newsletter under the heading "Let That Be a Lesson, Gladys."

No one had murdered anyone since, at least not in a way that required police paperwork.

Which is why D.I. Marsh was now blinking at Angie like she'd told him Father Christmas was under investigation for tax fraud.

"A murder," Angie repeated, enunciating clearly. "A man. His name was Tony Ferrari. It happened just before Christmas. I have reason to believe his death wasn't an accident "

Gary was watching from the sidelines with the sort of expression normally reserved for a man seeing a particularly daring pub brawl unfold.

The sergeant blinked, checked under his desk as if hoping for backup, and then said, "One moment."

He picked up the battered phone at his elbow and dialled a number that he clearly wasn't exactly confident was the right one. Following a brief pause as the D.I expressed his surprise at being disturbed so soon after breakfast, he muttered into the receiver,

"Yes, I know DI Marsh, yes, yes, but believe me you'll want to see this one. I have someone here says they want to report a murder from before Christmas."

"Yes a murder. No stop it, you'll get me going"

He put the phone down and gave Angie the kind of smile you give to toddlers and drunks. Both of which he had much more experience of reporting.

"Take a seat, miss. Someone'll be right with you."

Angie sat down primly on one of the battered chairs. I hovered beside her. Gary leaned against the wall like a bored bouncer.

The minutes dragged on. Somewhere in the building, a phone rang. Somewhere else, a copier jammed and swore electronically.

Finally, a door at the back opened with a squeak that suggested it was either haunted or extremely badly maintained.

Out stepped D.I. Marsh.

He was tall, thin, and his tie was trying to escape over his left shoulder. He wore the expression of a man who had long ago given up asking why life insisted on happening to him.

He approached, clipboard in hand, and fixed Angie with a look.

"You wanted to report a murder?"

"Yes," Angie said, standing up and offering a hand.

Marsh shook it warily, standing back, like she might launch her handbag at him at any moment.

Looking first at Angie, then at Gary "Well, come on then," he sighed, leading her through the door, followed by a beaming Gary.

I floated after them. Gary gave me a thumbs up.

"Good luck, mate," he muttered.

I was going to need it.

D.I. Marsh's pen hovered uncertainly above his notebook and gave Angie a careful, polite smile, the sort of smile you reserve for people who are going to waste your time.

"Right," he said slowly, the word stretching across several counties. "You'd like to report... a murder. From before Christmas."

"Exactly," Angie said brightly. She clasped her hands together in the universal sign of "I know what I'm doing, even if you don't."

Behind her, Gary shifted awkwardly in his chair, trying to both look supportive yet absolutely not involved. I, being currently invisible, and dead, made a noble effort to loom meaningfully. It's harder than it sounds.

"… and who, precisely," asked D.I. Marsh, tapping his pen against the desk as if hoping the rhythm would summon wisdom, "has been murdered?"

"Tony Ferrari," Angie said, enunciating like she was reading out a competition answer on the radio.

Marsh blinked.

"You mean like the car?"

"No, like the man," she said firmly. "He owned a bookshop in London. Finsbury Books. You'll find a traffic accident report filed, I'm sure."

I nodded helpfully. No one noticed, obviously.

"And you know this because...?"

"Because I'm a book expert," Angie said smoothly. "The books he was cataloguing at the time of his death have turned up. There's handwriting, his handwriting, in the margins. We can match it to previous samples from the shop records."

"You just happened to notice this?" Marsh asked, raising one sceptical eyebrow so high it nearly detached from his forehead.

Angie smiled serenely. "I'm very thorough when it comes to first editions and rare collections."

It wasn't technically a lie. She *was* thorough. Especially when said thoroughness involved listening to invisible dead people and occasionally bribing them with fig rolls.

Gary cleared his throat loudly, offering Marsh a thumbs-up for some reason even he didn't fully understand. Marsh ignored it with the skill of a man who had seen worse.

"And you think this Tony Ferrari was murdered?" Marsh said. His voice had entered the dangerous register known as *"Politely Disbelieving While Preparing the Tranquiliser Dart."*

"I don't think he was," Angie said cheerily. "I *know* he was."

I crossed my arms smugly. That's my girl, I thought proudly, before remembering I technically wasn't supposed to have paternal feelings toward the woman saving my ethereal bacon.

Marsh tapped his pen some more. Somewhere in the background, a radiator gurgled sympathetically.

"Right," he said again, filling the room with it. "Humour me. How was Mr. Ferrari killed?"

Gary leaned forward as if about to add something useful, then thought better of it and pretended to admire a health and safety poster titled *"Notice, Notify, Neutralise."*

Angie, for her part, leaned forward too, as if sharing a juicy secret.

"A taxi parked him in a phone box," she whispered. "Outside his bookshop."

Marsh sat back slightly. "Parked?"

"Or run over," Angie allowed. "There are technicalities. The point is, it wasn't an accident. It was staged. Someone made sure he was there at the right place, the right time."

Marsh scribbled something. I floated closer to sneak a peek. It said: *Murder? Mental health referral???*

Typical.

"…and pray tell, who do you think is responsible?" Marsh asked, as nutters always think they know who did it.

Angie didn't even blink.

"Lord Percy," she said sweetly.

There was a long, painful pause. Marsh's eyebrows attempted to vacate the premises.

"As in... an actual lord?"

"Yes," said Angie. "A very real one. Lives in Percy Hall. Lovely house. Appalling ethics."

Gary gave a helpless little shrug when Marsh looked at him, as if to say, *don't ask me, mate, I just drive the cab.*

"… and," Marsh said, voice now strangled slightly by disbelief, "this Lord Percy... had Mr. Ferrari murdered because...?"

"Because Tony accidentally acquired a set of rare books that Percy was trying to quietly fake and sell to pay for roof repairs," Angie said, speaking quickly, like a magician whipping the tablecloth off a set table and hoping no one notices the broken china.

There was another long silence. You could hear a dust mote drop.

Finally, Marsh took off his glasses and rubbed the bridge of his nose like a man realising his pension plan may not be enough for this.

"You realise," he said carefully, "how this sounds."

"I do," said Angie.

"… and you're not... concerned?"

"Not in the slightest."

Gary coughed in a way that suggested he was very concerned but also really needed a cup of tea.

Marsh sighed, deeply, the sigh of a man contemplating retirement.

"Alright," he said at last. "Supposing for one insane moment that I believe any of this, which, to be clear, I don't, you say you have *proof*. The handwriting."

"Yes," said Angie brightly. "It's on the margins of three volumes of *History of the Indian Tribes of North America* by McKenney and Hall. Originals. Currently in Braithwaite's Auction House."

Marsh made a noise like a clogged hoover. "Braithwaite's?" he repeated. "You're telling me you have rare books connected to a dead person, in the possession of an auction house, tied to a peer of the realm?"

"Precisely," said Angie, beaming.

Gary nodded emphatically, knocking a "Visit Kent" tourism pamphlet off the desk with the power of solidarity.

Marsh ran his hands through his hair, which promptly gave up and lay down in despair.

"Right," he said again. "Sit here. Don't move. Don't... don't do anything." Mainly looking at Gary.

He stopped himself mid-sentence and gave Angie a very cautious look.

Angie smiled her best "butter wouldn't melt" smile. I grinned invisibly. Betty would've curtsied if she had been here.

Marsh stood up and walked off toward a side office marked Serious Crimes Division and gave the sticky door a shove, muttering darkly about needing a "long, hard sit-down" and "maybe some biscuits."

As the door swung shut behind him, Angie turned to the empty air where I floated.

"Not bad, right?"

I gave her a thumbs-up.

"Where's Betty?"

I hesitated. "She didn't come."

Angie blinked. "Didn't come?"

"This morning, I went looking for her. She wasn't in the pub. I checked the bar, the office, even the radiator in case she was trying to contact you through Mavis."

"And?"

"I found her on the green I sighed. With the Indian Squaw, you know, the one with the papoose." They were sitting outside the teepees. Just talking. You know that kind of conversation men are not supposed to hear?"

Angie nodded slowly. "The one who always looks like she knows exactly how the universe works and is disappointed we've not figured out shoes properly yet?"

Angie gave a thoughtful hum.

"Then Bob came tearing out of a teepee, laughing like a loon, and ran behind Betty's legs to hide. The Chief came out after him, pretending to scold him, and Betty just knelt down, wrapped her arms around Bob like he was the only thing in the world."

Looking out the window we watched as a pigeon landed on the "O" of the POLICE sign and immediately regretted it.

"I floated over to them. Bob decided to chase me. Ran at me with his hands on his head like horns. Played ghost buffalo around the teepees. Betty was giggling it was all good. She was happy, not just 'I've-found-a-pound-in-my-old-coat' happy. Real, glowing, incandescent kind of happy. Then next time I looked 'pop' she caught my eye and, well, the smile just... left her face."

 "What did she say?"

"Not a lot. She strode back to the pub saying she had things to do today."

Angie sighed. "She's changing."

"Can ghosts do that?" I asked.

Angie gave me a sideways glance. "You tell me. I suspect you've created quite a bit of change for her"

"Tricky" came a high-pitched voice from the corner. Dressed for a summer BBQ, a ghost glided up through the floor. Hawaiian shirt, shorts and open toed sandals covering a pair of brown socks. "what've you done? Forgotten an anniversary?"

"No I haven't forgotten our anniversary" I admit coming out a little more aggressively than I intended. "Anyway, you shouldn't be eavesdropping, this was a private conversation" The new ghost shrugged and backed away.

"Touchy, aint we"

"Yes. I mean No! Who are you anyway?"

"Jeremy Philpot, you can call me Jez".

"Listen Jez, a bit of privacy please" said Angie a little more sweetly.

"Ok, Ok, I get the message, thought I'd tell you Marsh in on the phone to a Lord Percy"

Angie looked at me and gave me ethereal flick with her fingers which meant go eavesdrop in the next room.

Gary, oblivious that there was any conversation going on at all, picked up the "Notice, Notify, Neutralise" poster and began reading it aloud in a Welsh accent. Nope, no idea why.

Detective Inspector Geoffrey Marsh had spent the better part of two decades listening to people lie to him. It was always someone else who had done it. He could spot it in the way they picked their lips or didn't make eye contact, in how they leaned back just slightly when they spoke, like the truth had bad breath. So, when Lord Percy of Percy Hall answered the phone with the smooth, crisp tones of someone used to signing cheques larger than the GDP of small nations, Marsh's suspicion kicked in before the conversation had even properly begun.

"Thank you for your time Lord Percy, we are just following up on a few details regarding an accident before Christmas. I appreciate you're busy"

Marsh scribbled something on the printout of the accident report of the death of a Mr. T Ferrari. I peered over his shoulder interested to see what he had gleaned already. I was just a doodle of a pigeon wearing a monocle.

"Of course, of course. Always happy to help the boys in blue. Or whatever shade of navy it is these days."

Marsh made a noncommittal sound that could mean agreement or indigestion.

"There's a young woman here, says she's a book dealer," Marsh said. "Claims a Mr. Ferrari bought a set of rare books at auction from you, Native American history. Claims his handwriting appears in the margins of those same books, which she believes are now being presented as something they're not."

"Books?" Percy chuckled. "Good Lord. No, I believe Mr. Ferrari purchased some light fiction. Lord Peter Wimsey, I think it was. First editions, quite charming. Nothing so grand as Native American antiquities."

"Right," Marsh said. "… and of course you'd have the receipts for those, I assume?"

"Well, I'm not a Braithwaite's, dear fellow. I don't keep auction records. I just oversee the collections."

There it was. That hesitation. The minuscule crack in the marble statue.

"Of course. Would anyone else have handled the sale on your behalf?"

A pause. Short. But short is all Marsh needed.

"There may have been a clerk involved. A M-... Barker, perhaps. Not terribly important. Just administrative matters, you understand."

"I do," said Marsh. "Completely understand. Would this Mr. Barker be the same Mr. Barker who was interviewed at the scene of Mr. Ferrari's death, shortly after the accident?" The fellow had actually read the report of my death. I was impressed.

Another pause. This one not so short.

"I couldn't possibly say," Percy said, now clipped, precise. "I imagine if he were, it was coincidence. We do have business interests in the area."

"I see."

Marsh ended the call shortly after, polite as ever. But something stank. It wasn't the Wimsey novels or the ridiculous poshness. It was the way Lord Percy spoke like the world was his drawing room and everyone else was furniture.

He turned slowly in his chair, casting a glance through the reinforced glass into the hallway beyond, where Angie was still sitting quietly, flipping through her handbag like it was a treasure chest. Marsh let out a breath that whistled slightly through his teeth.

This woman, strange, stubborn, might not be entirely bonkers after all.

He picked up his phone again.

"Murphy? DI Marsh. Get me everything you can on a man named Barker. First name possibly Harry. Connected to Percy Hall, and possibly a licensed black cab driver. Cross-check with transport records and the incident report from December, yes, lookup file 1673863- Ferrari, yes, as in the car."

He hung up and stood, adjusting his tie like a man about to ask the universe some pointed questions. Then he stepped out into the corridor.

"Miss...?"

"Angie," she said, brightly.

"Yes, Miss Angie. I think we need to have another chat. Perhaps something a little more... thorough. Tea?"

As DI Marsh went off to arrange tea I filled Angie in on the conversation Marsh had had with Percy.

"He lied, dear," Angie said with a small, pleased smile, "And now… we can prove it."

Detective Inspector Marsh sat across from her with the look of a man who had been politely hit in the head with a Victoria sponge made of facts. His fingers drummed the side of the file folder in a 3/4-time signature that said, "I want to believe you, but you're either brilliant or deranged and I haven't yet ruled out both."

I, of course, was right there with them, hovering like a very well-dressed hummingbird of justice, occasionally whispering helpful things into Angie's ear like, *"Mention the catalogue number,"* and *"Don't forget the marginalia,"* and once, *"For God's sake don't touch the custard cream."*

Angie did not falter. If anything, she leaned into her element. She had entered full "Head Girl Who Knows Where the Exam Paper is Hidden" mode. Her voice crisp, her memory sharp, her handbag organised in a way that suggested colour-coded magic.

Marsh tried valiantly to keep up, nodding in all the right places, scribbling notes that became increasingly illegible. At one point he drew a diagram, which I believe was meant to represent the link between Percy Hall, Finsbury Books and the telephone box, but more closely resembled a sad pancake.

"And so," Angie concluded, sipping again from her mug like she'd just won tea-based warfare, "that's why the handwriting in the forged McKenney & Hall books is the key. It links the real volumes to Tony Ferrari and the forged ones to Lord Percy. You can see, can't you, how the timing of his death isn't… ideal."

There was a silence in the room, broken only by the hiss of the radiator who had clearly been keeping up with the conversation.

Marsh leaned back slowly, letting the full weight of this improbable, inconvenient truth settle into his bones. He looked like he'd just watched an opera sung entirely by people holding ducks.

"I'm going to need a minute," he said.

"Of course," Angie replied, gracious as a duchess.

He stood, shuffled his papers into a sort of apologetic pile, and left the room with the air of someone who needed both a second opinion and a biscuit. Possibly a biscuit with a shot of something stronger.

The moment the door shut, Angie folded one leg neatly over the other with a practised click, her coat falling back like a superhero cape in a romcom for paranormal librarians. She placed her mug, still inexplicably half full, on top of a towering stack of folders that had, judging by the dust patterns, not been touched since the days of Betamax video recorders.

"Well," she said, her tone bright enough to illuminate a crypt. "That went rather well."

I nodded, crossing my ghostly arms. "You had him spinning. I almost felt sorry for him."

"Oh, he'll recover. Probably. I'm very persuasive."

"You're like a wrecking ball made of cardigans and charm."

She gave a modest shrug, which in Angie-speak meant *"Yes, I know, I am magnificent, but I'm trying not to gloat because I'm a lady."*

"He's reasonable," Angie said, glancing toward the door. "He wants this to make sense. All we had to do was give him just enough absurdity wrapped in evidence that he can pretend it's his idea."

"That's dangerously close to describing all of British governance."

We both laughed. Or, at least, Angie did. I sort of vibrated with amusement.

It was in that moment I realised something: Angie wasn't just holding the pieces of this mystery together, she was also keeping *me* together

She gave me that little smirk again. "You really should've been alive for this bit. You would've had a field day."

"Oh, I am," I said. "Just not in a way that's admissible in court."

From beyond the glass window, we could see Marsh pacing, talking to himself, or to the tea mug. Same difference.

"You think he'll come round?" I asked.

"Oh, he's already halfway there. That call to Percy nailed it. He knew he was being lied to..."

"You're very good at this, even if he thinks you're two jam tarts short of a bakery counter."

She smiled. "Exactly. That means he's underestimated me, and you know what that means, don't you?"

"He's doomed?"

"I was once head of the school debating team. I got us through a whole regional final by convincingly arguing that custard should be considered a breakfast food."

"That… actually explains a lot."

Angie leaned back, exhaled, and allowed herself a moment of silence. The kind that says, *for now, we wait. But not for long.*

Somewhere in the building, a distant voice shouted something about a missing stapler. The police station carried on around us, completely unaware that it was now part of something much, much bigger.

"He'll start now," she said cheerfully. "Poking around, just far enough to get himself tangled up in something he can't ignore."

"And when he starts pulling at the thread…" I began.

Betty's voice would normally have finished that sentence with something pithy about unravelling cardigans of truth. But she wasn't here.

I floated slightly lower.

"You miss her," Angie said, without looking up.

"Did I say anything?"

"You don't have to. Your spectral sulking has a distinct hum to it. It's like an old kettle."

I tried to mutter something witty and failed. "She had things to do."

"She's allowed that, you know," Angie said, giving me a look that could have replaced fluoride in most municipal water supplies. "Even ghosts get a life. Or an afterlife. She's not your sidekick, Tony. She knows that justice may not be too far away now… and all that means…"

"I know that."

"Do you?"

There it was. The sting. Truth, wrapped up in sarcasm, slathered in affection. The Angie Special.

Before I could reply, the door burst open with all the subtlety of a pantomime villain.

Gary barged in carrying a sandwich the size of a small ferret. "Sorry, got lost. Ended up in Records. Lovely chap named Willy showed me his stamp collection. Fascinating stuff. I pretended I was from 'Post Office Security' to get away."

He took a massive bite of the sandwich, then paused looking at Angie. "You look serious. I have news though! Bloke in Taxi licensing, Millwall supporter, called me back"

"You found Clarence?" I asked, perked up. Angie repeated for Gary.

"Oh yeah. Full black cab licence. Name's not Clarence, though."

"Then what is it?" Angie asked.

Gary wiped a bit of mayo off his cheek with a speed that suggested years of sandwich-related trauma. "Colin Briggs. Born in Shoreditch. Clean licence. Bit too clean, actually."

"How so?"

"No parking fines. No complaints. Imagine a cabbie with no complaints. Nothing. Even his DBS check came back with 'suspiciously bland' stamped in the margin."

"Which means…?"

"Which means," Gary said, lowering his voice like a man who'd watched too many detective dramas, "he's either a saint or someone's been laundering his file. Colin, sorry, Clarence, he's been to Percy Hall a lot. Listed as personal driver for one Harry Barker."

"Oh ho," I said, which is not a phrase I normally use but felt entirely appropriate.

"Exactly," said Angie. "… and Harry Barker, as we all know, is…"

"Lord Percy's evil twin in a slightly less polished waistcoat?" I offered.

"More or less," Angie agreed.

The door creaked again, and D.I. Marsh stepped back in, holding a new folder and wearing an expression that was halfway between 'I have questions' and 'I need stronger tea.'

He looked at Gary, who gave him a cheery wave. Marsh ignored it with surgical precision.

"Miss…" he paused, then gave up and asked, "Can I just call you Angie?"

"You may."

"Does this informality mean you'll investigate?" Angie asked, hopeful.

Marsh looked down at the folder, then at her, then at Gary, who was currently trying to discreetly remove lettuce from his collar.

"I can't *not* investigate," he admitted.

"Thank you," Angie said, standing.

Gary stood too, still chewing.

"And thank *you*, Mr...?"

"Gary," he said. "Just Gary."

"Of course," Marsh said. "Just Gary."

As they walked out, Marsh glanced at the ceiling, as if asking an unseen deity why his planned afternoon of golf had evaporated.

Outside, the sky had finally decided it was late April, which meant it was raining sideways with a hint of smug.

I floated up beside Angie.

"You were amazing in there."

"I know," she said, brushing imaginary dust from her coat. "Now let's find Betty."

It was late by the time I floated back into the Rose and Crown, the kind of late that only ghosts and bakers truly appreciate. The pub glowed with its usual golden haze, the fire crackling like it had secrets to tell, and the smell of beer, crisps, and wood polish clung to the air like a stubborn relative. The lights were flickering happily on the Wi-Fi router as the photo of someone's dinner was posted on Instagram. The Reverend must be asleep somewhere dreaming of the speeches he wishes he'd made. The regulars were still muttering into their pints about local council conspiracies surrounding the building of the new supermarket and whether it was appropriate for the new vicar to be seen with chin stubble.

There she was, Betty, sitting by the hearth in a wingback chair that technically belonged to no one but had been claimed by her through sheer force of ghostly will. She looked thoughtful and beautiful. Not her usual 'should we rearrange the chairs for maximum haunting efficiency' thoughtful, but the sort of thoughtful that's usually accompanied by a distant gaze and violin music.

I drifted over and perched on the hearth next to her. Or as near as I could perch, since my backside and gravity had stopped working together around the time of my untimely phone box appointment.

"Evening," I said softly.

She turned slowly, a warm expression lighting her translucent face. "Tony."

"Missed you this morning," I said, trying for casual and landing somewhere between awkward and vague detective noir.

"I had things to do," she replied.

I nodded, and we both stared at the fire. It was the kind of silence that wasn't empty. The kind that fills up with all the things you want to say but aren't entirely sure how to say without tripping over your own metaphorical shoelaces.

Eventually, I caved.

"I went looking for you this morning, first thing."

She didn't say anything, but the corners of her mouth twitched.

"I checked the office, the bar, even the radiator in case you were trying to phone Angie via Mavis's central heating again."

That earned me a laugh. A small one, but genuine. Like hearing a bell ring far away on a foggy night.

"Then I saw you," I said. "With the Indian squaw. You were having one of those conversations' women have. The sort of deep, mysterious, emotionally profound conversation that makes men want to build sheds."

She looked away.

There was a long pause. The fire popped, and someone at the bar loudly declared that custard creams were a conspiracy by the French.

"He likes you," she said suddenly.

"Who?"

"Who do you think?"

It took me a moment. "Bob?"

She nodded. "He thinks you're brilliant. You make him laugh. He follows you around like you're his best friend."

"That's a lot of responsibility for a dead man," I murmured.

"That's the thing," she said. "You won't be dead much longer. Not like this. Not here. Not with us."

I looked at her then, properly looked at her. She wasn't being dramatic. She wasn't even angry. Just… sad. The kind of quiet sad that settles in your chest and makes tea taste wrong.

"You think I'll move on soon."

"Yes," she said simply. "You're getting justice. You're piecing it together. The universe doesn't let you stick around for that bit."

"Well, that's rubbish," I said. "The universe clearly needs a better HR department."

She gave me a smile that said this might not be the time for jokes. "It's not fair on Bob. He's already lost a family. He doesn't need to lose another."

"I didn't mean to be—"

"I know," she cut in. "I know. But it's happening anyway."

I tried to joke it off. "You know, I always imagined my afterlife would involve more clouds and less paperwork."

"Don't deflect, Tony."

"Would *you* miss me?" I asked, suddenly serious.

She didn't answer straight away. She stared into the fire like she was hoping it might change the subject for her. Eventually, she nodded.

"Yes," she said, very quietly. "I'm going to miss you."

"That's good," I said. "Because I'd miss you too."

She blinked, and I could see she was holding back something. Not tears, ghosts don't really do those, but the emotional equivalent. Teardrops of the soul.

"I've been dead for eighty years," she said softly. "Most of that time I've been... numb. Not unhappy, just... waiting. Like I was on pause. Then you turned up."

"Sorry about that," I said, weakly.

She gave a small laugh. "Don't be. You made me feel alive again, Tony, as mad as that sounds for a dead person. You made me laugh. You made me feel things; feel things I hadn't felt in decades."

I didn't know what to say. Before I could say anything.

"You made me feel less dead."

She looked at me, properly now, her eyes bright and haunted in the best kind of way.

"You made me want things again," she said. "A future. A family." Then a long pause as she looked away again "But that's not something I get, is it!"

… and there it was, the truth, laid bare between us like a library book returned late with a polite apology and biscuit crumbs.

"I don't know," I said. "Maybe we can write our own rules."

She shook her head. "It doesn't work like that."

We sat in silence again. Not the comforting kind this time, but the kind that presses on your shoulders like too many blankets.

Then the door opened and Angie strode in, a whirlwind of energy and resolve. She stopped when she saw us.

"Oh," she said, clearly sensing she'd walked into something heavy. "I was just looking for Gary."

She hovered for a second, then wisely retreated. "I'll, um... leave you two to it."

The door swung shut again.

Betty turned to me, blinking away the weight of the moment. "So... how did it go at the police station?"

It was such a mundane question that it made me laugh. A laugh that broke the tension like a dropped tray of teacups, but it didn't last long.

"We got him," I said softly. "Lord Percy. D.I Marsh, the inspector, is poking into everything now. Angie did great, had him eating out of her hand. He even knows Clarence's real name, Colin 'Bloomin' Briggs, curtesy of Gary no-less. There's movement, Betty. Real movement."

She nodded, and her face crumpled just slightly.

"So that means…"

We sat, shoulder to spectral shoulder, with nothing more to say. The fire crackled, the beer taps clinked behind the bar, and Bob's laughter, followed by the sound of a duck's insistent quacking, echoed faintly from the teepees on the green.

"I don't want to go," I said quietly.

She wasn't looking at me when she whispered "I don't want you to either" her shoulders dropped. "But the train has already left the station Tony, the police are following up and it won't be long now"

Standing up, placing a hand delicately on my shoulder, we looked at each other, no words, no drama, just that warm, ghostly pressure that still managed to say everything. Then, as if the very act of speech would have cracked something inside her, she turned and glided away. Her footsteps didn't echo, they never did, and of course never would, but somehow the air noticed she was leaving. She headed for the staircase that wound gently upward, curling around the great, uneven spine of the Rose and Crown. That staircase had seen generations of feet, boots, paws, and the occasional drunken tumble, but it had always saved a little of itself for Betty. Even now as I watched, it seemed to bend slightly toward her as she ascended. She passed the picture rail where her height had been marked in pencil over the years: Betty, aged five. Betty, aged nine (with a scrawled "won the Maypole race!"). Betty, aged twelve-and-a-half, with "still wants to be a pilot" written next to it in her dad's spidery script. Her form shimmered faintly in the low lamplight, her outline bending with the age of the place, like light filtering through whisky. Then she was gone. Just the faint scent of tea and lavender lingered, and a feeling in the chest, as though someone had pressed their cheek gently against your heart.

The Rose and Crown knew Betty. She'd grown up here after all. Her father had pulled pints, shouted at the darts team, and raised a daughter. Her room, Betty's room, was sacred ground. It was never let out. Not once. The passing hikers with plastic raincoats and mud-caked boots were welcome to any room, but not that one. Even the spreadsheet-savvy types who occasionally poked at the Rose and Crown's finances with polite frowns never dared question the blank square where Room 4's revenue should be. There was no rota for it. No bookings. It just was.

She passed all of it without looking back, and still, it looked after her.

She hadn't said goodnight. Not really. But ghosts, you'll learn, don't say goodbye like the living do. They *feel* their farewells. They send them in glances, in quiet gestures, in the way they disappear into shadow rather than light.

I turned back to the bar, where the fire still crackled, where the chairs still wobbled and the wallpaper still clung to the wall like it was doing it a favour. But none of it felt the same.

Because she wasn't there, and when Betty wasn't in the room, you felt the gap like a pulled tooth.

It struck me then; how strange this afterlife business was. I didn't think ghosts *changed*. I assumed we were fixed in time like old portraits or bad hairstyles. But Betty was changing. Not her face or her clothes, but something deeper. Something like... hope.

… and hope, for the dead I'm learning, is a dangerous thing. Because once you hope, you start to want… and once you start to want…

Well. That's when things get tricky. It almost feels like living.

Clearly I'm in trouble. Of all the times in my life to fall in love, I waited until I was dead. So much irony.

Feeling the weight of unspoken words and unresolved emotions, I decided to take a walk. The village green beckoned, its expanse bathed in the silvery glow of the full moon. The snow, though still present, had begun to melt, revealing patches of damp earth and the occasional brave blade of grass. Each droplet that fell from the trees seemed to echo the transient nature of my current existence.

As I meandered, the familiar quack of the village duck reached my ears. There it was, perched near the pond, eyeing me with a mix of curiosity and suspicion. I gave it a nod, a silent acknowledgment of our shared nocturnal habits.

Suddenly, a burst of laughter pierced the quiet night. Bob, the ever-energetic spirit of a child, came running towards me, his arms outstretched. I caught him mid-leap, spinning him around as his laughter filled the air.

"Time for bed, young man," I said, setting him down gently.

He looked up at me, his eyes gleaming. "Will you climb trees with me in the morning?"

I hesitated, the weight of impending justice and its consequences pressing down on me. "We'll see, Bob. We'll see."

He grinned like I'd promised him a trip to the moon. He didn't need certainty. Just the idea. Just the hope. To him, I was just Tony. The man who played buffalo and made duck noises. He gave a quick salute, his new thing, and ran off towards the pub with a joyful whoop, skipping in the kind of lopsided way that told you he'd never quite decided how knees were supposed to work.

I watched him go, and something in my chest twisted. In a good way, and in a bad way, and every way in between. That little boy believed in me. That was a miracle, in any form of life.

From the direction of the teepees, a soft chanting began, a melodic harmony that resonated with the very soul of the village. The notes danced on the breeze, intertwining with the rustling leaves and the gentle drip of melting snow. It was a lullaby for the restless, a balm for the weary.

The full moon hung low in the sky, its reflection shimmering in the puddles that dotted the green. The melting snow, once a blanket of purity, now revealed the imperfections beneath. It mirrored my own journey, uncovering truths, facing realities, and the inevitable change that follows.

The night deepened, and with it, the realisation that change was imminent. But for now, under the watchful eye of the moon and the comforting chorus from the teepees, I allowed myself a moment of peace, cherishing the present before the dawn of a new chapter.

For a loud American who always had a funny quip to hand. All the jokes had stopped.

CHAPTER ELEVEN

TIME DOESN'T SHOUT "SURPRISE!" BEHIND YOU

"Ferrari, get up, you lazy tike."

My eyes open blearily. Ghost sleep isn't so much sleep as it is an interdimensional pause with optional melancholia. We don't snore. We don't toss and turn. But we do... fade. Ghosts, you see, still need rest. Not for the body, which we left behind with taxes and sock elasticity, but for the mind. There's only so much brooding you can do in a day before your ectoplasm starts to vibrate at frequencies known only to abandoned fax machines, microwaves and Trevor.

In ghost-sleep, you don't dream in the normal sense. You relive things, moments, feelings, what you should have said, what you didn't say, and the time you misquoted a proverb during a breakup. Sometimes you dream you're alive again. The first few times, it's comforting. Familiar. But as the weeks go by, those dreams start to feel like lies your brain is telling itself for comfort.

Last night, I dreamt I was in the bookshop. Betty was humming softly behind the till, Bob was scribbling on a receipt pad, and I was polishing the front window while outside the snow fell sideways. I turned around, and there was the duck, wearing a monocle and reading Voltaire. That's when I knew I wasn't in Kansas anymore. Or, to be precise, not in Finsbury anymore.

When I "woke up," if that's what you call re-solidifying your thoughts enough to form a sentence, Reverend Miles Abraham was floating at the end of my bed looking like The Ghost of Breakfast Disapproval.

"Ferrari, you lazy tike, get up!"

I blinked. Which in ghost terms is more of a mental flicker than a physical one. "Why?"

"You have an appointment."

"With who?"

"Chief Ahyvda Wohali."

"Who?""

"Chief Thunder Eagle."

He didn't wait for follow-up questions. He vanished with a puff of moral superiority and possibly incense.

I got up, it was first light. The air was thick with the sense that something was about to shift. I drifted downstairs and out of the Rose and Crown into the cool, quiet of the village green. I had a preexisting appointment with trees and Bob so I couldn't hang around too long.

The snow was melting more quickly now, in that sad, splotchy way where everything's still technically winter but the season's clearly packing its bags. The duck, bless its cantankerous soul, winked at me from the edge of the pond like I was trespassing on its particularly sopping bit of real estate and it was keeping a close eye.

I took a few steps toward the firelight flickering between the teepees. My ghost-feet didn't leave prints in the half-melted snow, but I felt the crunch in memory. The air was thick with the scent of woodsmoke and something older, something that smelled like memory.

Chief Ahyvda Wohali stood near the central fire, his silhouette framed by the dancing flames. His regalia a tapestry of feathers, beads, and leather, each piece telling a story older than the apparition of the village itself. He turned as I approached, his eyes reflecting the firelight and something deeper. He had the same smile as when he chased Bob, mischievous I guess I would call it.

"Tony," he greeted me, his voice a low rumble that seemed to resonate with the earth beneath us. "Thank you for coming."

He gestured for me to sit beside him on a log near the fire. As I settled in, the warmth of the flames seeped into me, not physically, of course, but in that way that ghosts feel warmth: as a memory of comfort.

For a moment, we sat in silence, the crackling fire filling the space between us. Then, the Chief spoke.

"You've been making progress," he said, more statement than question.

"Progressing, Chief. Slowly, but surely. The threads are unravelling, and the truth is beginning to emerge. Angie's been incredible. She's got the police looking into Lord Percy. The books are the key."

He nodded slowly. "Those books are more than just pages and ink. They are the voices of my ancestors, the stories of our people.

They were never meant to be hidden away in private collections or government warehouses that do not understand their significance." His gaze drifted toward the horizon. "Justice is not merely about retribution; it's about restoration. For my people, for all those whose voices have been silenced, For the ancestors, for the land itself."

I felt the weight of his words settle over me. "I want that too," I said. "But I'm also aware that once justice is served, I might... move on."

He looked at me, his expression unreadable. "That troubles you?"

I hesitated. "Yes. There are people here I've come to care about. Betty, Bob... Angie. Leaving them behind isn't easy."

The Chief nodded. "Connections are the threads that bind us, in life and beyond. But sometimes, letting go is part of the journey."

We sat in silence again, the fire crackling between us. In the distance, I could hear the faint sound of singing, voices rising and falling in a melody that seemed to echo through time.

"The snow is melting," I said, more to myself than to him.

He looked out across the green. "Yes. A sign of change. Of renewal.

I pondered his words, the gravity of them settling in. "What happens when justice is served? What will happen to this village, this manifestation, disappear?"

A gentle smile played on his lips. "Some will move on, their purpose fulfilled. Many have been waiting for this moment, their souls yearning for closure, including mine. But not all. The justice this serves will not touch everyone and their journey will not end with it; it transforms. Those who remain will visit the ancestors, each in their own time, in their own way and walk the paths of their memories. Time, for them, is a dance between the past and the present."

He paused, eyes turned toward the horizon as if watching something move through the wind. Then, in a voice that shimmered like smoke from sacred fire, he said,
"Time is a woven sky, threads of spirit stretched across moments, past and yet to come. In life, your soul moves through this weaving with purpose. But in death... the thread frays. We scatter, like feathers caught in many breezes, a whisper in one age, a shadow in another. Still, we seek the others, our pieces, our people. For though we drift, we are not lost. We are always of the same cloth."

We sat in comfortable silence, the fire crackling between us, the village stirring with the gentle rhythms of life, or afterlife. Children's laughter mingled with the distant beat of drums, a symphony of continuity and change.

"Chief," I began, my voice part intrigue, part absolute confusion, "you mentioned seeking the other pieces. I understand that when we achieve justice, the fragments of our souls all come together, allowing us to *move on*. But are you saying that before you *move on* you can visit your ancestors? Or perhaps the parts of them that are scattered across different times?"

He reached for a small stick and began to draw in the melting frost at our feet. Spirals. Circles. Arcs that looped back and crossed over themselves like a plate of very philosophical spaghetti.

Looking at me, he knew I was struggling to understand "The river runs forward, yes, but it circles, too. It returns to places it once passed, carved deeper this time. So do we. Time remembers us. It waits where we laughed. Where we cried. It folds those moments and tucks them in a hollow tree, or a quiet song. We don't leave time. We walk it differently."

"So... not linear, then?" I offered, increasingly struggling.

The Chief gave me a look that could have fossilised a tulip. The kind of look that said, *you're asking the right question, but still making it entirely too complicated.*

"You keep thinking of time like a queue at a fish and chip shop. One thing after the other. Birth. Life. Death. Tuesday. Wednesday. Apocalypse. But that's not how it works, not here, not for ghosts and not for my people either. It's directional"

I blinked. "Directional?" Angie mentioned directional time, "I thought that was the same as linear time? This isn't easy, is it?"

"Well actually it is Tony," he said, voice patient like a teacher explaining fire to a damp log, "in this world, there is no straight line that doesn't bend when you're not looking."

"Time doesn't come from behind you, shout "surprise!" and head out in front of you. Time moves across the land. East to west, just like the sun. It's not about *you*, not your body, not your gaze. It's about the Earth. Time is tied to direction, not ego."

"So… instead of time happening *to* you," I said, trying to wrap my mind around it, "you move through it?"

"Yes. ". Time doesn't wrap around you like a scarf. You walk along it, like a trail. The trail doesn't follow you; you follow it. Time moves with the land. The wind. The sun's path."

He sat back, the firelight catching the lines of his face like tree bark full of memory. "When you die," he said softly, "you don't leave the path. You just stop needing feet to walk it. The trail?" He pointed up. "It's still there, it never left. It still goes on. You just see it all at once. The direction stays. The journey shifts."

I nodded slowly, but my brain was full. I had to think about this. I had the feeling like someone had just handed me the map upside down and it should suddenly make sense, but it didn't quite yet.

He gestured toward the teepees, where I could still hear faint singing. "My ancestors live there. Not just in place, but in moment. That moment can be yesterday. Or one hundred snows ago. Sometimes, it is now."

"But... how? How do you visit them? Those not in this present moment? Those pieces of soul lingering in the past?"

"My ancestors, and yours, linger in places of significance, in moments of strong emotion. They are the echoes of laughter by the river, the shadows of sorrow beneath a tree. Sometimes, when the wind is just right, and the spirit is willing, we can find these pieces, commune with them, and seek understanding."

He tapped his own temple and went quiet. He was searching for a way my poorly trained brain would understand. "The soul is a house with many rooms. In life, you walk through them in order. Kitchen. Hall. Bedroom. In death..." He spread his hands wide. "You realise the house never had doors. Only curtains. You can walk wherever your spirit remembers where to go."

My brain did a small somersault trying to keep up.

"So, I can walk," I repeated, "wherever my spirit remembers where to go?"

The Chief gave me a long look that managed to be patient, amused, reverent, and faintly patronising all at once, the look of a man who's been teaching cosmology to people who think the universe stops at the pub car park.

"Yes, Tony," he said, "if your spirit remembers it, you can walk there. Ghosts don't only haunt places. They haunt memories of places."

Tapping his head again, as if pointing out a particularly stubborn attic. "When you were alive you didn't visit the past with your feet, but with your heart and in your memories or daydreams."

I blinked. "Isn't that what haunting is?"

"No," he said, waving that away with a small puff of smoke from the fire, "haunting is loitering. This is different. This is travelling."

He poked the fire with a stick. "Every strong emotion leaves a thread. You've got thousands trailing behind you right now, Tony Ferrari. Like a cat who's fought a ball of wool and lost."

I looked behind me and grimaced. "So, I just follow the wool?"

He grinned. "Exactly. Tug the thread, and if the thread remembers you, it pulls back."

I stared into the fire. It crackled knowingly, like it had done this conversation before and was just waiting for me to catch up.

"Could I take someone with me?" I asked. "If… if I wanted? Or could someone take me to a place or time of their memories?"

The Chief looked at me thoughtfully. "Only if their spirit is good. Clean. Honest. Only if they wish to come. You cannot drag a ghost where their memory doesn't want to follow. That's possession and a side of the spirit world we don't follow."

"… and if they do come?"

He gave a small shrug. "Then they'll see what you see. Hear what you hear. Feel what you feel."

"But wouldn't that be… dangerous?"

The Chief's face creased with something that might have been laughter or indigestion. "Tony, you're dead. The only danger now is forgetting why you still care."

I thought about Betty. The look in her eyes when she hugged Bob.

About the smile that faded. I thought about how, despite being dead, I still felt incredibly alive whenever she was near.

"If Betty or Bob could take me with them" I said, slowly trying to piece together the scrambled thoughts in my head. "To walk with me, in the places their spirit remembers. Am I in the time they were there, or still in my time"

"So, let's say that Bob has a trail of wool thread behind him still," I ventured, grasping for understanding. "Then, could we pull on one of those threads and go back in time to when he was alive?"

The Chief shook his head slowly, "No, not to when he was living. The earliest you can go back is to when he first moved from the living plane and started vibrating in the dead one."

I frowned, the metaphor of vibrating in the dead plane conjuring images of spectral tuning forks and ghostly harmonics.

He chuckled, the sound rich and warm. "It's a way of saying that when a soul transitions, it leaves behind echoes, resonances. These are the threads you can follow. Not the moments of life, but the moments of transition, of significance. They're like footprints in the snow, fading but still traceable."

I considered this, the idea that I could follow these spectral footprints to moments of emotional weight. "So, if I wanted to walk with Betty or Bob, to share in their memories, I could?"

The Chief nodded. "If their hearts are good, and if they choose to walk beside you, they may follow. Ghosts move easiest through the places where their emotions held tightest. Joy is a strong current. So is sorrow. Love... even more so."

I shook my head trying get the jumble of thoughts in some sort of order.

The Chief's eyes twinkled with a knowing light, the fire casting dancing shadows across his weathered face. He leaned back slightly, the creak of his bones echoing softly in the stillness of the night. The village around us seemed to hold its breath, the murmurs of the spirits blending with the crackling of the fire.

My brain hurt. It wasn't just time going in circles.

He reached into his cloak and pulled out something small, round, smooth. A stone. He handed it to me.

"This is not magical," he said. "It will not open portals or summon storms. But it is real. Real things help focus the soul. Hold the stone in your hands, wrapped together tight, and then focus."

I turned the stone over in my fingers. It was warm, impossibly warm for a ghost to feel. Etched with something that looked suspiciously like a duck.

"Did you carve this?" I asked, squinting.

"No," he said, standing. "But the duck insisted."

With that, he gave me that mischievous smile and walked away, back into the shadows of time and smoke, his silhouette flickering between worlds.

I sat there, stone in hand, the firelight trying to warm thoughts that had long since gone cold. It cast flickering shadows that seemed to whisper *answers*, but only in a dialect my brain had never learned. I had learned something important, yes, but what exactly? Something about time not being a line, souls being rooms with curtain walls, and history folding like a particularly sentimental napkin. All very poetic, yes. All very spiritually uplifting. But I was still dead. Still stuck, and in any moment, I might go "phut" and disappear in a puff of remorse whilst clutching a stone like it might crack open the universe if I held it the right way.

What did it mean? What *good* was knowing that time was a spiral with commitment issues, if I still had no idea where I was supposed to go?

But then…. What if I could go back, back in time? That's the dream, isn't it? The impossible itch in every soul. To the time someone was just murdered, when there is still time to find justice for them. To a time where it isn't too late for Bob or Betty to find justice and *move on* like everyone else? I couldn't stop them from dying. I know that. I'm dead myself, which tends to bring a sort of clarity, in much the same way that falling down a well clears your schedule for the week. But maybe, just maybe, if I really am a detective, ghostly or not, trench coat optional, I can still solve something. I could still *matter*. Maybe I can be the hand that points, the whisper in the dark, the gumshoe who does more than haunt the scene of the crime.

If I could give them that, Bob, Betty, the Chief, the ancestors, the whole spectral troop, then maybe, just maybe, they could *move on*. Whatever that even means, because *moving on* could mean absolutely anything. No one knows, not even the Chief. A second place. A final place. A better place. Heaven, if you're feeling theological. Or maybe something stranger. A new dimension made entirely of Sunday afternoons and fond farewells. Was it a higher plane? Was there a gift shop? Did it include dinner? Or was it just the cosmic compost heap, the great starry mulch pile, where all souls are recycled, repurposed, and reborn. Perhaps I'll come back as a badger.

But then… what?

What if I helped them move on? What if I helped *Bob* move on?

Would Betty thank me? Would she *want* that?

What if moving on was just another kind of goodbye?

Wasn't that the big joke? The big cosmic laugh? Solve the mystery, win the day, uncover the ancient injustice, then poof! Everyone evaporates in a golden haze of karmic paperwork, and you're left alone on the green, waving goodbye to the afterlife's best moments, like a lonely man at a bus stop that only runs once every hundred years.

Was that what "justice" meant? That you got to feel righteous and bereft in equal measure?

What about Bob? The boy with a grin too big for his face and a giggle that made ghosts feel human again. What if I found a way to give him peace, and in doing so, robbed Betty of the one soul who kept her sane?

What if the reward for all of this, the investigation, the haunting, the spectral high-fives and low-grade ectoplasmic trauma, was that I got to watch everyone I cared about *move on and lose them*?

The fear hit me like a misplaced custard pie: comic, sudden, and vaguely sticky. In that moment of stickiness clearly some mental capacity became dislodged or unhinged and another thought scampered in.

Because if this all ended, if the final clue was found, and the final truth spoken, what was left?

The memory of softly crunching snow followed behind me as I stalked across the green, my brain leaking from the overflow of thoughts, questions, fears and hopes. The great oak tree that stood, timeless and slightly smug, in the beer garden of the Rose and Crown, waved at me in the morning breeze. It had been there for centuries, growing knotty with secrets, its branches climbed by the living, the dead, and, on one regrettable occasion, an inebriated vicar getting closer to God. The tree bore witness to love, laughter, ghosts arguing over pub quiz answers, and the peculiar intersection of the physical and metaphysical known only to those who'd once paid council tax and now passed through walls.

This morning, its bark glistened with melting frost, the faded moon still visible in the pale blue early morning sky, hanging like an ancient eye keeping its own kind of time. I could feel something gathering, not wind, not memory exactly, but purpose.

I was walking not just toward a tree, but toward a choice, maybe even a future. Not the kind measured in birthdays and council bins, but in moments that mattered, that stuck. I was no longer just chasing justice or dodging purgatory.

I was walking toward something that was… I can only explain as the feeling of – of family.

Because for all the uncertainty swirling in time's peculiar plumbing, one thing was clear.

What mattered most in life, death, or the afterlife, were the people asleep in the pub or swinging from a branch behind the Rose and Crown.

I had an inkling. Not a full-blown inkle you understand, not even a solid theory, but an idea that was brewing, skulking about in the attic of my brain, rattling the floorboards and refusing to come down for tea. It was hiding somewhere in the cluttered recesses of my mind, wedged between a half-remembered TV jingle and a growing suspicion that I should've paid more attention in Philosophy 101. But there it was, a slippery, half-formed notion that, if I could just coax it into the light, might let me lose and win at the same time. Which sounded suspiciously like cheating, or possibly enlightenment. Either way, I liked the sound of it.

I had no plan, no grand speech, no ghostly bouquet of spectral roses. Just the weight of what I knew, and what I feared… and something else.   Hope.

CHAPTER TWELVE

THE FLORAL NIGHTIE AND AN UPPITY MR CHURCHILL

Bob, being a ghost child, climbed in that very specific way children have; with absolutely no concern for gravity, authority, or any branches that might be structurally unsound. His little ghost-hands scampered from limb to limb, the way squirrels do when they're late for something important. Despite having no corporeal weight to speak of, he still managed to snap a twig or two as he went, possibly out of sheer enthusiasm.

Betty stood beneath the great old oak tree, her hands clasped in front of her as if she were praying to the Spirit of Sensible Behaviour. Her eyes, wide with concern, followed Bob's every movement like a nervous parent watching their toddler juggle knives.

"Bob, Be careful!" she called up, her voice half-maternal instinct, half spectral dread.

I stepped beside her, watching the small boy-ghost wriggle his way into the crook of a high branch like it was his natural habitat. I tried not to smile too much, but it's hard not to when the undead are frolicking like it's a school field trip.

"Betty," I said gently, "he's already dead. Falling won't do much more damage."

She turned to look at me, her expression the ghostly equivalent of a withering glance softened by affection. "Yes, well. You don't switch off just because the child is no longer technically subject to gravity."

She had a point. Ghost logic was still an evolving science, and Betty had apparently signed up for the advanced course in Spectral Nurturing.

"Besides," she added, "he's adventurous. Like someone else I know."

I raised an eyebrow. "Are we talking about me or the duck?"

She smiled. "Yes."

That was Betty. Queen of the one-word double meaning.

Bob sat astride a thick branch like a pirate captain surveying his leafy domain. Below him, the world stretched out into familiar pockets: the Rose and Crown's beer garden, the duck by the pond pretending it wasn't watching us, a small village of ghostly Indian teepees, and Betty still wringing her hands as if ghost-parental anxiety was a full-time occupation.

I hesitated, hand on bark, foot poised on the lowest branch. There is something deeply unspoken about climbing a tree after you've died. It's not about danger, obviously. It's not even about common sense. It's about dignity. Or the loss thereof, in front of a pretty girl.

"Come on, Mr. Slow Coach !" Bob taunted from above, his ghostly legs kicking in the air with all the smug enthusiasm of someone who no longer feared splinters or grazes.

I hoisted myself up with a grunt. Ghosts, as it turns out, can still grunt. Nobody tells you that when you die either. There's no welcome pamphlet. Just a vague understanding that you can float through walls.

Up I went, branch by branch, my dignity lowering like a flag in a stiff breeze. Bob laughed so hard he nearly phased out of the tree.

"You okay down there, Grandpa? Need me to pull you up?"

I shot him a look that would've made a librarian cry. "You know, technically, I died about 150 years after you."

By the time I was halfway up, I was clutching a branch like it might suddenly declare its intention to bolt. The wind whistled through the leaves with a sound that felt suspiciously like snickering.

"Ghosts don't get vertigo," I muttered to myself.

"Scaredy cat," Bob replied.

I looked down. Betty had taken to pacing. Trevor had also arrived and was clearly so worried he peed against the bottom of the tree as a sign of support.

"You okay?" Betty asked, a flicker of real concern in her voice.

"He'll be fine" I called down

"I wasn't asking about him!" she smirked

"Yes. Just... enjoying the view" I said whilst trying not to look down.

"That's a no, isn't it?"

"Firm maybe."

Bob wriggled along a branch like a lovesick squirrel "Don't worry, we're nearly there. This branch is my favourite. You can see everything from here. The whole village, the pond, even the lane…"

He stopped.

"Uh-oh."

Now, I'm not a fan of children saying "uh-oh." It's rarely followed by winning the lottery.

"What is it?"

Bob squinted, then pointed. "Taxi. Coming down the lane."

"It's probably Gary," I said automatically. "Coming to pick up Angie."

But I could see his face scrunching up.

"It's not Gary. It's a mean taxi"

I craned my neck, trying to peer through the branches. The taxi was crawling down the lane like it knew it didn't belong, all hunched shoulders and guilty headlights. It bumped along the potholes with too much familiarity.

Then I saw it. The dent in the wing. Just behind the driver's side. A jagged smear of red paint clinging to the metal like a bad memory.

The same dent that had pinned me to a phone box just before Christmas. A Tony shaped dent you might say.

The world seemed to tilt.

"Bob," I said quietly, "get down. Go to Betty."

He didn't argue. He knew the tone. He started scrambling down like a ghost on a mission.

I followed, slower, the vertigo forgotten in a rush of cold realisation. The man in that cab, Clarence, Colin, whatever his real name was, he was here… and that meant trouble.

Betty met Bob as he jumped from the last branch. She caught him by the shoulders, pulling him close. She didn't ask questions. She didn't need to.

I dropped down behind them. The duck waddled over, heading towards the arriving taxi, with what I can only describe as a grumpy quack, which is impressive from a bird with no known vocabulary.

The taxi was already pulling into the pub car park like it had somewhere better to be but was willing to commit minor crimes in the meantime. It coughed once, dramatically, and died with a rattle that could've belonged to a nineteenth-century school bell. The man who'd driven it that fateful day stepped out, straightening his tie, sniffing the air. He looked up at the sign over the Rose and Crown door as if sizing up whether it was the sort of establishment that might require small talk or just a punch.

Then he stepped toward the front door. Which would've been straightforward, except Trevor was now lying across the threshold like the world's laziest dragon.

Trevor, the pub's semi-official pub dog-slash-local authority figure, opened one eye. He didn't growl. That would've required effort. Instead, he slowly began chewing a single back paw with the kind of deliberate indifference only achieved by dogs and committee chairmen.

I felt something twist in my ghost-gut.

Betty leaned close. "That's him?"

"Yes… and if he's here, Percy sent him."

"Where's Angie?" I asked, panic settling in.

"Room two," Betty said. "Reverend Miles had to give up his room."

We stared at the man as he walked towards the pub.

Betty's hand found mine.

The enemy had arrived. My murderer had arrived.

Bob clung to Betty's hand. "I don't like him."

Clarence attempted to step over Trevor.

Trevor sniffed his shoe. Then his ankle. Then yawned wide enough to suggest he could've swallowed Clarence whole if only he could be bothered.

Clarence muttered something under his breath and finally made it inside.

Inside the Rose and Crown, it was that quiet time of day where the only action came from the low mumble of the coffee machine, the slightly sinister creak of the floorboards and an occasional surprised jingle from the fruit machine.

"Excuse me," Clarence said to no one in particular. "I'm looking for someone."

Mavis was sitting on her usual stool, polishing her glasses with the sort of grim dedication usually reserved for forensic work. She looked up, squinted, and gave him the kind of smile that could sterilise cutlery.

"Who is it you're looking for, love?" she asked.

"A woman," Clarence said, adjusting his tie as if that might upgrade his credibility. "Dark hair. Mid-thirties. Sharp voice."

"You've just described half the Women's Institute," Mavis replied dryly.

"No," Clarence said, stepping forward. "She would have been here yesterday, long scarf."

"Ah," Mavis said, "you mean the clever one."

Clarence smiled like a man who thought he was being agreed with. "Yes. Exactly. Her."

"Room two," Mavis said. "Up the stairs, last on the left. Though I'd knock loudly. She's a sound sleeper. They were hoovering at 9 this morning."

As Clarence started toward the stairs, Mavis turned and muttered, "Not that I think you'll like what you find!"

I was already inside by then, floating just above the banister with Betty at my shoulder.

"We need to get to Angie," I whispered.

"You're a ghost," Betty whispered back. "Why are you whispering?"

"Habit."

We zipped past Clarence on the stairs. I managed to blow a cold wind down the back of his neck as we passed, which made him shiver and mutter something about draughty inns.

Upstairs, room two's door was shut, we floated through...

Inside, Angie stood near the window, cup of tea in one hand, notebook in the other, fully dressed, fully alert. She was the human embodiment of "I dare you to try it."

She didn't even look up when I floated in.

Betty zipped in beside me. "Clarence is downstairs, Mavis just told him your up here."

"She's clearly more observant before the first Sherry," Angie replied, sipping her tea. "So. What's the plan?"

"Plan?" I blinked.

"Yes," she said, finally looking at me. "You're the detective, remember? What are we going to do about Clarence?"

"I was hoping to improvise."

"Of course you were," Angie muttered, just as the floorboards creaked outside the room.

Clarence was at the door.

He knocked once, tentatively, like a man unsure if this was going to result in a conversation or get a vase to the face.

"Is it room service." she said, brightly. "Unless you've brought marmalade on toast and strong tea, I'm afraid you're already starting on the wrong foot."

"I'm looking for Miss Angela Robbins," Clarence said.

"I'm Miss Robbins."

"You are?"

"I'm also rather busy. What can I do for you, Mr...?"

"Churchill," he said, though clearly it wasn't.

"Really? How terribly historic of you. Do you also have a fondness for cigars and mildly alarming facial expressions?"

"What?"

"Well, Mr. Churchill, what is it?"

"I need to ask you a few questions." A pause, then: "Miss Robbins, can we speak?"

"Yes"

"I mean with the door open. There are certain questions that need answering," the voice said more sharply.

"Gosh, no. That would be terribly forward. I'm in my nightie, you see. It's floral and quite disarming, and I wouldn't want to give you any ideas. I really didn't sleep very well, they were hoovering at some unearthly hour of the morning, and then there is this duck, did you see it when you arrived, it has a real attitude. Reminds me a lot of my Auntie Flo who…"

"Miss Robbins," Clarence said, trying to wrest control of the conversation with the grace of a man chasing a balloon in a hurricane, "can we speak?"

"Yes, what is it Mr Churchill?"

"I'm afraid this is not optional." There was a pause. Then came the faint rattle of the doorknob.

"Now, that's not very polite," she said. "You wouldn't be trying to come in uninvited, me in my nightie and all, what would people say? My how they gossip. Are from a small village Mr. Churchill?"

The man outside exhaled through gritted teeth. "Miss Robbins, open this door. Or I will break it down."

"Your obviously in a very uppity mood Mr. Churchill, did you miss breakfast? It won't take me long to get dressed. I asked them to put the hot water on first thing, well after they had finished the hoovering, but it's still rather luke-warm. Would you be a love and give them a nudge downstairs for me. It would speed things up enormously and save me the trouble of yelling out the window again. I'm fairly certain the receptionist is hiding in the linen cupboard."

"I know the police called Percy Hall," he growled. "…and I know who the so-called book expert is."

"Do you?" she asked with exaggerated wonder. "Is it me? I'd love to be a book expert. Do you get a badge?"

"You've made enemies, Miss Robbins." More door handle rattling "I will give you ten seconds—"

"Then I will give you eleven," she snapped, suddenly steel behind the silk. "To take your grubby shoes and your borrowed threats and walk off my doorstep. Because if you try to force your way in here, you'll regret it… not just because I've barricaded the back door with a Victorian hat stand. I am also a black belt in Karate"

Betty and I exchanged glances. This woman was a true force of nature.

Leaning his forehead with a dull thud against the door, he closed his eyes. This was not going to plan at all. People just don't understand the pressures hired henchmen go through. Clarence tried to compose himself. Breathing exercises, the book had said. Centre yourself. Visualise success. Clarence had visualised Angie Robbins opening the door, inviting him in, gasping in horror, and confessing to everything while he enjoyed a complimentary biscuit. Instead, she'd refused to open the door and accused him of having unpolished shoes.

He checked his watch. Still early. Too early for violence. Possibly too early for coherent thought.

"I'll be waiting!" Clarence yelled at the door. He gave it a swift kick, which did nothing more than scuff the toe of his already suspect brogues and trigger an indignant creak from the floorboards. The Rose and Crown, being the sort of building that had been disappointed in people since 1784, responded with all the menace of a sigh and a draft.

With a huff he turned from the door and immediately collided with what at first appeared to be a very erect, slightly waxy Victorian librarian. It was, in fact, Hector, the landlord.

"Sir," Hector said, his tone clipped with the kind of politeness that suggested he'd happily report you to the Queen, "we try to avoid guests raising their voices in the upstairs hallways. Unless it's singing. ... and preferably after pudding."

Clarence blinked. "I wasn't yelling."

Hector arched one eyebrow better described as Romanesque rather than neoclassical. "You rattled the door handle."

"It was a nudge."

"It was a full rattle. Possibly a jangle. Borderline clatter."

Clarence rubbed his temple. "Look, I just need to talk to the woman in that room. I'm here on official business."

Hector consulted his clipboard like it contained the lost gospels of hospitality. "Are you from the council sir?"

"No."

"Health inspector?"

"No."

"Plumber?"

Clarence paused. It was tempting. Plumbers had carte blanche to do just about anything short of minor surgery.

"No," he sighed. "I'm... private."

"Oooooh," said Hector, eyes glinting. "One of those. We had a private detective here once. Wore a trench coat. Made rather rude observations about the pork pies. Smelled of Old Spice cologne and dusty books."

"I'm nothing like that."

"Shame. He was quite funny."

Meanwhile, in the corner of the ceiling where I was hovering, all eyes of the ghostly community turned my way.

"I have never heard a more accurate description," Betty muttered. "Old Spice?"

"Possibly" I whispered, "perhaps yes." I frowned. "I really don't remember ever being here when I was alive."

"You don't remember a lot. But clearly, part of you does. Maybe this place matters."

Back in the corridor, Hector leaned just a little closer to Clarence. "So what's your business, exactly?"

Clarence bristled. "Private enquiry. That woman, Miss Robbins, is interfering in things she doesn't understand." Then tried to push past, but Trevor emerged from the stairwell, did a disapproving circle, and settled squarely across the hallway like a sentient velvet rope.

Hector folded his arms. "I wouldn't. Trevor's on a no-nonsense diet."

Clarence looked down at the dog. The dog looked up and smiled affectionately. Clarence lost.

Hector tapped his clipboard again. "Now, sir, I think you should leave. You're not welcome to upset our guests. Especially ones staying in Room Two."

Clarence clenched his fists, glared at the Trevor, muttered something about this "not being over," and stomped back down the stairs.

Hector turned back to the corridor. "Another fine morning at the Rose and Crown," he said to no one in particular.

From behind the door of Room Two, Angie raised her teacup and toasted the hat stand barricading her door. "Well done, Colonel. That's another one routed."

Betty Giggled.

Downstairs, the pub exhaled. Upstairs, I felt the memory settle into my ghostly gut like a long-lost penny finding its piggy bank.

Somewhere in The Rose and Crown, the past was beginning to wake up. Outside a black dented taxicab roared off down the lane before the first pothole took a hearty bite at the rear tyre like an angry badger with a grudge.

The car juddered, swerved, and let out a mechanical protest not dissimilar to a trombone being insulted. A low-hanging branch, which had never been low-hanging until just that moment, gave the roof a polite thwack.

The lane narrowed, the wind picked up, and a sudden gust caught the cab's wing mirror with an audible "tink," as though the village itself had flicked it on the nose. The mist rolled back in, dense and oddly sulphurous, like the memory of boiled cabbage at a school dinner, and the headlights flickered as though caught mid-blink.

Even the birds got involved. A murder of crows took flight as the cab passed, swooping dramatically in its wake. One particularly theatrical crow dropped what looked like an old dog biscuit on the bonnet, then cawed something that might have been an insult.

By the time the cab reached the bend at the edge of the green, the lane had committed to its sabotage fully. The gravel had formed ridges. The hedge leaned in slightly… and something, somewhere, was humming in a key that made the engine stutter.

The Rose and Crown didn't chase him away. It simply allowed the village to decide for itself.

Clarence's cab roared petulantly as it bumped, scraped, and shuddered its way out of view. The exhaust spat defiantly at a daffodil, which remained unimpressed.

Inside, the Rose and Crown stood quietly triumphant. The beer glasses on the shelf above the bar gently buzzed and rattled without reason. Mavis slipped off her stool to look out the window and up at the clouds. "They haven't done that since Concorde flew over" she muttered.

The door to Room Two creaked just enough to feel smug and up in the rafters, something ancient and unseen exhaled like a house settling its bones. The pub knew its people… and it did not care for Clarence. It didn't mind a little drama, but manners are manners old chap, and he had none.

"Angie, you were marvellous," beamed Betty, the admiration in her voice glowing like a Gaslamp on a foggy evening. She had the kind of smile that could warm a whole WI meeting room. "Are you really a black belt?"

"Course not, silly," Angie said, laughing, with a flick of her wrist that could've disarmed a particularly confused pigeon. "But I've seen all the films, and I can make all the right sounds—ahhh!

Huhh!" She demonstrated with a series of swishing hand movements that looked like she was either warding off invisible wasps or auditioning for a low-budget martial arts musical.

"It's all in the noise, really," she added. "Confidence. You flap with enough enthusiasm and they think twice. Worked on my year nine class during indoor PE. "

Betty nodded solemnly. "You were like a caffeinated Jackie Chan with curlers."

I gave a half-laugh, but my expression didn't follow through. "He'll be back, though," I said, watching the door as if Clarence might materialise through the coat rack like a budget Voldemort. "We need a better plan."

"Report his visit," I added, turning to Angie. "To the Sergeant at the station. Make it official. Paper trail. Something that says, 'Hello, someone threatened me, please put that in your nice filing cabinet and maybe give him a stern talking-to.'"

"Witness protection?" said the Reverend, appearing from behind a curtain as if summoned by the phrase, or possibly just eavesdropping with ecclesiastical flair.

He was holding a mug that said *'Caffeine and Confessionals'* and wearing the kind of expression that suggested he'd spent the last ten minutes listening in and waiting for the right line.

"I think you've been watching too much telly" I said.

"Possibly," he conceded, "but it's very educational. I watched *Line of Duty* last week. It's all corruption and acronyms and people being angrily interrogated under fluorescent lighting. Very cathartic. I'm convinced I now know how to break into a municipal council meeting."

"I don't need witness protection," Angie said, brushing a crumb off her skirt with the gravitas of a woman who has bested both Ofsted and several overconfident men in pub quizzes. "I need people to stop underestimating me."

"Still," I said, "Clarence turning up at the door wasn't just rude. It was strategic. Percy sent him, didn't he?"

Betty frowned. "Then he knows who she is."

"Which means," I said, rubbing my temples in a very noir detective way that would've suited a trench coat and low lighting, "we are now officially in the second act of a mystery. The stakes are up. The villain has entered the scene, and someone's going to make a very bad decision before tea."

"That'll be Trevor," said the Reverend, peering out the window as the dog attempted to eat a fallen scone whole.

"Reporting it is sensible," Betty said gently, the voice of reason wrapped in a cashmere cardigan of charm. "You were threatened, Angie. Even if he didn't get in, it was still intimidation."

"… and he said he'd be back," I reminded her.

Angie sighed, looking toward the curtains billowing in the breeze like they too were eavesdropping. "Ok. Fine. I'll go this afternoon. Gary's coming over, he can take me."

"I just wish I knew what Percy's next move was," I muttered.

In some stories, the cavalry arrives on horseback. In ours, it might just arrive with biscuits and well-filed paperwork.

"Right then, Ferrari," said the Reverend, pointing a spectral finger like a holy accusatory compass.

"You've been here before, haven't you?"

"I said that too, didn't I?" Angie chimed in, with the air of someone who always enjoys being right, especially when it's about someone else being wrong. "I *told* you, Tony, you must've turned up here when you were alive at some point."

"Well I never *saw* him," huffed the Reverend, folding his arms in the time-honoured tradition of men who haven't seen things but feel very strongly that they should have. He turned to Betty. "Did you?"

Betty tilted her head and squinted at me as if trying to read the fine print of my personality. "No, I don't think so," she said slowly. "But then again, he *is* terribly forgettable." She winked at me like a grenade with a faulty pin.

"Angie," I said, attempting to wrestle the conversation back from the brink of farce, "can you talk to the landlord? He seemed to remember me. Maybe ask him about the chat with Clarence? Mention a rude American detective in a trench coat who apparently smelled like 1978."

"Where *did* you get Old Spice, anyway?" Angie asked, her nose wrinkling as if the scent were trying to escape the memory unscathed. "They stopped making that decades ago. Surely?"

"I found it in a drawer at the bookshop," I said defensively. "One of those Christmas gift packs. Still sealed. Probably considered a historical artefact now."

"It was all the rage during the war," Betty added helpfully. "I liked it"

A little moral support there. I liked that.

Whilst Angie trotted downstairs to interrogate the Landlord in her patented mix of charm and passive-aggressive eyebrow work, about his offhand comment to Clarence concerning a "rude private detective who smelled like Old Spice and unresolved trauma" (which, of course, was me), Betty and I were left alone.

Well. Not entirely alone.

Trevor had managed to meander his way into room 2 and jumped on the bed, turned three times and was asleep before the third turn had completed.

The Reverend, on the other hand, had muttered something about Norwegian Psalms, spiritual fortification, and the pressing need to reorganise his ectoplasmic sermon notes, before vanishing in a dramatic swirl of superiority.

So that left me, Betty, and Trevor (who, to be fair, was doing his best impression of a pillow and succeeding admirably).

Now, let me be clear: I didn't plan to put my arms around Betty. It wasn't premeditated. I hadn't spent the morning thinking, *"You know what this murder investigation needs? A nice ghostly cuddle."*

But the idea, *the* idea, had finally crawled out from the shadows in the attic of my brain, brushed the cobwebs off its trousers, and started doing calisthenics behind my eyes. It wasn't fully formed yet, but it was loud and energetic and insisted I act now, immediately, without asking permission from the more sensible regions of my mind, which were still upstairs arguing with each other over whether this would be an emotional breakthrough or a deeply awkward spectral incident that would be talked about in hushed tones for the next hundred years.

I turned to Betty.

She was looking at the fireplace, or where the fireplace had been before someone bricked it up and put a commemorative plate of Princess Diana in front of it.

"Betty," I said, which was not the most romantic opening, but I stand by it.

She turned, mildly startled, as if I'd just asked her opinion on post-war British biscuits. Before she could speak, I stepped forward and did something bold, foolish, and completely against ghost protocol.

I put my arms around her.

Now, you have to understand; hugging is already complicated. There are arms to consider, and breathing, and social norms, and whether someone is holding a cup of tea. But ghost-hugging? That's an entirely different kettle of existential fish. There are no limbs, technically. No mass. No temperature. Just willpower, emotion, and the strange, wobbly metaphysics of the recently deceased.

Betty went stiff. Like she'd just been hit by a very polite emotional train.

I panicked, slightly. Not the flailing kind, but the internal kind, where you run in circles inside your own head and scream silently into a pillow that no longer exists. I was about to back off, apologise, maybe pretend I'd been possessed by a particularly affectionate poltergeist… but then...

She relaxed.

It was subtle. A shift in pressure that wasn't really pressure. A softening of presence maybe. A willingness to occupy the same quantum corner of reality with someone else.

Then it happened.

Our edges touched.

Not physically, because physics had long since decided we were someone else's problem, but spectrally. Our frequencies aligned.

Our vibrations harmonised. Our auras stopped glaring suspiciously at each other and instead said, "Oh, it's you. Fancy meeting you here."

There was no dramatic flash of light. No celestial choir. No glowing thread of destiny wrapping around us like a saccharine Christmas special.

But it was good.

More than good.

It was like discovering a song you didn't know you loved was already playing on a radio you didn't know you had inside you. The song was soft and warm and had a saxophone solo in just the right place.

We stood like that for what might've been a moment or an eternity. Ghost time is weird. It doesn't tick; it *meanders*. It doesn't count down; it *wanders off to make tea and forgets what it was doing*. But however long we stayed there, phasing together like two slightly embarrassed particles in love, it felt... right.

Trevor coughed and opened one eye briefly, which was impressive, because he did that without waking up.

Neither of us spoke. It didn't feel like a moment that needed words. Words would've gotten in the way, like trying to explain the punchline of a joke while the laughter was still hanging in the air.

But still, *the idea*, the one that had driven me to this moment like a sheepdog with boundary issues, refused to be ignored. It wasn't just about the hug. It was about the plan. The sneaky, twisty, probably ill-advised plan that had started forming as I had walked over from the teepee village.

"I think I've found a loophole" I blurted.

The inkling was now less inkling and part formed idea. It was the kind of idea that let you lose and win at the same time. That let you throw the game board in the air and declare yourself both victor *and* martyr.

Betty pulled back slightly, just enough to look me in the eye.

"So?" she asked, her voice soft, amused, and carrying the faint static of someone who suspected she was about to be dragged into something deeply theatrical. "What are you thinking?"

"I'm thinking," I said, "that sometimes the best way to win is to let everyone think you've already lost."

"What?"

"I mean, I don't have to throw the whole game, in order to win"

She raised an eyebrow. "That sounds like the sort of thing someone says before getting arrested. Or elected."

"I was murdered by 2 people, by Clarence who drove the Taxi, but also by Lord Percy who arranged it"

"I know all that."

"For me to get justice, *move on*… yada yada yada, I need justice from both. Not one. Right?"

I looked at Betty.

She looked at me.

Then she smiled, and I don't mean one of those tight-lipped, socially acceptable, "I acknowledge your existence and will not report you to management" smiles. No. This was a *smile*. It was the kind that started at the mouth, strolled confidently up the cheeks, took a quick detour through her dimple, and did a triumphant jig behind her eyes. Her entire face beamed with mischief and curiosity and maybe, just maybe, a little bit of hope.

"I'm listening," she said, leaning in slightly. "… and you think hugging me is going to help solve your murder?"

"I think," I replied, "that it helped me remember I'm not in this alone."

That seemed to strike the right chord. Not just any chord, a major seventh with emotional resonance. She beamed. Properly this time. A wide, eyes-sparkly, teeth-visible beam of a smile. Not the kind of smile you give to tourists asking where the nearest toilet is. Not the kind of smile you give to a tax inspector when they ask if you have any undeclared income and you definitely do. This was a warm, genuine, knee-wobbling kind of smile that had *possibility* stitched into its corners.

"So?" she said again, eyes twinkling, "what's the loophole?"

Ah yes. The loophole.

There's always a loophole. Life is full of them. So's death, apparently. Bureaucracy is one of the few things that doesn't stop when your heart does. It just gets more... metaphysical.

"If I can get partial justice," I began slowly, because you have to be careful with these things, especially when using the word *partial* in a conversation about murder, revenge, and the afterlife, "then the first step is making the books public."

"The dodgy versions?" Betty asked.

"The dodgiest," I nodded.

"If those books are out in public for all to see," I continued, "then the Cherokee Nation can pursue their claim in court. They should. It's theirs. All of it. That part's justice. Real, tangible, not-theoretical justice. But..."

Here came the twist. There's always a twist. If this were a musical number, the lights would dim and the piano would slow down.

"In doing so," I said, "we don't bring *both* Clarence and Lord Percy down at the same time. We only get one. Clarence."

Betty blinked. "So... you'd let Lord Percy go free?"

"That's the idea."

She pulled back like I'd just suggested we spend eternity haunting a motorway rest stop. "Tony, that man has the moral compass of a damp sock. *He's* the one who ordered you to be murdered! Clarence is just the tool he used."

"Exactly," I said, as if I hadn't just proposed the afterlife's version of a plea bargain. "Percy was always going to be the bigger fish to fry. But you don't fry a big fish all at once. First, you catch the small slippery one and let the big one think he's safe, *then* you bring out the harpoon made of public outrage and spectral stubbornness."

Betty crossed her arms. "… and you're okay with that?"

"No," I said, honestly. "Not *okay*. But strategic. Percy's got friends in high places. The sort of places that have red leather chairs and portraits of people who died of gout. We will get him, but not now, not yet."

That little word did a lot of heavy lifting.

"Yet," I repeated. "*Yet* is the key word. I don't get justice *yet*. Which, as it turns out, might be the most important part of all this."

She raised an eyebrow. "You're telling me this whole afterlife quest thing, you know, your entire reason for floating about being sarcastic and moody, is about *delaying* justice?"

"Delaying *my* justice," I said. "So, others can get *theirs*. Look, I've been thinking about this the wrong way. Everyone acts like justice is a one-time deal. You get it, a trumpet sounds, angels weep, and you disappear in a puff of satisfied morality."

Betty stared. "Is that *not* what happens?"

"Apparently it doesn't have to be," I said, gesturing to my very un-trumpeted, very un-vanished self. "If we do this right, I can control *when* it happens. I can make it *our decision*."

I paused. Took a deep breath. Not because I needed one, I hadn't technically needed oxygen in a while, but because some habits die harder than the people who practice them.

"We get to choose the moment," I said. "Not fate. Not Percy. *Us*. Me and you Betty, we choose when or *if* I move on."

There was a silence.

Not the awkward kind.

The kind that sits comfortably between two people who are very much on the same page, even if they're not quite ready to read it out loud yet.

Betty looked at me. Not through me, or past me, or over my shoulder at Trevor on his back, paws twitching in rabbit territory. She looked *at* me.

"You're serious about this?" She gave me a long, appraising look. "You really want to wait before moving on? To keep... haunting?"

"Not haunting. Sticking around with intent," I said. "There's a difference. This is sticking around with you and Bob."

"I suppose if you say it in a British accent it sounds classy," she muttered.

"It always does," I said. "Even tax fraud sounds noble if you say it in Received Pronunciation."

She snorted. It was a beautiful, genuine, unladylike sound that made her seem more alive than I'd ever seen her. Which, considering she was dead, was an impressive achievement.

"So let me get this straight," she said. "We make sure the books are bought by someone who will make them public... not hold them in a private vault. We expose Clarence. The Cherokee Nation use the books to further their case in the courts... and Lord Percy gets to prance around in his tailored waistcoats a while longer."

"Yes."

She grinned. "You're completely mad."

"Probably," I said. "But so was Sherlock Holmes and no one complained when *he* solved crimes while talking to a skull."

"That was Hamlet." Giving me a withering look. "So what do we do now?"

"First we will need to get back to Braithwaites when the books go back for auction and make sure one of the good guys gets the books" and then

"We wait for Angie," I said. "She's downstairs working her magic on the reason I was here in the first place. It has to be connected somehow."

"... by magic, you mean aggressive questioning and judging people silently with her eyes?"

"Exactly. She'll get what we need."

Betty sighed, walked over to the window and stared out at the village green.

"I hope you're right." She looked at me again. The glimmer of that earlier smile returned, just a flicker. "You're a very strange man, Tony Ferrari."

"Dead man," I corrected. "… and thank you."

I felt like a detective again.

One with a terrible aftershave, a spectral partner, and a very dangerous plan.

That's when Angie called from the stairwell.

"You're going to want to hear this!" she shouted. "Hector remembers more than just your cologne!"

There's a peculiar kind of frustration exclusive to ghosts. It's not the inability to touch things, or the way people walk straight through you like you're a disappointing breeze. It's not even the existential sting of your death certificate being filed under "Unsolved" with a sticky note that reads "bit suspicious." No, the real agony is this: when someone remembers a thing about you that you don't remember at all.

… and once they start they won't stop bloomin talking about it.

That someone was Hector, landlord of the Rose and Crown and unbeknownst reluctant confidant to the dead. He had the air of a man who could wrestle a beer barrel single-handedly and still find time to critique your choice in crisps. He also claimed, with the quiet certainty of someone recalling the price of eggs in 1974, that I had been in his pub. Alive.

Now, to clarify, I have no recollection of this. Not a flicker. Not a ghostly trace. Trust me, I've rummaged through my spectral brain like a pensioner through a charity shop bargain bin. But nothing.

Yet here we were, me hovering just behind the bar like a slightly concerned weather system, and Hector, drying a pint glass with the grim resolve of a man who knew it would never be clean enough for the 'real ale police standards', whilst talking to Angie like he'd known me longer than I had.

"Well, he smelled of Old Spice," Hector said, unknowingly accurately gesturing towards me with a bar towel, "and he was muttering about tribes and treaties and some missing chapter."

I blinked. Metaphorically.

"He read something in a book," Hector nodded. "Said it was flowery nonsense but important. Kept going back over it, mumbling to himself. Not three. Four."

"Did he say *what* that meant?" Angie pressed suddenly hopeful, doing that thing where her voice dipped into serious territory usually reserved for war crimes and tax audits.

"No. He finished his pint, made Duck noises at the Duck in the beer garden, and legged it."

"… and you didn't find that suspicious?"

"I run a pub, love. If I got suspicious every time someone drank alone and muttered about betrayal, or made Duck noises, I'd never get anything done."

In the spectral corner, Betty was pacing in mid-air, arms folded, ghostly lips pursed. "He remembered *you*, Tony. That's important."

Hector scratched his chin. "He mentioned Beddlestead."

Angie narrowed her eyes. "The village?"

"He was going on about a 'travelling inn', somewhere just in case."

"In case what?" Angie asked.

"'As I said, he legged it."

I floated down toward the bar, attempting to rest my elbows on it, and promptly passed through the varnish. "So, let me get this straight. I, alive, smelly, and wearing a trench coat, came in here the day *before* I was murdered, talked complete nonsense then left?"

Angie paraphrased back to Hector.

"That's about it," Hector confirmed, now polishing a new glass that had been clean for at least three hours.

"So where does Mavis fit into all this?" Betty prodded Angie, ever the detective.

"Betty says where does Mavis fit in?"

"Whose Betty?

"Sorry I was getting muddled" Angie backtracked "but where does Mavis fit in"

"Oh," Hector said with a grin, "she overheard it. Ears like a bat with broadband, that one."

Angie's phone buzzed. She glanced at it and sighed. "Gary's asked me out on a date" Then flicked it closed. It wasn't for debate.

The room was quiet for a moment, the way pubs go quiet just before someone does something truly regrettable involving karaoke. Then Angie turned back to Hector.

"Can you take us through everything again? Slowly?"

Hector sighed, sat down on the bar stool beside her, and leaned forward like he was about to explain algebra to a Labrador. "He came in around half past two. Middle of the day. Dead quiet. Ordered a pint of stout and asked if we had any books on the local history of Beddlestead or the pub. I told him we have a few books on the shelves, for display, but the regulars don't read - they look at their phones these days, although we do have the complete collection of Giles Cartoon annuals."

"He said he was looking for" and did the quote thing with his fingers "*A place that people come and go, that sees everything and remembers nothing*"

I turned to Betty. "That's got to be the Rose and Crown. A travellers' stop for centuries."

Betty nodded slowly. "… that sounds like a pub every Friday night."

"Then just before he left," Hector said, "he got a call. Took it outside. Came back in five minutes later looking... different. You know, not so cocky. None of the jokes about pork pies"

"How different?" Angie asked.

"Like he'd read his own obituary. He left a fiver on the bar, told me, 'If anyone comes asking, tell them nothing,' and walked out."

"That's the last time you saw him?" she asked.

Hector nodded with the solemn finality of a man who'd once seen a ghost, spoken to it, and was now forced to admit this was somehow not the weirdest part of his Wednesday.

Betty let out a low whistle. "Do you think this was anything to do with Indian books, or something else."

"No recollection whatsoever!" I muttered, my ghostly fingers attempting to drum on the bar and instead passing through it like a disgruntled cloud looking for purpose.

Before anyone could add another cryptic metaphor or nod sagely, the front door opened with a squeak that could only have been achieved through years of deliberate neglect. Two of Hector's regulars shuffled in, bundled in tweeds and rural conspiracy theories. They smelled faintly of Bovril, rain, and the kind of aftershave that doubles as a wasp repellent.

"Alright Hec?" called one, who bore an uncanny resemblance to a disappointed rabbit. "Has that duck of yours finally lost the plot?"

The other nodded sagely as if this was part of an unfolding prophecy. "He's out there doing laps of the beer garden, snapping at thin air. Looks like he's trying to exorcise the picnic tables."

"You ever think it might have mad cows disease?" the rabbit-man said, peering over his bifocals and wandered off to the far side of the bar, where the radiator was gurgling.

Angie turned back to Hector. "Any last clues you can give us?"

Hector rubbed his chin, scratched his ear, glanced sideways as though someone was watching and finally said, "Well… he had a cigarette with Mavis before he left."

Angie blinked. "Mavis? Mavis Mavis?"

"No, the *other* Mavis," Hector said, deadpan. "Of course *Mavis…* Mavis. Our Mavis. The one who talks to the gin bottle called Geraldine when she thinks no one's looking."

"She talks to me as well," I said. "But in fairness, I am a ghost. It would be more rude if she ignored me."

Do you think she remembers what they talked about?" Angie asked.

"She's Mavis" Hector replied. "She remembers what you wore the first time you came in, how many peanuts were in the bowl, and whether you paid in cash or card. If your 'American fella' so much as exhaled a suspicious noun, she'll have filed it somewhere in that soggy brain of hers, cross-referenced, underlined, and annotated with disapproval."

Angie stood up, chair scraping backwards with the noise of a sarcastic goose. "Right. We're talking to Mavis."

"Good luck," Hector muttered, returning to polishing a pint glass that had reached a level of clarity normally reserved for angelic visions. "She's been struggling with 7 across in The Times crossword for the last two hours and is getting tetchy. If she throws a pencil at you, consider it affectionate."

As we floated toward the Snug bar door, Betty in a glide and me with the jerky defiance of someone still not used to phasing through fire extinguishers (or, frankly, Victorian plumbing), I glanced back at Hector. There he was, behind the bar, a stalwart against the nonsense of both the living and the dead, like a ship's captain who'd just watched a kraken rise from the depths, offer him a pint, and then politely ask for directions to the courthouse.

"I had a cigarette with Mavis," I muttered. "How is that the only thing memorable?"

Betty patted my shoulder like a school nurse diagnosing a terminal case of denial. "Might've been the last normal thing you did before someone arranged your visit to the phone box."

"Comforting," I said. "Very comforting. I'll have that carved into my gravestone. 'Here lies Tony Ferrari: last seen sharing a smoke and being less interesting than a crossword.'"

The door creaked open with all the drama of a pantomime villain entering a budget theatre. The warmth hit us.

It was like stepping into the Caribbean. Not the postcard version, mind you, but the real thing, humidity, floral wallpaper, and the faint but persistent tang of something floral that could be potpourri or old gin regrets. The Snug Bar was exactly what the name suggested: too many doilies, too few windows, and the psychic weight of four hundred years of gossip pressed into its upholstery.

There she was.

Mavis.

Queen of the Snug. Empress of overheard conversations. She sat in her usual seat beneath the dartboard that hadn't seen a winning Rose and Crown team for many years, surrounded by a forcefield of crossword clippings, knitting needles, and tea cups arranged like defensive emplacements. The air around her vibrated faintly with the tension of one who had been thwarted by 7 across, 'Elephantine, possibly, but in short supply (7)' - and was now prepared to declare war on the English language itself.

Her eyebrows twitched when Angie entered, a movement so slight it could only be picked up by seismologists or very sensitive cats.

"Oh, it's you, the clever one," Mavis said, in a tone that could strip wallpaper. "Come to make my day worse, have you?"

Angie smiled. "Only if I have to, Mave. Mind if I sit?"

"You're going to whether I say yes or not, so let's not pretend this is a democracy."

I hovered by the fruit machine, that had a nice buzzy vibration about it. It seemed happy.

Mavis squinted and smiled. "Hi Betty, I can hear you."

Betty beamed.

Mavis turned her squint vaguely toward me. Her eyes narrowed further. "… and the air's feeling... twitchy. Is Hector burning incense again?"

Betty smirked. "That's Tony, actually. He's here too."

Mavis sniffed. "Geraldine? Can't really hear her until I've had a proper nip."

"Rude," I muttered.

Angie settled in with a theatrical exhale "Mavis, do you remember Tony being here before he died?" she asked."

Mavis looked up from her crossword, finally giving us the full power of her squint. "Remember? Of course I remember. He reeked of Old Spice. We had a ciggie outside", she pointed to the window "Hectors gone all modern and won't let us smoke in the pub, very lardy da"

Betty sat on the armrest of Angie's chair, hovering only slightly, like a particularly elegant fog bank with opinions. "What did he talk about?"

Mavis leaned back and crossed her arms with the authority of someone who has seen things, many of them in lowercase italics.

"Nonsense most of it. Obviously"

"Obviously!" Betty agreed, throwing me a smile that was either affectionate or accusatory, possibly both.

"Which bits were Victorian. Of course, ALL the pub is Victorian. Gothic Revival. Pointy windows. Stonework that's too fancy to trust. Same with St Margaret's and the post office. All built in a flurry of stone and piety when some duke had a bout of nostalgia and too much money. The pond and duck house too."

Betty perked up. "The pond?"

"Yes, dear. The duck pond. Out back, by the old orchard that isn't an orchard anymore, just a sad lawn with ideas above its station.?"

"Did he say anything about *four not three?* Angie asked, getting back on the mystery like a bloodhound.

Mavis considered, eyebrows knotting like two annoyed caterpillars. "No, I don't think so. He said that nothing adds up but everything points in the same direction."

"Vector," I said without thinking.

Betty and Angie turned to me like I'd just started speaking in Latin.

"What?"

"Vector. *Nothing adds up but everything points in the same direction,*" I repeated, feeling strangely proud.

"Crossword answer?" Mavis said putting her sherry glass down with the clink of revelation.

"Exactly."

Clearly, the last nip had opened her ears, or at least her internal antenna for cryptic innuendo. Although sometimes I think she only opened her ears when she wanted to, which was usually when she could correct someone or win a bet. "What do you think of 3 across?"

I floated over and peered at the crossword. 3 Across: 6 letters, second letter N.

"Onions," I said confidently.

Silence.

Mavis blinked. "*Experts in layers who often make you cry?*" she read aloud. Then she tapped the paper. "Of course."

"Prescient," I added.

"What?"

"8 Down."

"Stop it," Betty glared at me. "Focus, Tony. Focus!"

 "That duck… it's always out back near the pond, right?"

"For heaven's sake Tony, focus"

Mavis, now re-armed with her pen and sherry, didn't look up, but added helpfully, "Afraid that was it. Looked she had just had bad news."

"She?" asked Angie

"Geraldine!"

We all looked at each other. Dead end.

"If you find whoever wrote 7 across," she added without looking up, "tell them they're a sadist."

"Will do," Angie said, standing.

Just as we phased out through the door I whispered back "MAMMOTH"

312

CHAPTER THIRTEEN

EVERYONE'S GOT EARS, KEV

The taxi had a bit of an odd smell this morning. Damp polyester, weak tea, and discounted sushi. In short, it smelled like most London taxis, only slightly more philosophical. Gary explained, without prompting of course, that the bouquet was courtesy of a particularly strange fare from the day before: a man in a novelty Monkey suit who insisted on riding with three suitcases, a portable foot spa, and what Gary referred to only as "a spiritually unsettling flask of soup."

Angie sat in the back, arms crossed and jaw set, doing her best impression of someone who wasn't planning to help bring down an intergenerational conspiracy involving colonial theft, property fraud, and ectoplasmic emotional entanglement.

Betty and I were hovering on the back seat beside her, invisible to Gary, who, like most living people, had long ago trained himself not to see the weird unless it had its own YouTube channel.

"All I'm saying," Gary was saying, with the unstoppable momentum of a man who had discovered an audience and refused to relinquish it, "is that if the French had just accepted mayonnaise as a legitimate chip dip, we wouldn't have needed Brexit."

Angie, however, was deep in thought watching London blur past the window like a melancholic flipbook and decided today wasn't the day to get into Brexit with Gary.

"You sure you're ready for this?" I asked.

Angie continued to look out the window "Do I look unsure?".

We got the message and continued in silence driving up The Old Kent Road towards London.

Angie eventually broke the silence. "Right," she said quietly, addressing us ghosts. "We need this auction to go through and those McKenney & Hall's volumes to go public. That's the start. Once they're in the open, the Cherokee Nation can launch the court case." Then looking directly at me "Last time we tried this, you two had too much fun and literally brought the house down".

"Agreed. But this time, we've got a plan." I winked at Betty.

"You *say* that" Angie replied, "but your plans have the structural integrity of a flan in a thunderstorm."

Gary cleared his throat loudly. "Just so you all know," he said, not taking his eyes off the road, "talking to yourself in the back seat is how people get written up in the incident log at the cab depot."

"Sorry," Angie said, deadpan. "I have very strong imaginary friends."

I raised an eyebrow. "Imaginary?"

We drove in silence for a bit, which in Gary's cab meant only that Gary had paused for breath long enough to reload his conversational cannon. Gary didn't believe in silence. True to his

Taxi driver calling he believed in *monologue*. He treated it as a moral obligation to fill all available airspace with commentary, observations, and the occasional unsolicited culinary opinion.

When the silence hit the 14-second mark, his personal record for restraint, he exploded.

"Remind me again," With the eager tone of a man who never missed an opportunity to be reminded of a plot point if it meant he could insert himself into it like a human footnote. "Why would governments want to stop this? I mean, they already own all the good stuff. Roads, phone lines, the BBC. What more do they want?"

Angie turned her head, which was her way of preparing to explain something complicated to someone she didn't entirely trust not to eat glue.

"Because" Angie said, "when the Dawes Act passed in 1887, the U.S. government, bless their opportunistic cotton socks, 'reallocated' ninety million acres of land. Supposed to help the tribes. Instead, it helped speculators, railroad companies, and one bloke named Chet who later sold half of Oklahoma in exchange for a steam-powered cow milking machine."

"I think I saw something like that on Channel 5," said Gary thoughtfully. "The one with the bloke who renovates castles."

"Instead of building equity," Angie continued, "tribes lost generational homes, spiritual lands, and in one case, a sacred mountain that got turned into a novelty golf course."

Betty sighed the kind of sigh that carried centuries of diplomatic betrayal in it.

"…and let's not forget," she added, "that His Majesty's Government facilitated plenty of this nonsense through offshore deals, hush-hush land transfers, and a national strategy of pretending not to understand how treaties work. The British didn't technically steal anything. They just stood nearby while the Americans did it, took notes, and offered legal advice."

"Classic British diplomacy," I said. "If it's not nailed down, colonise it. If it *is* nailed down, annex the nails."

Betty shot me a look that could shatter stained glass.

But Angie nodded. "The books are evidence. Written proof of who made what promises to whom. If they go to private collectors, the chain of evidence breaks. If they're bought by someone working for the US or any other Government with an interest…"

"… they disappear," said Betty, grimly.

"Step One," I said, pointing a ghostly finger dramatically, even though no one could see it, "make sure the books are sold to someone who'll hand them straight to the Cherokee legal team."

"Step Two," Angie said, "get Clarence to do something so utterly and undeniably illegal that he's arrested before he can so much as sneeze on a catalogue."

"You missed Step One?" said Gary

Angie repeated, as of course Gary only hears Angie's side of the conversation.

"Right," said Angie. "… and we've got a bit of help there."

Betty raised a perfect eyebrow.

"I went to the police," Angie said, "as agreed" her voice casual in that way that people's voices only ever get when they're about to explain a very non-casual felony workaround. "Told them Clarence threatened me. Which he *did*, in that charming 'I'm not saying I'll bury you in a shallow grave, but I'm keeping my Tuesdays open' tone of his."

I whistled. "Classy."

"I also tipped off Detective Inspector Geoffrey Marsh," she added, throwing me a look. "You know. The same one we gave *no choice* but to look into your murder."

"Wait," said Gary, narrowly avoiding a cyclist with the same lack of regard one might give a persistent wasp. "So Clarence is already being watched?"

"Watched, listed, and probably halfway to being audited," said Angie. "I told Marsh that Clarence, sorry, *Colin*, if we're being formal, would be at the auction. That he'd be nervous. Probably twitchy. Likely to do something stupid."

Betty tilted her head. "How did Marsh take it?"

"Hard to say," Angie said. "He mostly stared at me like a man whose entire career had just been ambushed by a newspaper headline. You know that look? Like someone just handed him a live weasel and told him it was part of an official inquiry."

Gary coughed again. "You lot *do* know I can hear most of what is going on, and can make out the rest?"

Angie waved a hand dismissively. "Of course. You're a highly trained, discreet professional."

Gary preened slightly. "That's true."

"… and no one would ever believe a word you said."

The preening stopped.

"And then we have Hectors revelation to deal with" said Angie, whose mood was obviously lifting.

"Hector?" said Garry with that confused "no one ever tells me anything" expression in the rear-view mirror. "Who is Hector?"

I smirked. "Only that Hector the landlord most likely met me while I was alive." Angie relayed that to Gary.

"Is that possible," said Gary, reasonably.

"Looks like it," I said, unreasonably.

Angie groaned. "Why do I feel like my life has turned into one of those reality shows where no one does the dishes but everyone cries during the reunion special?"

Gary turned into a narrow lane with all the grace of a man who'd spent forty years driving in a city designed by drunk medieval goats. "We're about here. You lot ready?"

I adjusted my ghostly tie. "Emotionally? No."

Betty brushed invisible dust from her blouse. "Metaphysically? Barely."

Angie pulled out her phone, checked her messages, there were none, and tucked it away with a sigh. "Tactically? Let's find out."

"Alright," said Gary, pulling to a stop and throwing the gear stick into 'Heroic Neutral'. "What now?"

As Angie stepped out, Gary called after her. "You need me to wait?"

"No," she said. "If this goes well, we'll get a ride back with the police. If it goes badly… well, I'll call you."

Inside the cab, I held Betty's hand.

"Ready?"

"No." she smiled "But let's do it anyway."

Meanwhile up in the CCTV Room, Mezzanine Floor 2

"I still say the Panther Trifle was more dignified than the Lemur Eclair," Kev declared, wielding his plastic fork like he was about to knight his microwaved breakfast rather than stab it into submission.

Dave looked up from his tea with the weary resignation of a man who had been through this exact debate more times than he cared to count, dreamt about it once during a cheese-induced nap, and had considered filing an official grievance with the Pastry Council of Great Britain.

"Kev, the lemur éclair wasn't real mate. It was a novelty poster. For World Pastry Week. You hallucinated it. Or read it wrong. Or both."

"It had a paw print on it, Dave. A paw. With icing sugar. That makes it real in my book."

The CCTV room of Braithwaite's Auctioneers hummed, punctuated by the occasional mechanical sigh of expensive equipment pretending it was more important than it really was. Twelve monitors blinked at Kev and Dave like disapproving headmasters. The two of them sat in chairs that had started life as ergonomic wonders and ended up as collapsible regrets, one foam pad away from becoming sentient health hazards.

"Tell you what is real," Kev added, pointing a custard cream at Monitor 4. "Lot 17. Back on the menu."

Dave squinted. The camera feed showed a set of glass double doors through which the auction room slowly filled. Polished shoes clicked. Cravats adjusted themselves nervously. Several people moved with the twitchy energy of politicians pretending they hadn't heard the word "inquiry".

"See the guy with the ears?" Kev pointed

"Everyone's got ears, Kev."

"But his are listening to things."

Dave blinked slowly. "That's what ears do mate."

"Yeah, but his ears are... on duty."

They fell into silence, eyes drifting across the feeds. Gallery Two now showed the star of the day: the three volumes of McKenney & Hall's *History of the Indian Tribes of North America,* sat like royalty in their glass display case. Or prisoners. Or royal prisoners with historic value and criminally misbehaved wheels.

"You think they've fixed the wheel this time?" Dave said.

Kev gave a theatrical sniff. "Don't trust it. Wheel Four's got malice. You can feel it in the rotation."

"We don't need another security farce," Dave said. "Not after last time."

"Yeah, still picking cheesecake out of the ventilation shafts."

Dave sipped his tea. "That was your fault. When the lights went out you launched a tiramisu like it was a warning shot."

From one of the monitors, a new figure entered frame. Clarence. Resplendent in velvet. Sans limp today.

Kev nudged Dave. "Penguin Man's back."

Dave grunted. "Didn't he nearly crash the case into the Ming vase?"

"Yep, it's refusing to come out of storage"

As they watched, the Dereks emerged. Derek One, tall, worried, hands full of clipboard. Derek Two, shorter, rounder, possessed of the sort of moustache that could legally classify as architecture.

Kev leaned forward. "Here we go. The books are moving… and wobbling. Slightly."

Dave tapped Monitor 6. "That wheel's got ideas again."

Kev reached for his notepad, scrawled something, and held it up. It read: *Wheel Four = Gremlin*. Dave nodded. "Noted".

There was a knock at the door. Neither moved.

The door opened anyway.

Marcus, their supervisor, poked his head in. "Status?"

Kev gave a thumbs-up with the slow, deliberate, pride of a man with no idea - absolutely winging it.

"No chaos. Yet," Dave added.

Marcus grunted and vanished.

"We should get badges," Kev said.

"We have badges."

"Better ones. Ones with job descriptions like 'Spectral Containment Analysts or 'Temporal Anomaly Response Team.' Something with *gravitas*."

Dave looked over. "You still think that dancing static were ghosts?"

Kev glanced at Monitor 7, where the static had begun to fizz just slightly. The kind of fizz that suggests mischief. Or metaphysical interference.

"Yup, if we get interference the monitors freeze, not break into dance routines"

Dave reached for the Kit Kat. Broke it in two. Passed one to Kev.

"Let's not tell Marcus."

"Agreed."

Kev and Dave sat back.

"So," Kev said, "panther trifle. Best animal-themed dessert or just misunderstood?"

"Hold on… Penguin man is on the move" said Dave

Clarence who had been loitering in Row Three, aisle seat, pretending to read a catalogue, suddenly straightened. His eyebrows arched so high they tried to check out of his forehead. He folded the catalogue with more drama than necessary, stood, and casually moved four seats over and two rows up. Sitting behind a striking lady wearing wellington boots and a scarf wrapped like she'd won a competition in stylish defiance.

They zoomed in slightly. Clarence was now directly behind Scarf Woman. He adjusted his tie. Sat forward. Then leaned back like a man trying to appear inconspicuous and achieving the opposite.

"Now he looks like he's about to propose to the back of her head," Kev muttered. "Do we radio Marcus?"

But Dave wasn't looking at Clarence. He was looking at Monitor 7. The static was no longer subtle. Tiny fizzing bubbles of distortion now peppered the upper right corner. Like digital champagne. Or something trying to seep in.

"…Kev?"

"I see it."

They both leaned in.

In Monitor 7, the auction floor shimmered faintly. A bubbly slightly fizzing shadow in the shape of trench coat had just floated in, except no one in the room seemed to see it. It floated down the centre aisle, passing through the legs of a man fiddling with his cufflinks.

"and… static snow blizzard blowing in, see lower left quadrant, lady presence detected! Long coat, 1940s vibe. Is that… no… is she glowing?"

"Soft ochre."

Dave blinked.

Kev added, "Mood lighting for ghosts."

A sudden shift of light made one of the camera feeds flicker, and the scarfed woman turned briefly, brow furrowed. She shivered. Glanced over her shoulder. Then faced forward again.

"She *felt* them," Dave whispered. "as they went past"

Kev nodded slowly. "We are now officially in the vicinity of weird. Hold on."

Dave delved deep into his duffle bag and grabbed *the* packet of chocolate Hobnobs. He slid the packet across the desk with the solemnity of a man offering a peace treaty to a neighbouring biscuit-based nation.

Kev received it wordlessly, his expression shifting into something between reverence and suppressed glee.

In America, they might light a cigar for moments like this. In Britain, you break out the Hobnobs. Chocolate-coated. Emotional support tier.

No words were exchanged. None were needed. The Hobnobs had spoken.

They both leaned back, put feet on the desk and watched as the auctioneer took the podium and tapped the mic.

Kev cracked his knuckles. "This is gonna be grrreat."

Inside the Auction Room:

We floated in through the corniced ceiling with the gentle ease of ghosts who'd done this sort of thing before. Betty, as always, descended like an apparition from a painting.

The auction room was already a low buzz of anticipation. Wood panelling glowed. Gold-framed portraits loomed. The scent of polished leather and quiet desperation hung thick in the air. This was a place where fortunes changed hands with the tap of a hammer, and egos collided.

"They fixed the wheel," Betty whispered.

"Or bribed it," I muttered. "its going straight, but under protest"

Down below, the Dereks, who I was starting to suspect were not so much employees as a slapstick double act in disguise, were rolling in the glass display case like it had been baptised. The infamous Wheel Four glided along with suspicious smoothness, not a wobble in sight. I didn't trust it.

The counterfeit books looked as they always had, three glorious, leather-bound volumes, worn but noble. McKenney & Hall's *History of the Indian Tribes of North America.* My death sentence in hardcover.

The auctioneer, a thin man with a voice like someone had shaved a violin, breathed a visible sigh of relief. He tapped his papers on the podium and gave the nod. The crowd tensed.

"Alright," I said, glancing around. "Let's see who's here to pretend they don't work for a government."

We drifted through the chandelier, which buzzed slightly as our frequencies brushed against it. Betty floated elegantly toward the back row.

"There," she whispered. "Back right. Lapel pin. Who wears tan shoes in winter? Definitely American."

"…and no umbrella," I added. "Trying to blend in but carrying a notebook labelled 'Confidential'. Subtle."

She gestured toward a woman with military posture and a shark smile. "Australia."

"How do you know?"

"She's already judged everyone else's accent and thinks this whole thing could have been sorted with a rugby tackle."

I turned slowly. A man three rows from the front was watching the books with the kind of casual intensity that said 'civil servant' but screamed 'black-ops budget'.

"British Foreign Office?"

Betty nodded. "Or MI5's garden club. Either way, he's here to lose politely."

Then I saw Angie.

With the calm confidence of a woman who knew where the exits were, had memorised three different escape routes, and was carrying a handbag that could double as an evidence locker. Her scarf, navy blue, dramatic fringe, flowed behind her like a flag of passive-aggressive resistance.

"Oh good," Betty said, smiling softly. "She brought the scarf."

But I wasn't watching the scarf. I was watching Clarence.

He'd been seated in the middle of the crowd, flicking through the catalogue like he was hoping it had a centrefold. The moment he saw Angie, he froze. Then he stood. Moved casually. Too casually. Four steps sideways, two rows up. He sat directly behind her.

My entire ghost spine stiffened.

"He's planning something," I said.

"That's good we need him to do something."

Angie didn't turn around. But I saw her shoulders tighten. Her grip on the bag adjusted. She knew.

She knew he was there… and she was biding her time.

"She can't cause a scene yet," I muttered.

"Not yet," Betty agreed.

We hovered closer. Watching. The room had gone still.

The auctioneer stepped up.

"Ladies and gentlemen," he said, his voice echoing like buttered toast in a cathedral, "we come now to Lot Seventeen, an extraordinary offering: the complete three-volume edition of McKenney and Hall's *History of the Indian Tribes of North America*. A rare, invaluable piece of published heritage."

All eyes turned. Bidders raised their catalogues or paddles. The auctioneer smiled.

"Let us begin."

The first paddle hadn't even lifted when Betty leaned over and hissed through her teeth.

"Far left. Tweed jacket. Corduroy elbow patches. Eyes like a library cat."

I followed her gaze. Ah. Him.

"Jonathan Keegan," I said. "British Library. Chief Curator of Rare Acquisitions."

Betty tilted her head. "He smells faintly of typewriter ink." She turned to me. "You know him?"

"We met at the Hay Festival. Shared a panel on 'Lost Volumes and Found Scandals.' We argued about a misprinted edition of *Middlemarch*. He was wrong, obviously. But he bought me a pint anyway."

Betty gave me a look. "He's sweating. That's not a man confident about winning."

I studied him. He was sitting near the back, shifting in his seat. His catalogue had a small tear in the corner, folded and re-folded with nervous fingers. No paddle yet. No movements. Just tension.

"He doesn't have the budget," I said. "Probably scraped together what he could from his discretionary fund and the coin jar in the staff lounge."

Betty looked at me. "But he's the right one, isn't he?"

I nodded. "He won't hoard it. He won't bury it. He'll scan it. Log it. Share it. He'll get the information into the right hands, Cherokee historians, researchers, legal teams. He'll do what I should've done."

She hovered closer, her glow warming just slightly. "Then we make sure he wins."

I grinned. "Oh no. We interfere righteously. There's a difference."

Below us, the auctioneer raised his gavel.

"Shall we start the bidding at fifty thousand pounds?"

Hands twitched. The first paddle lifted, a private collector from China who didn't blink. Then the American man with the ears. Then the Aussie. The Brit followed. Prices leapt.

Keegan still sat, unmoving. Watching. Waiting. Or maybe just praying.

"Betty," I said.

She turned to me, already knowing.

"Go haunt the Australians."

When she returned "Is that the Australian delegate brushing invisible lint off her shoulder?" I asked.

"Not lint," Betty said. "I whispered that something with wings had landed in her hair."

The woman twitched again, brushing at her bun. Her hand snapped back to her catalogue. A second later, up it went. The paddle. Again.

"She's bidding against herself," I murmured, wide-eyed.

"Technically, yes. But emotionally? She's defending herself from an imaginary insect invasion."

Another swat. This time a full-on double-handed sweep through her hair. The people on either side of her leaned away like she'd announced she had nits.

"She's going to outbid her own embassy at this rate," I whispered.

"She just hit eighty thousand," Betty added, admiring the chaos. "The auctioneer is looking confused"

"Good. Keegan's still quiet. He's watching. Waiting. Probably hyperventilating into a folded page of *Antiquarian Weekly*."

Below us, the auctioneer paused. Blinked. Glanced at his assistant, who shrugged with the helplessness of a man trying to interpret if that last flail was an offer or an exorcism.

The Australian delegate slapped her head. Hard. Then smiled at the auctioneer. Then raised her paddle again

"Number 73 please refrain from bidding" said a distressed auctioneer "you can't push up the bids on your own. Now sit down please"

We watched as one of her diplomatic aides stood up and scurried to whisper in her ear. She batted him away like he was another bug.

"She thinks he's part of the swarm," Betty said, barely containing a laugh.

"What exactly did you say to her?"

"Only that a rare insect, worshipped by at least three South American tribes, had landed in her hair and was trying to communicate."

I stared at her.

"What?" she said innocently. "You told me to interfere righteously. I added whimsy."

The auctioneer cleared his throat again, then turned toward the confused clerk.

"We seem to have a very eager bidder," he said, chuckling nervously. "Can I confirm that last offer of ninety-five thousand pounds… was indeed intended?"

The Australian paused. Looked at her hand. Realised it was raised.

And for the first time in twenty minutes, she didn't move.

The hammer hovered.

Silence.

Then, finally, a new paddle rose.

Keegan.

"Good man," I said.

"About time," Betty added.

Let the real bidding begin.

The auctioneer barely had time to register Keegan's bid before another paddle went up. American. Confident. The kind of confidence that comes from being backed by a department whose budget was more a concept than a number.

Betty floated back toward me, her hands clasped behind her back like she was strolling through a gallery of chaos she had personally curated.

"Yank's in," she said. "Eyes on the prize, jaw like it's carved from Mount Rushmore."

I squinted down. He had one of those takeaway coffee cups with a logo that probably said something ironic about capitalism in cursive. He was sipping it like he had all the time in the world and had never knowingly overthrown a government by accident.

"I'm going to knock that cup over," I said.

Betty raised an eyebrow. "That's petty."

"It's also justice."

I swooped down, brushing the tabletop just enough to send a ripple of ghostly static through his fingers. The cup tipped. It teetered, then, glorious in its inevitability, it fell.

Hot coffee splashed across his suit trousers. He jerked up with a yelp, flailing for napkins, dignity, and a paddle that had clattered to the floor.

The auctioneer hesitated, confused as the American stood, sat, stood again, mopped at his knee, and then, while half-standing, accidentally raised his hand.

"Bid accepted at one hundred and twenty thousand pounds," came the announcement.

The American blinked. "Wait, what?"

Too late.

The crowd turned like a school of predatory fish. The Foreign Office rep adjusted his tie with the grimness of a man about to spend someone else's money. His paddle went up. One twenty-five.

Keegan followed. One thirty.

Betty swooped low, eyes gleaming.

"I've got the Brit," she said. "Watch this."

She floated behind him, hovered for a second, then reached out with her ghostly fingers and began to tickle. Not obvious. Just enough to create the sensation that perhaps a spider was delicately Charleston-ing across his ribs.

The man twitched. Scratched. Tried to remain composed. Failed. Giggled. Shifted in his seat. Raised his arm instinctively.

"One hundred and thirty-five!" the auctioneer declared.

He looked startled… and a bit betrayed by his own limb.

"What are we up to now?" I asked.

"Chaos," Betty said. "But measured in thousands."

Paddles were going up and down like a flock of confused flamingos. The Australian had resumed bidding, still swatting periodically at her head. The American was trying to salvage his coffee situation with the emotional grace of a wet napkin. The Brit had given up all attempts at decorum and was now shifting side to side like he needed the loo, giggling like a schoolgirl.

Clarence leaned forward, his breath warm and conspiratorial against Angie's ear "I don't know how you're doing this," he hissed, menace dripping from every syllable, "but I know it's you. Stop it."

He gave the leg of her chair a sharp, petulant kick, the kind of kick that said 'intimidation' but felt more like a toddler losing at tiddlywinks.

"Stop it. Now." His hand quivering with rage temptingly close to the scarf around Angie neck.

Angie didn't flinch. She smiled sweetly, eyes still on the auctioneer.

"Oh, is that you Mr. Churchill," she whispered back, "if you think I'm in control of this, I'm flattered. But at this point, even I'm just enjoying the ride."

She shifted in her seat and added under her breath, "… and you should probably stop kicking. By the look of things, chairs here bite back."

Keegan stayed still. Focused. Paddle gripped in both hands. Waiting.

"C'mon, Jon," I murmured. "Time to pounce."

He did. One forty.

Immediately countered by the Brit. One forty-five.

Betty was now humming the theme to *Mission: Impossible* while ghost-tickling every few seconds.

"Stop doing that," I said. "He's starting to enjoy it."

"He's very British," she replied. "If it's mildly unpleasant and expensive, he assumes it's a privilege."

The American raised his paddle again, wincing as he shifted. One fifty.

The Aussie, somewhat dishevelled, shouted "One fifty-five!" while batting at an entirely imagined swarm.

"Are we the bad guys?" I asked.

Betty looked at the spiralling chaos. The paddles. The flailing. The slight smoke curling from the American's trouser leg.

She shrugged.

"Only if we lose."

Keegan steadied himself. Took a breath. Raised his paddle.

"One hundred and sixty," the auctioneer called.

Silence. For a beat.

Then:

"One sixty-five!" yelled the Brit.

"One seventy!" snapped the American, still blotting coffee.

"One seventy-five!" cried the Aussie, who now had one shoe off and was shaking it upside down.

Keegan. His jaw tightened.

"Do it," I whispered.

He raised his paddle.

"One hundred and eighty thousand pounds."

Even the auctioneer paused.

This was it.

The Aussie delegate wasn't paying attention, she had other things on her mind. Following a side swipe at an insect suspected of nibbling her earlobe and inviting friends, she tripped over her handbag and landed in the lap of the Chinese bidder.

The American opened his mouth to speak, then looked down just in time to witness the remainder of his coffee, stage a dramatic escape, cascading over his tan shoes like a caffeinated protest. He swore - loudly and with the confidence of someone used to getting answers.

The Brit, already fraying at the edges, finally snapped. He dissolved into helpless giggles, high-pitched, wheezing ones that echoed off the mahogany panelling like an old kettle nearing retirement. This time, there was no regaining composure. His shoulders shook. His monocle popped. Somewhere, decorum quietly died.

The room froze.

Except, of course, for the back row, where a flurry of distinctly unladylike giggles erupted from a group of horrified diplomats.

A sharp expletive, possibly Mandarin and definitely heartfelt, rang out near the display case.

Above it all, the American stood up and bellowed, "Who's responsible for this madness?!"

It was a question that, under the circumstances, would've required a spreadsheet, a séance, and a small army of lawyers to answer.

The auctioneer lifted the gavel.

I held my breath.

"Going once…"

Meanwhile up in the CCTV Room, Mezzanine Floor 2

"No more, stop! Look over there. No… what the—" Kev wheezed, spraying a half-laugh, half-crumb combo across Monitor 3. The CCTV screens flickered with chaos. The auction room looked like someone had opened a portal to a slapstick theatre production halfway through a history conference.

Monitors 1 through 4 showed various angles of mayhem: flailing arms, rising paddles, a spilled coffee tsunami engulfing expensive leather shoes, a woman shaking out her hair like it was auditioning for a L'Oréal ad under duress. Somewhere in the corner, a diplomat was arguing with a shoe.

Kev was now folded halfway over his chair, crying with laughter and pointing at Monitor 2. "She's waving her shoe like it's a weapon, Dave! You seeing this? Dave?"

Dave didn't respond.

He was still, rigid, mouth open mid-bite, a chocolate Hobnob hovering in arrested motion between hand and mouth. His eyes were locked on Monitor 6, where the British bidder had completely unravelled into helpless giggling fits.

Kev leaned over. "Dave?"

Dave blinked. Slowly. Like someone rebooting. He turned to Kev with the expression of a man who had just watched Parliament perform *Cats* in Latin.

"What… what are we looking at?" he asked faintly.

Kev gestured to the monitors, crumbs flying like celebratory confetti. "This is it, mate. The big one. The moment. The ghost tsunami. The supernatural finale. It's like watching the Queen's Speech rewritten by Monty Python."

They turned back to the screens.

Monitor 5 showed the American delegate still demanding answers with the righteous fury of a man whose espresso had staged a betrayal.

Monitor 4 caught the auctioneer attempting to maintain composure, sweat glistening at his temples as he tried to confirm if the last seven bids were legitimate, delusional, or possibly Morse code.

"Look, look—Monitor 7!" Kev slapped Dave's arm.

Betty had drifted into frame, smiling like an angel caught moonlighting as an agent of chaos. One of the British aides flinched and looked behind him, brushing at his shoulder like he'd walked through a very judgmental curtain.

"That's her, right? The ghost lady?"

Dave, recovering slightly, set down the Hobnob. "Definitely… and if I'm not mistaken…" he tapped the zoom on Monitor 8, "…that's the trenchcoat ghost. He's the one torturing the America, isn't he?"

A chair fell over on Monitor 2.

"Another one down," Kev murmured.

Dave rubbed his face. "This is madness."

Kev clapped his hands. "This is *entertainment*. We should've sold tickets."

The Australian delegate had taken off both shoes now. She waved one triumphantly, like an Olympic torch, and shouted something about "divine whispers in her fringe."

"Did she just say fringe?" Dave squinted.

Kev nodded. "Yup. Classic."

Monitor 9 showed Clarence stiff as a board behind Angie, eyes flicking wildly from paddle to paddle, lips moving but body frozen. He looked like a man who'd just realised his secret plan was being outwitted by a woman in a scarf.

"Oh look," Kev whispered. "He's glitching. He's got that 'I'm a villain and things weren't supposed to be this funny' face."

Angie, meanwhile, sat serenely. Unmoved. Calm in the storm. Occasionally raising her eyebrows like she was internally rating the unfolding spectacle.

Monitor 10 blinked violently.

The Foreign Office bidder had just sneezed himself into another accidental bid. The clerk raised his hand to clarify, but the auctioneer had already shouted, "One hundred and eighty-five!"

On Monitor 3, Keegan still sat, still calm. His paddle rose once more.

"One ninety," the auctioneer confirmed.

The other bidders were not even paying attention

Kev leaned closer to the mic. "I think… I think that was it."

The auctioneer raised the gavel again. "Going once…"

Dave whispered, "Do it."

"Going twice…"

"Do it."

"…Sold, to the gentleman at the rear for one hundred and ninety thousand pounds!"

Kev threw both arms in the air, knocking over his own tea. "YEEEEESSS! "

Dave stared at the monitor, mouth twitching. "You think we just watched a spectral sting operation?"

Kev nodded. "I love this job."

Dave picked up the Hobnob, now slightly damp but emotionally intact. "You think Marcus will want a debrief?"

Kev shrugged. "He'll get one. Eventually. After we edit the footage to remove the bit where I laughed so hard I dislocated a kneecap."

They sat in silence, watching the chaos ebb. One diplomat began to cry quietly into her microphone. The Brit was being escorted out, giggling uncontrollably.

Clarence's eye was twitching on Zoom "He's wound tighter than my nan's Hoover cord," Kev observed. "Best Tuesday I've had in years."

Dave raised his biscuit in salute to monitor 3.

Somewhere, as the feed flickered softly, a book spine glinted beneath glass, and a ghost smiled.

Inside the Auction Room:

It was dawning on Clarence, very slowly, like a hangover at a silent retreat, that the auction had just concluded for a fraction of what Lord Percy was expecting. A *very* small fraction. An embarrassingly un-Percy fraction.

The plan had been simple. Elegant, even. Let the government bidders fight each other tooth and cheque book, watch the price skyrocket into the millions, and then funnel that money into Percy Hall's structural repairs, ongoing litigation defences, the extensive sherry cellar and Colin's bonus. Instead, the final hammer fell at just under £200,000.

Clarence blinked at the number.

£190,000.

He tried to process it, like a laptop being asked to load a high-definition video using dial-up.

This wasn't a sale. It was a robbery. Someone had swindled Lord Percy, swindled him. Someone had outplayed the outplayer.

His eyes darted around the room, scanning the flotsam and jetsam of shaken diplomats, giggling historians, and a woman still cradling her shoe like it held secrets.

…. and then his eyes rested on the chair in front.

Angie Robbins.

Calm. Composed. Smirking like someone who had just pulled the correct thread in a very expensive jumper.

Clarence's blood boiled. If he were a teapot, he'd be shrieking on a hob. His face flushed redder than his velvet jacket, and his fingers clenched around the auction paddle with the white-knuckled rage of a man who had just realised *he* was the patsy, *he* was the fall guy in a clever swindle.

He didn't know *how*, but he *knew*.

Maybe it was the American's coffee cup doing a cartwheel. Maybe it was the way the British bidder had giggled like a schoolboy after three pints and a trifle.

Angie had orchestrated this.

That was the moment, the moment Clarence, logical, velvet-clad Clarence, snapped.

He coiled his arm, paddle in hand, and drew it back in a full, theatrical arc, clearly intending to bring it down on Angie's unsuspecting head like she was a very stylish piñata.

Unfortunately for him, theatricality left a lot of time for interception.

Out of nowhere, a firm hand caught his wrist mid-swing.

A voice, cool and dry as a gin-and-tonic left out in the English sun, rang out.

"No you don't, sonny."

Detective Inspector Geoffrey Marsh stood up slowly, the way old oak trees might if they had knees and a police badge.

Clarence froze.

The room had gone silent again. Even the ghosts were watching.

Angie turned slightly in her chair, eyes wide but unafraid. "Oh look, Inspector Marsh. So nice of you to join us."

Clarence spluttered. "She, she, she rigged the auction!"

Marsh didn't blink. "You tried to cave her skull in with a souvenir paddle."

Clarence looked around desperately. "She *provoked* me!"

"By ….   By sitting aggressively?"

"She - she *knows* what she did!"

"Colin Briggs," Marsh said, releasing his grip only to produce a warrant from his inside coat pocket with the air of a magician who'd finally grown tired of your nonsense. "Also known under the alias of Mr. Churchill. You're under arrest for conspiracy to commit fraud, obstruction of justice, intimidation of a witness, and attempting to bludgeon a woman in full view of an international audience."

Clarence blanched. "Fraud?! What fraud? I'm just the… logistics manager!" He puffed his chest so full of pompousness his cravat popped and flew across the room. Landing in the leaves of a beautiful potted example of Nepenthes Rajah.

"Then you're about to find out what logistics look like in a holding cell."

He turned to Angie. "Miss Robbins, thank you for the tip-off… and for not retaliating with the paddle."

"I prefer verbal evisceration," Angie said, folding her arms and doing a curtsy.

Clarence was now being firmly but politely handcuffed by two officers who had appeared like bureaucratic ninjas.

"But, but Lord Percy, he said, he said it was all above board!" Clarence whipped his head around. "You - you *set me up!*"

"No, Mr Churchill," said Angie, brushing a bit of ghost static from her coat. "You did that all by yourself. I just gave you the stage."

The auctioneer cleared his throat. "Well… that concludes Lot Seventeen. Please feel free to collect your bidding paddles, those that remain unbroken, and do visit the bar for refreshments and perhaps emotional counselling."

Betty floated down beside me, smug and glowing.

"I saw Marsh warming up in his chair the moment Clarence twitched," she said. "He's been waiting for this."

Tony nodded. "He's an old-school copper. He doesn't run. He doesn't shout. But he's got a grip like Thor's handshake."

Betty grinned. "Do you think that's it then?"

Tony looked around. "For Clarence? Oh yeah. He's toast. But for Lord Percy…? I think the game's still afoot."

Clarence was gone. The door swung shut behind him with a satisfying *clunk*, like punctuation at the end of a long, badly written sentence.

The room exhaled. Chairs creaked. Whispered conversations resumed. Somewhere near the back, a diplomat laughed too loudly, the kind of laugh that says, "thank god it wasn't me."

I floated over to Angie's side. "That went… well?"

Angie, still composed, brushed a hair from her face and stood. "Clarence out. Books secured. British Library winning the bid. The Cherokee will have what they need. A good day at the office me thinks."

I looked at our little team, ever so proud. "So, shall we go?"

Betty looped her arm through mine. "One last float-by of the books?"

"Obviously."

We passed Keegan, who was cradling his paddle like it was a newborn manuscript. The British Library would get their treasure. More importantly, they'd share it.

As we floated through the chandelier one last time, Angie looked up and mouthed "See you outside,"

Angie stepped out into the brisk air and pulled her scarf tight. London moved around her, oblivious. Pigeons cooed, buses honked, a man in a kilt argued with a fox terrier over a croissant.

Behind her, the chaos of the auction slowly faded. But the consequences would ripple.

She turned her phone over in her hands. One new message. Gary. She smiled

"What now?" she Betty asked.

I looked up at the sky. "We have all the time in world to work out what to do next"

Betty grinned. "Excellent. I've always wanted to haunt the aristocracy."

Angie smiled. "Let's go home."

"And tell Bob"

With that, simply, we made our way back to The Rose and Crown…… Home

CHAPTER FOURTEEN

TEMPORAL LOOPHOLES & OTHER ROMANTIC GETAWAYS

The Rose and Crown was unusually still tonight, the kind of stillness that happens when something knows it's been part of a fiasco and is quietly pretending it wasn't. The chaos of the auction house was technically behind us, but the air still smelled faintly of scorched wallpaper, and something else I remembered from my youth, excitement for the future. A strange thing to find in death.

I'd escaped to the roof. Not because I'm dramatic (though I am), but because ghosts don't really get privacy, and this was the closest thing to solitude the afterlife provided.

Betty was already up here, legs swinging off the edge. She always looked comfortable in places that shouldn't be comfortable, like rooftops and ration queues.

"I heard one of the CCTV operators, Kev, tried to sell it," I said casually.

She glanced over, eyebrow arched. "The cravat?"

"eBay. 'Vintage ethereal neckwear, lightly possessed, may whisper unsolicited opinions about marmalade.'"

"Did it get any bids?"

"One. From a user named 'LordChuffington33.' I think Clarence has an alter ego."

She laughed again, and this time it was richer, darker, like she'd stirred something deep. "I love this ridiculous afterlife."

"Yeah," I said. "Surprisingly theatrical."

We sat there in that sort of post-spectacle silence, legs dangling over a pub that had seen too many weird nights and somehow remained the most grounded place I'd ever lived.

The silence wasn't awkward. It was the good kind. The kind that sits beside you like a friend who doesn't need to fill space to prove they belong there.

Still, I fidgeted. Adjusted a coat that no longer had weight but still carried meaning. Something was rattling around in my ghostly brain like a loose screw in a very complicated machine.

She noticed, of course. She always does.

"You've got that look," she said.

"What look?"

"You're clenching your jaw like someone just knocked on your door trying to sell you a vacuum cleaner."

"I wanted to ask about… Well ... About your 'before.'"

She gave me that look, one that makes you feel like you've just handed her your soul wrapped in butcher paper.

"My 'before'?" she repeated.

I nodded. "You were humming something earlier. That tune, it sounded familiar."

"Probably from the war," she said. "Everyone hummed it. My mother used to make stew to that tune. Mostly turnips. Once we had pie made from mushrooms and a tin of spam."

I laughed. "Sounds almost edible."

We smiled at each other, soft and sideways, like kids at a dance who've just realised they don't actually hate each other.

"You were different back then?" I asked.

"Aren't we all?" she said. "Before the war. Before death. Before rationed lipstick and knowing what it feels like to be forgotten."

"You're still loud," I offered.

She elbowed me. "You're still charmingly inappropriate."

The silence came back, warm and friendly.

"Why now?" she asked.

"What?"

"Why are you asking about my past now?"

I looked out at the sleeping village, all bricks and hush.

"Because I think we're heading into something," I said. "I want to know who I'm taking with me."

She turned away, but I caught the smile. It was the kind of smile you store in a memory box and open on days you forget you're worth something.

"I should warn you," she said. "I wore trousers before it was fashionable. Smoked French cigarettes."

I tried not to look delighted. Failed utterly. "Scandalous."

"I almost joined the navy. But I disagreed with the hat."

"Any other confessions?"

"I liked Glenn Miller but loved Billie Holiday. Wore red lipstick that wasn't rationed."

"Did it help?"

"No. But it was satisfying."

I grinned at her. "You're… remarkable."

"Flattery?"

"Not flattery," I said. I meant it.

Above us, the stars blinked like they were in on it all, whatever that was.

Below us, the pub exhaled.

Between us, something threaded itself quiet and sure, a connection that had nothing to do with death and everything to do with being seen.

Even ghosts, it turns out, can fall.

Me? I was already halfway down.

"You remember what I told you the Chief said?" I asked, carefully not looking directly at her in case the weight of the conversation spooked us both. There's something about moonlight and memory that makes a man more nervous than he'd care to admit.

Betty gave a soft *hmmm* in response, not her usual humming tune, but a thoughtful sound that landed somewhere between curiosity and caution. She was always like that when the air thickened, testing to see whether a moment was about to bloom into truth or backpedal into humour.

I pressed on. "About the threads? About how we're not necessarily stuck in time the way the living are."

"Visiting their ancestors?" she said, kicking her foot idly into the moonlight. Her boot traced a soft arc in the air, like she was sketching something unspoken. "Yes. I remember. So?"

"Right," I nodded. "He said the soul is loudest in moments of intense feeling. Especially…"

"… the moment we die," she finished for me. Her voice softened, as if the words had unwrapped something neither of us wanted to hold too tightly.

I settled into the memory of the Chief's words. It wasn't just the content; it was the way it felt. Like truth wrapped in metaphors and dipped in something eternal.

"He said we leave behind threads," I continued. "Like spiritual footprints. Except instead of feet, it's whatever your soul was screaming at the time."

"Poetic and rather scary," Betty murmured.

She glanced at me, the movement small but deliberate. "You think this is a real thing?"

I nodded slowly. "Yeah. I think it might be."

Her expression changed again, so subtly you'd miss it unless you were looking for it … and I was. Always am. It's the kind of attention you give to someone when every part of you is bracing for an answer you're not sure you deserve, one that made my stomach do a sort of ghostly loop-de-loop.

There was a pause then. A gentle one. Like the kind you find in a jazz tune between the notes that matter. We sat in that quiet with the ease of two people who didn't need to perform. I didn't need to impress her. She didn't need to question. We just… were.

"I keep thinking about it," I said. "Because if those threads are real, if we can travel them, then maybe we don't have to guess what happened to us."

There it was. The thing I hadn't wanted to say. The thing that had been twitching in the back of my ghostly mind like an unanswered phone. Saying it out loud felt like exhaling something I'd held onto so tightly it left fingerprints on my thoughts.

Betty didn't answer right away. She kept watching the stars, but her breathing had changed. Slower. Like she was trying to decide whether to keep something inside or let it bleed gently into the open.

"Tony," she said, gently. "Why would anyone want to go back to that time. It would be so painful surely?"

I shrugged. "Yes. No. Maybe. It feels like unfinished homework…"

She drew her knees up, arms looped around them, chin resting just above the curve. She looked smaller suddenly. Not fragile, Betty could out-stare a mirror, but more… raw. Someone who'd just been told the end of a story they hadn't agreed to finish.

"You're braver than me," she said. "I've been dead for… a long time, and I still don't know if I want to know."

"Because of who did it?"

"No," she said. "Because of who I was."

That one hit me somewhere between the chest and the part of my soul that remembers birthdays I didn't celebrate.

"What if I go back," she continued, voice quiet but certain, "and I don't like the girl I used to be? What if I was weak? Or cruel? Or forgettable? I was different back then"

"You weren't."

"You don't *know* that."

"I don't need to," I said. "You're here now. You're fierce, and kind, and remember you once told me you threatened to haunt a man because he refused to return a library book. That tells me everything."

She smiled, but it trembled at the edges. "What if they never thought of me again? The people who killed me. What if they just walked away? Had tea. Got married. Raised children who never knew their parent once snuffed out a life like blowing out a candle?"

I leaned closer, not touching her, just… orbiting.

"Then we name it," I said. "We find them. Even if they're gone. We say it out loud. We remember. We carry it until the story doesn't feel lost anymore."

She looked at me then. Fully. Like she was reading a map of every version of me she'd met since I woke up dead.

"I don't want to be forgotten," she said, and it wasn't a whisper, but it *felt* like one.

"You're not," I said. "Not by me."

Another long silence. The kind that folds you in like a blanket. I think she would've cried if she still could, and I would've held her if I had arms worth a damn.

"You seriously think the Chief was right?" she asked after a while.

"I do," I said. "… and not just about time. About people like us. People with unfinished chords still echoing through the song."

Betty tilted her head. "He's annoyingly wise, isn't he?"

"You know what gets me?" she asked.

"What?"

"If times like a charity shop, and our memories are these dusty knick-knacks, who decides what's valuable?"

"We do," I said. "We're the ones still walking through the aisles."

Another silence.

"Tony," she said, voice softer now, "if I go back with you… if we pull on the threads, there's no guarantee it leads to something nice."

"I know."

"There's no promise of what happens when we get answers."

"I know."

"But you still want to do it?"

"With you? Always."

She let out a long breath. Then nodded. Slowly. Like she was shaking hands with fate.

I offered her my hand, not out of ceremony, just instinct.

She didn't take it straight away.

But when she did, the stars flickered just slightly.

The moment held, and so did she.

We sat like that for a long while, me, her, and the hush of a village that didn't realise two of its residents were currently renegotiating the laws of time, memory, and posthumous justice.

Betty's hand still rested in mine. Neither warm nor cold. Just… there. A presence rather than a temperature. Like the moment you remember a dream just before it slips away.

"I keep asking myself," I said eventually, "what does 'moving on' actually mean?"

She didn't let go.

"I don't know," she said. "You'd think there would be something on Google by now. I looked. Nada'"

I smiled. "Chapter One: Congratulations, You're Transparent."

She chuckled, but her eyes stayed serious. "What if we do this, go back, pull the thread, dig up the bones of our own endings, and all that the justice leads to … *isn't peace. Not ascension. Just absence. The light flicking off, and no curtain call?*"

I knew what she meant.

"Then maybe it's not about where it leads," I said. "Maybe it's about *why* we do it."

"To feel useful?"

"To feel *finished*."

That landed.

She pulled her knees up to her chest again and rested her chin there. "I don't know if I'm ready to finish."

"You don't have to be," I said. "But Bob might be."

She went stiff and didn't move for a long time. Just breathed, or pretended to, the way ghosts do when they need to remember what it felt like to be afraid and hopeful in equal measure.

"That's what's supposed to happen, isn't it?" she said at last. "People are born, they grow up, they drive cars, they argue about petrol prices, they dance terribly at weddings… and then they die after all that."

I didn't interrupt. This was her path now. I was just here to walk beside it.

She turned slightly to look at me. "But Bob didn't get the rest. He didn't get the long years of weird haircuts and worse decisions. He didn't get to fall in love. Or get dumped. Or eat a whole packet of biscuits in one sitting just because he could."

"Or regret a tattoo," I added.

She smiled, and her voice softened. "Or get arrested for reversing up a one-way street."

I blinked. "That's a weirdly specific fantasy."

"Everyone deserves to mess up at least once and survive it," she said. "Bob didn't get that. He didn't even get a dog."

"He has Trevor"

"Oh, sorry I forgot. I love Trevor but he is much more gravy sponge than dog. He doesn't chase balls or snuggle into bed."

I looked down toward the glow of the pub windows below us. Somewhere inside, Bob was likely asleep dreaming of racing cars.

"He could still have that," I said. "Not the dog. I mean… maybe. But something more. Something next."

"What if 'next' isn't better?"

"It might not be," I said honestly. "But staying stuck, here, between what was and what could've been, that's not better either."

She was quiet again. Her thumb brushed across mine. I don't think she noticed.

"If it gives Bob the chance to move on," she said at last, "to *whatever* is next… then yes. I'll do it."

The breeze picked up slightly. It tousled her hair in that way British breezes are contractually obliged to, politely but with intent.

"I want him to have another go," she said. "A proper one. Maybe next time, he's not eight. Maybe he's twenty-eight and learning to bake. Or thirty-two and learning to dance with someone who doesn't mind his stutter."

"Or sixty-five and deeply obsessed with pigeon racing," I offered.

She gave a soft laugh. "Maybe he gets to live. Really live. Not just exist in a pub with a ghost dog and a dubious collection of crisps."

"Trevor *is* a very judgmental dog," I said. "You try existing with dignity when he keeps walking through you with gravy on his chin."

She leaned her head against my shoulder then. Even though we didn't weigh anything, I *felt* it.

"I want to believe," she whispered. "That something good is waiting."

"I already found something good," I said. "You."

She lifted her head and gave me a look, half surprised, half something else I didn't dare name.

"Careful," she said.

The silence that followed was full of the space we'd made for each other. Room to speak. Room to not speak. Room to be scared and still say yes.

"I want to do this," I said. "Not just for me. Not even just for Bob. I want to do it with *you*."

"Even if the truth hurts?"

"Especially if it does. At least then we're hurting for something that matters."

She reached for my hand again, and this time, she didn't let go.

We sat there, two ghosts on a rooftop, making plans not to haunt but to *un-haunt*. To travel backwards, through time and trauma, in search of the truth that might let someone else go forward.

"Tony?"

"Yeah?"

"We do this for Bob. Not me, at least not yet."

"We can do that. Time is the one thing we now have plenty of."

Her head was still against my shoulder, "Don't forget, there are still a lot of questions in *our* time we need to find answers to."

"Like what?" I asked, though I already knew the list. We were ghosts, not goldfish.

She sat up slightly and began counting off on her fingers. "Why you were here at the Rose and Crown at all, for starters. Why *you*, an ex-cop from New York with a trench coat and an excessive relationship with Old Spice, ended up haunting me at British pub in the middle of nowhere."

I held up a hand. "For the record, it was aftershave. Not a lifestyle."

She raised an eyebrow. "Was that why Reverend Myles Abraham said you smelled like a discount haberdashery?"

"That man thinks lavender water is a bold fashion choice," I muttered. "… but thank you for the support!"

 "Anything else on the List of Cosmic Loose Ends?"

"Why, whilst breathing, I was interested in Victorian pubs in Beddlested at all. Don't forget that mystery?"

She nodded. "Then, when we confront Lord Percy, how we make that oodles of fun?"

 "If we're going to take him on," I said, "we need more than charm and a ghost dog. We need a plan."

"We need Angie," Betty said firmly. "Her laptop, and her glares."

"… and her tea. She makes aggressive tea. The kind that tastes like decisions."

"She'll help us. Even if she rolls her eyes … and sighs first."

"Especially if she sighs. That's how she casts her spells."

We paused, sharing a look that said: yes, the living are strange, but also kind of brilliant.

Betty leaned back again, brushing against me just slightly aura gently fizzing. "Then," she said, "there's the matter of Percy Hall itself. All those ghosts. All those stories. We woke them up, Tony."

I nodded slowly. "We did. We definitely owe them something."

"They were counting on Lord Percy to fix the leaky roof. To finish what his ancestors started. We scuppered that plan."

I exhaled. "So now we're ghostly roofers, too?"

She grinned. "We're many things, Tony. Detectives. Historians. Matchmakers. Social justice phantoms."

"Of course, there is the question of what we'll do when we get to Lord Percy's vault, whether those original volumes of the Cherokee books are safe, and if the tribe ever actually gets the justice they deserve."

"Oh, just a light to-do list then," I muttered. "Bring justice to colonised peoples, expose historical corruption, fight a murderous aristocrat, and explain to Angie why she's going to have to be on retainer indefinitely."

Betty tilted her head, mock-thoughtful. "Do we ever explain anything to Angie?"

"True. She explains things to *us*. With tea and passive-aggressive scones."

"… and then there's Gary."

I frowned. "Gary?"

"Yes. Whether Angie goes on that date with him. You saw how he looked at her when she fixed the jukebox yesterday. Like she'd invented music."

"Oh God," I groaned. "That man has the conversational depth of a novelty tea towel."

"He did compliment her handwriting," Betty said.

"He said it was 'legible in a sexy way.'" I shook my head. "If Angie falls for that, I'm haunting her toaster."

"Yes, but toast is personal and he did fix the toilet"

"He broke it first!"

"She doesn't know that. Then, of course… the duck."

I sighed. "What *about* the duck?"

"Do we think it has mad cow disease?"

"Betty."

"It's a valid question. I've seen it try to eat a beer mat. Twice."

We fell into a fit of laughter that echoed around the village square, which fortunately was too asleep or too English to question spontaneous rooftop giggling.

When we calmed down, I glanced at her. "You're right, though. There's still a lot here. Still knots we haven't untangled."

She smiled. "Lucky we have eternity."

"No pressure, then."

"None at all." She nodded slowly. … "and if we're going to do this thread-travel thing properly, we have to decide *where* to go first. We can't just fling ourselves backwards and hope the universe provides."

"Well, technically we can," I said. "But it would be wildly irresponsible."

"So your usual plan, then."

"Touché."

We sat in silence for a moment, both of us staring down at the pub below like generals plotting a whimsical but morally satisfying war.

"I think Bob's thread is the one to start with," I said. "It's clearest. Strongest. I can feel it pulling already."

"And you get easily bored of the other challenges!"

She knew me so well. But still agreed "It's always been strong. You can see it in the way he moves. Like something's unfinished, even when he's trying to be a kid."

"He doesn't know he's missing something," I said. "But he *feels* it."

Betty's voice softened. "That's the worst kind of grief, isn't it? The one you don't remember collecting."

We sat for a long time, thinking about Bob. About the way he sometimes stares out the pub window. About the stutter that gets worse when he's near the cellar. About how he clutches his Matchbox cars like they're lifeboats on a ghostly sea.

"We need to follow his thread," she said finally. "Back to the moment. Or as close as we can get. See what happened. Who did it. Why."

"Then?" I asked. "What if we find the answer?"

"Then we make it known," she said. "We tell it. Out loud. In front of witnesses. Ghosts or not and let justice happen."

I nodded. "No more secrets."

"No more unfinished stories," she added.

We'd need time. Focus. Maybe snacks.

But mostly, we needed to be *ready*. To face what might not want to be found.

"I'll be with Bob," Betty said. "He knows me. He trusts me. If he's scared…"

"You'll be the one who makes it okay."

She looked at me. "… and you?"

"I'll be there too, to keep you out of trouble!"

"Ha! You are the trouble!" and on reflection she may have been right as Beddlestead had probably been pretty quiet before I turned up. But then an English county village without a settlement of teepees *is* so last season.

So the rooftop, once a place of reflection, became our launchpad. Our war room. Our whispering place.

We were going back in time - to start a future. Weird.

Into memory - into death — to find new life. Weird.

… and back into the moments where for some of us, everything went wrong. Maybe, just maybe, we'd come back with the truth.

Because I have learnt that justice, love and life doesn't end with a heartbeat.

Sometimes, it appears, it begins just after it stops.

I have never felt so alive or happy … and yes that all may be pretty weird for a dead guy.

ABOUT THE AUTHOR

I divide my time between Cornwall and Mallorca, where I live with my family, a dangerously unstable tower of books that I fully intend to read one day, and a very unreliable herb garden that defies both weather and reason.

Rudely Interrupted is my first novel, and certainly the first one to feature pub-haunting romantics, spectral red tape, and the surprisingly complicated love lives of the recently deceased.

When not writing or loitering in pubs, (for research, obviously), I can often be found exploring historic streets, wandering through bookshops, or testing the patience of my family with "just one more" story idea.

Rudely Interrupted is my first foray into romantic comedy with a supernatural twist. I hope you like it. If you laugh, cry, or feel the sudden urge to hug a ghost, I'll consider my work done, and if you hear a suspicious rattle in the grate, don't panic, it's probably just a ghost trying to get your attention.

Or it's the wind.

But mostly the ghost.